Venetian Rhapsody

by

Tonya Penrose

Venetian Rhapsody

Cover Art by *Jennifer Greeff*

The Wild Rose Press, Inc.
PO Box 708
Adams Basin, NY 14410-0708
Visit us at www.thewildrosepress.com

Publishing History
First Edition, 2023
Trade Paperback ISBN 978-1-5092-4894-0
Digital ISBN 978-1-5092-4895-7

Published in the United States of America

"Pardon me, señorita, but your case's hook tore the pocket right off my jacket." He handed the piece of material to her.

"Excuse me, but I see this a bit differently. Your droopy pocket snagged my briefcase as I was dashing for cover. And thanks to you, here we sit in a mud pit alone in the middle of a drenching. Everyone else made it inside clean—" Didn't he recognize her?

"Clean and dry." His anger turned to surprise. "It's you." He tried to stand, but the slick mud offered no traction.

"Of course it's me. Who else would I be?" Sofia attempted to scoot sideways into the grass. The rain shower may have passed, but not her predicament.

"Please, still yourself."

"I will not still myself, Signore Whoever."

"It's Señor Eduardo Diaz. Please continue your ranting, if you find it helps," he replied, his tanned face accentuated by his brilliant white teeth.

"Yes, it helps, Señor Diaz," Sofia replied with a huff. "I'm soaked, covered in red mud, my favorite silk blouse is ruined, and I need a bath."

His hand pointed to their problem.

"What now?" huffed Sofia.

Eduardo's cognac eyes twinkled and distracted her.

Sofia saw the laptop case strap wrapped around his ankle. "Oh. Good grief." She bent over to untangle the strap only to butt heads smartly with the man, who still looked eerily familiar.

Dedication

Dedicated to David Bazo and his amazing song that launched this story's gondola. Our best is yet to come.

A Special Musical Offering!!!

Venetian Rhapsody has a companion album.

By: David Bazo
Award-winning Composer, Producer, Performer

Let the songs take you on an unforgettable romantic journey with Sofia and Eduardo...where barriers of time's constraints fall away.

Find the album details at:
http://davidbazo.info/

The First Encounter

Chapter 1

With two weeks left in Venice to complete her Museum Studies Doctorate, Sofia Martin sat enjoying a cappuccino at one of Chicco di Caffe's outside tables. Observing the boats on the Grand Canal drifting by, a melancholy feeling washed over her. The thought of returning to Boston and her work at the museum had Sofia questioning her path. Still, it's where the next chapter in her life awaited, or so she believed.

Taking the last sip of coffee, Sofia's gaze was drawn to a table a few yards away. A strikingly handsome man chatted with a male lunch companion. He glanced her way and smiled. Sofia watched the emotions play across his face as if he recognized her. A frown creased his forehead, showing confusion.

Did she know him? Maybe. Sofia's hand moved without her approval and sent him a shy wave.

He nodded, and the smile returned.

Mortified by her actions, Sofia dropped the sunglasses over her eyes and pretended interest in her cell phone. Secretly, she made a study of him. The tan sports jacket defined broad shoulders. He'd probably tower over her five-foot-five frame. A sigh escaped. Her attraction to men with black hair and firm jawlines had proven her downfall more than once. Yet something was captivating about his face. Perhaps a simple explanation was that European men exuded an appealing sophistication. Sofia shook her head to clear the thoughts and stole another glance. If asked to describe him to someone, a single word would suffice. Charming.

A sip of mineral water cooled her flushed face. Tucking the cell phone back into her handbag, she wondered what took Ginny so long to pay for their lunch. For some reason that defied logic, her eyes traveled to where he sat in easy conversation.

The dapper-dressed man at his table signaled the waiter for the check and resumed talking. Moments later, both men stood and shook hands. "Dapper" waved and hurried off. Sofia's breath caught as Signore Charming seemed to move her way. At the last moment, he veered to greet a young woman dressed for a day of shopping. An unexplainable disappointment filled Sofia as the couple headed down the sidewalk and disappeared into the crowd of tourists.

"Hi there. What did I miss?" Ginny's eyes squinted in the direction Sofia had turned.

"Nothing. Someone looked familiar to me, but I guess I was mistaken. Did you find our waiter and settle the bill?" Sofia stood and reached for her straw handbag.

"Yes. He was flirting with some young *signorina* at the coffee bar. Shifting topics, I've saved a timely question for you until the end of lunch. Intrigued?"

"Of course, I'm all ears." Sofia bit her lip.

"Would you like to polish your dissertation one last time for me?" Ginny waited.

"You're shifting to Professor Greco?"

"Yes. I'm versatile. Some might say extremely accommodating." Ginny's smile lifted the corners of her mouth. "Well?"

"Hang on. I require a bit of clarification. Does this mean you'll allow me to include my research using esoteric specialized knowledge at museum heritage sites?" Sofia's delight rang warmly in her voice.

Ginny peeked at her gold watch. "Oh no. I'm late for class. Quick, there's the water taxi pulling up. Come on." Ginny grabbed Sofia's arm, pulling her along, laughing.

"But my answer—?" Sofia gave one last glance at his empty table.

"In a minute. Hurry."

Both women climbed aboard and claimed seats for the five-minute ride to campus.

Sofia touched her stomach. "After that mad dash, I feel my second cappuccino sloshing around."

"Poor you. That look on your face is begging for sympathy. Here's a peppermint. It should do the trick." Ginny nodded to a student across the aisle.

"Thanks." Sofia popped the candy into her mouth. "Okay, enough of the suspense. May I include my research on esoteric—?"

"Yes, yes. On the condition that you don't ask for another revision."

Sofia clapped her hands, drawing the smiles of the other passengers. "Professor Greco. I promise this inclusion will improve—"

Ginny shook her head. "Ever the perfectionist. Listen, your research paper has already been fully vetted by the department and deemed publishable."

"You're kidding? Publishable?" Sofia's hand fanned her face.

"Very publishable. I sold your brilliance in

incorporating esoteric thought into deserving exhibitions. You've got until the end of the week to get the dissertation back to me. Agreed?"

"Agreed. I'm beyond grateful. You've been my advocate from day one." Sofia's affection for her professor and friend bubbled up.

"Your passion for becoming a curator has been infectious to our department. We're not supposed to have favorites in the doctoral program, but you, Sofia Martin, captured our hearts." Tears brimmed in Ginny's brown eyes.

"How I'm going to miss you and the friends I've made here." Sofia smiled rather wistfully. "You know, I'm even going to miss the library niche I inhabited this year. Its smell of stale coffee and old leather enveloped me each visit."

Ginny touched Sofia's arm. "I shall miss you tremendously, my American friend. You're with us for another week?"

"Yes, and I admit to feeling conflicted about leaving Venice. It's been an amazing experience here. You'd think at twenty-seven, I'd know my mind."

"Then why not stay?" asked Ginny.

"Stay?" Sofia's brows drew together in a frown. "I can't stay. The museum in Boston has funded part of my doctorate program. They committed to me, and in turn, I committed to the directors and the retiring curator. My dream job awaits. I have to go back."

"And so, you shall. Here's our stop." Ginny rose.

"And so, I shall," repeated Sofia with resignation coloring her words. She followed, wondering what had dampened her enthusiasm to become the curator. They walked in silence across the campus.

The ringing of Ginny's cell phone punctured the silence, causing both women to stop.

Sofia stood, savoring memories of her time in Venice. An unexpected gust of wind released her honey-blond hair from the cloisonné barrette. She reached to adjust the clip and felt a strange nudge to look to her left. The back of a man wearing a tan jacket and jeans entered the Business Studies building. Was that him? The guy from the bistro? Her heart fluttered wildly.

Chapter 2

Ginny tossed her phone into the tote. "Sorry. Milo's return flight from Peru arrives tonight instead of tomorrow. It's been a long month of missing that husband of mine. Wow, I've got seven minutes before class begins."

"You need to have a celebration. Invite a few friends in. It's Thursday, so you can make it an early evening," suggested Sofia.

"Hmm, I like your idea." Ginny's mouth twisted to the side, contemplating that thought.

"Of course you do. I'm a legend for great ideas." A teasing smile crossed Sofia's face.

"Okay, come tonight for dinner. Dress super casual. I will run with your idea and invite three or four people to celebrate Milo's homecoming. He'll relish the chance to have an audience hear about his month in Peru."

"I'd love to come on two conditions. One, I bring the dessert." Sofia hesitated. "Why the frown?"

"You don't bake or, for that matter, cook."

"You're right, but I'm smart. I write a publishable dissertation, and I happen to know where the best bakery is downtown. I've got dessert."

"And what's your second condition? This ought to be good." Ginny began walking.

"Second, you don't invite a date for me again."

"But—"

"No, but. The last guy wore a bow tie that talked. I've never been so happy to see a battery die."

Ginny burst into laughter. "He's a professor of Medieval Literature. English professors love to wear bow ties."

"Ties that quote Chaucer over and over? Besides, he was shorter than I am. No fix-up. End of discussion. Let's slow-jog to your class?"

"Walk, not jog. I'm in my new sassy red heels." Ginny pointed down.

"They're quite fetching. I don't know how I missed them." As they passed the Business Studies door, Sofia cast a hopeful look.

Ginny pointed to the entrance. "With any luck, Milo's grad students will have his mug glaring at them next quarter."

"See? You have another thing to celebrate." Sofia grabbed a breath. "Didn't you tell me Milo's best friend stepped in and is teaching the classes?"

"Yes. Good memory." Ginny adjusted the tote strap higher on her shoulder. "Anyway, his best buddy knew the opportunity to launch an identical program at an institute in Lima meant recognition and more grant money for Milo's department. He jumped in to help."

"A chance too good to pass up," said Sofia. "Does his friend live in Venice?"

"Unfortunately, no. He flew in from Spain a few days before Milo departed to go over the course's curriculum. From what I hear, the grad students adore his unique teaching style. I've got four minutes. We'd better pick up the pace."

Sofia held the door. "He sounds like one amazing

7

guy."

"Most definitely." Ginny bobbed her head. "Milo's mother and I have cooked dinner for him a few times. He's got those impeccable swoonable Spanish manners and looks."

"Swoonable? I don't think it's a word—" Sofia smiled at their flight of fancy.

"Trust me. If you met him, you'd swoon. Here's my class. Where are you headed?" Ginny stepped aside for a student to enter.

"Where else? To my beloved library niche after I grab my laptop from your office. It seems I've some final dissertation polishing to do for my favorite professor. Catch ya later." Sofia waved and hurried down the hall.

"Swoonable," Sofia said aloud and thought of her mystery man. Would their paths ever cross again? Spending the last few days in Venice ensconced in a library corner, she'd be lucky to see daylight, much less him. She wondered why it mattered.

Crossing the courtyard, Sofia noted the darkening clouds choking the sunlight. Her deep aqua eyes willed the rain to wait five minutes until she reached the library. Clearly, her direct line to the rain gods didn't connect. The first gentle drops falling teased Sofia to believe the slight dampness to her yellow silk blouse and linen slacks could be forgiven. She'd even excuse the mud splatters on her strappy gold sandals.

The rain's voice shifted in an instant, from tinkling like a wind chime to a thudding drumbeat. A construction site she'd have to navigate loomed ahead. The deluge turned the mound of excavated dirt into a moving muddy mess headed in her direction. A small group of faculty and students ran past her, hurrying to escape the drenching.

Closing her eyes for a second to wipe away the water, Sofia heard the distinct sound of fabric ripping. Her laptop bag belt hooked onto something unyielding and propelled her backward. Unable to maintain balance, Sofia's sandals sank into the mud. Her bottom followed.

"What have you done to me?" said a nearby masculine voice. Losing his balance, he plopped down within a foot of Sofia. Mud splatters mixed with rain covered his face and clothes.

Sofia swiveled to look into eyes the color of rich cognac. The tan jacket resembled a leopard, but the face dotted with dirt belonged to…him. "I'm the one who should say, 'What have you done to *me*?' Just look at my laptop case."

"Pardon me, señorita, but your case's hook tore the pocket right off my jacket." He handed the piece of material to her.

"Excuse me, but I see this a bit differently. Your droopy pocket snagged my briefcase as I was dashing for cover. And thanks to you, here we sit in a mud pit alone in the middle of a drenching. Everyone else made it inside clean—" Didn't he recognize her?

"Clean and dry." His anger turned to surprise. "It's you." He tried to stand, but the slick mud offered no traction.

"Of course it's me. Who else would I be?" Sofia attempted to scoot sideways into the grass. The rain shower may have passed, but not her predicament.

"Please, still yourself."

"I will not still myself, Signore Whoever."

"It's Señor Eduardo Diaz. Please continue your ranting, if you find it helps," he replied, his tanned face accentuated by his brilliant white teeth.

"Yes, it helps, Señor Diaz," Sofia replied with a huff. "I'm soaked, covered in red mud, my favorite silk blouse is ruined, and I need a bath."

His hand pointed to their problem.

"What now?" huffed Sofia.

Eduardo's cognac eyes twinkled and distracted her.

Sofia saw the laptop case strap wrapped around his ankle. "Oh. Good grief." She bent over to untangle the strap only to butt heads smartly with the man, who still looked eerily familiar.

"Damn." Eduardo pulled away, rubbing the top of his head.

"Yes, damn." Sofia touched her forehead.

"Señorita Whoever, what do you have against me? You've stripped the pocket off my jacket, pulled me into this mud crater, and now brought me to near unconsciousness. I fear I'm not long for this world." A thin smile edged his full lips.

"I'm Señorita Sophia Martin. And ditto from my side of the mud crater," replied Sofia. "There. You're free."

Eduardo succeeded in standing. He extended his hand to Sofia. "Please, allow me."

Sofia accepted his hand, and her breath hitched. Who was this guy, and why did he have such an immediate effect on her senses? She pulled her wet blouse away from her skin. "Ugh. What a disaster."

Eduardo's eyes remained fixated on her. "Have dinner with me."

A surprised Sofia tilted her chin up to meet his

eyes. "What? Have dinner with you? I don't know you. No."

"I don't know you either. Nor can I explain why I'm compelled to risk another encounter with you." Eduardo responded with a hint of mockery in his voice.

"You're under no risk, Señor Diaz. We're not having dinner tonight or any night." Sofia lifted her laptop case, ignoring the blobs of mud clinging to the leather. Her hair felt like limp spaghetti. She was an utter mess inside and outside. "*Arrivederci.*"

"Probably not, Señorita Martin." Eduardo wore an amused expression, watching as Sofia's muddy hands hung the case strap over her shoulder.

Gathering what little dignity remained, Sofia took her first steps and realized her sandals hadn't come with her. "Could this day get any worse?" she mumbled, glancing at a grinning Eduardo dangling her sandals in each hand.

"Your once golden slippers, lovely damsel."

"Give me those." Sofia snatched them from his outstretched hands, turned, and hobbled away barefooted. His laughter stayed behind her, but not the undeniable and confusing attraction Sofia felt for one Eduardo Diaz. Glancing heavenward, her eyes caught sight of the unexpected...a glorious rainbow.

Chapter 3

Entering her rental condo, Sofia deposited her case and handbag on the quartz kitchen counter. They'd have to wait for their cleanup. A shower was her next stop. If only she could dismiss Eduardo Diaz from her thoughts as easily.

While dressing, her practical mind formed a plan to save her afternoon. If she hurried, there was time to get a few hours of work done at the library before Ginny's party. She'd scoot downstairs to Lucia's Bakery, choose a decadent Italian dessert, and leave it in the condo's fridge to grab and go later.

Tossing her mud-stained clothes into the trash, Sofia answered the ringing cell phone. "Hey, Melody. I'd planned to call you later."

"Baby sister, that's what you always tell me. I thought I'd check in and see how you're progressing with disentangling from your life in Venice. We're all counting the days until your plane lands at Logan."

"It's progressing. I bring happy tidings. Ginny has granted me a last revision to my dissertation—"

"Wait. You're not delaying the trip home because—"

"No delay. I promise you. Tell me. How are my niece and nephew hooligans?" Sofia put the phone on speaker and applied her coral lip gloss.

"They're busy in my living room making

decorations for the museum's welcome-back-Sofia party. Your kindly and gracious curator, Bill, assigned my hooligans the beverage table to festoon. Let's just say I'm confident glue and glitter have permanently adhered to Aunt Louise's antique wormy chestnut coffee table."

Sofia gave an indulgent laugh. "Make sure you tell them I'm excited to see their creations. Oh, and tell that husband of yours, I'm expecting his outstanding barbecue ribs my first Sunday back."

"Duly noted. Hang on a sec. Andrew, what are you doing with my permanent glue?"

"That doesn't sound good. I'll let you go." Sofia gave her hair one last brush, waiting for Melody's reply.

"You did not just glue your little sister's hand to my amber crystal vase. Sof, I need to go adhere someone's butt to the naughty chair. Talk to you later." Melody disconnected.

Sofia gave a chuckle, grabbed her wallet, and headed to the bakery. The aroma of fresh-baked Focaccine Veneziane danced in her mind's eye. The sweet buns had become a favorite of hers since arriving. With any luck, Lucia would have a few left.

"Here's my lovely Sofia coming to make my day *bellissima*. What have I to offer you?" A pleasingly plump Lucia wiped her hands on a flowered apron.

"Hello to you, my friend. You can offer me three Focaccine? And I need a dinner dessert recommendation." Sofia peered into the pastry case and felt her mouth water.

"Si, I box now while you look at my Pinza Veneta just there." Lucia pointed to a row of cakes cooling on a rack. "These are famous in Venice. Big hit for you to take, Sofia."

"Pinza? I don't believe I've ever had one."

Lucia tied burlap string around the box of buns, set them by the cash register, and joined Sofia. "What should I tell you about the pinza?"

Sofia nodded, knowing to hurry off would appear rude. "I'd love to learn about the cakes."

"Good, good. We care only for the Venetian version. Inside this cake…" Lucia broke off a large chunk and handed it on a white napkin to Sofia. "First, you must taste."

"My, what pure deliciousness." Sofia tried to identify the unusual flavors.

"You cannot guess? No?" Lucia smiled with satisfaction.

"No clue. What's in the cake?"

"The recipe, it varies from region to region, but I make pinza with white and yellow flour, a special yeast, sugar, and always fresh eggs. You mix this first. Understand?"

"Yes, this is your basic recipe?" Sofia nodded.

Lucia frowned. "I don't know basic, but I continue. I make my own candied fruits to use. I add dried figs, currants." The baker leaned closer and whispered, "Shh, my secret ingredients are fennel seeds and a bit of cinnamon. No share."

"I wouldn't dream of telling your secret." Sofia patted the baker's forearm.

"Good, good. Bake in the oven. *Voila.* You make the pinza. You want one boxed?"

"Nope," replied Sofia.

Lucia's face fell.

"I want two pinzas boxed. One for me and one to take to the dinner party."

"*Eccellente*." Lucia completed the order. She paused and studied Sofia. "You know I have…how you say…psychic ways?"

"Yes, I recall you sharing this." Sofia swallowed, unsure what was coming.

"Tonight carries something you mustn't ignore, Sofia. Follow your heart." Lucia's face changed to a knowing smile.

"I don't understand—"

Lucia shook her head. "No, but you will." Her hands passed the three boxes to Sofia. "Soon. You will. I see you again later." Lucia moved to a couple waiting.

"Thanks, Lucia." Sofia opened the shop's planked door taking her puzzlement upstairs with the bakery items.

****

Stepping onto the sidewalk, Sofia decided to give herself the luxury of ignoring time. She'd enjoy a leisurely stroll to the library and pretend it was her first day taking in the City of Love.

Sofia approached a tourist kiosk and smiled at the middle-aged man standing inside. "May I take a couple of brochures from your red carousel display? I want to refresh my memory on Venice's story."

He smiled back. "But of course, *signorina*. Perhaps these two will do."

Sofia squinted at his name badge. "Thank you, Aldo." Sofia stood to the side and read aloud. She marveled at how the city was built so long ago using wood pilings.

Hearing her speak, Aldo raised his head. "Might I

share some history about Venice and the names my city is called?"

"Sure. You've got me captive." Sofia moved closer to the kiosk.

"I begin by telling you the name, Venice, comes from the ancient people called Veneti. They occupied the area back in the 10th Century B.C. A very long time ago, yes?"

"Very." Amusement glinted in Sofia's eyes.

"Venice enjoys many names like City of Canals, which you've learned is a good name. Also, it's recognized as the City of Masks, City of Bridges, The Floating City, and the City of Love. I always say a secret passion beats in Venice's heart and in those who love her. You understand this?" Aldo's eyebrow lifted.

"Such beautiful words, but I'm not sure I understand—"

"Ah, I believe tonight you shall comprehend." Aldo smiled a little.

"Comprehend tonight? Still, I don't—"

"Patience, *signorina*. Tonight comes as it will. Please excuse me." Aldo turned to greet a small group of tourists, offering them Italian candies from a nearby bowl.

Sofia waved and continued down the sidewalk, puzzled by another cryptic message coming to her after Lucia's. Shrugging, she read more of the brochure describing how Venice was steeped in culture, education, and commerce. Glancing around at her surroundings, Sofia thought Venice had no peers.

Thinking about leaving in a few short days brought the melancholy feeling back for an encore. "Maybe this self-guided tour wasn't such a great idea after all."

Scolding herself, she tucked the brochures into her handbag. Noticing the approaching water taxi, she waited to board. She'd escape to her library cubby and immerse herself in the latest concepts for designing museum educational programs.

****

Arriving home late, she rushed to find an outfit that fit Ginny's idea of casual. Translated, it meant no high heels, layers of gold jewelry, or a full face of makeup required. If they dined on the patio, muggy air would be a dinner guest.

Sofia pulled a pale-yellow, peasant-style blouse from the closet. The embroidered colorful daisies always made her smile. Dare she risk wearing white jeans? Ginny's menu usually included a red sauce, which inevitably found a welcome home on Sofia's lap.

"I'm in the mood for jeans, and I feel lucky."

Sofia dressed, adding her latest purchase of Italian gold hoop earrings. They'd serve as lasting mementos of her time in Venice. Slipping her feet into a pair of straw-colored espadrilles, Sofia gave the mirror a nod. Retrieving the pinza, it was time to celebrate Milo's happy return home. As for what the night held for her, according to Aldo and Lucia's strange prediction, she'd wait and see.

Chapter 4

Standing outside Ginny and Milo's front door, Sofia paused to admire the quaint two-story stucco home tucked down a side street in the historic district. The jade-green shutters with the cocoa-colored window boxes full of red geraniums made her smile. Milo took full credit for keeping the boxes happy as he described his efforts. The couple's restoration efforts never seemed to end, which was typical for canal homes.

As Sofia reached for the bell, the front door swung open by a smiling Ginny. "You're late. I almost had to worry. Come in."

"Apologies. My water taxi thought he could take the long way and run the meter. He was mistaken." Sofia accepted the hug from her hostess. "Here's dessert. Has Milo arrived?"

"Can't you hear him?" Ginny's eyes glimmered with laughter. "You'll find his audience in the courtyard."

"I beg your indulgence, but not everyone is his audience." Surprised cognac eyes locked on dark aqua ones.

"You again? How's this even possible?" Sofia turned to Ginny, confused. "You know this man?"

"Yes, I do, and it seems introductions are unnecessary. How do you know each other? Something tells me it's a much more interesting story than mine."

Ginny's eyebrow lifted.

"He caused me—"

"She caused me—"

Eduardo and Sofia spoke in unison. They stopped and stared at each other with confused expressions.

A distracted Ginny tucked the cake into the refrigerator. "Tell you what. I'm going to slip out to the courtyard so you two can get your stories straight. Join us soon." Bestowing a wink, their hostess disappeared.

Sofia planted her hands on her narrow hips. "How did you finagle an invitation to my friend's home?"

"Finagle? What's this finagle word? I don't think I like it." Eduardo's eyes narrowed with the words.

"You aren't supposed to like it," said Sofia. "Why are you here? I don't understand how—"

"It's quite simple. I'm Milo's friend. I've been teaching the courses in his absence."

"You're his best friend?" The explanation sank in.

"Yes, and now that we've established why I belong here, maybe you'd enlighten me how you finagled, yes?" Eduardo paused.

"Yes, finagled is the word, but I did not finagle an invitation." Sofia's voice rose a few octaves. Eduardo was trying to get her goat and succeeding.

"Please, so that I may finish. How did you finagle an invitation to have dinner with me? I find myself feeling pleased with this change of plans. Señorita Sofia, you're a most resourceful woman." Eduardo moved closer.

"Oh, for pity's sake, you've got everything wrong. I'm in the doctoral program under Ginny. We're friends." Sofia stepped back and, meeting an unyielding chair, collapsed onto the cushion.

Eduardo's laughter rang out. "As anyone can see, you possess the dexterity failings that caused our afternoon mud bath."

Sofia spun her legs around to sit upright. "I refuse to rehash the whole mud—"

Eduardo extended his hand. "Come. Let us enjoy dinner together as the stars have ordered this night."

"Fine. Let's make the best of this night for our friends and suspend arguing." Sofia's traitorous hand went to his. Charming defined him—as for swoonable? She was nearly there.

Eduardo escorted her to the courtyard. "Pardon the delay. Sofia—"

Sofia glared darts.

"Sofia and I required a few moments to clear the smoke as Americans—"

"Clear the air. It's clear the air," Sofia murmured before turning to the group. "Welcome home, Milo. Hi, Annie and Bruno." Sofia always enjoyed being around Ginny and Milo's friends.

"It's great to be home, Sofia." Milo leaned over and kissed Ginny. "I hear I owe you for the dinner party idea."

"Only the idea. The preparations and decorations are your wife's work," said Sofia.

"We join Milo in thanking you. I got out of cooking dinner tonight," chuckled Annie.

Eduardo held Sofia's chair. "You smell like jasmine blossoms," he whispered in her ear. "I'm so pleased you agreed to have dinner with me."

Sofia's retort froze on her lips seeing his teasing expression. "Señor Diaz, I see it as fate conspiring against me."

"Possibly not, Señorita Sofia of the Mud." Eduardo's voice held a distant note as he watched her pour tea into the glass.

Sofia studied him. He was as perplexed as she about their encounter. Choosing to let the title slide, she chuckled at the reference. "Would you care for tea, Señor—"

"Please, call me Eduardo. And yes, thank you." As he moved his glass closer to Sofia, his hand brushed hers.

They pulled away as if the other's hand was a fire starter.

Eduardo reached for the sugar bowl and held three cubes suspended. "You take three?"

"Yes, but how did you know?" Sofia stirred the cubes into the glass.

"I have no idea." Eduardo's eyes held hers.

Ginny tapped her glass. "Can I have everyone's attention? Raise your glasses in a toast to my Milo's safe return. And our two-week getaway to Croatia just days away."

"Salute!" chorused everyone seated.

Bowls of mushroom risotto and garden salad moved around the table. A basket of crusty Italian bread was torn for dipping into individual dishes of olive oil and herbs. Fresh-cut flowers in a bright orange ceramic vase served as the table's centerpiece. Sofia could tell the blooms came from the small courtyard garden lovingly tended by Ginny. White lights draped around the privacy wall added ambiance to the relaxed evening.

Milo spent the next hour regaling everyone with Lima stories until nine o'clock when jet lag deflated him like a tire. Ginny sent Milo off to bed. After helping to clear the table, the group made their way to the front door saying good night.

Sofia stepped onto the cobbled walkway and took a deep inhale. The smell of the sea combined with food cooking defined Venice. Children not yet called home from a day of playing outdoors skipped the last round of rope. Off in the distance, Sofia heard a musician playing the mandolin.

"The music makes the essence of Venice. Does it not?" Eduardo came alongside her. He'd slung his jacket over his shoulder.

"Yes," sighed Sofia. "Venice has such a unique vibe. It's ever-changing, but then not really. Does that make sense?"

Eduardo took in the scene around them. "But of course, you make sense. The city's history and culture are solid and poured into rock, as you say. It is the coming and going of its ever-changing people…adding the flavor." He paused to gaze at her. "Do I get the gold star?"

Sophia lifted her head to meet his gaze. "It's poured in stone. And I award you the gold star, Señor Diaz." Where had her breath gone?

"I will trade you my star to hear you speak my name as Eduardo."

His voice cut across her thoughts. "Keep your star, Eduardo. Well, good night." Sophia untied the scarf from her handbag.

"Allow me." Eduardo draped it around her shoulders. "There. You're ready to enjoy Venice at night with me."

Sophia's head popped up. "What? No, I am not

ready to enjoy Venice—"

"Ah, but you are. We both know this…somehow."

Sophia found her gumption. "I don't know this. I don't know you well enough to sightsee. What I know is I'm going home now to polish my dissertation."

The front door opened, surprising both Eduardo and Sofia.

"Enough of this bantering." Ginny stepped outside and got between them. "Sofia, accept Eduardo's kind offer to show you Venice at night. As your doctorate professor, I'm giving you the assignment to enjoy an evening in our city." Ginny raised her hand. "Not another word."

Sofia closed her mouth and kept her objections inside.

Ginny pivoted. "Eduardo, I trust you to see Sofia safely home after your excursion."

"Do not trouble yourself on this matter." Eduardo did a mock bow.

Stepping back to her doorstep, Ginny turned. "Why are you both still here? Leave me in peace with my kitchen work. Get lost." Ginny made shooing motions with her arms. A hint of a smile graced her lips.

Eduardo evaluated Sofia's shoes. "They're walkable, yes?"

She rolled her eyes. "Yes, they're walkable—within reason. What do you have in mind because I don't—"

Eduardo lifted his hand. "Please. Allow me. There's someplace I'm sure you've not visited, which I'd like very much to show you."

"How do you know I haven't visited this place?"

Eduardo's expression appeared thoughtful. He

shrugged, offering another dazzling smile. "Somehow, I just know."

His charm was irresistible. With only a few days remaining in Venice, Sofia saw no harm in enjoying more of Eduardo's company. "Okay, I'm intrigued."

He nodded and offered his arm. "Shall we discover why this night has beckoned us together?"

"I suppose," Sofia said, trying her best to avoid his eyes. No man had ever looked at her that way. On some level, it felt like Eduardo knew her soul. Dismissing the thought as mere whimsy, her mannerly self wrapped her arm around his. "Let's go discovering."

The evening breeze stilled as they strolled along the streets of Venice. Eduardo supplied interesting information about the city that wouldn't make a tour guide's list. Sofia learned he'd graduated college there and often returned to see friends and family. Sofia became more fascinated by Venice and the man introducing her to its hidden charms.

"We arrive at our destination," said Eduardo.

"Wow, we're only a few blocks from my place."

"This is good to know. I shall walk you home. Assuming, of course, your feet agree?" He slowed their pace and glanced down.

"Shoes and feet are simpatico. Hurry up. My enthusiasm is undiminished," said Sophia.

"Up ahead, you may see it now, Saint Mark's Square." Eduardo pointed. "You've not been here yet. Is time, I think."

Sophia shook her head. "But how? I can't believe you brought me here. I purposely saved visiting it for my last week in Venice. I wanted a fresh memory to take home."

"I cannot explain. I can only say I felt the pull to bring you here tonight. I wonder why? Do you wonder?" Eduardo's expression held perplexity.

"Yes, I wonder." Sofia paused, letting her mind absorb his cryptic words. "Standing in front of this historical place, I'm wondering what you'll share right now. Enlighten me, kind sir."

"The church is closed, but we didn't come to visit it."

Sofia frowned. "No?"

"No. We came to see the Pilastri Acritani." Eduardo walked them closer to the two marble columns. "In English, they're called the Pillars of Acre. History tells us these two grand works were part of the looting that took place in 1204 at the sack of Constantinople. Crusader armies swooped in and confiscated much of the Byzantine riches. It's an all-too-common story, which I'm sure you know far more about than me working in a museum."

Sophia nodded. "The passion for antiquities is long-held and sadly by many unscrupulous collectors. So, I'd like to hear more about the Pillars of Acre. I sense you're saving the best for last."

"This is true, señorita. Do you see the monograms?" Eduardo indicated with his hand.

"I do."

Lowering his voice, Eduardo moved closer to Sofia. "They're Egyptian-Syrian monograms that I don't believe anyone has ever been able to decipher. You see, a great mystery exists around these inscriptions."

"Quite the captivating mystery. Well done, Señor Diaz."

Eduardo's eyebrow raised in objection.

"Correction, Eduardo." Sofia emphasized his name. "Is there more?"

His lips smiled faintly. "Some say the site is one of the most esoteric places in Venice. And the pillars represent a portal that leads to other dimensions. Since I was a young boy, time travel has held me spellbound. For you, the same?"

Sophia adored his way with English. "And yes, the idea of time travel fascinates me too. The whole going-to-the-past-and-future thing."

"Yes," said Eduardo. His eyes took in the scene. "It may sound strange to you, but I felt required to bring you here. To share a place…a story about the unexplainable. Do you not find an eerie similarity to our encounters? Are they not unexplainables?"

Sofia met Eduardo's gaze and experienced a strange fluttering in her stomach. "Perhaps, but I'm trying to ignore our unexplainable."

A smile spread across his face. "I don't think ignoring is working. Do you?"

"Nope. Not a bit." Amusement bubbled up in her. "Maybe if you could dial back the charm a skosh?" Sofia's hands flew to cover her mouth. What made her blurt those words to a man she'd just met?

Eduardo frowned. "What is dial back the charm? Never mind. I do not wish to dial back if this makes you like me a little."

Sofia felt her barriers crumbling. Panic overrode his male charm. "It's getting late."

"My apologies for keeping you out so late. Please allow me to walk you as we agreed. I want to hear more about your work in Boston." Eduardo's hand touched

Sofia's waist, moving her away from a teenager skating past.

Sofia's breath hitched as the heat of his hand penetrated through the fabric. "Okay. My place is maybe ten minutes from here." Surely, she could fortify her defenses for the stroll to her rental condo. A breeze with intention swept the scarf from her shoulders, sending it fluttering toward the ground.

Ever the gentleman, Eduardo caught it. "May I?" His fingers touched her neck as he draped the scarf once again. "I think maybe I'm getting trained tonight in the ways of scarves."

His warm breath fanned her skin. Her emotional fortifications turned to powder and followed the warm breeze. Thankfully, words stayed inside of her.

He stepped back, surveying the scarf placement. "Looks good." Eduardo held out his hand expectantly.

The phrase "moth to a flame" finally made sense to Sophia as her hand found his.

His genuine interest in her studies and work kept her chattering as they strolled. Sofia detailed what exhibits and programs she'd plan as the new museum curator. Eduardo seemed to catch her enthusiasm and had little difficulty understanding English. Discovering he could speak five languages certainly stomped all over her rudimentary Italian.

They reached Lucia's Bakery. "This is it. I'm upstairs." Sofia turned to face Eduardo.

"You chose an excellent location to live in Venice. Lucia's loaves of bread rate high on my list."

"Alas, I find myself in her bakery most every day. I'm going to miss her Zaeti cookies most of all." Sofia released a sigh.

Eduardo's expression grew thoughtful. "I've got an idea you might appreciate. Would you like me to introduce you to my friend, Tomas, who runs an eclectic gallery? He displays mainly twentieth-century pieces. Quite extraordinary finds, Tomas tells me."

"That would be amazing. Our museum has a tiny section from the same period. Where's the gallery?" asked Sofia.

"It's tucked away on a quiet side street." Eduardo paused. "Yes, you must see the pieces. Who knows? You both might arrange an exchange exhibit. I think you call this meeting idea synchronistic in English." His eyes held her captive.

Sofia's inner war broke out. Eduardo Diaz's charm was seductive to the senses. Her rational mind screamed not to spend another minute in his company. To risk getting involved with someone when her flight to Boston loomed ahead was lunacy. "Thank you, Eduardo. I'd love to meet him whenever it's convenient. I'm flexible." The words were out. Someone needed to tattoo "fool" on her forehead.

"Excellent." Eduardo beamed a smile. "I'll arrange the appointment. Write your cell phone number on this card." He passed Sofia a pen.

"Here you go." Sofia watched as he tucked everything into his pocket. Even his movements were deft and aristocratic.

Eduardo reached for her hand, letting his lips brush softly across. "Now, I bid you *buenas noches*."

Sofia's breath quickened. "*Buenas noches*." As she watched him go, the remembrance of Lucia's words that the night held something she shouldn't ignore came calling. Glancing up at the stars dotting the velvet black

28

sky, Sofia made a vow. Should any more invitations come from Eduardo Diaz, she'd graciously decline...somehow.

Chapter 5

"Finally, I find you." Ginny slid a metal chair over to the niche, where Sofia sat working. "This isn't your usual place."

"Hi there. I know. The newest library volunteer assigned my usual to another research graduate. I'm technically labeled a *fondatore*, which I think means a floater in Italian." Sofia adjusted her chair to face her friend.

"Would you like for me to pull some strings and reclaim your space?"

"No, but thank you. It's hardly worth it for the sake of a few days." Sadness at the thought of leaving came calling once more.

Ginny reached out and touched her arm. "I can read your face. Stay here with us. Listen to me for a sec."

Sofia's eyes, brimming with tears, turned to her friend. "I don't know what's gotten into me acting all clingy to my life here. Venice was never meant to be permanent."

"No, it wasn't meant to be permanent, but we change. We grow. We discover new things about ourselves. And if we're wise, we course correct when a path opens, bringing new opportunities to grow and prosper. It's what I did by leaving the States," said Ginny.

"But I want the curator position in Boston that's promised me. I've so many creative ideas to implement after working on my doctorate. It's my chosen path. Besides, it's not like I've had any job offers here…"

Ginny's expression changed. "Not yet."

"Oh, let's not talk anymore about this. Tell me why you came looking for me." Sofia forced a smile, hoping it would lift her mood.

"My curious genes wanted to hear about last night with Swoonable? I left you two outside ready to tussle."

Sofia recalled the scene and welcomed the distraction. "We behaved. Eduardo escorted me to the Pillars of Acre and then walked me home. All very tame."

"Then why are your cheeks flushed the same rose shade as my blouse as you tell me of this tame outing?" Ginny shook her head. "Tame and Eduardo do not compute."

"You're probably right. You know the guy."

"Hmm." Ginny's eyes studied her friend. "I want to leave you with some advice, and you'd do well to take it. If you see Eduardo again, keep things light. Guard your heart if you're bent on returning home." Ginny stood wearing a grin. "My students await my brilliance. I'll see you tomorrow. Maybe we can grab lunch."

"Sounds good. Thanks for the wisdom on all fronts." Sofia gave a wave and returned to her dissertation.

The screen stared at her, and Sofia stared back for the next hour. The face of a suave and debonair man from Spain held her captive. Sofia considered Eduardo's manners and his endearing way of speaking.

She envisioned him attending a ball in Jane Austen's time, all decked out in finery. Closing her eyes, the image came to life. Eduardo held her in his arms as they led a waltz in a grand ballroom. Her green satin gown was sprinkled with seed pearls reflecting the candlelight as they moved on the dance floor. Tiny white rosebuds were tucked into her honey-colored hair styled in an upsweep. A dainty cameo attached to a black velvet ribbon touched her throat. Mesmerized, Sofia watched the scene unfold. Their dancing mirrored a shared passion for each other. Her mind didn't intrude with its usual chatter, but a voice did.

"Señorita, may I interrupt your nap?"

Sofia's eyes flew open. "Excuse me? It's you."

"Who else would I be?" answered Eduardo, parroting her retort to him from the day before.

"Very funny. I wasn't napping. I was—oh never mind, you startled me."

"For that, I do apologize. When you didn't answer your cell phone, I called Ginny, hoping she might know where I could find you. Obviously—"

"She did." Sofia saw a slight smile flicker across his face. "What's the big rush to talk to me?"

Eduardo claimed the empty chair. "My rush brings an invitation to meet Tomas today, if you agree. Would you give me the afternoon?"

Sofia remembered Ginny's warning to guard her heart and the vow she'd made to herself the night before to do the same. "Thank you for setting this up. Surely, we don't need an entire afternoon to visit Tomas's gallery."

"This is true, but I require an afternoon to show you more of the City of Bridges. I wish to send you

home possessing wonderful memories, so you return."
Eduardo flashed a smile at her anxious face.

"Look, Eduardo, I don't think us hanging out is sensible. I would like to visit the gallery, but—"

"I agree with what you say. In fact, I told myself this all morning."

"You did?" Sofia felt confused and amused by this beguiling man.

Eduardo gave a solemn nod. "Yes, and I didn't listen to myself. Instead, I listened to… I do not know who, but here I find myself."

Sofia flashed to the image of them waltzing. Nothing about these encounters made a lick of sense. It was up to her to lay down some boundaries. She'd get the gallery's address and go visit Tomas on her own. Her heart would stay protected. Easy enough to accomplish. Sofia turned her gaze to the rakishly handsome face and lost another inner battle. "What time?"

Surprise danced in Eduardo's eyes. "Time? Now. Yes, now is excellent for us." He stood.

"Now? But I'm working on my dissertation."

Eduardo leaned in close to look at her laptop's blank screen. "I think not."

She smiled sheepishly and failed at ignoring his proximity. "Okay. Help me pack up. I need to go change before we head off for the afternoon."

"May I drive us part of the way? Apologies, I must leave my car in a parking lot. Venice offers no welcome for vehicles having wheels. Just say, 'Yes, Eduardo," he said with a slight laugh, taking her case.

Sofia released a sigh. "Yes, Eduardo." She'd become putty—malleable putty—in his hands. Where had her willpower gone? Sofia admitted she possessed none. All of which made little sense to her logical, always-in-control self. Maybe he wouldn't ask to see her again. A wave of sadness at the thought followed her out the library door toward Eduardo's car.

"You travel in style." Sofia climbed inside the expensive black Italian sports car, feeling the luxurious leather seat enveloping her.

"What is the saying? When in Rome, do as the Romans do." Eduardo fired up the engine. "She purrs. Yes?"

A smile tugged at Sofia's lips, thinking of men and their love of cars. "Yes, she purrs nicely." Sofia watched Eduardo deftly shift gears. He was the master of the machine. A happy Sophia gazed out the window, anticipating an afternoon of the unexpected.

****

Taking her cue from Eduardo's attire, Sophia hurried to change into jeans and a daisy-printed cotton shirt. Slipping on a vintage white lace duster, her eyes surveyed the look in the bedroom mirror. Borrowing from Italian women's iconic style, Sofia added a gold chain and earrings. "I'm good. Understated but right for the gallery and whatever the day holds," Sofia told the mirror. Grabbing her tote bag, she hurried downstairs.

Sofia spied Eduardo, arms folded and leaning against a post. She'd gladly give more than a penny for his thoughts. It was a sin for any man to look so dashing yet unaware of the fact. Charming and swoonable were a lethal combo. "Sorry I took so long."

Eduardo's lips parted to reply but stopped. His eyes took in her attire. "You look very nice. Daisies become you. Pardon me if I overstepped." Eduardo cleared his throat.

"Thank you for the compliment." Sofia beamed.

"Of course." Eduardo's lips smiled faintly. "We shall walk the few blocks to where my car is parked. Venice isn't friendly to automobiles, as you know."

Eduardo and Sofia exchanged glances while three chattering tourists pointed at every window flower box along their journey. Venice's afternoon light seemed to awaken the flowers' kaleidoscope colors. The water's calmness made the walk even more enjoyable.

Sofia turned to Eduardo. "So, what's the plan?"

"Yes, the plan," Eduardo replied. "I like your enthusiasm. Yes is the word?"

"Enthusiasm is the word." Sofia gave him a half-smile as they walked a couple of blocks to Eduardo's parked car.

****

Eduardo closed the driver's door and continued, "I rang Tomas while you did the change of clothes. He's waiting for us. If you agree, we can take lunch afterward? There's this place—well, you shall see. I think you'll approve."

Sofia nodded and relaxed into the seat, releasing a happy sigh. Her afternoon held promise.

"Do you know your smile rivals the sun?" Eduardo glanced sideways at her. "I fear I overstepped again." He shrugged broad shoulders that any athlete would covet. "Do you mind my words terribly?" He steered the car onto a main street.

"No, not terribly." Sofia watched him maneuver the vehicle easily around delivery trucks.

"You're teasing me, but I don't mind this." Eduardo reached for her hand. "Please, don't mind this either. It cannot be helped, these feelings…these outbursts."

A feeling of excitement fluttered inside her at his touch before surprising them both with laughter.

Eduardo frowned and released her hand. "Should I feel offended?" He studied Sofia's face for a few seconds while stopped at a red light. He joined her, laughing. "I should feel pleased. Much better all around."

Sofia's laughter retreated, but her smile remained. "Why pleased?"

Eduardo's voice softened. "Pleased because I see in your eyes that you suffer the same as me."

"I have no idea what—"

Eduardo raised a hand. "Do not deny, Sofia. We suffer together this strange magnetism for each other. I feel we must have some destiny to encounter. Shall we see where it leads?"

"Look, I'm here for a few more days. There's no time for us to see where anything leads." Sophia's tone was tinged with something that defied naming.

"You're wrong." Eduardo turned into a small lot and parked. "We have been brought here to this moment—to Tomas, to his gallery, to our next experience. After our visit, I will feed you well and show you a bridge or two if you're amiable. Amiable?"

"Yes, amiable," agreed Sofia but said no more. They were at a point where she needed to make her position clear.

"What's to object to? I see nothing." With those words, Eduardo exited the car.

Sophia hopped out before he could open her door. "Okay, let me make a few things crystal clear. I'm not looking for any week-long dalliance with you."

"No dalliance? How unfortunate for us." A smile edged Eduardo's mouth.

"Would you stop teasing?" Sofia continued to drive her message for both of their sakes. "I won't deny seeing Venice from your perspective is rather enjoyable. If you choose to view these outings as your destiny, fine. For me, it's fun without strings or anything else."

"I see." Eduardo's frown turned into a grin. "Still, you avoid our attraction. The pull of the magnet, so to say."

Sofia released an exasperated breath. "Okay, I will agree to feeling a strange kind of connection to you, but I'm able to disregard what you label as destiny. You should too." She marched toward the gallery's entrance and felt angry at her uncharacteristic harshness.

Eduardo approached and tapped her gently on the shoulder.

She spun around, and he leaned forward, his warm lips touching hers. The kiss, though brief, carried a message as old as eternity.

Eduardo broke away. His eyes held hers. "Our destiny, Señorita Sofia, is *ours* to experience and cannot be so easily disregarded."

Chapter 6

Diffused sunlight from the gallery's skylights cascaded into a hexagon-shaped reception area. A Roman-style fountain stood in the center on a gleaming marble floor. The water's voice created an ambiance of serenity. Sofia found the opalescent wall color fascinating and the ideal backdrop for the few watercolor paintings displayed. Two gold brocade chairs tucked in corners invited visitors for a brief sit. Despite the small gallery, she sensed it housed treasures.

"The space speaks to you?" asked Eduardo.

"Very much." Hearing footsteps approaching, Sofia said no more.

An impeccably dressed man in his early forties approached. He wore his Italian heritage well. Tomas's eyes found Sofia for a brief moment but turned to Eduardo. "*Mio amico*."

"In English, my friend," said Eduardo. "Tomas, allow me to introduce you. This is Sofia Martin."

"Hello, Sofia. A pleasure, *signorina*." Tomas's hand reached out in greeting. "Welcome to Galleria Alcova."

"As in Alcove?" asked Sofia.

"Yes, that's correct." Tomas moved an easel a few inches. "It's a surprise for many to discover the Alcova hiding down the narrow cobblestone street. To surprise is to delight. Right, Eduardo?"

"*Exacto*. It's why I brought Sofia here." Eduardo inclined his head her way.

Tomas opened a hidden paneled door. "Would you prefer my quick guided tour or a self-guided one?"

"Whatever you think," answered Eduardo.

"Let me at least make the introduction. I confess to having an unexpected dealer arriving in fifteen minutes. It's a meeting I could not decline. Apologies, but allow me to show you my favorite room."

Sofia shook her head. "Please, no apology is necessary, Tomas. I'm sure Eduardo can fill in for you."

"Absolutely. And, if questions come to Sofia, we can always return," said Eduardo.

"But of course. In fact, I hope you will do so. Shall we?" Tomas extended his hand for them to enter the next room. "I call this the Gilded Room."

Sofia glanced at the shimmering gold walls and carved marble rosette molding traveling the room's perimeter. "The name fits," she whispered and stepped inside. Baroque carved display cases took center stage and grabbed Sofia's breath in awe.

Jewelry had always been a passion. As a little girl, she'd lose an afternoon sifting through her mother's jewelry armoire. Sofia loved the gems' colors and how each carried a unique fingerprint. Artisans of jewelry design understood they were creating time stamps of beauty. Telling their story in amazing ways had become the heart of Sofia's dissertation.

Forgetting both men, she hurried to the closest exhibit featuring early 1900s Edwardian-era designs from the United Kingdom. Sofia peered inside the case, admiring Tomas's lovely collections of the dainty platinum filigree pieces encrusted with diamonds. Rings cast as flowers defined this popular style. Sofia glanced at Tomas and Eduardo.

"Your face tells me you know the Edwardian pattern," said Tomas. "It's most distinctive. Obtaining these fine pieces has been a satisfying journey. I've combed many antique shops in Europe and bid on inventories at estate sales to collect what you see in the Gilded Room."

Eduardo approached Sofia's side. "Did you know the word jewelry is derived from the Latin word *jocale*?"

Tomas glanced at his gold watch.

"The English translation means plaything," supplied Sofia, moving to the next display. "What other trivia do you have to dazzle me with?"

Tomas chuckled.

Eduardo cut him a glare. "I shall make another jab at—"

"Stab," said Sofia softly.

"Fine. I shall make another stab at dazzling." Eduardo paused. "Did you know originally, I mean back in time, jewelry was made from materials like fish bones, shells, and teeth?"

"You left out insects," supplied Sofia.

Eduardo raised an eyebrow at Tomas. "Is Sofia correct about the bugs? What woman would wear a bug? I don't know such women."

"Sofia is correct." Tomas covered his grin. "Perhaps allow her to answer your question about women's tastes. Unfortunately, I must leave you both to further enjoy the Gilded Room without me. If you're interested in art or sculpture, please wander through the large adjoining room. My assistant is nearby should you have questions."

Ignoring Eduardo for the moment, Sofia held out her hand. "Tomas, thank you for allowing me to visit and admire Galleria Alcova's collections. I've enjoyed meeting you as well."

Tomas released her hand. "You're most welcome, Signorina Sofia Martin. I feel quite sure we'll meet again. For now, I bid you *buon pomeriggio*." He disappeared behind a door.

"I like your friend tremendously."

"Yes, he's a fine man. We hope to explore a business idea very soon." Eduardo's hand touched Sofia's elbow. "Would you like to see more of the jewelry or move to the last room? There's a painting I promised Tomas I would show you."

"Do we have time for me to do both?" Sofia raised her eyes to his face and felt the crazy flutters return.

A smile tugged at Eduardo's lips. "I devote to you my day."

Sofia moved toward the next showcase. "I promise not to dawdle with the gems. I am intrigued to see the painting." Pleased she'd succeeded at forming a complete sentence, she peered into the next display of Art Deco pieces. The room housed a kind of jewelry time capsule. Sofia delighted in each showcase's contents and wished her museum could offer an exhibition of the entire collection.

Moments later, Eduardo ushered Sofia into the next room, where a guard stood discreetly in a corner. "Come just here." He positioned her in front of the oil painting. "There."

"My gosh! It's a Picasso. How did Tomas ever—?"

"He has a patron who adores him. The collector donated the Picasso to the gallery a few months back. It's Tomas's treasure and quite valuable, as you can imagine."

Sofia studied the painting. "It's also quite extraordinary."

"Yes. This is true." Eduardo's teeth flashed in a smile. "Like you."

Sofia felt his charm affecting her from six feet away. She needed air. "Are you hungry? I'm starving." Great. Her nerves had her babbling. "Let's go find lunch—something refreshingly cold." Sofia hurried the gallery's entrance before blurting out any more embarrassing declarations.

Amusement colored Eduardo's eyes a richer cognac as he caught up with her. "I see you're running away."

"Running away? I don't run—" Sofia bit her lip.

"You run. I understand it. I want to run too, but from myself. I don't know how." Eduardo grinned at his joke.

"It's just you—"

Eduardo waved his arms in frustration. "Yes, I speak without thinking when I'm around you. I cannot explain my behavior, as I've said. I cannot explain much when I'm around you."

"Let's not discuss our word filtering issues." If her rubbery legs could make it to his car, she'd have Venice's sites to distract them as they drove. "Let's go find lunch," repeated a flustered Sofia.

"Finding lunch isn't necessary." Eduardo winked at her. "I know where it waits for us and maybe another pleasant surprise."

Chapter 7

Seated back in the car, Sofia watched Eduardo send a text. She'd popped gum into her mouth to distract her.

"Now, I deliver on my promise of lunch. But first, we must drive for a time. Agreeable?"

"Yes, I'm most agreeable. In the past year, I've seldom left Venice proper. I'd love a drive and the chance to see new things. A car is a luxury in Venice. I think. Don't you agree?" Great, she was blabbering. Sofia stole a peek at Eduardo and saw more amusement in his twinkling eyes.

"I think you always chatter when you're nervous," offered Eduardo.

Sofia pondered the statement. "Hmm, I suppose I do." She sensed a flush creep up her cheeks. "But hey, it's my only character flaw." Sofia offered a sheepish grin. "Wait. How do you know this about me?"

"I just know." Eduardo winked.

His irresistible charm continued to surprise her.

Eduardo pushed a button, and the car's convertible top folded back, revealing a brilliant azure sky. "We have a beautiful day. All are simpatico."

While stopped at a light, Sofia breathed in the scent of flowers from a vendor and relaxed more into the seat. "Yes, a confusing simpatico appears to define us. I plan to pay it no mind. After all, I hardly know you, Eduardo Diaz."

"Perhaps this may change. We have time to know more on this ride." Eduardo engaged first gear.

For the next half hour, their route took the couple along the countryside. Villas and small villages greeted them as they traveled. Italy's enchantments were evident. While the miles ticked by, their conversation centered around each completing their work in Venice and returning home. Both acknowledged a bittersweetness to the ending.

Sofia clipped her wind-blown hair and wished she'd brought a hat. "So, I know about your teaching for Milo. I'd love to hear what work you do back in Spain."

"So, you wish to know about my real world. Will you return me the favor?"

"You mean tell you about my real world in Boston?"

"Yes. Will you?" Eduardo's eyebrow lifted.

"Deal. You go first." Sofia waved to three children selling vegetables from a roadside stand.

Eduardo thrust a hand through his black hair. "For generations, my family has owned Olivar Siete Colinas, or you might call it Seven Hills Olive Groves in the Andalucía region of Spain. Soon my father wishes to step aside. As the eldest son, I'm to assume my rightful role to run things, as you say it."

Sofia studied Eduardo's face and sensed he was holding back. "That's quite a heritage and responsibility. Is it what you want to do?"

"Yes, but I want the freedom to make changes or improvements to our enterprise." Eduardo paused.

"I gather you've been met with resistance?"

"You read me well, señorita. My father and I aren't

in harmony on this subject. Milo's request for teaching help came at a good time."

"I think I understand. You needed some distance to clear your head and hopefully give your father time to reconsider his position. I'm sure you offered wonderful ideas to explore." Sofia watched his frown lines ease.

"You grasp my goal perfecto." His face beamed. "I've created a proposal detailing the goals and profit projections for the next five years." Eduardo glanced at Sofia.

"Have you presented this proposal to your father?"

Eduardo shook his head. "No, when I left, he was not in the mood. My younger brother, Ernesto, had announced his desire to play music in Ireland. It's where his latest girlfriend resides. He likes to follow his desires."

Sofia could envision their father's disappointment if both sons weren't involved in tending the groves. "Dare I ask what kind of music?"

Eduardo's jaw clenched. "I believe Celtic. The style matters not to my father. He gave Ernesto thirty days to return home, or he'd cut off his allowance. You now get an idea of my family and world. Let us not talk more of this and ruin our day."

"Okay." Sofia felt herself falling more under his spell. Eduardo had solidness and loyalty at his core, and those rare traits earned her respect.

"There's the entrance. Do not look. I wish to delight you with the best view."

Sofia closed her eyes, smiling. "Okay, you big tease, tell me when I can look." The car slowed to a stop. Hearing the convertible top raising followed by the driver's door opening clued her they must have arrived. Sofia waited for Eduardo to set her free. Those three words took flight in her mind. Did she want to be set free? Free from what? And why did Eduardo's face become the answer? The door opened, and his hand clasped hers, awakening the annoying butterflies.

"You may stand and open your eyes. This place is historical as much of Italy is."

"How incredible. I—" Sofia dropped the rest of her words as her eyes took in the most spectacular botanical gardens she'd ever encountered. "Eduardo, this place is breathtakingly beautiful."

"I think you mean breath-giving beautiful. Beauty gives breath to us. It does not take. See? I can offer you help with the English words too."

Sofia pondered his answer briefly and turned a face full of happiness toward Eduardo. "You're absolutely right, and thank you. Breath-giving it is."

Eduardo grabbed a blanket from the car's trunk. "Let's head right, toward the gate."

Sofia took his hand without hesitation or thought. Her excitement and happiness trumped her mind's attempt to rain on the day. Up ahead, Sofia spied two things. Gardens of vibrant colored flowers were laid out like a patchwork quilt, and a man waved, approaching Eduardo.

"Thank you, Roberto, for this exceptional kindness."

"My pleasure, Señor Diaz. May I look forward to seeing you before your return home?"

"You may count on it, my friend." Eduardo tucked the blanket under his arm and accepted the basket.

Roberto dipped his head to Sofia and turned toward the parking lot.

"We now have our lunch. Shall we?" asked Eduardo.

"I have to say, Eduardo, you know how to dazzle a girl. First, by bringing me to this incredible botanical garden and now having our lunch delivered. You must rank as somebody special." Sofia stole a quick glance at his handsome face.

"I see this differently." A grin touched Eduardo's mouth.

Sofia tilted her nose in the air pretending to take offense. "I await your version."

"It's simple. I see it this way." Eduardo paused, staring at her. "I am not the somebody special. Instead, I'm with the somebody special." He bent down and kissed her forehead.

"Oh. That was another surprise." Sofia's fingers nervously touched the place his lips had been.

Eduardo released a loud laugh. "Tell me, do we like the surprise?"

Sofia rewarded him with a dazzling smile rivaling the sun overhead. "We did, though it's unwise to. Now, will you please feed me what's in the basket before I start gnawing on tree bark?"

"Of course." Live music played nearby as they walked to where Eduardo had chosen for the picnic. "What a perfect song for the gardens. It's very Venetian in melody. Do you hear the influence?" asked Eduardo.

"Yes, and I'm picking up on an underlying mystery threading with the guitar. Maybe even a dash of passion accompanying the piano." Sofia paused, studying Eduardo's face. "You think me crazy interpreting music in such a way."

"On the contrary, I think you speak music fluently.

We must listen and soak in more."

Sofia's eyes met Eduardo's serious ones. "Okay, I'm listening." She took advantage of the music's gift and did some reflecting as they strolled through the central gardens.

Roses were Italy's flower, and their passion for them was evident by the many varieties showcased in the main garden. Sofia chose a favorite color only to abandon it seconds later for another. The fragrance of the blossoms fed her spirit more joy, bringing a wispy memory of another time with Italian roses. Sofia dismissed the thought, stealing a peek at the man walking alongside.

Eduardo's treatment of her, while both charming and often infuriating, seemed laced with respect and good manners. Even the brief unexpected kisses were placed respectfully. The latter sadly missing from her dismal dating history with men back home.

Sofia's definition of true love had proven evasive in finding. An engagement ring never tempted her finger. Countless times, she'd refused to settle for the tepid relationships that had befallen her. Sofia admitted honestly, Eduardo was anything but tepid. No, he was a fascinating enigma with way too much appeal.

Stealing another peek at her charmer produced a sigh. There were only a few days left in Venice. The very thought caused her throat to tighten with emotion. The music faded away. Eduardo's voice brought her into the present.

"I draw your attention to the tall hedge. See the private opening?"

Sofia gave a slight nod. "Are we heading there?"

"Yes, inside is a grass-like velvet carpet. It's our

special place." Eduardo waited for Sofia to go first.

"Special? Do you mean just our place to picnic?" Sofia kicked off her sandals and felt the soft grass under her feet. The same familiar knowing she'd experienced the first time seeing Eduardo returned. The knowing they'd managed to side-step. "Eduardo? Tell me you meant it only as our place to enjoy lunch."

Wearing a frown, Eduardo spread out the blanket. "Yes, I meant our place to take lunch."

"Whew, that's a relief because silly me—"

"But, Sofia, surely you feel the strange connection here to us? Is somehow familiar?"

"Nope. Sofia surely doesn't want to feel the strange connection or take this subject further. We're about food and flowers. Flowers and food…" Her voice trailed off, seeing the sandwich Eduardo handed her.

"Either I'm your prince or your servant." A mask of reserve seemed to cover Eduardo's face.

Sofia swallowed. "How did—? How could you know peanut butter, honey, and bananas is my favorite sandwich? I haven't eaten one in a very long time. Eduardo, explain."

"I think I'm to be called Prince Eduardo by you. Let us hope answers may come later." He unwrapped his sandwich and lifted the top slice. "*Manda narices.*"

Sofia reacted to his word and peered at Eduardo's lunch. "Roberto left off your tomato relish. Disappointing." She shrugged and took a bite of her sandwich. "So good."

Awareness hit them at the exact moment.

"How did you possess knowledge of my relish preference on my roast beef?"

Sofia stopped chewing. "This is insane, Eduardo.

We can't possibly have this information about each other's likes and dislikes. We've only just met. Hells bells, we live on different continents. We speak different languages. We—"

"And yet, Sofia, we share this strange bond, I call it. From the moment my eyes saw you sitting at the table sipping your cappuccino, I felt a tug here." Eduardo touched his chest. "My heart recognized you. I cannot explain the how. I cannot explain the feelings, except to say they grow by the minute…by the second. I'm powerless over this tugging. Is it the same for you? Do not lie to us."

Sofia laid her sandwich aside and stood. "It's all closing in on me. Nothing makes any sense. This whole lunch—" Her breath felt trapped inside. "Please understand. I need a few moments alone to walk around and collect myself. Maybe I will have an answer to bring back…for us."

Eduardo's voice came from a faraway place. "I will wait for you."

Chapter 8

Sofia's appetite for food abandoned her. In its stead came a hunger for answers. Answers that are usually hidden in ancient texts or held by monks sitting on a mountaintop chanting single-syllable words. She had access to neither. Hearing the musicians playing once more, Sofia walked toward the sound. A green wrought-iron bench scrolled with flowers waited for her up ahead. Taking a seat, Sofia closed her eyes, letting the song's calm melody do its magic until a woman's voice intruded.

"Hello there. May I share this seat with you?"

"Sure." Sofia scooted over, wondering if leaving to reclaim her peace on a different bench made sense. She observed the older woman adjust her yellow straw sunhat. There existed a refinement around her and something else Sofia sensed but couldn't name.

"I find music a lovely portal to gaining a greater understanding of one's quandaries." Her eyes fixated on the gazebo where the trio was playing. "The composer of the piece understands this. And the musicians bestow the gift to listeners who possess such awareness."

There was no desire to engage in some elevated chatter with the woman. Sofia wanted time alone to figure out what was happening between her and Eduardo. She'd give some polite answer and make an excuse to go.

"I hope you'll choose to stay so we can enjoy a nice visit."

Taken aback by the woman's words, Sofia turned to face her. Odd, the woman's English lacked any accent, even a regional one from the States. "Thank you, but I've someone waiting for—"

"Perhaps you can spare a few moments. I'm called Dina, and you are?" The woman smiled sweetly.

Sofia couldn't behave rudely. "Sofia." Now what? She waited for Dina's pleasant visit to continue, and hopefully end soon.

"Sofia, we share something in common." Her bench buddy smoothed a wrinkle from her linen skirt. "Would you care to know?"

"Yes, I suppose so." Sofia noticed the song changed. There was a playfulness to the tune which lifted her spirit. "What do we share?"

"The names Sofia and Dina mean the same. Wisdom. I find that a most interesting association."

Puzzled, Sofia gazed at the woman.

"You appear confused, but I sense it's around someone other than me and our names." Dina's eyes scanned Sofia's face. "And it's been my experience when I see that particularly confused demeanor on a woman's face, it usually involves a man. Being drawn to the intended one can throw one off-kilter." Dina swayed with the music. "Are you finding this so?"

"Very so. I don't understand a whit of what's happening, nor can I explain why I'm telling this to you. Calling him 'my intended' adds to my…well, it's adding something. I just don't know what yet. Please excuse my rudeness." Flustered, Sofia exhaled loudly.

"Rudeness is merely expressing frustration." Dina

paused. "Life's complications between two people can often cloud their destiny." The woman made a tsking sound. "Such a sad thing to witness."

For some reason that defied her logical mind, Sofia liked Dina's company and didn't abandon their bench. "I've never considered destiny as something real, especially in romance. I'm too pragmatic." Sofia paused to assess her situation. The whole thing flirted with lunacy. Here she sat, discussing relationships and destiny with someone named Dina. At the same time, a man waited in a private garden for her return. Not just any man but Eduardo, the man who caused her butterflies and knew her peanut butter sandwich preference. "You seem like a wise woman. You really believe in this whole destiny business?"

"I not only believe it, but I also live it."

Sofia peeked at her gold watch. She needed to return to Eduardo.

"Give me a few more moments to gift you what I brought. Discounting destiny often leads one off their life path. The secret, Sofia, is knowing how to distinguish destiny's direction from the mind's misdirection. Do you understand?" Dina asked.

"I'm grasping some of this. Yes, I can see the difference between destiny's direction and the mind's misdirection. Actually, your words are profound."

"The mind delights in misdirecting us in order to keep control. When you sit with those words, I'm sure they will find a home," said Dina.

Sofia swallowed her hesitation, desperate for someone to listen. A stranger like Dina was a gift. Sofia wouldn't have to worry about being judged or her crazy thoughts getting out to others she knew. "Okay, sage

Dina. Would you please help me understand why my last few days in Venice have been so mystifying?"

"Why don't you elaborate? To do so might help illumine the answers you seek." Dina opened a bottle of water and took a sip.

"Well, I need some fast answers, so here goes. It all began with seeing this incredibly handsome man named Eduardo at a café yesterday. I sensed something familiar about him. You know, like I'd met him before but couldn't place where or when. We didn't communicate or anything other than me waving to his nod."

"What a lovely first introduction to your destinies," said Dina.

"If you say so." Sofia felt the last vestiges of worry about sharing evaporate. "Less than an hour later, we were thrown together, literally in a pit of mud." A laugh escaped her recalling their mud bath.

Dina clapped her hands. "A funny first encounter always sets the tone of future interactions. Do go on."

"You'd be right. We were a mess and declared the other at fault. If recorded, our performance would have gone viral." Sofia grinned in eagerness to continue.

"Fate's sense of humor can become formidable."

Sofia nodded. "Later that evening, we found ourselves invited to the same dinner party. I mean, what are the odds in all of Venice we'd end up seated next to each other sharing a meal and the same friends?"

"Quite extraordinary." A glimmer of amusement shone into Dina's eyes.

"On that, we can agree. If those encounters weren't crazy enough, Eduardo and I are discovering we know unexplainable things about each other."

"For example?"

"For example, today we came to the botanical garden to enjoy a picnic lunch. Eduardo produced my favorite sandwich since childhood, peanut butter with bananas and honey. And I, in turn, notice and lament the tomato relish left off his roast beef sandwich. How could we possibly know these preferences about each other?"

"Yes, I can certainly see why you'd question those powerful examples."

"Dina, I don't understand why I'm sitting here pouring out my last two days with someone who plopped down on a bench, inviting me to have a little chat. I don't understand why my world has stopped spinning normally on its axis. I don't understand this strong attraction I feel toward this guy. And I really don't understand having a flight of fancy seeing myself dancing at some ball in his arms." Sofia grabbed a breath.

"And you have one more statement which needs a release," said Dina.

"Of course, and somehow you know this. I need to bring some nebulous answers to Eduardo, assuming he's still waiting for me."

"I'm sure he waits." A smile crinkled Dina's mouth. "Would you like me to offer a fresh approach?"

"Offer me anything rational and grounded in reality."

"I offer you a single word. Acceptance. Pour it like concrete into your and Eduardo's relationship foundation. Let it set without disturbance. Continue to allow destiny to draw you two closer. Allow things to unfold naturally without your interference. For it is said, time and destiny keep good company. Trust and believe, time will reveal all you need to know if you but accept." Dina lifted her hands to punctuate her words. "Accept things as they appear."

"Wow, you're speaking high-minded concepts, well above my ken. You're suggesting I accept all of this and keep moseying along with Eduardo?"

"Or you can choose to end things now and go your separate ways. How do you feel—not think—about taking that direction?" asked Dina.

An empty ache entered Sofia's solar plexus, scattering the Eduardo butterflies away. She drew a shaky breath. "I can't end us. I don't know how there can even be an us, but—"

"Destiny knows. Try by accepting this truth and one more." Dina rose. "Never forget you always have free will."

Sofia stood. "Free will is highly overrated."

"But necessary in this life," added Dina.

"You're a wonderful sage, and I'm grateful for the unexpected gifts you brought to me. Though I don't understand why you appeared on the bench." Sofia raised her arms in surrender.

"Destiny, my lovely Sofia. Destiny deemed our meeting. Now, I must go so you can return to your debonair Eduardo Diaz."

"Perhaps it is destiny. Goodbye, and thank you for the incredible sharing." Sofia walked a few yards and stopped. How did Dina know Eduardo's last name? She'd never shared it with her.

****

Entering the private garden spot, Sofia observed Eduardo engrossed in reading a small leather-bound book. Once again, she felt smitten just gazing at him. His coal-black hair was cut to perfection, and his olive skin complementing those cognac-colored eyes made him irresistible. While Eduardo Diaz didn't have a bodybuilder's frame, Sofia knew his physical strength hid behind the clothes, and his inner strength showed in words. He'd become an undeniable, potent aphrodisiac from the first moment seeing him at the bistro.

Eduardo looked up. "Ah, Sofia, you return finally. Your face tells me we're better to continue being an us?"

A smile played about her lips. "Yes, we're better to continue being an us."

"Tell me how you came to know this." Eduardo patted the place beside him.

Sofia sat facing him. "I had another strange encounter. While sitting on a bench contemplating *us*, I met a wise woman named Dina. We chatted a bit about…well, you and me. Don't ask me to explain the impossible, but Dina gave me a word to bring back in answer to our confusion." Sofia peered inside the basket and retrieved her sandwich.

"Yes, please, eat. And the word?" Eduardo opened a bottle of mint green tea and placed it next to Sofia.

"Mint green tea? How? This is making me—" Sofia grew quiet. Accept things, her mind chided. "Mint green tea is—"

"Another favorite? I remain a puzzled prince in good standing." Eduardo did a mock bow. "Enough delay. What's this word?"

Sofia swallowed her bite. "Accept."

"Accept," Eduardo repeated. His eyes followed two blue butterflies frolicking around a bed of daisies.

"Yes, and we have two options of acceptance. We can accept and not question what's happening between us. Time will show us what we need to know. Or we can simply cease being an us starting now."

Eduardo said nothing but stood and walked around the garden area.

Finishing her lunch, Sofia allowed him space to contemplate. Unable to get a read on his changing expressions, a worried frown appeared on her face. Until now, she'd never considered Eduardo might choose to end things. Sofia chased her fear with a gulp of tea and reached for the abandoned book. Seeing the title, a sigh escaped her lips. It was *Don Quixote* by Cervantes.

Chapter 9

Eduardo returned to their blanket. His face wore frustration with a resoluteness.

Sofia's throat tightened in expectation and she wondered why his answer mattered so much. "Well? What's it going to be? Pack up now and go our separate ways, or continue seeing each other?"

A look of high emotion flashed over Eduardo's face. "A moment, please. I need to collect my ideas."

"Thoughts. You need to collect your thoughts."

"Whatever you say." He stood and walked toward the daisy garden.

Sofia found a bag of Zaeti cookies in the basket. How could Eduardo know they were another of her Italian favorites? She munched one while waiting.

Eduardo returned and sat next to her. "I bring you a third option." He held a daisy in his hand. "Let us have fate decide and be done with this inner affliction."

"How do you propose to contact fate?" Eduardo's suggestion caught her by surprise. This wasn't what she'd expected from him. Her heartbeat pattered with apprehension.

"The daisy has our answer." Eduardo plucked the first petal. "Stay." He placed it in Sofia's hand. "Go." The second followed. "Stay. Go. Stay."

"This is crazy. You're letting a daisy determine our—"

"Go," Eduardo's voice whispered as he handed Sofia the last petal. "Fate has decided for us. Agreed?" His eyes were fixed on the last petal.

Sofia's mind ran through a myriad of responses. Recalling Dina's words, her mind rejected all, save one. "I *accept* the fate your daisy declared. It's probably the wisest action for us since I leave for Boston soon." Sofia sprinkled the flower petals in a nearby planter.

"I don't like how wise feels." Eduardo reached for Sofia's hand.

"Me neither, but the daisy is right. It's for the best."

A grin replaced Eduardo's frown. "Fate didn't say we have to end us this moment."

Sofia shook her head, confused. "No?"

"No. I'm claiming the rest of the afternoon as ours before we part. Will you spend it with me? Make more memories?"

"I don't think—"

Eduardo pulled Sofia to her feet. "Do not think, señorita. Come. The gardens have much to show us."

The idea pleased her. He led her to the main walkway. Her mind said a few more hours wouldn't matter either way. Sofia's heart tried to tell it differently.

They strolled along, taking in nature's beauty. The blooms' fragrance was intoxicating when they toured the expansive greenhouse. Sofia and Eduardo were delighted at seeing the orchids and acknowledged they appeared like living sculptures. After an impassioned discussion, they found agreement, awarding one yellow orchid first place for elegance.

Eduardo excused himself and returned with a

surprise for Sofia. He'd purchased a dainty yellow orchid corsage from a sidewalk vendor. "For your Venice memory collection." His breath stirred her hair as he pinned the flower to her blouse.

"It's lovely. Thank you." Sofia stepped back, feeling a flush tinge her cheeks. How her heart dreaded their parting. Eduardo brought her unexpected pleasure and happiness. Anticipating the withdrawal of those feelings left an ache. Sofia touched the flower and stole a glance at the man who'd cast a spell on her.

"Listen." Eduardo halted. "The music, it plays once more with a happy voice." His body swayed, catching the rhythm. "It's very nice. You agree?"

"It's very nice. I hear the happy voice too." Sophia's laughter bubbled up as Eduardo waltzed around the sidewalk. His arms wrapped around a pretend partner.

"We must match the happiness. Yes?" Eduardo swept a surprised Sofia into his arms and continued the dance to the delight of watching tourists.

"That's what I call grand passion. Why don't you ever dance me around like that, Abner?" A woman standing a few feet away poked her husband in the ribs.

"Because we aren't svelte like those two. That's why." Abner chuckled and winked at Sofia as he waddled past.

The music ended, and applause replaced the silence. Eduardo bowed deeply. "It's a day for memories. We must now go make more," he told their smiling audience.

Sofia couldn't recall ever feeling carefree. She often pondered what the emotion meant when she heard others proclaim the experience. Eduardo had just given her carefree, wrapped in his charming ways of interacting with the world. And she wanted more.

They wiled away the afternoon, enjoying paddling a canoe around a small lake. Visiting an aviary gave Eduardo a chance to show off his knowledge of water birds. Her only contribution was saving him from a heron who wanted to leave a lasting impression on his shirt.

A melancholy feeling came calling. Sofia nodded to Eduardo's questioning expression. He felt it too. They walked toward his car. Their memory-making was setting with the sun. Her mind chastised her for allowing emotions for a man she hardly knew to intrude. Yet she did know Eduardo on a level they both couldn't explain but for the moment accepted. All thanks to the synchronistic Dina encounter.

Sofia watched as Eduardo touched the button to open the car's convertible top.

"The sky changes as night paints it a deeper shade. We must enjoy this on our ride back," Eduardo said.

"I agree." Sofia stole a peek at her watch and sighed. Time had turned against them.

****

Eduardo pulled into a short-term parking slot. "May I escort you to your condo door and say goodbye?" He raised an eyebrow with hope.

"Let's say goodbye here." Sofia fought back tears. "Eduardo, I've really enjoyed spending this amazing and confusing time with you. I can promise I'll never forget a moment. Thank you." Leaning in, her lips kissed his cheek. Quickly opening the door, Sofia tried to make her escape. Eduardo grabbed her hand.

"Wait. Please. Allow me to have some say."

"A say," said Sofia. The first tear fell.

"Yes. I say *gracias*, my Sofia. I can't begin to explain us, but I can tell you I'll never forget us. If only…" Eduardo's eyes, full of confusion, stared out the car's window.

A rush of emotion stormed through her body. Sofia had to escape before she'd start begging him to see her again tomorrow. She opted for humor. "Make sure you avoid the mud pit. So long, Señor Diaz." Not giving Eduardo a chance to answer, Sofia swallowed back a sob and rushed away.

Arriving at her condo, Sofia's tear-stained face ignored Lucia standing outside the bakery, waving a fresh Italian loaf her way.

Once inside, Sofia snagged a box of tissues and collapsed on the leather sofa. She'd never been a crier until now. A big, soppy wet cry was imminent and with good reason. She was completely besotted with a man she'd just met. A man her heart recognized from the first moment she laid eyes on him.

Sofia's rude cell phone rang as her hand pulled another tissue. "Hi, Melody. This isn't a good time." Sofia blew her nose.

"You're crying, which means this is a perfect time for me to call. What's up, baby sister?"

"It's nothing. Hormones." Sofia knew her sister's powers when it came to extracting information. She'd better cut her off before spilling every detail.

"Your hormones are kind to you, unlike mine." Melody hesitated. "Nope, your voice has the distinct sound of man troubles. My money is on the hot guy from Spain that you wrestled in the mud."

Sofia hiccupped and wiped her eyes. "Have I ever

told you how much I hate your ability to intuit me?"

"Many times. Stop stalling, and for Pete's sake, shut off the waterworks and tell me what's happened." Melody hollered to her husband to deal with the kids. "Hurry. I've got a war breaking out over an oatmeal cookie."

Taking a deep breath, Sofia tossed the tissue onto the pile. "You're right. It's about the guy from the mud pit. And I don't need reminding we only just met."

"I'm always right about these things. Go on," said Melody.

"Eduardo is amazing. He's wonderful. He's charming. He's handsome. He's thoughtful. He's everything. And I'm never going to see him again." Sofia went to the refrigerator and pulled out a soda.

"I knew you wouldn't listen to me. I told you to avoid any male involvement. You're leaving in a few days for home. This isn't the time—"

"To lecture me," finished Sofia. "I messed up. Okay? I admit my judgment was flawed. I never dreamed we'd make this strange kind of connection. It was like a magnet-to-steel kind of thing. No. It was like this attraction which transcended—"

"Oh boy. You're in trouble." Melody released a loud exhale. "You've fallen for this guy. Can you get an earlier flight home? You gotta get out of Venice."

"No, I can't leave yet. I've got a few more hours of work on my dissertation. Plus, Eduardo and I aren't seeing each other…ever…again." Sofia's throat tightened. She took a sip of the cold drink.

"Well, that's a relief. Listen up. Everything is going to work out," offered Melody.

"I suppose."

"You'll forget this guy soon enough. Go get something decadent from Lucia's Bakery. I'll ring you later."

"Okay. Good luck with the war of cookies." Sofia disconnected and forced a smile. Walking back to the sofa, she heard a ruckus in the condo building hall. It sounded like all of her neighbors were chatting and laughing. Unable to deny her curiosity, Sofia opened the front door to a dramatic scene.

Chapter 10

Sofia's amused neighbors were standing in their doorways, watching Eduardo knock on another condo door. He held a single daisy in his hand. "Perhaps you know Sofia Martin?" he asked the man.

"I'm here," said a confused Sofia. Her grin was as wide as the Mississippi River.

Eduardo apologized to the man next door and approached Sofia. "Hello again. *Uno momento*." He turned to his audience. "I found her. All is good."

"I don't understand what's happening. What are you doing here and holding a daisy?" Sofia whispered and waved to her neighbors.

"I'm miserable," Eduardo said, keeping his voice low. "I want what you call a do-again." He pointed to the petals.

"You want a do-over." Sofia's laughter rang out.

"If that means we give this well-behaved daisy a chance to make things right for us, then yes, I wish a do-over." Eduardo glanced to see the residents hadn't budged. "I think she likes me."

Sofia yanked him inside and shut her door. "This isn't a good idea. Are you forgetting we've known each other barely two days? We need to forget—"

"You've been crying, my Sofia." Eduardo's fingers touched her cheeks. "Do not cry for us." He tilted her head to meet his eyes.

Sofia tried to look away. Melody's warning words danced across her mind. She met Eduardo's eyes and melted.

"Your eyes are the color of the Adriatic Sea. I get lost in them."

Her heart filled with emotion. "The daisy?"

Eduardo held the flower between them. "Yes, I've got the right formula for our fate this time. Please put out your hand. I shall demonstrate for us."

"Is that so?" Sofia asked.

"Pay attention." Eduardo's expression grew serious. He touched each petal. "Stay, stay, stay." He paused. "You approve of the new method?"

"I shouldn't, but yes. Please continue."

The corner of his mouth twitched slightly. "Stay, stay, and…stay." Eduardo touched the last petal and closed her hand around his. "As you can see, destiny declares we must enjoy us. We stay and not go."

Sofia's words leaped to her lips before she could filter them. "Eduardo, I'm still not sure it's wise to…enjoy us."

"Let's not be wise like owls. Let's be like pigeons." He tried to pull Sofia into his arms.

"Pigeons? I don't want to act like a dirty pigeon." Sofia reclaimed her wits and stepped back.

Eduardo rubbed his forehead. "Perhaps I chose the wrong bird." He reached for Sofia's hand. "Do you prefer doves?"

His touch sent a warm tingling up her arm. "Doves?" Sofia took a breath. "Forget the birds. I'm trying to use good judgment despite your rigged daisy method and this…whatever this is that we feel. I realize I'm all over the place about us. When I have my wits, I know I'm leaving in a few days, and spending time with you is a really bad idea."

Eduardo's eyes narrowed with worry. "Why do you say such things? I've shown you respect, and what's the word? Tolerance?"

"Tolerance? Really?" Sofia's hands flew to her hips. Her body moved closer. "Just what have you tolerated, Señor Diaz?"

"Right now, I'm asked to tolerate your washy-wishy ways about us. And I find my tolerance slipping away, Señorita Martin."

"Wishy-washy," replied Sofia feeling her anger ebbing.

Eduardo waved his arms in the air. "There. Another example of my tolerance."

"What are you going on about now?" Sofia's voice raised a few octaves.

"I tolerate you constantly fixing my English. I'm quite gracious on this matter."

"You are, huh?" How she adored this man. Denying the truth was making her *wishy-washy* and feeding Eduardo's frustration. He returned, bringing the daisy and ridiculous petal plucking because he wanted more time with her. Sofia watched as he plopped down on her sofa.

"I sit. You think about us."

"Trust me. I am." Sofia went to get him a glass of tea. "Here. Cool off."

Eduardo nodded and took a long sip, eyeing Sofia all the while.

She returned to the kitchen and let her mind whirl with questions and possibilities. Didn't she want the exact same thing as him? For them to spend the next few days together and accept, like Dina said, what destiny delivered? Fear was running her show at this moment. Is that what she wanted? Sofia reminded herself that she'd been a sobbing mess minutes ago, missing his face and charming speaking style. Spending the following days with him might prove smart. Maybe this crazy magnetism or whatever would evaporate. Maybe he'd kiss her for real, and she'd feel zippo. Maybe not. Her cell phone rang. Horrified, Sofia watched Eduardo grab it off the end table, push the speaker button, and answer.

"Hello. This is Eduardo Diaz answering for Sofia Martin, who is presently having what you call a snit." His eyes blazed in Sofia's direction.

"Excuse me. This is Melody. I'm Sofia's sister. What's going on? Hold the fort. You're Eduardo. The Eduardo that's got my sister all—"

Sofia hurried to the sofa to take the phone, but Eduardo was stealthy and dodged her.

"Yes, I'm the Eduardo that has been very tolerant of your sister's—you see, she's cast a spell upon me. Did you know this, Melody? I'm what you call besotted. I fear this is true."

Sofia snagged the phone from behind and turned off the speaker. "Hi, Melody. Listen, this isn't a good time, as you can tell. May I ring you back later?" Tossing the phone on a sofa pillow, an amused Sofia turned suddenly to face Eduardo. "You're correct. I was having a snit."

"A proper snit. It was becoming. Do you know I can feel your moods, my Sofia?" Eduardo's voice softened. "Do you not feel mine?" He moved closer.

"I—" Sofia swallowed, liking too much how it felt

having his arms wrapped around her waist. She gazed up at Eduardo. "Did you say you're besotted?"

"I may have in the heat of the moment." Eduardo's eyes were fixed on Sofia's lips. His fingers traced their outline.

The butterflies fluttered at his touch. Was as he going to kiss her? Was she going to kiss him back?

A tap at the front door caused their moment to pass. Sofia recovered first. "Excuse me. I need to answer—" She hurried to see who waited on the other side. "Lucia."

"*Buona sera*, Sofia. I saw your gentleman come call. I had these leftover meat pies." Lucia handed the first box to Sofia, craned her neck to see inside, and offered Eduardo a shy wave.

"How thoughtful and observant of you." Sofia's voice held amusement.

"Yes, well, I thought you might like to have them for dinner since you no cook."

Eduardo approached, turning on his charming smile. "Sofia doesn't cook?"

"Not a bit, signore, though our Sofia has many other fine traits." Lucia giggled.

"This is good to know." Eduardo took the box from Sofia. "I confess to liking meat pies."

"I appreciate you both talking about me like I'm not here." Sofia's good mood was fully restored. "What's in the other box, Lucia?"

"Fregolotta. You call it a giant cookie. I felt compelled to write something in buttercream frosting. I cannot explain why. Please, both of you enjoy. I must go now."

"Thank you, Lucia. I can't wait to ring the dinner

bell." Sofia closed the door, wondering what was written on the cookie. She lifted the lid and slammed it shut.

Chapter 11

Eduardo came up behind Sofia. "What says the fregolotta?" His hands reached for the box.

Sofia smacked his hand away playfully. "The cookie talks to me and not you."

"Ah, now I really must see what the talking fregolotta says." Eduardo snagged the box and headed to the living room. His laughter rang out as Sofia chased behind him. He held the box in the air.

"Give me that box." She jumped up, trying for it.

Eduardo moved behind the sofa and lifted the lid. "*Segui il tuocuore.*" He passed the box to Sofia. "This is what you call a smart cookie. You should listen." Eduardo followed her back to the kitchen.

Sofia laid the carton on the counter and got plates for their meat pies. "What do you know about a smart cookie? Could you please translate it for me? I only know the word heart in Italian, and that was enough to alert me this message spelled—something." Sofia lifted her palm.

A teasing smile crossed Eduardo's face. "The fregolotta says, 'Follow your heart.' Is a smart cookie."

"Isn't that just swell? Now, I'm getting directions on how to live my life from a cookie? And craziest of all is you're listening and agreeing. Do you want a salad?"

"A salad? You change the topic fast. Lucia said

you and the kitchen are not simpatico. I'm not sure if I dare eat—"

"Oh, for pity's sake. You don't cook a salad." Sofia emptied the container of fixings into a wooden bowl and pulled a bottle of dressing from the fridge. "Toss it while I warm the pies."

Eduardo delivered a smart salute and took the salad tongs. "So, I'm wondering since you sort of invited me to dinner and we've reached an understanding to keep us going—what now?"

Sofia grabbed the tongs. "You're beating the lettuce like it's an egg. Gently toss it like this." Sofia demonstrated, showing a gentle hand. "And I thought I had kitchen lacks. What were you saying?"

"I'm told by many I have few lacks in any department." A smirking Eduardo moved the salad into the waiting wood bowls. "Never mind. I was saying would you like for me to show you more of Venice after we dine on my beaten salad and Lucia's pies?"

"Hmm, a man with few lacks offering to show me more of Venice," Sofia pondered, her face bemused.

"You mock me. I shall ignore this." Eduardo took the salads to the dining table. "We can bring pieces of the fregolotta to eat while we follow your heart."

"Who's mocking now?" Sofia removed the pies from the microwave onto two colorful plates that reminded her of ripe mangos. "Here's yours and a bottle of sparkling mineral water. Let's go eat and discuss your idea, Man of la Mancha."

"Andalusia. I'm a man from Andalusia," said Eduardo.

"I was merely referencing the book you're reading, *Don Quixote of la Mancha*." Sofia gave a little shrug letting him have his win. "I stand corrected. Wow, this chicken pie tastes incredible. Lucia has a way with herbs."

"She does. I'm glad Lucia brought four. I find my appetite is much approved since the afternoon miseries." Eduardo took another bite.

"Improved. Your appetite is improved." Sofia smiled across the table.

"They sound very much the same. We let this one go. Eat faster. I have an idea for where I must take your heart." Eduardo's cell phone chimed. He paused to see who was calling. "*Un momento*, if you please."

Sofia listened to the Castellano words flying around the room as Eduardo paced. He was a man full of confidence and passion. She'd always admired those qualities and found them missing in the men she'd dated. Eduardo first experienced his world from a sensory place and then let his mind interpret it. For her, it had been the opposite. Her mind called the tune before she could taste life's gifts.

An awareness hit her. Fear had driven too many of her life's choices. Passion and confidence sat in the back seat of her mind's constant chattering and dictates. Eduardo's influence was shining a light on her own lack. She'd always heard when you point a finger toward someone else's flaws, it really should be turned back on oneself. Eduardo had tolerated her 'wishy-washy' ways as a gentleman of refined manners. Sofia recalled his rant stating that fact. He showed up at her door with the ridiculous daisy because he'd chosen to follow his heart back to her. What did it mean to follow her heart? She wanted to find the answer.

Sofia stole a glance Eduardo's way. He smiled

faintly at her, said a few more words, and disconnected.

"A thousand pardons, señorita. My father had a business matter needing immediate attention." Eduardo joined her at the table.

"I understand and hope you got things resolved. I don't speak Castellano, but it sounded intense." Sofia lifted his plate. "I can reheat this for you."

"Let me do it. You finish your meal." Eduardo set the microwave and turned to Sofia. "My father holds strongly to the old methods of operating our olive groves and running my life. This I've told you. Those methods are shunning him because of technology. He resists, and I persist." Eduardo returned to the table.

"I feel sure the groves and business would thrive under your singular care." Sofia finished her last bite and folded the floral napkin. She studied the man while he ate. Eduardo's hair, the color of ink, touched his collar, giving a slight rebel impression. His broad shoulders and strong biceps came from some activity requiring strength. It wasn't a body built from steroids and hours a day in a gym. Her mind wondered if he played a sport. No, Sofia dismissed him as a player. Eduardo did things with intention. Still, she'd like to know more about what he enjoyed doing. "Hey, do you play sports or something?"

Eduardo choked and coughed. "Play sports? Me?" He shook his head and coughed again.

"I didn't mean to—"

"No, it's fine. I didn't expect the question." Eduardo's white teeth gleamed in a half-smile. "I shall answer. I don't play sports. As for me, it makes no sense to chase a ball around the ground or air, for that matter. I prefer to boat, to horseback ride, to meet nature. You understand me?" Eduardo placed his napkin next to Sofia's.

"Yes, I understand you…" Sofia's breath caught as he gently pulled her from the chair.

"You know me well, I think." Eduardo's eyes fixated on her lips.

Sofia drew a shaky breath and stepped back. Her hormones had never misbehaved like this. "So, tell me, what's your idea for us tonight?"

"You wish to distract me from kissing you. For the moment, I will obey. Yes?" Eduardo took his plate to the kitchen.

"Yes, obey is a good choice, though I feel sure you don't mean it." No man had ever taken her on such an emotional roller coaster. Didn't she want him to kiss her? Yes. Then why pull away? Fear. "Ugh."

"Ugh? I haven't even told you my idea, and I hear an 'ugh'? Surely that wasn't meant for the kiss." Eduardo returned. His hands lightly caressed her shoulders.

A sigh caught in her throat. "No, the…ugh…was for something personal." His fingers reached to stroke her arm.

"Your skin feels like silk." Eduardo moved slowly, his lips claimed Sofia's for a moment, but it was enough for both. "Yes, satin, like a gown I see you wearing to waltz with me. Do you know such a satin gown?"

Sofia closed her eyes and did the unexpected, returning Eduardo's kiss. In an instant, her mind flashed an image of a grand ballroom staged in another time. She was waltzing happily in a man's arms. Dressed in a satin gown, the color resembled lilac's first blooms.

Sofia failed to make out the face of her partner before Eduardo's husky voice brought her back. Her eyes opened.

"You know the gown? I know the gown. How? I do not know, but I see this dance with you." Eduardo wrapped his arms around Sofia, pulling her close. His lips whispered in her ear, "Dare I scare us both and tell you the color of your dress?"

Sofia took an inner leap and let go of her fear. "Tell me. Maybe you'll be wrong."

"Lilac. A beautiful lilac so pale it looked like moonbeams floating on the floor. You danced only with me. I think. We see this somehow." Releasing her, Eduardo gazed into Sofia's eyes. "Who are we?"

Chapter 12

"I have no idea." Sofia's expression grew thoughtful. "Nor do I have a clue how to find the answer. If I let myself think about these connections we keep discovering, like meeting Dina, and now Lucia's cookie with a message, I'd book the next flight home."

Eduardo's voice cut in. "Yellow. Any shade of yellow."

"What are you talking about?" asked a perplexed Sofia, returning to the sofa.

"Yellow is your favorite color. Yes?" Eduardo came to sit next to her, touching her hand. "This yellow I know."

"Nope, blue is my favorite color." Sofia's mind rebelled. She'd break this spell on them.

"Sofia? Do not lie to us. Yellow makes you happy. Any shade of yellow makes you smile. Wait."

"Where are you going? This is nuts. We're nuts," said Sofia.

"Nuts? You like macadamias most of all." Eduardo went to the kitchen and got a dinner plate from the drying rack. "This color you love more than blue. Shall I go to your closet and see what it presents? I'm sure—"

"Don't you dare go to my closet—okay, you're right. I love yellow. Blue is my second favorite color." Sofia rubbed her temples.

"And your nuts?" Eduardo returned the plate.

"Yes, I'm definitely nuts, but that's not what you mean. I can't get enough of macadamias."

"Now, tell me something about me. We must explore a little more. Then I promise to take you somewhere to distract us from this craziness." Eduardo touched Sofia's cheek. "Let me hear one thing."

Sofia closed her eyes. An image came immediately. "You wear handmade black leather boots for riding. You prefer the Andalusian horse breed because of their long Spanish heritage." Sofia's eyes opened in time to catch Eduardo's stunned expression. His frown she couldn't ignore. "Enough. I told you two things. I'm going to change so we can go." She moved toward her bedroom.

"I adore Andalusians. It's the only horse I ride in my black boots," Eduardo said to her, retreating. "How can we know these things? Feel this way?" he mumbled to himself, watching Sofia close the door.

Pulling her favorite yellow blouse from the closet, Sofia hesitated. "I refuse to wear this color tonight." Her hand tossed it on the bed only to pick it up again. Fastening the buttons, Sofia gave her mind free rein to try and apply logic to what just happened. The images coming to her felt real, though she'd never experienced anything like them before. She'd seen Eduardo riding across a pasture full of wildflowers. However, one part of the vision troubled her most. The part she intentionally left out in her recounting. She'd been riding alongside him.

Applying coral lip gloss and a spritz of jasmine fragrance, Sofia searched for Eduardo. The living room had been tidied and cushions put in place, but a handsome male presence was absent. She noticed the front door ajar and heard voices in the atrium hall. A puzzled Sofia found the source. The corners of her mouth turned up faintly.

"I see your problem. The spokes they are bent here and here." Eduardo's long tapered fingers pointed at a red bicycle's wheel. "Get me a pair of pliers. I can fix this for you, Phillipe."

Sofia watched a young boy around twelve years old disappear inside one of the units. "Hiya. I see you've made a new friend."

Eduardo remained squatted, holding the bike's seat. "Yes, while you dressed, I heard the bike metal noise in the hall. I met Phillipe pushing his problem. He tells me he had a run-in with a competitor in a race."

"I see." Sofia focused on Eduardo's sexy dimple appearing when he smiled. How had she missed it?

"His bicycle won't pedal, but I can fix it easily enough for his return to Verona. You don't mind waiting a few moments?"

"No, I don't mind waiting at all. You're a great guy, Eduardo. A really great guy."

"As I've been trying to tell you, señorita. You look lovely tonight in yellow." Eduardo stood. "Would you come closer? I can't leave the bike, or it will topple."

Sofia felt his charm embrace her from five feet away. "Come closer? No, I—"

"Here are the pliers, Eduardo." Phillipe bent down, touching the damage.

Eduardo winked at Sofia. "I do not like fate's interruptions." He went to work with the pliers.

Sofia left them to retrieve her crossbody bag and secure the condo. Her mind wondered what the night had in store. With Eduardo, the unexpected was expected.

"It's fixed as good as can be done. You must ride with caution until you go home to Verona. You understand me, Phillipe?" Eduardo handed the bike over.

"Si, signore. *Grazie*." Phillipe walked his bicycle inside his grandparents' condo.

"Ready to experience more of Venice? I've arranged for us a little amusement." Eduardo offered his arm.

"Am I dressed right for this little amusement?" Sofia looped her arm through his and thought how natural it felt.

"You're perfect." Eduardo's eyes scanned her. "Perfect in all the ways which matter to me."

"Oh, wait. I forgot to bring Lucia's cookie for us." Sofia tried to turn back.

"We don't need that talking fregolotta cookie. I've something more in mind, more to our liking. You trust me on this?" Eduardo's expression turned playful.

"Yes. I'm all for leaving the cookie." Sofia wrinkled her nose. "You've got me so curious about our evening. Give me a hint where we're going," Sofia asked, hurrying with excitement down the stairs.

"A hint you require. Tonight we'll savor the sweetness of others' talents. Our destination is maybe seven blocks. We shall walk."

"Walk, of course. No boat ride. We've got a full moon and a warm breeze." Sofia adjusted her annoying handbag strap and set their pace. As they ventured down the canal side, Eduardo kept her enthralled with his knowledge of Venice's illustrious history. Sofia learned the city rested on one hundred and eighteen islands, all separated by approximately one hundred and fifteen canals.

"Did you know Venice is well known for its lace and glass?" asked Eduardo. He nodded to an older gentleman who waited for them to pass.

"I know zip about the Venetian glass," said Sofia. "Should you want to change profession, consider becoming a tour guide. What else?"

"I guide only for you. Let me think. Did you know Marco Polo was a Venetian? Or that the Rialto Market is about a thousand years old? One more. Are you aware Venice is shaped like a fish?"

"Nope. I wasn't aware of those facts. A fish, huh?" Sofia scrunched her face. "Hey, I've got one for you."

Eduardo shot a grin her way. "I'm ready to hear."

"Did you know Venice invented the concept of quarantine?" Sofia punched his arm. "I surprised you, right?"

"Yes, you did, but surprise seems to like us." Eduardo pulled Sofia closer and kissed the top of her head. "I have the last fact to give you. Many gondolas you see are black."

"Really? I never noticed. Are you sure?" Sofia squinted at two nearby gondolas.

"I'm never wrong. Surely you know this about me?" teased Eduardo.

Sofia rewarded his words with another playful poke. "On the contrary, I find men are seldom right. Haven't we covered this topic before?"

Eduardo rubbed his torso, grinning. "I'm a different kind of man for you, my Sofia. Let us leave this subject alone."

"That's probably wise." Sofia's eyes noticed a

small group of people ahead, walking and chatting merrily. Their brisk pace signaled time mattered.

Eduardo's hand touched Sofia's waist. "Follow the group. We walk down the dark lane to the right."

Giving a quick nod, Sofia followed, admiring the flower window boxes overflowing with geraniums and petunias. Her curiosity increased as they greeted the smiling face of a middle-aged actor in full theatre makeup and attire. He looked as if he'd stepped off the Shakespearean stage. Sofia's curiosity soared. She smiled at the gentleman as Eduardo shook his hand.

"Patron Diaz, welcome." His British accent was unmistakable.

"Hello to you, my friend. Are we late?" Eduardo glanced at his watch.

"Not at all. Please go right in." Giving a slight bow, the actor opened the wood-planked double doors.

Sofia's breath caught. "Eduardo, thank you." The scene unfolding in front of her offered pure enchantment, as did the man standing beside her.

Chapter 13

Eduardo led Sofia to their first-row seats. "Have you been to a theatre in the round before? Of course you have. Boston is known as a hip culture center."

"Listen to you saying hip." Sofia chuckled. "Yes, though Melody and I were young when our parents took us to see a fairy-tale performance." Sofia scrunched her nose and leaned in. "One of the actors slobbered when he talked. We had front-row seats then too."

"You carry a memory best forgotten." Eduardo nodded to a refined older couple a few yards away. "Would you excuse me? I must greet my uncle and aunt."

"Please, go." Sofia took the opportunity to study the theatre. She counted the rows and seats and determined a hundred theatergoers could attend a performance. The chairs upholstered in a moss, brocaded fabric were incredibly comfortable and roomy. Colorful designed Venetian masks decorated the walls. Their history had fascinated her ever since arriving in Venice. At different times, the law forbade wearing masks and then changed to requiring them. Sofia thought of Shakespeare's *Romeo and Juliet*. A masked ball allowed a person to be equal no matter their station in life.

The earlier vision of waltzing with Eduardo

interrupted her ponderings. Had they danced before? The scene seemed so real. Sofia relived the exhilaration of his hand on her waist as he led them around the dance floor. Passion was married to love in how they looked at each other. Sofia had never touched drugs. Was it possible someone could have slipped magic mushrooms in their lunch? No, she admonished herself for such a notion. It began at the café when she'd sensed Eduardo's presence. In that first encounter, he seemed so familiar, and a strong attraction pulled her toward him.

Destiny had seen fit to bring them together; although, she couldn't fathom for what reason. Nor could her rational mind explain how they knew things, personal things, about each other. Glancing at her yellow blouse, Sofia exhaled a sigh. Their mysterious meeting defied earthly understanding. One fact seemed certain—her confounded mind didn't have the answer. Who did? She'd leave the question open to fate, destiny, the universe, or her unreliable fairy godmother.

The theatre lights dimmed. Sofia craned her neck around to see where Eduardo had gone. She caught sight of him heading her way, bringing a smile bright enough to spotlight the actors. He was dashingly handsome like some rogue in a historical romance novel, especially when riding his beloved Andalusian.

"I beg forgiveness for being away so long. I brought you the program. I neglected to tell you about our play." Eduardo sat and positioned his long legs so others could pass.

Sofia glanced at the program. "It says this is an original play."

"Yes, the troupe performs original plays they write.

Their talent is quite extraordinary. You will agree soon enough. I confess tonight's play strikes me as fitting of us. We might learn something to help explain the unexplainables. The story of Eduardo and Sofia." He paused, staring longingly at her.

Sofia arched her brows. "Let's call it the story of Sofia and Eduardo. I'm a modern woman, despite the lilac ball gown we hallucinated earlier."

Eduardo's laugh was spontaneous, complementing his rich baritone voice.

"Shh, people are staring." Sofia glanced around, seeing smiles and nods.

"They stare because they like what they observe. Venetians thrive on romance and passion. We show both to those that can see. Shall I kiss you here?" Eduardo leaned over and tipped Sofia's chin.

"What? No. You shall not kiss me here. What makes you say things like—?"

"I'm taken by you, Sofia Martin. I'm a man with little wits or control. Lean closer. I want to—"

The theatre grew dark. The silk curtain opened as the musicians began to play.

"Fate taunts me," whispered Eduardo.

"Thankfully, or you'd make us a spectacle," Sofia whispered back.

Eduardo kissed Sofia's hand and directed her eyes to a discreet screen where English subtitles appeared.

The unexpected kiss and the haunting melody played by the orchestra melted her heart a little more.

Eduardo pointed to the line describing the play. "We're about to time travel with two lovers."

"Of course we are. And I'm not even a teeny bit surprised." Sofia turned her attention to the stage.

****

During the brief intermission, Sofia noticed Eduardo seemed withdrawn and lost in thought. While he went to get drinks for them, her thoughts reflected on the play. The setting was a small European farming community in the early eighteen hundreds. Two childhood friends had grown up carrying their parents' expectations of marriage. And though they shared a love for each other, passion was absent. The story unfolded with their dilemma of how to honor their family's expectations, yet be with the one they truly loved. Sofia appreciated the comedy as they maintained the charade for their families of acting like a couple in love. Seeing Eduardo coming her way, Sofia smiled. He truly belonged in another era where chivalry, dashing looks, and manners were intoxicating to the opposite sex. She could certainly attest to the appeal of such a man. "I'm just as besotted as you, Eduardo Diaz," Sofia mumbled under her breath.

"I chose cherry lemonade for us. I know we share a sweet tooth." Eduardo passed Sofia a frosty glass. He nodded to a woman dressed casually in white jeans and a flowered vest. Italian gold chains dripped from her neckline.

"This combination tastes amazing. Good choice." Sofia sipped from the straw.

"Yes, I've impeccable tastes in many things." Eduardo's eyes glinted.

Sofia was pleased to see his somber mood lift. "So you keep telling me. What do you think of the play? It isn't true time travel, but simply traveling back in history. The theme is timeless."

"Do you find the play boring? If so—"

"Boring? Oh, quite the contrary. I'm thrilled there isn't some mystical message in it for us. I feared any moment an actor would step off the stage and proclaim I must follow my heart or walk a labyrinth."

Eduardo's laugh rang out. "How you captivate me."

"And how you charm." Sofia rolled her eyes. "Anyway, I find everything about the play and performance delightful and entertaining. I can't wait to see how Winston and Sara resolve their dilemma and get to marry who they really love." Sofia glanced at her watch.

"I'm pleased the plot has your interest." Eduardo's tone chilled.

"You don't like the theme—?"

"No. Parents shouldn't interfere in matters of love." The lights flickered. "We must return to our seats." Eduardo handed their glasses to a passing server.

Sofa's brows creased. "I see you have a strong feeling about parental influence. Would that apply to your own children, assuming you want children?" Sofia headed in the direction of their seats, letting her question taunt him.

Eduardo pulled her to the side. "Wait. Allow me to answer. I want my children to have the freedom to choose who to love."

"Lucky for them," Sofia tossed back and continued walking.

"Can we abandon this subject? I wish to enjoy your company and not discuss fictional matters."

"I agree." They settled into their seats.

"I beg forgiveness for my mood." Eduardo sat and reached for Sofia's hand. "A personal matter from an earlier phone call has occupied my mind. Let us continue to enjoy being us. Yes?"

"Yes." Sofia sighed and squeezed Eduardo's warm hand. His touch made her feel all mushy inside. "Since your mood has improved, may I ask for something?" Sofia batted her lashes.

"The eye fluttering isn't necessary for me to say yes, though I find it amusing. Ask, quickly. The curtain is pulling back."

Sofia leaned in. "Can we go for gelato after the play? I've been craving a—"

"Peppermint dark chocolate. Yes, we must get you this. I know the best place, and it's nearby."

"Hang on." Sofia gulped. "You said peppermint dark chocolate. How did you—"

"I spoke without thought as if I knew because I did." Confusion washed over Eduardo's face. "You want the biggest gelato. No tiny cup." His eyes looked haunted. "Who's putting these things into my head?"

Sofia's shoulders lifted in a shrug and searched for a lighthearted response. "It's gotta be me. I'm warning you telepathically about ponying up big bucks for my ginormous gelato."

The lights dimmed, halting the conversation.

****

Over the promised and delivered confection, Sofia detailed to Eduardo her next few days' commitment to finishing her dissertation. Then she'd turn attention to packing up her last year in Venice and saying *arrivederci*.

Eduardo listened, nodding at the appropriate times, but otherwise stayed silent.

Sofia sensed he was still distracted by the earlier

phone call at her condo. She'd left the subject alone.

As they strolled back to the condo, she recalled Ginny's text stating she and Milo were leaving for a two-week trip to Croatia.

"Your thoughts hold your interest?" asked Eduardo.

"I was thinking about Ginny and Milo departing tomorrow afternoon for a holiday in Croatia. I'm meeting her in the morning for an espresso and to say goodbye." Sofia felt her throat tighten with emotion. "I hate goodbyes."

"Maybe you could say goodbye for now to Ginny. 'For now' feels better. Yes?" Eduardo pointed to a small pond. "Let's go there."

Sofia refastened the clip on her handbag and adjusted the strap. "For now? I don't see a return to Venice in my crystal ball."

"Perhaps your crystal ball needs a polish." Eduardo's smile didn't meet his eyes. "See here. The timing is perfect. We've arrived at the wishing pond."

"How enchanting, Eduardo." The water glistened like sparklers from the gold lights encircling it. A couple kissed on a nearby bench.

"We go this way." Eduardo led them up a narrow wooden bridge.

Sofia leaned over, gazing into the still water. "What do I do now?"

Eduardo reached inside his pocket. "It's simple, really. We toss a coin for each wish over our shoulders. Let me position you properly."

"Okay." Sofia relaxed her body while Eduardo had her lean back against the bridge's wood railing.

"Open your hand. I have a coin for you."

Sofia laughed. "I need more than one coin. How many do you have?" Her hand remained outstretched.

"Señorita, I think you're a greedy wisher," Eduardo said in an amused voice as he dropped coins into Sofia's palm.

"I am not greedy. I simply have more wishes." Sofia counted her coins. "Okay, you've given me three wishes. I need a moment to decide."

"I didn't know this stop would involve such…I don't have the word."

"I'm glad you don't have the word. I didn't need it. Now please be quiet so I can think." Eduardo's hand steadied her elbow. Sofia took the first coin and tossed it into the water. The splash confirmed her success.

"One wish up. Next." Eduardo waited.

"Here goes." Sofia sent the second coin soaring high. It held the wish for her return to Venice.

"Your arm movements show enthusiasm for the wishing. Make the third a good one. Put your everything in the toss."

Sofia nodded, amused, and swung her arm around like a baseball pitcher. She released the coin and more. The loud splash alerted her something had gone awry in her coin delivery. Her shoulder felt lighter.

Eduardo's eyes mirrored back Sofia's panic. He leaned over the railing peering into the water. "It sunk."

"Oh my gosh, I'm sunk, too. I can't believe I just tossed my purse into the water. It had my cell phone and favorite lip gloss." Panic washed over her.

"Take a breath. What else was in the bag? It was tiny, so maybe things aren't so dire." Eduardo hugged her to him.

Sofia twisted her lips, pondering. "I think I only

had my phone, gloss, a small amount of money, and mints."

"What about a key to your condo or a wallet?" asked Eduardo.

"I enter the condo with a keypad code. Thankfully, I left my wallet at home. The stupid strap clip kept opening since the mud pit debacle." Sofia shook her head and looked into the water. "What a klutz move. You encouraged me to put extra oomph into—"

"This klutz you blame on me?" asked Eduardo.

"Well…" Sofia read his face and checked her following words. "Forgive me. I did the klutz move."

"I shouldn't have encouraged your vigor to toss. I will pay for a new cell." Eduardo looked remorseful. "Still, it could have been worse. You can replace your phone tomorrow, but better to play it cautious and request a new number."

"Safe. Play it safe," responded Sofia absently. "Yeah, you're right. New phone and number to start my day. Thanks, but you're not buying it." Sofia bopped her forehead. "I can't believe I tossed my phone. Does that mean my third wish is ruined? Because I really want my third wish to come true."

"What was this wish that means so much?" Eduardo wrapped his arms around Sofia and pulled her back against him.

Sofia turned her head to the side. "I can't tell you my wish, or it definitely won't come true. You know the rule."

"How about I give you my coin that I was going to wish on? You can have a do-over."

"I can't take your coin. Make your wish and walk me home before I have some other calamities befall me." Sofia pulled away so he could do the setup.

Eduardo paused, leaned backward, and released his coin. "We can go now and bring our memory of the wishing—"

"Fiasco," supplied Sofia. The hilarity of it all was replacing her mortification. "It was a wishing fiasco. I have zero faith that any of my three wishes will see the light of day. Zero." Sofia's index finger and thumb made the sign.

"We leave it to fate, my Sofia." Eduardo reached for her hand. "It's late. I must see you safely home."

"Thanks. I'll cling to being escorted safely home since my phone abandoned me. As for fate, I remain open but skeptical."

"Your words just taunted fate. Now I must worry about another mud encounter."

Sofia tapped lightly on Eduardo's shoulder, causing him to stop. "You know what I think?"

"You think—"

"Don't answer. That question was rhetorical."

"Rhetorical. I know the word. It means I'm not required to speak." Eduardo's tone held a coolness. "So, tell me what you think?"

"I think there's something much more important worrying you, Señor Diaz. Something which has hung a gray cloud over you the whole evening. Something you'll need to attend to soon." Sofia continued walking.

Eduardo caught up and tapped Sofia's shoulder. "Know what I think? It too is rhetorical."

"Touché. What?"

"I think you think too much."

Sofia weighed his words in silence until they reached the condo building. "I do live in my head.

Maybe if I devour Lucia's 'follow your heart' cookie, I can shift more in the heart's direction." Sofia leaned against the building's entrance door, wondering what was next for them.

"Before I bid you good night, would you like to have dinner tomorrow night? I have another bridge to show you, if you like." A grin broke across his handsome face. "You must promise to let me hold your purse should you feel the pull to throw more coins."

"Yes, to everything you asked. What time?" Sofia matched his grin. Tomorrow looked promising because Eduardo still wanted to be an "us".

"I will knock on your door at eight o'clock. Until then." He leaned in and brushed her cheek with his lips and walked away.

Sofia watched him go. A gloomy feeling washed over her. It wasn't just the disappointment that Eduardo didn't try and kiss her on the lips. The feeling was somehow attached to that earlier phone call. Heavy raindrops splattered the sidewalk. Sofia glanced heavenward as lightning created a fracture across the sky. "Swell, a portending."

Chapter 14

Eduardo greeted the morning with a bullfight happening in his stomach. He turned the bottle of antacid up and chugged it, and flicked on the satellite radio choosing something calming. The song changed to what reminded him of a waltz and the woman's face that haunted his days and nights.

Meeting Sofia had proven the most incredible experience of his life in two short days. Sofia Martin was a woman like no other he'd known. Was he in love with her? A cynical laugh escaped his lips. Madly and forever, it seemed. And while he couldn't explain rationally anything about their connection and feelings for each other, he was clear on one hard fact. His life in Spain presented complications, insurmountable ones based on last night's phone call from his father.

"I have but one option." He grabbed his suitcase and threw in a few necessary things. After making a phone call, he headed out the door to his first destination.

Eduardo rang the doorbell. Waiting a few seconds, he rang again with more urgency.

The door flew open with some Italian expletives. "It's you. Whatever has you looking like a matador about to enter the ring?" Milo grinned and took a sip of his coffee.

"I am about to enter my father's ring of fire. I need

your help. Can we go somewhere private to talk?" Eduardo's eyes peered inside Milo's foyer.

"Ginny's not here. She's meeting Sofia for espresso and to say goodbye. You're safe. Come on in." Milo chuckled and stood aside for Eduardo to pass. "And to think if you'd arrived on my doorstep two hours from now, I would have missed this show."

Eduardo glared. "This isn't the time for your jokes when my life is a crumble."

"Your life isn't a crumble. It's not possible." Milo's expression couldn't hide the concern in his eyes.

Eduardo pushed past toward the kitchen. "Pour me a cup of that Turkish brew. I need fortifications."

Milo set the bright yellow mug on the table in front of Eduardo.

"Yellow. You give me coffee in a yellow mug?" Eduardo drew in an image of Sofia's face and groaned.

"What's wrong with yellow? Not masculine enough for you, matador?" Milo slapped Eduardo on the back. "Get over the color yellow and get to the telling of your woes."

Taking a large gulp of the strong brew, Eduardo gathered his thoughts. "My life has become full of complications."

Milo took a seat across the kitchen table from his friend. "What's caused these complications? I know your father's expectations weigh heavily, but I thought you'd agreed to the commitments he asked for."

Eduardo waved his arms in the air. "Yes, yes, I did this, but things have changed. I feel trapped by these agreements and—"

"Stop there, amigo. Does this have anything to do with a woman? Because it sounds like woman woes to me." Milo's eyebrow slowly raised. "But you're not currently seeing anyone, right?"

"Wrong." Eduardo stood and paced around the large kitchen. "I've seen her for only two days, and I'm taken over. We have this…this something I cannot describe without you insisting I'm loco. Who am I teasing? I am loco."

"Kidding. It's kidding, I think." Milo twisted in his chair to see Eduardo. "Your kind of loco for a man usually means he's in love. Still, two days to fall in love—who is this woman that's achieved the impossible? Roped the bull, Eduardo Diaz."

"You make the jokes when I'm in this state? It's Sofia."

Milo's expression registered surprise. "Sofia? The Sofia you fussed with the whole night at my party?"

"Yes, her." Eduardo knew he sounded edgy to his friend, but he didn't need lectures. "Do not ask more questions or offer advice. I must depart for Spain, and I need your help."

"Okay, I won't offer any of my wise advice, at least right now. I assume Sofia knows nothing about your complications."

Eduardo dropped his head. "No. I've not found the proper time to tell her. We've moved so fast in these feelings. She's a modern American woman who cannot understand my world."

"True. What can I do to help?" asked Milo.

"I've written Sofia a note telling her I have to make an unexpected trip home. I need you to deliver it before you and Ginny leave for Croatia."

"Why do I—"

"Please, let me finish. We're supposed to have

dinner tonight. I can't call Sofia because her phone was dropped in the wishing pond last night."

Milo laughed. "I'm not going to ask any questions. In fact, I wouldn't know where to begin after hearing all of this. You're right about one thing. Your life is full of complications. Give me the note."

Eduardo placed the envelope on the table. "Thank you, my friend. I shall owe you."

"I like the sound of being in Eduardo Diaz's debt. Get out of here before Ginny comes home and wheedles this story out of me. You have my word. I will take the note to Sofia's condo within the hour."

Eduardo shook Milo's hand and rushed out the door, wondering what destiny had in store for him next. At least he was listening to the cookie's message and following his heart. Would Sofia? The answer waited in the future.

****

"I've got two iced espressos with a dollop of whipped cream." Lucia set the glasses on the table. "The freshly baked cinnamon buns are on the house as you say. Enjoy, my friends."

"I'm going to miss Lucia and her delectable treats." Sofia took a bite of the roll. "So, tell me, when do you and Milo leave?" Their friendship had blossomed into something Sofia would always treasure.

Ginny glanced at her cell phone. "I need to head home in fifteen minutes. That doesn't give us much time, but then, it's probably easier to say fast goodbyes. I feel the tears building."

"Me too. I can't begin to thank you for everything you've done for me over the past year. I have something to give you as a reminder." Sofia placed a tiny foil-wrapped box in front of her friend.

"It's been my pleasure to companion you toward obtaining your doctorate. What have we here?" Ginny unwrapped the paper and lifted the lid. "Oh my, Sofia, it's lovely. A gold book charm, and you had it engraved with my initials. Thank you."

"I'm so glad you like it," said Sofia.

Ginny's cell rang. "Excuse me. It's Milo."

"Of course." Sofia glanced out the window, memorizing the scene she'd come to love. The boats moved along the canal, carrying passengers and goods to their destinations. She'd missed seeing Milo talking outside as he headed upstairs to tape Eduardo's note to her condo door.

"What do you mean you misread our departure, Milo? You navigate jungles and somehow you can't manage—fine. I'm coming home." Ginny tossed her phone into her tote. "Well, as you heard, my husband has upped our departure time to now. I'm so sorry to have to rush off." Ginny took the last sip of her espresso and rose.

"I want a hug and a promise." Sofia stood and embraced her friend.

"A promise?" Ginny draped her bag over her shoulder.

"Yep. Promise me we'll find a way to see each other next year." Sofia dabbed her eyes with a napkin.

"I promise. And it's a promise I will keep. We'll chat once you get settled in Boston." Ginny gave Sofia a final hug and dashed out the door.

Lucia filled the empty seat across from an emotional Sofia. "Goodbyes ask so much. Do they not?"

"Yes. I'm going to miss you both." Sofia managed a smile for Lucia.

"And my cookies with special messages?" teased Lucia.

"Most definitely, though I don't know where you're getting these messages?" Sofia drank her coffee and prepared to leave.

"The messages come to me, and I deliver. It's what you call my gift to give." Lucia nodded and gathered the empty plates. "I wish you a day of satisfaction with your writing."

"Thank you. It's the wish I needed. I plan to spend the next two days in the library to finish my dissertation. That'll leave me a couple of days to pack up."

"It's a bittersweet time for you, my Sofia. I'm nearby if you want company. You go. I have cookies to make and maybe messages to deliver." Lucia winked and bustled off to the kitchen.

Sofia stepped outside the bakery debating whether to walk or take a boat. She opted to walk and let thoughts keep her company. Her first stop was the campus store, where she'd purchase a new cell phone, and then on to her library niche. Replaying the last two days with Eduardo brought joy to her heart. Sofia marveled at the speed at which they'd connected. Or was it reconnected? While what they were experiencing and feeling remained a mystery, one constant couldn't be denied. She, grounded Sofia, had managed to fall in love with Eduardo Diaz.

****

Glancing at her new phone, Sofia smiled at the daisy-festooned case she'd chosen. Her favorite flower now carried the imprint of Eduardo. She gave the case a little peck and hurried to choose her outfit for their night out. She'd been unable to focus on her dissertation earlier for thinking about him…them.

Sofia nodded approval, holding up a hanger with a pale-yellow sundress and matching shawl. The condo seemed eerily quiet. No sounds of her neighbors' doors opening and closing. It was as if everyone had vamoosed. "Music. I need music to match my happiness. I know it's temporary. And I've got to return home, but not tonight." Searching the internet, she found an instrumental song that captured Venice's mysterious side. Sofia felt transported back to 1162 and the Carnival of Venice. Her mind could envision the bejeweled masks made of leather, glass, or porcelain on faces as they danced in the streets near her condo. The song ended, taking the images. Sofia was left wondering why she'd felt such a strong attraction to the City of Love from the moment her plane landed. And why did it feel as if she was stepping off her path away from lasting happiness?

Sofia focused attention on styling her hair in an upsweep. The happy mood returned until she noticed the time was eight-thirty. Where was Eduardo? A myriad of emotions came calling to her. She realized he'd never given out his cell phone number, nor did he have her new one. Calling Ginny and Milo wasn't an option. Eduardo seemed lost to her. Refusing to accept he'd dropped her, Sofia spent the evening waiting for a man who never showed.

Chapter 15

Sofia woke the following day on the sofa, still dressed for her date with Eduardo. Her muscles protested as she stood. "I guess it wasn't a bad dream. Maybe Eduardo had been a dream?" She found that idea a lot more appealing. Seeing the wilted daisy on the coffee table confirmed he wasn't a dream.

Opening the refrigerator, Sofia took out two cucumber slices, tilted her head back, and laid them on her swollen eyes. The cell phone chimed. Her hand felt for it and answered. "Hi. It's Sofia."

"What's with the new cell number?" asked Melody. "I got your text last night."

"I dropped my old phone in a pond by accident and had to get a new one. Is everything okay?" Sofia tried to make her voice sound normal.

"Yeah, yeah. I need to get your cake frosting preference for your welcome home. It's a yellow cake. Are you listening?" asked Melody. "You don't have an overnight guest there?"

"I'm here and no guest. What are my choices?" Sofia couldn't care less what frosting covered the cake. Melody could spread peanut butter on it.

"Well, that's a relief. You came to your senses. No time for a man until you get home."

"The frosting?" Sofia wasn't engaging. Just saying Eduardo's name would be enough to release the tears.

"Coconut pecan, dark chocolate, or lemon. And the winner is?"

"Coconut pecan sounds about right." Sofia didn't bother adding she was close to being nuts wondering what happened to Eduardo.

"You got it. Now, tell me what news I've missed hearing?"

"I'm busy trying to finish my final dissertation, so I'd better ring off and get to campus. Thanks for calling and the cake. I promise to eat a big slab of it." Sofia removed the cucumber slices and dropped them in the garbage can.

"Okay, I won't keep you. Are you sure everything—"

"Yep, everything is just peachy. Talk to you in a day or so. Love ya, sis." Sofia tossed the phone in her handbag and released a heavy sigh. "Just peachy. That's me. I've got the world on a string. A short, tattered one."

****

Mustering a heavy dose of determination, Sofia prepared to leave for the library. She opened the condo door only to find her neighbor's hand ready to knock. "*Buongiorno*, Rita and Rosa." Sofia reached down to pet the pug.

"We come bringing a sorry. I fear my Rosa was very naughty." Rita shook her finger at the dog.

"I don't understand." Sofia gave a bewildered look to the petite gray-haired Italian lady.

Rita held out a chewed-up envelope. "I think this belongs to you. See? It says 'Sof.'" Rita pointed to the letters. "Rosa's wet mouth made the ink disappear. 'Sof' is you."

Sofia took what was left of the envelope and an illegible paper inside. Her heart fluttered. Was it from Eduardo? He hadn't any other way to communicate with her.

"We go. Leave you with our sorry. I bake you something to make up," offered Rita.

"No, please, don't trouble yourself. Thank you for bringing me this." Sofia looked at Rosa and grinned when the dog whined. "I forgive you, Rosa, but don't eat any more notes of mine."

"She's been punished. No treats or toys all day. Bye, Sofia. Sorry." Rita scurried home.

Sofia closed the door and inspected the envelope and paper, hoping to confirm it was indeed from Eduardo. Going into the kitchen, she spread the papers on the counter and grabbed her magnifier. "Eureka! I see the signature ever so faintly. At least I know Eduardo tried to contact me." Fearful thoughts gathered momentum like a snowball rolling down a hill. What if the note was a goodbye? It made perfect sense. Eduardo had a change of heart about them being an us. Why spend more time with her if she was leaving in three days? Things were over between them. That had to be it. Her nose sniffed back a sob.

Sofia grabbed a box of tissues. "I listened to a stranger named Dina and let a cookie lead me astray. I followed my heart, only to end up heartbroken." Sofia blew her nose, allowing inner anger to fill the emptiness. "I'm done. No more men. No matter how charming, or handsome, or dashing, or mannered, or sexy, or…" Sofia emptied half the tissue box before her usual composed self made an appearance.

Applying her second favorite lip gloss since her

first favorite was at the bottom of the wishing pond, Sofia gazed at her reflection in the mirror. With head held high, she marched out of the condo. Her dissertation needed finishing, and life in Boston waited. Eduardo Diaz could take a flying leap off the wishing bridge. She wouldn't give him another moment of her time, even if he dared show his face. "If only you would," Sofia whispered and walked down the stairs.

Chapter 16

Eduardo knocked on his father's study door at the appointed time. The pending discussion boded the usual outcome. The elder, Señor Diaz, would demand his expectations and dictates be met by his sons. Freedom to explore interests while gaining knowledge of the family business he would allow, but only for so long. Venturing out, like Ernesto was doing, flirted with mutiny in their father's eyes. Today's meeting was more than obligatory. It was a call to action for both brothers.

"Enter," said a rough, masculine voice. Hector Diaz sat behind his meant-to-intimidate antique carved mahogany desk. The room's décor exhibited a strong male influence with the paneled walls and massive pieces of furniture. A tapestry depicting a bullfight hung on one wall, while leather-bound books lined shelves on the opposite wall. Light poured in from the group of lead glass doors leading to a veranda.

"Hello, Father." Eduardo chose the brown leather wingback chair. It was the chair he always chose. The word always bothered him more today than ever before. He always did as his father asked. He always tried to behave as his father asked.

Hector laid his glasses aside and gazed up. "My son, I'm pleased you heeded my call home. A wise decision. Your brother is tardy, as usual."

Eduardo offered a perfunctory nod. His fingers thumped the chair's arm.

"You seem agitated, Eduardo. This behavior isn't of your character. After our meeting, why not take your horse and check on the new plantings? A ride will release whatever is bothering you." Hector placed two folders on the desk's corner.

"Perhaps." Eduardo turned, hearing the knock.

Ernesto entered, wearing the smile of a man in love with his lady and life. "Hello, brother. Father." He plopped in the matching wingback chair. "So, what's so important that we get this summons to come home? I have a gig to play tonight, so—"

"You're wrong to think I care about your gig." Hector sat up straighter. His physique, while intimidating to most, matched his sons. "Let me remind both of you what I do care about and why you're sitting across from me this day." Hector paused. "Do not interrupt me. Do I have your attention?" Hector stared at his sons.

"Yes, Father," Ernesto's voice sounded monotone.

Eduardo gave a cursory nod.

"Very well. The time has come when I require you both to return home…for good. I'm ready to turn the running of our business and estate over to you. I've had our attorney prepare the documents detailing what role you each will assume. I've based this assessment on what talents you possess." Hector passed each a folder. "We will discuss the particulars this evening. Everything is spelled out clearly. I advise you to take time this day to read and compile any questions or clarifications you might need." Hector sat back. "Now, I will entertain a question or two."

"Can we meet earlier? I've got a flight back to Dublin at—"

"As I stated, Ernesto, I have no interest in your gig, as you call it. And you'd be wise to abandon this folly of playing your guitar."

"You care only for—forget it. I'm wasting my words." Ernesto stormed out of the study.

Ignoring his youngest son's departure, Hector turned to Eduardo. "Questions?"

Eduardo stood and tucked the file under his arm. "Mine can wait. I'm going to take that ride." Giving Hector a nod of respect, Eduardo left the room. His father could keep the chains that bound him a while longer. He needed to ride like the wind, away from his problems and Sofia's complications. Space was what he needed. Space to think. Space to breathe. Space to feel. And most of all, he needed space to choose.

Leaving the grand estate and his father's demands, Eduardo strode to the barn.

"Señor Eduardo, it's good to see you home." The stocky-built barn manager offered his hand. "Hearing of your arrival, I've groomed Rio and told him to expect you. You'll find him waiting in the last corral." He closed the tack room door.

"TJ, it's always good to see you here. Thank you for saddling Rio." Eduardo lifted his suede hat off the hook and grabbed two apples from the hanging basket.

"Those are fresh apples my Lola picked this morning." TJ gave a wide-toothy grin.

"She's still married to you, huh?" A teasing Eduardo slapped TJ on the back. "How many years have you both been at Olivar Siete Colinas?"

TJ scratched his chin. "Let's see now. You were

three when we came."

"My family has been privileged to have you and Lola with us for many years. I should thank you more for such loyalty." Eduardo studied TJ. "In fact, it's past time I do something to honor your commitment to Olivar Siete Colinas and our Andalusian horses."

"Señor Eduardo, this isn't necessary. I'm paid well for my work." TJ followed Eduardo outside.

Catching sight of something belonging to the barn manager, Eduardo knew just the right thank you gift. "You're a good man, TJ." Eduardo gave Rio the apple and patted his neck in greeting. "Listen, if anyone looks for me, I'm heading out to the newest grove we planted. Has there been rain?"

"I believe there's been enough to please those trees, Señor Eduardo. Enjoy the land. I think you want to ponder some pressing problems. It's a fine day for doing this." TJ ambled back to the barn.

Eduardo shook his head. Not only was TJ an Andalusian whisperer, but the manager also seemed to have picked up on his inner turmoil. Once Eduardo had ridden Rio out of range of TJ's hearing, he made a call. "This is Eduardo Diaz. I'd like to purchase and arrange delivery today of a new red pickup truck. Please bring it to the barn and present TJ with the keys. He'll give you any information you need for licensing. Thanks." Eduardo tucked the cell phone in his pocket and sent Rio on a gallop.

His thoughts turned to Sofia as he rode. What was she doing? He envisioned her in the library typing and mumbling to herself. He imagined sitting next to her and taking in her cuteness and sassiness. Until he met Sofia, he didn't know feisty women were so appealing.

Why couldn't the woman who tormented his dreams have come into his life before commitments had been agreed upon? Having a future with Sofia rested on Eduardo finding a solution to the complications. While he couldn't find any rational reason for falling in love so fast, denying his feelings meant denying happiness and destiny. One question lingered. Would Sofia approve of him following the cookie's instructions too? Eduardo was banking his future on it.

The folder held Eduardo's life planned out, as designed by Hector and the family attorneys. Eduardo and Ernesto had named them *controlling folders*. They'd been created at different times in their lives, spelling out responsibilities, goals to reach, and consequences if not met.

Eduardo planned to review the contents later and approach his father before the official meeting. Some kind of compromise seemed the best case he could hope for. And the worst case? Eduardo chose to ignore the roadmap there.

Coming upon the young olive trees, Eduardo got off Rio and tied him to a limb near a stream. "Enjoy refreshment, my friend." He bent down to examine the growth since his last visit. Eduardo let all his senses inform him about the trees. As a young boy, he had learned from their Field Operators about caring for olive groves. He felt a kinship to the trees and their well-being. He still did. "You're all looking healthy and robust," said Eduardo, touching and smelling the leaves.

"Do they still talk to you, my brother?" Ernesto dismounted and joined Eduardo. He was a mirror image of his brother, only missing a couple of inches in height. The same chiseled jaw and olive skin were framed by black hair, a little too long. Ernesto wore his carefree spirit, well symbolized by jeans and a partially unbuttoned white cotton shirt. "What secrets do the trees tell you this day?" Ernesto's face broke into a lazy grin before turning serious.

"Want to know what this one said?" Eduardo stood wearing a matching grin.

"Never mind. I changed my mind. I'd rather hear what you thought of becoming bound to Olivar Siete Colinas? Did you see the insanity cooked up by Father?" Ernesto wiped his forehead with a bandana.

"I'm ignoring my folder until this afternoon. I needed to come out here and gain some clarity about what I want to do with my life." Eduardo went to check on Rio.

Ernesto followed. "Clarity about your life? Hilarious. You're the one who always has it together. I'm the one TJ nicknamed Tumbleweed." Ernesto parked himself on a nearby boulder and popped his soda tab. "Want to go first and tell your problems?"

"No, I'm going to spare you this time. Let's talk about you, Ireland, and the folder." Eduardo squatted next to his brother. Even though they were opposites in many ways, their bond was ironclad. Eduardo knew he could trust Ernesto with his life. "What's her name again? Maureen?"

"Maude. Wait till you meet her. She's a redhead and everything that goes with it. I'm hopelessly entangled with Maude. The insurmountable problem is she's tied to this little village outside Cork where her mom lives alone in a shabby cottage. Maude can't leave her mom, and I can't leave her. I'm trapped." Ernesto rubbed his face.

"Can you make a living playing Celtic music?" Eduardo knew his brother liked fine things, and this was his Achilles heel.

"You know the answer. Dammit, don't you dare say you can't live on love. Maude's mom has sung that song to us nonstop."

Eduardo stole a sip from his brother's soda can. "Sounds like the woman knows your song." Eduardo laughed and dodged his brother's slap. "Tell me what this folder is demanding. We must first work from its dictates."

"For a change, it's straightforward: Come home, take over the Andalusian horse breeding, and handle the philanthropy interests of our family dynasty. In return, I'm rewarded handsomely and get to call Villa Blanco my new home."

"Hmm. It sounds like a good proposal, Ernesto. Father is generous to give you the villa on the far property line. With all our family land, you should enjoy privacy from him, unlike myself having to remain in the main house. Plus, isn't there a small house near it?" Eduardo's face lit with an idea.

"Yes, but why are you looking like you've got the winning lottery numbers?" Ernesto retrieved his soda.

"Because I'd like to offer you a new song to sing." Eduardo's excitement escalated. "Maybe you can have your cake and chew it too."

"It's 'you can't have your cake and eat it too,'" said Ernesto, snickering.

"Don't you start with the corrector, or I won't give my brilliant idea."

"Fine. No more corrector. Tell me," said Ernesto.

"Do you want to marry Maureen?"

"Maude, and yes."

"Invite Maude and her mom to visit here. Sell them what a grand life they will enjoy. Show the mom the wee house that can become hers. It's far from shabby."

"Wee?" Ernesto chuckled. "Continue, oh brilliant brother, with a flair for the Irish brogue."

"If destiny is to be believed, your two women will accept. And you all will live happily ever after."

"Yes, I like your idea. Fact is, I love your idea." Ernesto paused, frowning.

"What did I forget? Wait. It's the music." Eduardo nodded.

"Yeah, my love to play. Where does that fit in?"

Eduardo stood. "Look, you must trust the music will get played. You first settle things with your redhead and fulfill your obligations to the family and business. Yes?"

Ernesto jumped up and ran to his horse.

"Where are you going? We haven't discussed the newest grove's needs," hollered Eduardo.

"I'm going to sign the blasted papers, give them to Father, skip the meeting tonight, and go get my two women. When I get back, we'll tackle your complications. Adios, and thanks!"

Eduardo watched him gallop off. "Unfortunately, my complications won't wait for your return, my brother."

Chapter 17

A fine mist of rain fell as Sofia hurried up the sidewalk to her condo entrance. If anyone cared to ask about her day, she'd answer it was a day of endings and closings. The final dissertation waited for Ginny's blessing. She'd closed out all accounts with the college. Her last stop at the condo rental office finalized the lease obligations. Shutting down her life in Venice had caused another crying jag. "Endings and closings. Who likes those?" She entered the building's atrium.

Smiling, Lucia appeared behind her, bringing an answer. "You should like them because of what they offer, my friend."

"Hey, Lucia. You surprised me." Sofia stopped walking. "Okay, I'll bite. Why should I like endings?"

"It's simple. Because you make a new beginning. And beginnings bring growth and opportunity. Do you not find it so?"

"I adore you, Lucia. Your face is exactly what I needed to see." Sofia hugged her soothsayer. "You're holding a couple of pizza boxes. I didn't know you delivered."

Lucia shook her dark curls. "I do not deliver the pies. I bring the pies to share a dinner with my friend who's making a new beginning. You don't have any plans?"

"No plans. Your timing is perfect. Let's go devour

the best pizza in all of Venice."

"You're too kind. I took a chance on your toppings. I hope you like it." Lucia followed up the steps. "Look there, at your door. Someone has left a sweet pie."

"I guess it's a pie-kinda night." Sofia punched in the code while Lucia grabbed the dessert.

"There's a note with only one word. 'Sorry.' Does that make sense?" asked Lucia, closing the condo door.

Sofia laughed. "It does, and I'll explain after we eat. In fact, I'd welcome your interpretation of something." Sofia headed to the kitchen, placing her laptop case and handbag on the chair.

Lucia deposited the pizza boxes on the dining table. "It's good to sit down. I had a busy day at the bakery. Tomorrow I'm considering taking off and letting my workers handle the shop."

"Good for you."

Lucia twisted to see Sofia. "Do you need help?"

"Nope. Stay seated. I've got this part. Green tea, mineral water, or juice?" Sofia opened the refrigerator door and peered inside.

"Green tea for me." Lucia studied the dessert. "Very unusual. The pie is fresh peach with macadamias."

Sofia poured tea into the glasses and brought plates and silverware to the table. "Macadamia nuts are my favorite. What's my pizza? Smells divine."

Lucia peeked inside the top box. "This one is yours. And I made a sausage one in case you didn't like yours."

Sofia closed her eyes, pulled a slice from the box, and took a bite. "Oh my gosh. It's mixed olives and your fresh mozzarella. This is so good."

"Those aren't just any olives." Lucia bit into her sausage slice.

"No?" Sofia chewed, savoring the salty and earthy taste.

Lucia shook her head. Her eyes held a secret smile. "The olives are imported from the Andalusian region of Spain. You've heard of it?"

"Yes." Sadness choked in Sofia's throat thinking of Eduardo's home. Olives were one of his family's enterprises. Were they the Olivar Siete Colinas olives? "Lucia? Whose olives—where—why?"

"Shh, I answer. I felt the nudge again. I was to order three cases of these after tasting them at my aunt's party. The label says Olivar Siete Colinas. Would you like a few jars to take home?"

"No, but thank you." Sofia's good manners trumped her desire to dump the pizza in the garbage can. Taking another slice, her mouth tasted anger and hurt instead of flavorful olives. *Change the subject.* "It's so nice to eat with someone. So many nights—"

"I understand. I also eat alone at home. It's too bad you're leaving after you and the gentleman met. Maybe he's coming around later? So little time to follow your heart." Lucia snagged another piece from her box. Her eyes watched and waited.

"No, my handsome man has gone, disappeared, evaporated into the ethers." Sofia waved her hands in the air. "Do you see the tattered paper laid out on the coffee table?"

Lucia turned. "Yes."

"That's what a Dear Sofia letter looks like." She closed the pizza box.

"A Dear Sofia letter? I don't understand—"

"It's a letter saying he no longer wants to see me." Sofia gave a little sniff, but refused to cry.

"You know this letter says these things?" Lucia's hand reached over and touched Sofia's arm.

"Well, not exactly. But I've heard nothing from him since the letter—"

Lucia went to the coffee table and peered at the wrinkled paper. "I see nothing but runny ink and a few letters I can hardly make out. Come. Show me where he tells you it's finished."

Sofia joined her friend. "I can't actually show you where he wrote those words, but I'm sure they were there before Rosa slobbered and chewed my letter."

"Who is this Rosa to do such a thing?" Lucia snorted.

"Rosa is a pug who belongs to Rita. They live next door and are why we have a peach pie with unusual macadamia nuts for dessert. It's an 'I'm sorry' pie." Sofia collapsed on the sofa, grabbed the box of tissues, and let fresh tears run free.

Lucia sat next to her and pulled out a tissue, handing it to Sofia. "You can choose to cry more. I see your face puffed like a soufflé from this crying." Closing her eyes, Lucia laid her fingers on the note.

Sofia dabbed her cheeks. She watched, confused as Lucia said nothing but reminded herself this was the same woman who baked her a talking cookie.

"Look at me. His name?" asked Lucia, her tone serious.

"Eduardo." Just saying it made Sofia's heart flutter.

"Hear my words and do not doubt them. Eduardo did not leave you a Dear Sofia letter here. This doesn't feel like that. You must wait to learn what it contained."

"But I may never hear from him again. I have a new cell number, which he doesn't know. I don't have any way to reach him. Our mutual friends are on holiday, so they wouldn't have any information for me. I don't know where Eduardo lives in Venice, or if he's even still here. Plus, I'm leaving in less than three days."

Lucia raised her hand. "I understand all of the impossibles. I repeat. His note wasn't a farewell. Now, how about some of that sorry pie?"

"I hope you're right, Lucia. I'd like to say a proper goodbye to Eduardo. Thanks for helping me feel a little better about things." Sofia stood. "Two big slabs of sorry pie coming up."

****

Sofia watched the stars flicker out her bedroom window and wondered if Eduardo had the same sky above him. Where was he? If Lucia was right, what could have caused him to miss their date? Eduardo had no way to contact her except to come to the condo. Once again, Sofia recognized time had turned against them. Even if he was around, what future did they have with two days left to spend together? They'd make a few more memories and experience a few more woo-woo exchanges. All of it still led to a big dead end. "My future lies in Boston, curating at the museum." Sofia fluffed her pillow and turned over. Dreams of Eduardo waited, assuming she slept.

Chapter 18

Eduardo returned to the main house in the late afternoon. He stayed away, preferring to avoid interacting with his father until fully prepared. He'd studied the folder's contents, which confirmed his suspicions. Hector had planned every detail of Eduardo's life, including one part that would become the centerpiece of their upcoming meeting.

Entering the kitchen, Eduardo gave Lola a hug as she finished giving instructions to a delivery man.

"I've been expecting my hug all day." Lola handed a clipboard to a cook and turned her attention to Eduardo. "So, how long will you stay?"

"I need to fly out tomorrow." Eduardo snagged a carrot stick from a cutting board. "Tell me. How is my favorite señora?"

"You're still the charmer of the Diaz men. I'm well and trying to get TJ to eat more vegetables. He's fat." Lola laughed loudly.

"Only a wife could get away with such words." Eduardo grinned. He took in the busy kitchen scene. "So, what's with all the commotion?"

"Señor Hector has invited the Reyes to dine this evening. I've been instructed to oversee the menu and table since Chef Inez is off for a few days." Lola studied Eduardo. "What's that face? You no like the company?"

Eduardo ignored her question. "How many Reyes are dining with us?"

Lola held up two fingers.

Eduardo sighed until Lola pushed a third finger up and shrugged. "You're unsure who's coming?"

Lola nodded. "Two. Three. It's all the same for me. We cook plenty either way. It's how your father prefers. That is why my TJ is fat. He comes around for leftovers. Now, kiss my cheek and scat. I've much work to do."

Eduardo bent down. "You know I love you, Lola. Thank you for taking such good care of us. I'll see you later."

The terracotta floor tiles announced Eduardo's movements. He ran up the wide staircase, ignoring the wrought iron banister's support. Escaping his father's dinner expectations was a worthy goal. He headed down an open hall that overlooked the courtyard below. The home's architecture appeared timeless. He'd always admired his ancestors' tastes and how each generation honored the estate's grand heritage and nobility.

Entering the carved walnut double doors to his suite, Eduardo's body relaxed. He felt like when he was a kid hiding to avoid his father's wrath after he and Ernesto had gotten into trouble. Only this time, he hadn't confessed his trouble but left it simmering away. Eduardo's thoughts turned to Sofia. Did she miss him? How he longed to return to her. Tomorrow couldn't arrive soon enough. He headed to the shower, taking with him the hope he'd see only two Reyes at the dining table. Three would add another complication to his life.

****

Heading down the stairs, Eduardo could hear Hector's baritone voice booming from the expansive foyer. The fountain's noisy water proved no match for Señor Diaz. Greeting their guests had begun. Putting his smile in place, Eduardo entered the room, glimpsing Señora Reye dropping a coin into the fountain. He sighed, relieved to see the couple arrived alone.

"You caught me making my wish, Eduardo. You know the fountain has blessed me many times over the years. I never pass up the opportunity."

"You've been most devoted to feeding our fountain." Eduardo smiled wistfully, thinking Alice Reye's American accent reminded him of Sofia and the wishing pond. He wondered what those wishes were that she'd made.

"Eduardo, please." Hector Diaz's harsh tone got his son's attention. "Greet—"

"Good evening, Señor Reye." Eduardo extended his hand to shake. "It's nice to see you both looking so well."

Señor Reye took his measure of Eduardo. "Thank you. I'm looking forward to finalizing our plans very soon." Not waiting for a response, he followed his wife and Hector into the dining room.

Eduardo stood by his chair until everyone was seated. "Señor Reye, I've heard Lola has asked the kitchen staff to prepare your favorite dish."

"How lovely. Isn't it, my darling?" Alice touched her husband's forearm.

"Yes, yes, thank you." Señor Reye's dark eyes narrowed on Eduardo. "So, I understand you've finished teaching a graduate business course as a favor to Milo? I sincerely hope you're home and ready to assume your rightful position? Your father has been exceedingly patient with you, and frankly, so have I."

"Please, dear, let's enjoy a pleasant evening in our friends' company." Alice once again intervened, giving Eduardo an out.

A server dressed in black entered, carrying a silver soup tureen. "Pardon. Tonight's soup is a sherry crab bisque served with homemade bread sticks." He ladled the first serving into Señora Reye's fine porcelain bowl before moving to her husband. Once he'd made the rounds, he quietly exited.

A relieved Eduardo listened as his father discussed experimenting with a new organic fertilizer, promising to increase the groves' yield by up to twenty percent. He waited to see if his father would give him credit for the find or ask him to elaborate on the research. Remaining invisible in the conversation had its advantages. His father could own the night's stage with Eduardo's blessing.

"Tell me, Eduardo, have you and Isobel enjoyed some time together in Venice this past week? I expected her home this afternoon, but her flight got delayed."Alice provided Eduardo with the explanation for Isobel's absence at dinner.

"Regretfully, our schedules haven't aligned. Of course, I picked her up at the airport a couple of weeks ago. We did manage to meet for dessert once. Isobel and her friends must have shopped Venice empty by now." Eduardo waited for the server to remove his bowl.

"I believe you're correct judging by the parcels arriving daily." Alice stared off. "Your dear mother, may she rest in peace, always said you could pass for brother and sister. Isobel has always been devoted to you."

"And I to her, Señora Reye. Your only daughter means a great deal to me. May I ask you a personal question?"

Alice smiled across the table at Eduardo. "What would you like to know?"

"Did you mind too much leaving America to marry Señor Reye? I mean, did you have the homesickness?" asked Eduardo, curious to hear the response.

"What an unexpected question, Eduardo. I'm not sure where it came from, but I shall answer. I was very young, and marrying a handsome man from Spain felt exotic." Alice's eyes glistened. "As for feeling homesick, maybe a little at times. At first, I missed certain foods and my friends, but I soon adapted and made a wonderful life. I wouldn't change a thing. Does that answer your question?"

"Most certainly. Thank you, Alice, for being so candid." Eduardo grew silent as the main course arrived.

Alice merely smiled.

Table conversation shifted to the upcoming Festival of Olives and the roles each grove owner agreed to play. Anticipation of the event by everyone at Olivar Siete Colinas was evident. Eduardo had noticed a job sign-up board in the bunkhouse earlier with a few empty slots left. He smiled at his choice. Giving grove tours to the children would teach them good land stewardship.

The Reyes made their leave after dinner, promising a forthcoming invitation to brunch at their estate once

Isobel returned. Alice left another coin in the fountain as they bid good night to both of the Diaz men.

****

Eduardo glanced at his watch. The eleven o'clock meeting with his father loomed. A sudden look of determination passed across his face as he walked toward the study. He held the folder in one hand while he rapped on the door.

"Come in, my son." Hector sat in the wingback chair, smoking a cheroot. "Take your usual seat, and let's put a stamp on our agreement."

Eduardo laid the folder on the side table which separated them. He'd start the conversation by making pleasant talk. "The evening with the Reyes was enjoyable. They're loyal friends and neighbors to us."

"What purpose do you have for stalling? The hour grows late." Hector leaned in and pointed to the folder. "Do you have questions? Or might I have the good fortune that my son signed everything and merely wants to pass the time with his father? Perhaps you'd enjoy a snifter of brandy? Both seem highly unlikely, but I remain optimistic."

Eduardo ignored the taunt and opened the folder. "Let's talk. I'm agreeable to everything regarding my role in running the estate and businesses. I would go so far as to say I'm enthusiastic about the enterprise and have spent the last six months formulating plans to update and improve production."

"I'm not sure your timing for such expenditures—"

"Father, I ask your indulgence while I make my response." Eduardo cocked an eyebrow, signaling his father for an answer.

Hector took a puff of his cigar and squinted at his

son. "Very well. Continue."

"I have ideas for expansion to attract tourists. I'm happy to do a formal presentation later, but for now, know that I have a vision."

"I've been hearing about your vision from TJ and others."

"It matters to me you know I'm committed to Olivar Siete Colinas. Nothing changes there. What might change is the agreement particulars regarding my personal life. With respect, I'm requesting you make me a compromise."

"What kind of compromise? That's not my negotiating style." Hector's tone chilled.

Eduardo's body went rigid. "We're talking about my life and not a bottom line. I refuse to go along with an outdated and outrageous arrangement entered into by my parents when I was three years old."

"Your English improves with anger. Did you notice this?" Hector rose and poured two cups of coffee. He placed a cup in front of Eduardo and sat. "Drink. Gather your wits. See reason."

Eduardo took a gulp. "I've gathered my wits, and I see my reasons clearly." Eduardo went to the window and caught sight of TJ entering the side door, probably to bring Lola home. He spun around to face Hector. "I've met someone. No, let me say it this way. I've met who I think is the one. And that means I cannot abide by the arrangement. Strike it out of the document, and I shall sign this tonight. You will have me devoted to Olivar Siete Colinas for my lifetime, assuming my someone agrees to live here."

Hector jumped up. His flushed face rivaled the nearby bowl of red apples. "I will not agree to these absurd terms. I will not dishonor my name by going against a longstanding agreement with the Reyes. You will marry Isobel next month. Our lands will join and create the most extensive holdings in the south of Spain. These two facts are not open for further discussion. Sign the damn papers, Eduardo, and we'll forget this momentary lapse in judgment by you."

"And if I refuse to marry Isobel? What then? Do not answer until you're calmer." Eduardo returned to his chair, wondering if his blood pressure rivaled his father's.

Hector drained the coffee cup and glared at his son. "Who is she? This woman who's robbed my son of his brains. Of Ernesto, I'd expect such folly. But not you."

"Her name is Sofia Martin. She's finishing her doctorate in Venice and returning in a couple of days to Boston."

"There." Hector waved his hand in the air. "You see, time takes care of this folly. The young woman leaves soon. Sign the contract."

"I don't want her to leave. I'm in love with Sofia. We've got this something I cannot explain which defies—"

"Answer me. How long have you known this Sofia?"

"Not long enough to suit you, but long enough for me to know what I want. It's to spend my life with her, if she'll have me." Eduardo's voice softened.

"You've saddled your horse to an American gold digger." Hector looked toward the heavens and exhaled loud enough to wake his mastiff lying in the corner.

Eduardo tried to remain calm but failed. His tone rose three octaves. "She's not a gold digger. The fact is,

Sofia remains unaware of the wealth we possess. Am I to understand you wish to force Isobel on me, knowing I love someone else?"

"That's exactly what I'm doing unless you come to your senses. We honor our word at all costs. And from where I stand, love costs little here."

"Father, surely you know Isobel and I love each other like brother and sister. I don't believe she feels any different than I do on this subject."

"You make a mistake thinking love sways me. I wasn't in love with your mother when we married. It, too, was an arranged union. Over time, we both grew to find love in our way. You and Isobel will do the same. Let's say no more." Hector opened the folder and reached for a pen. "Come and sign."

"What if I refuse?" Eduardo walked toward the study's door.

Hector switched off the desk lamp. "If you don't agree, then you're on your own, Eduardo. You will make your way in life without the advantage of this family. Am I understood?"

Pain and disappointment crossed Eduardo's face. "I will give you my decision in seventy-two hours when I return from Venice. Good night, Father."

Chapter 19

Standing at Sofia's condo door the next afternoon, Eduardo rang the bell. He thrust a hand through his black hair.

Rita stuck her head out the door. "Sofia, she's home. Rosa and I are very sorry. Ask for some pie." The door closed, leaving Eduardo with a confused expression.

Sofia stood in the doorway. "What are you doing here? You've got a nerve, mister, showing up after leaving me a Dear Sofia letter."

"This is not the greeting I anticipated for the last two days." Eduardo pushed past and entered. "What is the matter? You know I couldn't call you. I didn't have your new number." Eduardo reached for Sofia's arm, but she shook it free.

"So, okay, you couldn't call me. I get it, but to leave me a Dear Sofia and then come around here now?"

"What is this 'Dear Sofia' you keep saying to me?" Eduardo moved closer.

Sofia pointed to the coffee table and the tattered paper. "That's a Dear Sofia telling me you didn't want to see me again."

"I wish to examine this lying paper," said an exasperated Eduardo.

"Fine, examine away." Sofia took stock of the man

in front of her, trying desperately to find something unappealing about him. Anything at all would do. A thread hanging off the black polo shirt displaying his broad shoulders and washboard stomach, or where he missed shaving his strong chin. A belt that didn't match his leather loafers. Anything to calm her heart flutters seeing him again.

"Please, come here. Show me where it says that I don't want to see you again. And please also explain what you did to my note? It looks like—"

"A dog chewed it? That would be Rita's dog, Rosa, who lives next door."

"The woman who spoke nonsense to me about a pie?" asked Eduardo. "I grow more confused by the second."

"Yes, that's her. Rita baked me a sorry pie for Rosa doing that." Sofia pointed to the note.

"I ask again with great patience to please show me the words where I said—"

Sofia huffed. "I can't show you the exact words, but it's so obvious. You leave me a note, and I hear nothing from you. Any woman would assume—"

"Ah, assumption. That's your mistake. To assume such a thing about me tells me you don't believe in us. I would never take a note you left for me, which I might add is illegible, and think such meanings."

Sofia felt a grin threaten. How she adored Eduardo Diaz's choice of words. Her soul sang in joy. He'd come back to her.

"No corrector right now. It fuels my anger. I left you a note saying I'd return in two days. You think so little of me. Why?" Eduardo pulled Sofia into his arms and looked at her. "Why do you think so little of us?"

He stroked her cheek.

Sofia's cheeks grew warmer at his touch. "You're wrong. I think too much of us, and it hurt to think you'd just disappeared. Without your cell phone number, I couldn't call you."

"That mistake belongs to me. I forgot to give it to you before leaving. I'm sorry, my Sofia." Eduardo's lips brushed her hair. "My father called me home for a meeting the night I was here at your place. You remember the call?"

Sofia nodded. Her body felt as if it was floating in a sea of happiness once she heard Eduardo's explanation.

"I came back as soon as I could." Eduardo's fingers traced the outline of Sofia's lips. "We waste precious time on this subject. I missed you. Did you miss me?"

"Uh-huh." Sofia managed to deliver two syllables. Eduardo rendered her witless. His eyes looked at her in a way no man had before. Her few defenses crumbled. She'd missed him every minute. And too much. "Uh-huh," Sofia repeated in a whisper.

"I think that means yes." Eduardo's grin lit the room. "May I kiss you now?"

"Uh-huh." Sofia closed her eyes and lifted her chin. She'd waited a lifetime to feel this way.

At first, Eduardo's kiss held promise, like the opening chords of a love song. The way his lips touched hers felt tentative, yet so familiar. Pent-up passion intruded on the sweetness, sweeping them to a place where feelings wouldn't be denied. The single kiss stretched into minutes as love spoke what words could not.

Eduardo pulled back. Her name broke from his lips. "Ah, Sofia. What have you awakened in me? This grand passion? I haven't a name for it. But there is something I know." Eduardo's voice was laden with emotion. He drew Sofia into his chest. His fingers stroked her head.

Sofia drew a breathless sigh. "What do you know, Eduardo Diaz?" She wanted to freeze time to remain wrapped in his strong arms, maybe forever. "Tell me." She looked into his eyes, begging for another kiss.

"It is this, my Sofia. You may doubt the sun will shine tomorrow. You may doubt the stars' gift to life. You may even doubt the moon's influence on our moods. But, Sofia, promise me you will never, *never* doubt us again."

Feeling enraptured by Eduardo's beautiful images and words, Sofia found herself unable to speak. He was asking her to trust what? That they belonged together? How when she was flying home soon? A practical Sofia sat up and turned to face the man who captured her heart. "You surprise me again with how you compose thoughts into such lovely words. You're quite the romantic."

"I am waiting for your answer about us."

"I know, Eduardo." Sofia's expression grew wistful. "What I doubt is time being a friend to us."

"This remaining doubt of yours, I understand, but only for the moment," Eduardo said cryptically. "Come. Before I left for Spain, I promised to show you a bridge. And if you deny me, I shall stay here and give passionate love—"

Sofia laughed and hopped up. "You say make passionate, though I can see why you'd choose the word give." Sofia witnessed Eduardo's frown. "Never mind. I would never deny you showing me a bridge. I need to grab my new handbag."

"I plan to watch this new bag carefully. You don't have a good history of avoiding mishaps," Eduardo said, teasing, heading toward the front door.

Sofia puffed up, acting insulted. "That's not true. I'm known for my dexterity and athletic—"

"One word I give to you: mud. Now let us go introduce you to a famous bridge." Eduardo opened the door just as Rita was about to knock. He stood aside for Sofia to greet her.

"Hello, Signora Rita. What have you got?" asked Sofia.

"I bring more sorry for him." Rita pointed to Eduardo. "He's the one who wrote?"

"Yes, he did, but you didn't need to bake another pie." Sofia watched, amused as the pie passed to Eduardo.

"*Grazie*, Signora Rita." Eduardo set the pie inside on the foyer table.

"It is what you call a cherry." Rita bobbed her head and scurried back to her condo.

"The poor woman has plenty to feel sorry about with her dog chewing my note, but two pies seem a bit much."

Sofia twined her fingers around Eduardo's and grinned up at him. "I agree, but the woman can bake a mean fruit pie. You'll see later. Time's a-wasting. Take me to this bridge you're all aflutter to show me."

****

Eduardo pointed up. "What you see is the Bridge of Sighs."

Sofia gazed at the structure. "What an unusual bridge. It's small, relatively speaking. Tell me about this Bridge of Sighs."

"The bridge has a remarkable history. You see, of course, it's enclosed and made of white limestone. The windows have bars. The bridge designer was named Antonio Contino. Guess when it was built?" Eduardo stopped walking and turned toward Sofia.

"Hmm, how about 1746?" Sofia glanced at the two buildings it adjoined.

A smile tugged at Eduardo's lips. "Interesting guess, but alas, wrong. The Bridge of Sighs was constructed in 1600. You can see it passes over the Rio di Palazzo. What it connects to I find most interesting."

"And that is?"

"The bridge's history connects New Prison to the Doge's Palace interrogation rooms," explained Eduardo.

"Not exactly a fun place to go visiting back then. And you brought me here, why?" Sofia gave a little shiver.

Eduardo chuckled. "Come. We can go inside. Then I shall tell you what Milo told me. A legend goes with the Bridge of Sighs."

"A legend? I've always had this thing for myths and legends. The mystery and all." Sofia's excitement caused her to set a fast pace.

"I know this about you. Don't ask me how. It's one of those 'us' things again. I wish to bring you enjoyment. It's my pleasure to do this. You understand me?" Eduardo held the door open.

Sofia touched his cheek in passing. "It's one of the things I find irresistible."

"I must find ways to bring you more enjoyment, so I remain irresistible," said Eduardo.

"By all means. Don't hold back," Sofia teased.

As they began to cross the bridge, Eduardo's hand halted Sofia. He pulled her to the side, away from people walking past. "It's time I give you the legend."

"Okay." Sofia waved to a toddler who held up her lollipop.

Eduardo gazed into Sofia's eyes. "It is said that if two lovers kiss on a gondola at sunset under the bridge as the Saint Mark's Campanile bells toll, then they will be given forever love."

Sofia looked out the window into the water, needing to keep things light. Her heart was in jeopardy of breaking at the thought of saying goodbye to this wonderful man. "I guess they'd better make sure they love each other before they take a ride on the gondola. Forever is a long time."

"This is true. But for the rare love between two people who feel such a strong connection, forever may not be long enough." Eduardo sealed his words by giving Sofia a brief kiss.

She glanced around and saw a couple smiling their way. "That was unexpected."

Eduardo brushed his lips across hers again. "I no longer feel the need to ask permission to show you my feelings. You may show me your feelings too."

Sofia tugged Eduardo's belt closer and kissed him with a wantonness that surprised them both. Releasing him, she stepped back. "Those are my feelings, Eduardo Diaz." A breathless Sofia adjusted her drooping sunglasses. "So, shall we cross the rest of the way, or do you have more to show me?"

Eduardo's face transformed into a cheeky smile. "I fear we'd get arrested if I show you more feelings. Maybe we should finish our tour of the Bridge of Sighs."

"Sounds like a safer plan. I'd hate to be exiled to New Prison." Amusement coursed through her until Sofia glanced at her watch. Time had sped up.

Chapter 20

Evening shadows claimed the sidewalks as they strolled alongside the canals. The sky, now painted a stormy charcoal with splashes of coral, gave foreboding to those who could see. Street vendors displaying their wares called out to the couple in vain. Storefront lights came to life, but the two witnessed none of the changes in the landscape. If asked, onlookers might describe them as lost in each other. Eduardo and Sofia were simply an us—an us like no other.

"Hungry? May I feed you something rich? Perhaps it will feed you the wish to remain in Venice." Eduardo pulled Sofia closer.

"Please, don't ruin our evening by reminding me I leave soon. You know I can't stay. My work waits in Boston. Furthermore, has it escaped your mind that you don't live in Venice?" Sofia playfully tapped Eduardo's temple as they waited to cross the alleyway.

"No, my Sofia, it has not escaped me. I carry a heavy burden as we walk." Eduardo's voice held a distant note.

Sofia pulled Eduardo to a nearby bench. "What kind of burden? Do you want to share it with me before we have our decadent dinner?"

"Not yet. I must labor through it more, but tell you I will." Eduardo drew a deep breath.

"Okay, you work through whatever this problem is,

and I won't press you further tonight." Sofia's happiness returned, despite Eduardo's troubling words. She refused to lose a second of joy being in his company. Making memories was her mission over the next day and a half. Lots of beautiful memories with a man her heart adored. "Hey, handsome."

"You speak to me this way?" asked Eduardo.

Good. He's back in the present. "Will you please feed me dinner, or I will be forced to go home to a sorry pie."

"The pie must wait. We're to dine on Luigi's fresh-made risotto, which, I assure you, Señorita Martin, tastes like no other. We must experience it together." Eduardo checked the time. His brows furrowed. "Now. Time moves too fast this night. Come dash with me."

Sofia took Eduardo's hand as they rushed down the alley. "Risotto? I adore risotto, especially when it has—"

"White asparagus and wild mushrooms. Yes, I know this already. Luigi's preparing it just so," said Eduardo, glancing sideways at Sofia.

"How? Why? I don't think I'll ever understand—"

Eduardo shrugged and hurried them inside the restaurant.

"My favorite guest, Signore Diaz." Luigi nodded to Sofia.

"You're too kind, Luigi. Thank you for this special meal prepared for us."

"My pleasure. Your corner table awaits on the patio. Very few diners tonight. Most unusual. You'll find the place almost deserted. Follow me."

Sofia took in the restaurant's charming atmosphere. At least a hundred aqua-colored candles lit their way. It was the same color as the water in Venice's canals.

White tablecloths with sparkling crystal glasses waited for the waiters' water pitchers. Sofia's eyes focused and stopped on one feature that caught her breath: Hand-painted murals of great beauty covered the walls, depicting scenes of Venice. Sofia assumed it was Luigi's vision of the City of Love's history. "Luigi, the murals are extraordinary."

The restaurant owner seated Sofia. "*Grazie*. My papa had them commissioned many years ago. I'm their guardian now. Please enjoy your special dinner."

Eduardo nodded to the waiter who approached. "Sofia, what drink would please you most? Cranberry and fresh lime or—"

Sofia nodded in disbelief. "You've chosen everything perfectly for me." She looked at the waiter. "Cranberry over ice with lime is fine."

"And for you, Signore Diaz?"

Sofia jumped in. "I think ginger ale and a splash of lime."

Eduardo's head jerked up from the menu. "How did you know this desire?"

"It seems I possess the same connection to your likes as you to mine." Sofia batted her eyes as the waiter disappeared.

Eduardo sat looking at her, his face unreadable. "What shall we ever make of this us? I speak without thinking what you like. The magnet inside you pulls at me constantly to touch you, to kiss you. I will say no more."

The waiter set their drinks on the table and left.

Three women musicians appeared on a cobalt-blue tiled dais. Their violin, guitar, and piano played the first notes, resetting the room's mood. A playful and vibrant melody sparked Eduardo's eye toward the dance floor. Two couples found their moves, and smiles broke out as the tempo increased into a version of a tango.

"It's not our waltz, but it will do." Eduardo came around to Sofia and extended his hand with a bow. "May I have this dance?"

On a sigh, her eyes took in his European charm and dashing self. "Swoonable. Ginny's one hundred percent right." Sofia rose, letting him guide her.

"What was this you just said? I didn't hear it all." Eduardo pulled Sofia into his arms. "You talk of math when I ask for a romantic dance? I fail to understand American women," said Eduardo, his breath against her hair.

"Forget the math. I don't tango or flamenco. What are you doing?"

Eduardo dipped her body and leaned over her, grinning. "We do the Eduardo. Follow along if you dare."

With one hand on his shoulder, Sofia lifted her chin. "Me, follow a man? Never." She took the lead, but only for a few seconds before Eduardo claimed her body with a simple look. His sexy, dark eyes taunted her to discover the depth of their passion in dance. Sofia gave way and followed her heart's desire.

Over the next half hour, they danced while saying nothing but feeling everything. The music awakened dormant love and, if they spoke of it, memories. Unexplainable memories of passion and a love so grand it defied boundaries.

The smiling waiter retrieved their dinner and carried the untouched plates back to the kitchen. "No problem with the risotto. *Amore* is the problem," he explained to a puzzled Luigi.

"Ah, it's about time Signore Diaz meets his destiny." Luigi turned to the chef. "Dump this risotto. We make them fresh. Add *amore* to the recipe. We help things along. You understand me?"

The chef nodded and held up a special bottle of dried Italian herbs.

The trio took a break, forcing Sofia and Eduardo back to their table. The music had brought them closer to recognizing and accepting the depth of their love and bond. They knew the future was undecided, but the present moment belonged to them.

Sofia sipped her juice. "I'm going to need a refill. I wonder what happened to our risotto?"

Eduardo lifted his glass, signaling the waiter. "We're about to find out. I fear Luigi's emotions are hurting."

Sofia tapped Eduardo lightly on the arm. "We don't want to offend Luigi."

"Luigi's feelings are fine, signorina. Here's a fresh risotto. Is better than the first. Made with amore herbs. You like. You see." Luigi placed a plate in front of Sofia and then Eduardo. "*Buon appetito*."

"*Grazie*, Luigi." Eduardo glanced at their risottos. "What's different?"

"I want to know what's in amore herbs. Should I worry?" Sofia sniffed. "Smells divine."

Eduardo lifted his spoon. "Let's show bravery. Yes?" He took a bite.

"Better to show trust, I think." Sofia scooped up the rice. "Oh my gosh. This is amazing." She swallowed, never taking her eyes off Eduardo. "I'm in love."

"Me too." Eduardo ate another spoonful and looked up at her.

Taking a sip of water, Sofia's eyes glinted. "It's the herbs. We're acting sappy happy."

"Maybe we'd better avoid a fried cream for dessert."

Sofia wore an impish smile. "Know what I want for dessert?"

"Me?" teased Eduardo. "Sorry. That's not a reply of mine."

"No, it isn't, but it has a cuteness." Sofia winked, grinning.

"I don't like me cute. What dessert?"

"Another gelato. I can't get enough and since I'm to go—"

"Do not speak of it. Speak of the gelato, so your beautiful smile returns." Eduardo laid his napkin aside. "Yes, gelato sounds *perfecto*. We should go soon before they close the cart." Eduardo motioned to the waiter for the check.

Sofia took the last sip of her drink. "Why is the waiter shaking his head no?"

Luigi appeared at their table before Eduardo could reply. "I hope you enjoyed the meal."

"It was most excellent. Thank you for the great kindness." Eduardo rose and extended his hand to the owner.

Sofia stood. "My risotto was delicious. The best I've ever eaten, and I've eaten my way through Venice on risotto."

Luigi bowed. "Now, you allow me to treat you to this dinner. Such love, I've never seen between two people. We've all taken great pleasure in your presence this night. Please, you must return again soon."

Eduardo's and Sofia's faces displayed surprise at hearing Luigi's words. They thanked him and waved goodbye to the musicians and staff.

"Gelato?" asked Eduardo, standing outside the restaurant.

"Definitely gelato." Sofia put her arm around his waist. "And it's my treat."

"No, I want—"

"Nope. Say no more. I've got our gelatos, and I'm going for a new flavor. I don't know what yet, but I feel adventuresome." Sofia glanced up at the sky in time to see a shooting star. Venice imbued love upon couples. Simply breathing the air seemed to awaken the heart. Venice also carried a mystery in the air. It reminded her of New Orleans in that regard.

A chill crawled down her back. Sofia saw the woman before Eduardo did. Dressed like a gypsy in a flowing bright-colored skirt and peasant blouse, her fingers beckoned Sofia to her booth.

"Come. Bring your love. I have something vital to share. I charge you nothing." The fortune teller's bangles clanked as she motioned for them.

Sofia noted the woman's smile possessed a kindness, unlike fortune-tellers she'd observed in the past hanging around Venice. Pausing a few yards from the fortune-teller, Sofia glanced at Eduardo. "Tell me this isn't yet another weird encounter for us." Sofia pulled closer to him.

"It is. What do you make of her? Her face looks friendly, but dare we venture closer to hear her words? I do not know," whispered Eduardo. His fingers gripped Sofia's.

The fortune-teller abandoned her post and approached them. "Don't worry. I bring you a missive from someone you know." Her hand held a blue envelope in the air.

Sofia spoke first. "You must have us confused with someone else."

"She's correct. It's an error you make," added Eduardo.

"No mistake. You're the Eduardo and Sofia who hold a grand love. We know about you." The woman's expression warmed as she reached them. "Excuse my English. I'm from another place."

"I don't understand any of this. I mean, I understand what you're saying but not what it means. Eduardo?" Sofia's body hummed with nervous energy.

"Who knows about us? Us?" Eduardo repeated and looked at Sofia.

The fortune-teller shook her head. "I can say only these words. You belong together. The stars decreed this long ago. Take the envelope, please. I must go." She placed the missive in Sofia's hand. Instead of returning to her booth, the woman hurried down the sidewalk.

Mouth open and eyes wide, Sofia turned to Eduardo. "Why do these strange encounters keep happening to us?"

"Why do these remembrances keep finding us?" Eduardo pulled them to stand under a light pole. "Will we ever understand us?"

Sofia laid her head on Eduardo's shoulder and pulled a matching pale blue paper from the envelope. "There's one sentence written in a copperplate style."

"What is the copperplate?" Eduardo studied the

words. "I see. It looks like old-style writing. Is most curious."

"Copperplate is the handwriting style used in the American Constitution. It's written with what looks like a quill. Fascinating."

"Please read the words to me. I care most to hear them." Eduardo spoke in barely an audible voice.

Sofia frowned and read the message under her breath. She swallowed and twisted to face Eduardo. "The message is addressed to me from…Dina."

Chapter 21

Eduardo drew in his breath sharply. "Dina? The Dina from the botanical garden? What is this insanity?" A flicker of impatience and irritation shone in his eyes.

"Yes, that Dina. As far as the insanity part, I'm just as confused as you are, maybe more."

"Well? Shall I risk going more crazy by asking what Dina wrote?"

Sofia looked up at him. "She wrote my three wishes had been received."

Eduardo stepped back. "I can hear no more. Let's do something normal. Eat gelato. The largest one they can make."

"I'm all in for the largest gelato." Sofia tucked the note into her handbag. She'd have plenty of time once home to try and make sense of her last week in Venice and the man called Eduardo Diaz. For the time being, Sofia wanted to just have fun and forget the unexplainable things.

Eduardo greeted the young girl serving the treat. He read the flavors aloud, stopping at the black cherry. "Sofia, what do you choose?"

"I want a large fresh peach with amaretto in a cup. And he wants a large black cherry in a cup. Thank you." Sofia glanced at Eduardo, judging his mood. "You, okay?"

He gazed at her and grinned. "No, I am not okay.

Maybe yes, after this gelato settles me." He accepted the cup from the server. "Thank you for treating me."

"Of course." Sofia spooned the peach gelato into her mouth. "It tastes so good. Yours?"

"The same." They strolled to a nearby table with two chairs. "What are these wishes? Can you not say to me?"

Sofia shook her head. "I told you already. If I tell you, they won't come true."

"You hang onto this belief, despite what goes on around us? What follows and finds us? This fortune woman brings a message from a woman you met at the gardens about these wishes of yours. This crosses the line. And you worry about wishes not coming—"

"Chill. Treat yourself to a deep breath." Sofia paused. "Remember Dina said we should accept what comes? You must accept."

"I'm not a man to accept what I cannot understand. I try, but it's not me, Sofia. You know this." Eduardo looked off and returned to his dessert. "Did it escape your notice we ordered the same fruit gelato as our sorry pies?"

Sofia shook her head. "I knew but figured better to stay silent on yet another whatever we're calling this."

"I need—"

"You need fun. I need fun. We need fun. Let's keep things light and...fun. Yes, fun. Don't think about...well, you know." Sofia presented a bright fake smile to Eduardo. "Fun," she repeated and offered a loopy grin.

"You did a drip on your shirt." Eduardo pointed. "Would you like for me to wipe it? That would make fun." He lifted a napkin and reached across the table.

Sofia smacked his hand away from her chest. "You get a gold star for a fast pivot. Give me that napkin."

"You keep my fun from me," said Eduardo, pulling a pretend sad face.

"Not at all. I see fun differently. Lean over here." Sofia dabbed his hair. "When you got all amped about my wishes, your spoon flung gelato into your hair. You've got a sticky glob. Oh, it's a piece of a cherry." She chuckled.

Eduardo touched the area. "This is the end straw. I'm not going around with globs. Can we go back to the condo?"

"Good idea. My safe little nest." Away from amore herbs, fortune-tellers bringing Dina missives, and everything else Sofia chose to shove into the recesses of her mind.

On their silent stroll to her condo, Sofia's thoughts came calling with a fresh worry. Would Eduardo ask to stay the night? It wasn't her style to enter a physical relationship with any haste. The fact was, she barely needed one hand to count them. Nerves fluttered in her stomach, only to awaken and quicken her pulse. The logical Sofia intervened, reminding her of the upcoming flight departure. They were entangled enough to baffle a magician. Adding the anticipated physical combustion would likely ignite the condo building if unleashed. Her neighbors deserved a peaceful night's sleep. She'd forgo one herself, thinking of what her spirit missed sharing with the man who'd captured her heart. The decision made, Sofia's pulse quietened, and the butterflies took flight.

Approaching the condo building's entrance, Sofia waved to Lucia as her friend locked the bakery door.

"Have a good night."

"You two the same," replied Lucia.

"She's a very nice person, I think." Eduardo followed Sofia up the steps.

"Very. Someone else I shall miss." Sofia punched in the door code and turned the knob. "Let me grab your sorry pie."

"Sofia?" Eduardo's manners kept him at the threshold.

She returned, handing him the pie. "Yes? Oh, forgive me. Thank you for introducing me to the Bridge of Sighs and for the amazing dinner."

"Sofia?" He laid the pie on an oak table outside her door.

"And for the dancing. I really enjoyed the dancing. The gelato, I don't much remember how it tasted." The way he said her name sent panic waves through her body.

Eduardo stroked his finger against her cheek. "My Sofia." He pressed her to his body. "Do you not want us together tonight?"

"I do. So much, but—" Sofia buried her face against his chest and noticed a gold chain. Her eyes focused on a charm hanging inside his shirt.

"But?" asked Eduardo.

"But I'm leaving Venice, and it's hard enough to say goodbye. If we made—if we—I can't." Rivers of tears fell down her cheeks.

Eduardo's arms held her tighter, whispering words that were loving and comforting.

Forcing her composure back, Sofia stepped away. "I'm sorry." Standing on tiptoes, she'd let her kiss speak for her. "Good night, Señor Diaz." Sofia closed the door on a stunned Eduardo. His reaction to the kiss made her smile inside, yet saddened at the same time.

A soft tap sounded on the door.

"Sofia?" Eduardo's voice was low.

"Yes, Señor Diaz?"

"May I have the honor of calling on you tomorrow after lunch?"

"I regret that I'm busy tomorrow afternoon packing and closing out things." She loved their playful side. It helped her move past the rejection she'd delivered.

"This is too bad. I must see you again. Surely you want to see me again. Yes?"

Sofia heard her neighbors' doors opening and some words directed at Eduardo.

"Sofia? Have some mercy. We have an audience," Eduardo pleaded.

She laughed, imagining her neighbors' faces peeking out their doors. Poor, proper Eduardo having to endure strangers listening to him beg for a date. "Eduardo? Are you still there?"

"Si, yes, but I warn you, not for long. This is too much. What you put me—"

"Through." Sofia's hand muffled her laughter.

"Enough. I'm leaving."

"No, don't leave her. Signore. Sorry. More pie?" Rita's voice rang out.

"Sofia, give the guy a break," said the man from across the hall.

"Okay. You all win. Eduardo, how about you come around tomorrow night at seven o'clock? I don't want to eat dinner at the typical late hour here."

"Seven o'clock. You promise to open the door to me? Say yes, and I shall bring you something special."

"I'll open the door even if it's just you standing there."

"Everyone, go to your homes. All is working now. Thank you for the help," said Eduardo.

Sofia giggled, loving Eduardo with every beat of her heart.

"Are you still there? Sofia?" Eduardo whispered louder.

"Yes. I'm here. What else do you have to say?"

"Tomorrow is important to us. This I know, and now so do you. Good night, Sofia."

Chapter 22

Sofia awoke to her cell phone ringing. "Hi, Melody. What's the question needing an immediate answer?" Sofia's voice held amusement. Her sister's calls had increased as the arrival date closed in.

"Hey, this will only take a sec. I can't break away to get you at the airport. But not to fret, I've worked it out," said Melody.

"Worked out how?" Sofia frowned. "I sense meddling."

"You sense wrong. I've called in a favor from Albert. He's got your photo, and the kids made a sign last night. He'll hold it up so you recognize him. Problem solved."

"Hang on. Who is this Albert?"

"Oh, we call him Amazing Albert. I think I hear the doorbell," replied Melody.

"Don't you dare disconnect. I can't believe you're making me pull a simple answer out of you. First, who is the 'we' that calls some guy Amazing Albert?"

Melody released a heavy sigh. "'We' are the kids and me. Albert is their pediatrician."

Sofia rubbed her forehead. "Your matchmaking has gone too far this time. You've suckered your kids' doctor into—"

"Stop. It's all dandy. Albert is invited to your welcome home party, so no biggie. Besides, unlike your

Casanova, he speaks perfect English and lives here. He's amazing."

"So you said. Okay, fine. There's no point in arguing, but I'm not interested in dating anyone right now. Leaving Venice has become—never mind. Go answer the phantom at your door. We'll talk tomorrow morning before I board."

"Just make sure you get on the plane, Sofia. Counting the hours. Bye."

Sofia rolled out of bed and padded over to the window. Rain pelted the glass. Colorful umbrellas painted the sidewalks as people scurried. Hunger claimed her attention. A quick shower and a trip to Lucia's for a latte and some decadent pastry sounded right. Acknowledging this was her last visit to the bakery caused her eyes to tear.

Prepare yourself. The tears will follow you all day, along with the symbolic rain. And with good reason. You don't want to leave Eduardo or Venice. In less than a week, you've managed to fall in love and upend your goals and plans. Way to go, Sofia Martin. Way to go.

For once, Sofia admitted her mind had it right. She'd managed to walk away from the scene at the mud pit with no dignity, but at least she'd walked away. Her agreement to let Eduardo see her home after Milo's party was where she'd gone off track. Well, going back wasn't an option. She'd put on her big girl britches, tap into her stiff upper lip, march downstairs to the bakery, and then take charge of the day's list. "I'm going home to Boston. I'm going to take up the curator's job...my dream job. I will say goodbye to Eduardo and ignore the whole follow-your-heart dictum. Yep, I've got a plan, by golly. I'm meeting Amazing Albert at Logan

Airport and going to party like I mean it." Sofia got in the shower and let the spray wash away the tears as they fell.

She dressed in her baggiest black jeans and sloppiest tee to mirror her mood. The tissue came out of her pocket as Sofia entered the bakery.

"Buongiorno, Sofia. I hoped you'd pay me a final visit. I baked you a special something this morning to go with your latte." Lucia held up a finger. "Wait. I shall get. Take a seat."

"How sweet of you." Sofia sat at a corner table, soaking up the bakery's vibes to take home with her. Lucia had created a relaxed atmosphere, causing patrons to linger longer. The smell of rich coffee married with the sweet deliciousness of baking intoxicated the senses. Sofia's mouth watered as she waited.

"For you, my friend. Three bomboloni, which I filled with custard. A new recipe called the Sofia Bombolone. Taste." Lucia set the latte next to the doughnuts and kept her smile in place.

"I'm beyond honored you named a dessert after me. This is too much." Sofia squeezed her eyes, forcing tears to stay at bay so she could take a bite. "Oh, my gracious, Lucia. It tastes incredible."

"Yes? Is good?" Lucia clapped her hands and hollered to her kitchen staff, "Sofia likes."

"No, Sofia loves. Thank you for your friendship and for feeding me each day. I'm going to miss you terribly." Sofia dabbed her eyes with a napkin.

"No cry. You'll return to us." Lucia leaned down and hugged her.

"I don't know. I guess anything is possible."

Lucia straightened to look directly into Sofia's eyes. "If you follow your heart, you shall return. Here, I kiss you and say see you next time. Now eat, drink, and smile past all tears. My gift to you."

With a nod, Sofia watched Lucia disappear into the kitchen. "Follow my heart. Lucia keeps telling me this even on a cookie, but I can't." Sofia finished her breakfast. With one final glance at the bakery, she went upstairs to face the open suitcases and let the landlord know about her departure plans.

The morning gave way to the afternoon as Sofia scurried around packing her year in Venice into a few suitcases and making the condo sparkle from her labors. Pausing to admire the unit's loveliness, her mind wondered about the next tenant. Would they adore living there as much as her? On a whimsical feeling, Sofia wrote a welcome note to leave with a P.S. warning that the hot and cold water valves were reversed. The smile returned, remembering her chilling discovery in the shower.

Sofia's eyes settled on the daisy's sad face, matching her own. Her fingers plucked the flower from the vase, meant to revive it. "You're going home with me. We can share our sadness at losing him." She pressed the flower between wax paper and tucked it inside her copy of *Don Quixote*, the same title Eduardo had been reading at the botanical gardens. Her breath caught in a sigh. They were quite a remarkable us.

****

Sofia recognized the tap on her door. He'd arrived early, way early, judging by her watch showing five o'clock. She hadn't dressed for their evening, but then she'd neglected to ask what he had planned. His cryptic parting words from the night before had followed her around most of the day. Her mind wasn't any closer to understanding what Eduardo meant, saying tonight was important to them. Time had hurried the answer to her.

She opened the door. Eduardo wore a tux and held a boxed corsage in one hand and a garment bag in the other. The handsome smile was the bonus. Her heart melted even more. Eduardo Diaz lived to surprise and charm her and had made a success of his enterprise in a few short days.

Two condo doors opened. "Too handsome," Rita told her neighbor, pointing at Eduardo.

"Not for me," replied the older woman grinning and waving.

Even her neighbors fell under Eduardo's spell. His teeth flashed a smile as he waved to them. "Holy smokes, Eduardo. You're all gussied up, and here I stand in jeans and a t-shirt. Are you sure you've come to the right place? Your timing is a bit off." Sofia motioned him inside.

He paused to kiss her cheek. "My timing is impeccable. You should ask me why."

"Why?" answered Sofia, feeling happiness infuse her for the first time that day.

"Because I wish to arrive before you dress. I've taken some liberties, as you call them, for our special evening."

Sofia's eyebrow shot up. "What kind of liberties?" Never had she known a man like Eduardo. He didn't belong in the current time.

"I shopped for you while I waited for the afternoon to pass. I bring you what matches your eyes, like the Adriatic Sea. The saleswoman assured me it was

perfect. I showed her your size with my hand like so."
Eduardo spread his hands and fingers apart. "You see?
This is your waist. This is your hips, which I like. This
is your bosom, which I like even more."

Her cheeks flamed. "You're quite creative in
taking a measure of me, but—"

Eduardo's grin escaped. "Please, allow me to
complete this measurement story. I regret I failed at
bringing you glass slippers. When I tried to measure
your feet, the helpful woman said my beloved was
blessed with such generosity in feet that she could not
fit her." Eduardo glanced at Sofia's bare feet.

Sofia's eyes followed his. "Are you trying to tell
me I have big dogs?" Her hands went to her hips.

"Dogs? I don't speak of dogs. I'm apologizing for
offering no shoes to go with the dress because your
feet—"

"Listen up, buster, I'll have you know my shoe size
is an eight, and while that might be a tad large for my
five-foot-five self, I wouldn't call my feet—"

Before Sofia could finish, Eduardo swept her into
his arms. "Say no more on this. I adore you and your
dog feet." He kissed her thoroughly, igniting a passion
that tested their willpower to pull away. Eduardo ended
the kiss, but the fire for Sofia remained in his eyes.
"You're what I think is called a vixen." A corner of his
mouth quirked in amusement. He touched the tissue
wrapping his gift.

Sofia gathered her few wits and found some air.
"First, you insult my feet, and now you tell me I'm a
vixen. Do you even know what it means?"

"Of course, I know what vixen means. I said it."

"May I remind you, sir, that you say a lot of things

incorrectly." Sofia grinned and tried to steal a peek at the dress.

"Vixen means what Sofia does to Eduardo. There. You see no corrector needed. Now we see this. Yes?" Eduardo pulled the bag away, revealing a beautiful aqua lace dress.

The design wasn't flowy, which never suited Sofia's small frame. Eduardo had chosen an A-line style meant to hug curves and show off shapely legs. She gulped, recognizing the famous designer's label. How could he afford such luxuries? Surely an olive grove couldn't produce—

"Well? You say nothing of the dress." Eduardo's expression looked hurt.

Sofia wrapped her arms around his neck. "I adore the dress as well as the man who chose it so carefully for me." She kissed his cheeks, leaving his lips for last. "Did you like my answer?"

"I fear too much. You're killing me. Go dress while I get something cold to drink. A night like no other waits for us, my Sofia."

Chapter 23

The lace dress fit perfectly, as if specifically designed for her. It was amazing how Eduardo could know her so intimately. Fortunately for them both, she'd resisted the desire to cross that line in their short-lived relationship. Her few remaining wits told her that adding more reasons to grow closer to Eduardo would only leave her in emotional tatters. Still, Sofia marveled at how he'd captured her size. Another enigma to add to the list.

Eduardo promised them a night like no other. Walking next to him, those taunting words whirled in her mind. Why would their last night together deliver him to her door in such high spirits? Eduardo's mood remained a puzzle, and Sofia expected time would soon reveal the answer. Inhaling the pale-yellow rose corsage's lovely fragrance helped artificially buoy Sofia's spirits as they approached the destination. Eduardo's voice pierced the silence.

"It's good the rain moved on, leaving everything refreshed and renewed. The sun's fullness shines on us a while longer. Right here, my Sofia." Eduardo pointed to a wrought-iron gate. "Close your eyes. I will direct you inside."

"Again, with the eyes closed? Okay, I'll trust you and go along." Sofia smiled and lifted her hand for Eduardo to guide her. Her skin felt the coolness of shade as her feet took small, unsure steps.

"Now your chair waits." Eduardo's hands guided Sofia to sit. "You may open your eyes and behold our evening."

Sofia gazed in awe at the magical scene before her. "I've never seen anything so romantic. You arranged all of this for—"

"For us, yes. Excuse me for a moment while I attend to something."

Her eyes took in the twinkling gold lights woven around a canopy of greenery made for the private courtyard's ceiling. Sofia spied a raised wood floor on the far side. Multitudes of yellow flowers in colorful ceramic planters marked the patio's perimeter. Breathing in the atmosphere, Sofia closed her eyes to commit it to memory.

She felt his kiss on the nape of her neck. "Eduardo, I can't believe any of this is real. Surely, I'm dreaming you." Sofia accepted another brief kiss before he sat down.

"Rather, I'd like to hear you dream of me. Yes, I think it's better you do this because, my Sofia, every night since we met, I dream of touching you, loving you completely, like you should be loved." Eduardo lifted Sofia's hand and kissed it. His lips lingered for a few seconds, his eyes never leaving hers.

Desire coursed through her. She felt her pulse racing and the familiar tingling before she experienced the waltzing flashback. Her eyes closed, and the image filled in the darkness. They were alone in an impressive, ornately decorated bedroom. A mural of resplendent gardens embraced a wall, where a chaise lounge beckoned. Heavy drapes closed out the night and them to the world. Eduardo returned to their bed after tending to the fireplace. Wrapping Sofia in his arms and bestowing a tender kiss on her lips, he resumed reading from a leather-bound book to her. Sofia listened, smiling up at him while clasping a gold locket hanging around her neck. The vision faded. Their all-encompassing happiness caused tears to pool in Sofia's eyes. How they loved each other then. Then? When? How? Sheer fantasy, her mind answered.

"Did you experience us just now? You must tell me." Eduardo still held Sofia's hand.

"Possibly, or my imagination is on steroids. Okay, I think it must have been the same period as the waltz, judging by the room's decor. You were reading to me. It was quite a lovely moment we shared. I'd prefer to leave it there. Let's stay in this present moment that you've created for us."

"I agree. This is our night, happening here." Hearing voices, Eduardo released Sofia's hand and turned. The three musicians stepped onto the wood platform and began playing a classical piece, threading romance through their interpretation.

Her Prince Charming had surprised her once again. "My stars and garters, they're who played at Luigi's. I adore their original compositions. How did you arrange all of this, Eduardo Diaz? You're going to have to work the groves yourself to pay for—"

"My Sofia?" Eduardo placed his fingers across her lips. "I arrange the night as I know you would love because—"

The same waiter from Luigi's came to their table. "Good evening again." He poured water into the goblets. "Signore Diaz, may I serve your antipasti?"

Eduardo looked over at Sofia. "Yes?"

"Yes. I'm excited to taste what awaits me." Sofia tucked the yellow linen napkin onto her lap and waited for the waiter to leave. "Eduardo, you chose everything yellow, knowing it's my favorite color." Sofia glanced around the courtyard.

"Of course. To show you my feelings for you requires many kinds of expression. Words can never be enough for us." His gaze roamed over her hair and face. "You look exquisite tonight." Eduardo raised his hand. "I need no corrector. Those words I made sure were proper."

Sofia smiled a little, touched by his efforts to make the night perfect for her. "I've never known anyone like you, and I doubt I ever will again."

Eduardo looked heavenward. "What need do you have for another me when you have me? Sofia Martin, you make little sense. Perhaps you need a corrector or some food." He nodded to the waiter to approach with the antipasti.

Relieved he had shifted them to banter before she declared undying love, Sofia replied, "How you've managed to remain single is a mystery to me."

"There is no mystery. I simply do not say, 'I do.'" Smiling, Eduardo pointed to their plates. "Do you know this?"

"No, but it looks delicious. Introduce me." Sofia picked up a small fork.

"It's called prosciutto e fichi, and it's famous in Venice. You have two ingredients of fresh figs and rolled prosciutto. The crusty bread accompanies. Shall we savor each bite?" Eduardo built the bite with his fingers and offered it to Sofia. "Try my way."

She leaned in and let Eduardo place the small piece into her mouth. The intimate gesture activated her flutters. She'd have to feed herself or risk starving from her stomach putting on a show. "I like the combination of sweet and salty. The different textures make it—"

"Sofia? Relax. I see my touch excites you too much. You may eat your way." Eduardo held amusement in his tone.

"I am not excited because you put a morsel into my mouth. I'm simply an enthusiastic eater." Sofia built an identical bite for Eduardo. "Let me offer you a taste from my plate." She licked her lips to torment him and fed him a small piece of bread topped with meat and fig. Sofia wiped a crumb from the corner of his mouth.

Eduardo stopped her hand. He kissed each of her fingers. "Sofia?"

"Hmm?" Her eyes closed, thinking of herself a volcano about to erupt.

"I fear you overestimate my power of will around you." Eduardo's voice sounded raspy.

"Do I?" Sofia mumbled, trying to breathe.

"I think it's best we feed ourselves." Eduardo emptied his water glass.

Sofia's brain kicked in. "Feed ourselves. Gotcha." She flashed a grin and took a hefty bite. Chewing proved an effective cooldown activity. She'd employ it over the next courses.

They sat in silence, waiting for their next course and enjoying a unique atmosphere: music to feed their souls. The happy melody being played seemed to capture the essence of their mood. Eduardo clasped her hands until the waiter brought their entrées.

Sofia studied her plate, holding her fork and knife

suspended.

Eduardo released a chuckle. "Your fork and knife show confusion over the national dish of Venice. Let me tell you the story of baccalà mantecato. It's a salted cod. Please taste." Eduardo took a bite. "Oh, this is very good. Luigi prepared it to perfection."

"That's not much of a story." Sofia chose a tiny morsel to eat.

"No, I continue. This dish is considered by many Venetians to be the most important traditional food to eat. I read somewhere the dish dates back to around 1431 when a ship from Venice carrying spices encountered a storm. Blown off course to an island off Norway, the sailors learned from the locals how to salt cod. They brought the method home. I guess baccalà mantecato came after their education."

"What a fascinating tale, pardon the pun. Get it, fish? Tail?" teased Sofia.

Eduardo's brow creased. "Please, the corrector. You speak of the wrong tail. My story tale isn't the same tail as a fish. It's okay, Sofia. I help you learn the proper words too."

"I know the difference. It was supposed to make you laugh. Never mind. The grilled polenta tastes nice with the fish. I'm a fan of Venice's national dish and wonder how I've missed so much flavor of the city."

"Easy answer. You were waiting for me." Eduardo pushed his empty plate to the side.

"Of course. You're right. I *was* waiting for you." Sofia grinned at his forthright responses. Eduardo possessed no filter, which only enhanced his charm. Yes, she'd been waiting for him her whole life, only to say goodbye. Sofia placed her napkin to the side.

"Would you dance with me, my Sofia?" Eduardo rose and extended his hand. He signaled the trio, and immediately, the music changed to an ethereal sound and yet compelling.

Sofia nodded, telling herself going anywhere near Eduardo's arms rated high as a risky move. "Moth to a flame," muttered Sofia, feeling Eduardo's hand touch the small of her back in a sensual way. Someone had better save her.

Dancing their first few steps, the music acted as a transporter. Sofia's eyes closed and immediately flashed back to the ball. This time, they stood close on a veranda, letting a cool breeze refresh them from dancing. The night sky's canopy twinkled with stars as they embraced. An exquisite filigree-styled diamond ring on her left finger caught her attention. The shimmering yellow stone had to be priceless. A full moon appeared, bathing them in blue light as they kissed, and the scene faded away in slow motion. Sofia's body gave a little jerk. She opened her eyes to see Eduardo watching her.

Their movements stilled. The music ended, matching them.

"The ball again, yes?" Eduardo asked. His voice held a distant note as if he'd traveled there too.

Sofia nodded.

Eduardo's arms released her. He bowed and escorted her to their table.

His manners didn't jive with the current day. Nothing about Eduardo fit. He practically defined Jane Austen's version of polite society. The whole evening reflected this puzzling truth. Sofia studied his formal yet friendly manner as the waiter delivered their decadent Venetian Carrot Cake.

"Please extend my gratitude to Luigi, the musicians, the staff, and, of course, yourself. Everyone did an excellent job. Now, please excuse us. We wish to enjoy each other's company alone."

"As you wish, Signore Diaz. It's been an honor to serve you and the Señorita Sofia. *Buonanotte*."

"Thank you, and good night." Sofia watched as the waiter and musicians quietly withdrew through a side entry.

Eduardo's focus turned to Sofia. "At last, I have you alone. I felt their eyes on us all evening. Nice, caring eyes, but intruding. I require time alone with you, to speak, and to discuss us. First, I sweeten your disposition for my words. I think carrot cake makes you supremely happy."

"Eduardo, my disposition is quite sweet for whatever you want to discuss, and the carrot cake does make me happy."

"I make a success of our evening so far. I shall endeavor to construct more." Eduardo took a bite of the cake.

"It's better to say you shall endeavor to build on it," replied Sofia.

"That too. Do you taste rum or brandy in the cake? I think the chef took liberties."

Sofia's laugh rang out. "Eduardo Diaz, I say again, you're unlike any man I know. What century did you abandon for this one?" The unexpected question surprised Sofia, but not Eduardo.

Answering without a pause, "The century you keep going to spy on us. We know this already. It's the how and why we're missing." Eduardo said no more, leaving

Sofia to digest the surprising reply along with the rest of her cake.

Chapter 24

Eduardo scooted his chair back and stood. He gazed at the sky and then at his watch. "The sun has dropped, making our time shorter. I cannot wait longer to speak of heart matters." He came to her side. "Shall we?"

Sofia rose, uncertain of his words and direction. "Shall we what?" A nervous smile punctuated her feelings.

"You'll see in a moment." Eduardo escorted them around a partition to reveal a private romantic oasis.

Sofia sighed. The yellow twinkling lights and greenery remained as the canopy. A three-tiered bronze fountain added the soothing sound of water. A velvet-cushioned metal bench waited in front of a lush garden of ferns as green as juicy limes. A bouquet of yellow roses, matching Sofia's corsage, rested on a table next to a journal.

She turned to face Eduardo. "I can't believe you've arranged this beautiful night so perfectly. I've never felt so—I've never been so—" Sofia threw her arms around his neck, paused a second to memorize their moment unfolding, and let her kiss fill in all the blanks her words could not.

When the kiss ended, Eduardo's arms remained around her. He buried his face in her hair. "Sofia, there is much for me to say." He pulled her to the bench.

Sofia bent to smell the roses. "And I want so much to hear what you have to say."

A bottle of sparkling champagne waited in an ice bucket next to two fluted crystal glasses. Eduardo popped the cork. "Let us toast. To the forever us." He touched his glass to Sofia's, and they drank.

"It's a lovely evening, is it not?" His fingers touched her lips.

Sofia swallowed and failed at ignoring the flutters' arrival. "Yes, a lovely evening," her mouth parroted.

"It's our night, Sofia. Our night for declaring our feelings and affection. I must go first."

An unsure Sofia could only nod. What did Eduardo mean? Declaring their feelings to what end? Her flight was leaving in hours. Still, her heart held hope.

Eduardo rewarded her with a smile. "Ah, how I adore you. You must know I'm so in love with you I can scarcely think of anything else but us. It matters not the little time we've spent together. We know each other in ways we cannot explain, but it's real. *We're* real. Tell me, do you feel this way about us?"

She waited for a beat, then breathed, "Yes."

Eduardo's eyes flicked over her. "Want to know what I see when I gaze at you?"

"Yes." His look was melting her with a slowness like honey dripping from a bottle. The butterflies were multiplying faster than rabbits inside of her. *Find some words, any words to break this spell*, Sofia scolded herself. "What do you see?"

"I see your face and the way you scrunch your nose when I say the wrong words. You delight me. Maybe I say the wrong word sometimes to see you make the face." Eduardo kissed the tip of her nose.

"Do you really?" Sofia gauged his expression. "You do, you scoundrel." Her hand smacked him lightly, but then her expression turned serious. "What else do you see?"

"Sofia, my love, I see your eyes, the color of the Adriatic Sea. Do you know how much I want to gaze into them for always?" Eduardo's fingers traced Sofia's brows and withdrew. "I see your lips, so full and begging for the kiss."

"I don't beg—"

Eduardo touched her bottom lip. "Shh, I see your intelligence which keeps me on my feet—no. Toes." Eduardo grinned. He caressed her cheek. "Most of all, my Sofia, I see your inner beauty, your soul that calls me home to your arms. These are the things I desire in a woman called Sofia Martin." Eduardo reached for both of Sofia's hands. "I love you fully. The way a man must love a woman. I feel forever love here." Eduardo touched his heart. "For you, Sofia. Only for you. And I want very much to propose marriage to you, but there are complications to my proposal. You must hear them and accept them before I get on the knee."

Sofia's pulse quickened. For once, her mind offered no help. Eduardo wanted to marry her. Did she want to marry him after only knowing him for a few days? Following her heart led only to one place, to Eduardo Diaz. Stunned with happiness, Sofia could only sit and wait for Eduardo's next words.

"I have a plan for us. It's a plan I wish to explain." Eduardo paused. "I notice you say nothing. Should I worry about your loving me as I love you? Did my talk of marriage cause you fright?"

"On the contrary. I'm quiet because I'm struggling

to take in all of this and manage my worry." Sofia leaned over and pecked his cheek with a kiss. "Though your way of bringing up marriage to me doesn't exactly fit the romantic Eduardo Diaz persona I've come to adore."

"That Diaz is waiting for his moment." Eduardo smiled. "What worry causes you to frown before I even explain the complications? This isn't going as I planned it."

"I worry about how we can possibly make us work. The distance and all, for starters." Sofia paused. "I'm afraid to hope there can even be an us." Sofia squeezed both of Eduardo's hands. "I've never believed love like ours existed except in books. Here's what I want you to hear. If there was a stronger word for the love I feel, I'd claim it this moment for you." Sofia inhaled deeply. "I'm ready to hear and keep hoping you have some way for us. Please share your plan. Hold nothing back."

"Very well. The whole story you shall have, but promise me you won't judge until I finish?" asked Eduardo. "It's long and complicated, but I'll try to shorten it because we still have something to enjoy together."

"I promise to keep an open mind and not judge until you're finished. At this rate, I may turn gray waiting to hear this plan." Sofia interjected a grin to ease them into the next moment.

Eduardo leaned against the bench's back and hesitated a few seconds. "I begin in the middle, reminding you of my father's phone call at your condo. This you remember?"

"Yes, and you were agitated the rest of the night."

"Indeed, it was because he called me home and

demanded I do certain things."

"Like take over running Olivar Siete Colinas?" Sofia asked.

"Yes, operations are one part, but there are many complexities around my family and business. I've not told you much regarding the Diaz workings. First, you must know my father is unbending on matters he thinks important. He's ready to hand over the running of our business to Ernesto and me, but with certain stipulations. I did agree to all these stipulations before meeting you. Now, things have changed." Eduardo's mouth gave a slight twist.

"See? It's my fault your world has turned topsy-turvy. We need to forget—"

"What's this topsy-turvy?" asked Eduardo.

"It means things turned upside down and causing problems," explained Sofia. "It's best if I go—"

"Please, give me a chance to state my plan for you. I tried to negotiate with my father, but a compromise wasn't for him. I agreed to move home permanently, but I wanted to bring you if you'd agree to become my wife."

"Me, move to Spain and not return to Boston? I need—"

Eduardo raised his hand. "There's more. The hard piece comes now." He swallowed. "My father refused to release me from a pledge made by my parents when I was three. You see, our land adjoins the Reye land. It's been a long-held desire to join our lands and enterprises. You understand me?"

"I do. Bigger is better," offered Sofia. Her senses screamed troubled words were coming her way next. Her pulse felt like a jackhammer. "So?"

"So, to meet this goal, both families agreed to an arrangement of marriage. You see, Isobel Reye and I grew up as childhood friends. Our parents saw to it we'd spend time together and would naturally care about each other and accept our future planned out. We have done this."

Sofia's heart sank. "Are you telling me you're supposed to marry Isobel and yet you're wanting to propose to me? I'm so confused."

"Yes. I wanted my father to release me from this arrangement so you and I could spend our lives being an us. He refused and gave me a choice of doing what is expected or being cut loose from the family." Eduardo's voice held a bitter note.

"Hang on a sec. Let's go back to you and Isobel. Do you love her? Does Isobel love you?" An ache ran through her body just posing the questions. Sofia supposed it was possible to be in love with two people at the same time. No, she was lying to herself. It wasn't possible. "What do you feel for Isobel?"

"I cannot lie. I do love Isobel but as a sister, Sofia. Only as a sister. I've never been in love with her. I was willing to settle for this arrangement and type of love. Why? Because I'd never found love with another woman until you. Now, I can't imagine settling when there's my Sofia sitting next to me." Eduardo paused for a breath.

"And does Isobel love you?" Sofia pressed.

"She says yes. Perhaps she's not in love with me either. Perhaps we lie to ourselves. I don't know."

Sofia shook her head in disbelief. "Let me see if I've got this story down. Your family and Isobel's arranged when you were young for a marriage to take place to merge your lands. You and Isobel grew up together and developed a love for each other as time passed. Only your feelings for her are the brotherly kind. Your father has called you to honor this agreement and assume your business responsibilities to the family. You tried and failed to negotiate yourself out of the marriage. Your goal was for me to marry you, move to Spain, and live at the olive grove. Does that cover it?"

"Said your way sounds not like me." Eduardo's expression showed frustration. "No, I do not like the way you tell of my complications. You leave out how much I love and want to be with you. You do not yet have my plan for us."

"Fine. What's this plan?" Sofia didn't hide her exasperation over the mess Eduardo laid at her feet.

"My plan, my Sofia, is to release my ties to the family and move to Boston."

"What? Move to Boston? Are you daft?" Sofia's voice rose a few octaves.

"Yes, move to Boston, where your sister and the museum await. I shall find work and become a success there. Of course, it means I come to you having little funds. I'm hopeful your love for me will forgive this. Sofia, we belong together. The last few days keep showing us in ways we can't explain. I can never love anyone but you, maybe for all time." Eduardo shrugged. "Your visions show something similar. Yes?"

"I can't think about the flashes right now. I'm struggling over your giving up everything and your life in Spain for me."

"For us, my Sofia. For us, it's not giving up. No, it's a go toward everything I love and want. I go to you.

I go to us. Surely you see my love for you knows no boundaries. If you agree to my plan for us to spend our lives together, I can properly propose to you now. What says, my Sofia?" A smile of hope played around Eduardo's mouth.

Sofia rose. "I need a few moments to process what you've said. This is huge, Eduardo. And I'm so in love with you it's coloring my practical side right now."

"Forget the practical. Feel the coloring toward our love. Feel the coloring toward saying yes to us being together. This grand, unexplainable love of us. Don't you see? We're like no other couple we know. There's something special happening." Eduardo's eyes followed Sofia as she paced around the small space.

She returned to his side. "Give me a coin," said Sofia. This fascination with coin wishing made little sense. She'd add it to her growing list of unexplainables. "Just one." Sofia smiled faintly.

Without asking for an explanation, Eduardo reached into his pocket and handed her a silver coin.

Sofia walked to the bronze fountain and whispered, "I need a sign. I can't let him walk away from his world for me unless I know it's our destiny. For the past few days, I've been asked to trust and not question what makes zero sense. I need some guidance here. I know I keep relying on coins, but it's what I have near. Nothing earth-shaking, just an itsy-bitsy nudge. Give me a sign of what I should do next." Sofia tossed the coin into the fountain and waited.

Chapter 25

Eduardo's cell phone rang. He answered in Castellano and within seconds hung up. "Apologies."

She'd been given her answer. Sofia joined Eduardo on the bench. "I assume the caller was Isobel. I don't speak your language, but I heard her name."

"Yes, Isobel had texted me an alert earlier, which I ignored. I had to make sure my father's heart hadn't taken a turn." Eduardo laid his phone on top of the journal.

Sofia's concern for Señor Diaz trumped the crushing disappointment of the sign. "I'm glad your father is okay. And Isobel?" What made her push to feel more pain?

"Isobel wanted a ride if she decided to return home. Nothing more. Please, this is our evening. Will you accept my plan so that I might get on my knee?" Eduardo leaned in, bestowing a kiss to Sofia. He pulled back. "What's wrong? You didn't return my kiss. Tell me."

Tears tumbled down her cheeks. Eduardo pulled her into him, mumbling consoling words into her ear. Minutes passed as Sofia cried for what she must do. Accepting Eduardo's handkerchief, she turned to face him.

"Now, will you please tell me what's upset you so? Let me remedy it so we can plan our future." Eduardo's eyebrows were pulled downward, lips taut.

Sofia's finger trailed along Eduardo's jaw. With every bit of inner grit her mind possessed, her eyes met his. "I asked for a sign of what to do when I tossed the coin. Isobel's call brought me the answer."

"What madness do you speak?" Eduardo's anger surfaced.

"Shh. It's my turn to have the floor and your turn to listen to my plan. All right?" Sofia's voice held a resoluteness that surprised even her.

"I'll listen."

"I love you more than the stars in heaven. Never forget those words. How I wish I could say yes to marriage, but I can't. I won't. I'm touched deeply by the idea of your plan. It shows me how much you love me and want a forever us."

"I'm not liking where you're taking this."

"Please, Eduardo. I need to finish while I've got the inner strength. I can't let you walk away from your family, your dreams for the groves, your commitments, and most importantly, your honor. Even though our time in Venice has been brief, I know your honor defines the man you are. It's one of the many character traits I love and admire in you." Sofia placed her hand over his mouth as he was about to speak. "Not yet. I've one more point. If we married and you moved to Boston, in time, you'd grow to resent me. Regret would become our shadow. Our love deserves higher-minded choices. The honorable ones." New tears pooled in her eyes. Her throat contracted as Sofia said the final words. "Go home, Eduardo. Marry Isobel. Find your way to love her as a husband. Honor yourself and the agreement. In doing this, you honor the man I love, and you honor us." Sofia closed her eyes and felt Eduardo's hand wiping her cheeks. Her eyes opened to see the tears in his.

His voice matched the pain in hers. "I don't want this plan for us. I won't feel the resentment or the regret you speak of. I want only for us to be together, to hold you each night next to me."

Sofia shook her head. "Our timing is off. We can't begin our life by causing others' pain."

"Is there nothing I can say to change this course you're charting for us?"

"It's the only way, Señor Eduardo Diaz, the man who holds my heart and my love. Trust me. It's the only way." Sofia released his hand and returned to the fountain. She watched the water trickling down into the lower bowl. Surprise washed over her. She searched for the coin. It wasn't there.

Eduardo came to her side, pocketing the small journal. "Despite the sadness we're feeling, I beg you to accompany me to make our next memory. Would you like to take a gondola ride? I've saved this outing for our romantic night."

"I would like nothing more." They were making their last memory together. Sofia did not ask about the journal. As they left, she gave a glance over her shoulder at their magical place. She'd left her 'if only we could have' behind, where it now belonged.

They strolled along the canals as the orange setting sun prepared to give over to the night shift. Eduardo led them down a narrow cobblestone lane where gondolas waited for lovers. Sofia watched as he pondered which boat met his approval.

"Hello. Come over to my boat." A smiling

gondolier dressed in Old World finery beckoned to them.

"Eduardo, I think he's calling us," said Sofia, waving to the friendly face.

"He is, and we shall answer the call." Eduardo gazed down at her. "His boat is the one I looked to find."

Those cryptic words occupied her mind while Eduardo and the gondolier had a brief exchange. Her efforts to stay in the moment and not think about their parting weren't working. A big cry skirted and flirted with erupting like Mount Vesuvius at any moment. She'd been second-guessing her decision ever since leaving their romantic courtyard. Still, the sign given to her seemed unmistakable. Sofia could only hazard a quirky guess where the coin had evaporated to: Maybe it went through the same wormhole as the gypsy and Dina. To share this week's adventure with a rational person would prompt an offer for a psychiatric workup.

Eduardo motioned. "Sofia, we must hurry. The sun's movement beckons us." He helped her board gingerly in her lacy dress and pumps. A long-cushioned seat welcomed them as the gondolier took his standing place at the stern. "Say *ciao* to Angelo."

"*Ciao*, Angelo. Thank you for the ride." Sofia managed a warm smile. "This is my first time on a gondola." She noticed a bouquet of daisies in a vase mounted near the bow.

Angelo grinned. "It's my first time too." His English carried no accent. "I must make this a ride to remember." He grabbed the oar.

"Angelo assures me he's got the perfect route meant just for us." Eduardo gave a dismissive shrug of his shoulders. "We go with the stream."

"You mean, 'We go with the flow.'" Sofia felt awash in sadness, thinking that may have been the last time she'd need to correct Eduardo. Sofia took a second look at him. "You set me up. You knew it was flow."

"Perhaps. I needed to have my Sofia back." He tucked a strand of hair behind her ear. "Please, let us remain Eduardo and Sofia these last minutes together. Yes?"

"Yes." Sofia's lips quivered. Eduardo covered them with his own. They kept the kiss alive until Angelo cleared his throat.

"Pardon the interruption. I've brought you to the Bridge of Sighs at the exact time the legend decrees. It's sunset, and the bells of Saint Mark's should chime at any moment. I invite you to please kiss…" The bells tolled. "Kiss now to have your love sealed forever."

Eduardo embraced Sofia with an urgency she'd never experienced from him. His kiss, full of passion, carried them both to another time, to another place where being in each other's arms held no sadness. Too soon, the gondola's movement ended the kiss and the connection. Eduardo recovered first. "Did you know, my Sofia, gondolas used to be what you call a status symbol to transport the nobility?"

Still reeling from what they'd just shared, Sofia clipped her hair back and glanced around at the other boats. "Really? Venice is unique in so many ways." She nodded, taking in the passing gondolas. Glancing up, the sky's color had taken on a deep purple glow. Sofia chose to ignore the darkening shade, proving time had truly turned against them once more. "What else, my gondola expert?"

"You appreciate my knowledge." Eduardo cupped her chin and grinned. "Let's see. It's stated in books the gondola has existed in Venice since the 11th century. Back in the 17th and 18th centuries, there were approximately ten thousand boats, but today maybe four hundred. It is sad to me there are so few."

Sofia looked over her shoulder, wearing a grin. "Hey, Angelo, are his facts correct?"

"I believe they are, Miss Sofia."Angelo steered them into a narrow, private canal and raised his oar. "May I have your permission to play a song I wrote? It's been waiting a very long time for the two people who share a grand love like no other."

Sofia looked at Eduardo, seeing the same surprise in his expression. A random fact popped into her head. The name Angelo meant angel messenger. "What's one more unexplainable thing?" she said in a low tone.

"I'm collecting them," Eduardo answered and twisted to face Angelo. "We'd be honored to have you play the song."

Angelo unwrapped a mandolin from a blanket. He propped his leg on the steering platform and adjusted the instrument. He touched his nearby cell phone to bring on accompanying instruments. Satisfied, he smiled at the couple. "Sofia and Eduardo, I call your song 'Venetian Rhapsody.' It belongs only to you and is a testament to the timeless love you share." The haunting melody unfolded, telling their story with musical notes.

Emotions embraced her while listening. With eyes closed, those sentiments transported her back to their ornate bedroom. Wrapped in Eduardo's arms, Sofia witnessed their unbridled love. Releasing a sigh, she could almost hear Eduardo singing words to their song. Her eyes opened. His expression was so full of passion, heartache, and pleading as he gazed at Sofia.

Angelo's mandolin ended their song.

Sofia held onto Eduardo, memorizing what they shared. "You've gotten into my soul. I'm going to love you forever, Eduardo Diaz. Tonight may be the best and worst night of my life."

"Ah, my Sofia, you must always believe in us. You must." Eduardo pulled her against his chest as the gondola set a course home. No words were spoken. None were left to say, save goodbye.

Darkness wrapped them in silence as the boat glided over the calm water and into its parking slip. Once off the gondola, Eduardo and Sofia turned to thank Angelo for the ride and gift of "Venetian Rhapsody."

Angelo came alongside the couple. "Sofia and Eduardo, I have more words to share." He paused. "Your amazing love truly defies time. Trust in it. I leave you with the words of Dylan Thomas: 'Do not go gentle into that good night.' There are many kinds of death to triumph against. To allow the death of such love like yours should not become your fate. I bid you farewell—for now." Angelo tipped his cap and steered the boat down the canal.

A stunned Sofia stared at Eduardo. The steady stream of tears hadn't ceased. Sofia doubted they ever would. "I'm at a complete and hopeless loss."

"I know. It's the same for me. One day we might understand, but not tonight." Eduardo held her hand. "Come, my love. Let me walk you home and make our last memory for us. We've said our words to each other.

A farewell for now and a kiss are all I ask."

Sofia nodded. Make more memories? She was overflowing with them and close to becoming a living puddle. To say goodbye to Eduardo in a few moments would surely shatter her heart. But say goodbye, she must. They had a different path to travel. Somehow, she'd find the courage to walk up the condo stairs and not look back. Somehow.

The Second Encounter
One Year Later
Chapter 26

Surveying the one-bedroom condo over Lucia's bakery, Sofia felt at home. Overall, she'd done a respectable job of unpacking and settling in. The balcony view of Venice's Grand Canal left her awash with memories. Memories of a face that still had the power to melt her and rob her of breath. Memories she'd clearly lied to herself about burying. Returning inside, Sofia plopped down on the floral sofa, hugged a pillow, and released a sigh. Why did fate seem bent on delivering her back to the City of Love? The place where her heart had shattered into a million pieces.

Hearing the cell phone chime, Sofia grabbed it from the marble coffee table. "Hi, Melody. I was about to call you." Sofia coaxed her voice to sound happy.

"Hi, baby sister. Are you satisfied with the condo you rented? I know it's the same building as before, but you're picky about where you stay. Are you going downstairs to the fab Italian bakery?"

"Yes, to all of your questions and any that I cut short." Sofia laughed and twisted her honey-blond hair into a topknot.

"Great. You didn't let me ask my last question. So, I should presume your yes to my questions means you've decided to accept Aaron's marriage proposal. I know he's a bit uptight and all, but you're never going to find another—cancel that last part. Need I remind you that you're edging toward thirty? Tick-tock," chided Melody.

Momentarily thrust back into her Boston life, Sofia didn't take her sister's ticking-clock bait and chuckled at the ploy. "No, I did not agree to marry Aaron before I left. I need more time to consider if I want to be anyone's wife. Besides, I plan to enjoy the time here and prepare for the symposium with my Italian colleagues." Sofia felt the beginnings of a headache.

"Okay, you've already slipped into the Dr. Sofia persona. I promise not another word from me about Sir Uptightness. You're back in Venice. The place where you and...never mind. I'm going to hang up and chase my kids out of the pool."

"Good plan." Sofia smiled wistfully. "Tell your hooligans to behave while Aunt Sofia is gone. And tell Mike I already miss his Sunday barbecue ribs."

"Righto. Let's chat again in a few days. Be sure you find time for fun. Please text me at least once a day. Make me jealous of what you're doing in the City of Love. Bye." Melody disconnected.

Sofia laid the phone aside. Another unwanted memory flashed of him, saying her eyes were as blue as the Adriatic Sea. That he wasn't Aaron. A knock on the door brought a welcome interruption. Sofia opened it to a smiling older woman holding a plate of cookies.

"Hello. Are those what I think they are?" Sofia bent down to look. "Because when I was last here, I ate Zaeti cookies every single day."

The woman's eyes crinkled from a wide smile. "Yes, I bring you nice Zaeti to welcome you. My name is Marie. I'm a new neighbor and live next to Rita.

Your name, please? I struggle much with the English." Marie passed the cobalt glass plate into Sofia's outstretched arms.

"Your English is lovely. My name is Sofia Martin, and thank you so much for this gift." Sofia took a bite of the cookie. "So good. Did you soak the raisins in wine?"

Marie gave a sheepish nod. "Shh, mustn't tell Luis, my husband. I took from his bottle of vino. Our secret, yes?"

"Yes, our secret." Sofia felt an instant liking toward the sassy, petite woman. She could use another neighbor friend. Hearing Rita was still living in the building brought an instant grin to Sofia's face. "Won't you come inside?"

Marie shook her red curls. "Not this time. Luis waits for his meal."

"Then I shall look forward to your visit soon." Sofia waved and closed the door, stuffing another baked treasure into her mouth. The thought of her beloved espresso from Chicco di Caffe came calling.

Glancing at her gold watch, Sofia nodded. There was enough time to indulge before her first meeting. Seeing Ginny later promised a lovely evening ahead. Sofia grabbed her straw tote bag and headed out the door.

Blending in with the locals, Sofia walked down the narrow sidewalk. She'd dressed in a bright sunflower-printed skirt. A yellow top and cream lacey scarf draped casually from her shoulders. Gold hoop earrings and a long strand of lapis lazuli beads completed her look. Well, almost, Sofia thought, seeing a stylish straw hat moving atop a beautiful Italian woman's head. She made a mental note to purchase one on her next outing. "Or now." Sofia spotted a vendor's cart displaying hats and caps.

"*Ciao*," Sofia said, greeting the man. Within a few seconds, her hands found the one. A white straw hat with a wide brim and a bright yellow ribbon ran around it. "I'll take this. " Sofia placed the cheerful bonnet atop her head, stooping to see her image in the small mirror hanging from the cart's canopy. "Hmm, it's interesting how a hat offers such mood enhancement," Sofia mused.

A spring in her step accompanied her to an outside table for two at Chicco's. The azure-striped tablecloths and matching umbrellas set the inviting mood for customers. Chalkboards on metal easels announced the chef's lunch specials. Sofia smiled, noting the restaurant's layout hadn't changed an iota since she'd left Venice. For her, everything had changed. The melancholy feeling tried to intrude. Sofia willed it away, only to have a nudge replace it. A nudge she'd not experienced since a year ago on this same date.

He was nearby. Her whole body sensed his presence. "Impossible," Sofia whispered. The nudge came stronger. Twisting in the chair, she scanned the location where she'd first laid eyes on him.

Eduardo looked up from the menu and saw her. His expression of disbelief mirrored her own as he slowly rose from his seat.

The waiter appeared. "What would you like?"

"Good afternoon." Sofia tried to keep her voice steady, seeing Eduardo's approach. "I'd love an iced espresso with almond milk and a dollop of—"

"Whipped cream," said an amused male voice.

Sofia's heart leaped as she gazed into Eduardo's cognac-colored eyes. She turned back to the waiter. "What he said." Sofia felt the familiar flush come to her cheeks. "Hello, Eduardo Diaz."

The server typed the drink order on his tablet and disappeared.

"Hello, Sofia Martin." Eduardo motioned to the empty chair. "May I sit for a moment? I must say, this is a surprise."

"Please, sit. It seems fate delights at throwing us together in Venice."

"Yes, and this fate still defies my understanding." Eduardo's tone sounded cold, distant. He studied Sofia's face. "Tell me, what brings you back?"

"I'm attending a three-day museum curators' symposium, but I added a few extra days to my itinerary for vacation time." Sofia held her head high. "And you?"

A mask of reserve covered Eduardo's face. "I'm here until Friday to assist my uncle in a business matter. Are you staying in the same condo above Lucia's bakery? I recall you enjoyed the location."

Sofia gave a brief nod and smiled. "Your memory is correct. As it happens, the condo management company had a short-term rental unit that I was able to snag for the week."

"How nice for you." Eduardo diverted his attention to an older, debonair gentleman entering the dining area. "Please excuse me, Sofia. My uncle has arrived for our lunch meeting. I hope you'll enjoy your time in Venice. Just so you know, your favorite gelato cart is still around the corner."

"Thank you, Eduardo. I can't believe we—" Sofia

gave a shake of her head. "It was nice to see you again," she said, evading his eyes.

Eduardo's jaw clenched. "Goodbye, Sofia Martin."

Crestfallen, Sofia watched him escort his uncle to their table. Waves of emotion washed over her as memories of the time they'd shared engulfed her. To see him was fate acting its cruelest.

The waiter brought her iced espresso and straightened the napkin disturbed by Eduardo before departing.

Sofia's hand trembled while lifting her iced coffee. Glancing Eduardo's way, she caught him looking at her while talking to his uncle. His expression held anger and something else she couldn't identify. Her ire rose to meet his. She'd be wise to leave before marching over to his table and demanding why he'd just treated her like a block of ice. Grabbing her tote, Sofia left money on the table and walked toward the sidewalk without a glance back.

Only when she'd turned the corner did her breathing return to normal. Every flavor of confusion accompanied her to the college campus. Sofia tapped on Ginny's office door and entered.

"I want a hug." A smiling Ginny came from around her desk to embrace Sofia. "Gosh, it's so fantastic to see you. I've been waiting all day."

"I promised you I'd return for a visit." Sofia delivered a hug and claimed the wingback chair. "You've redecorated your office, Professor Greco. I like it."

Ginny chose the matching wingback chair. "Thanks. I let Milo pick the color scheme. He's good with that sort of thing."

"I agree." Sofia's fingers fiddled with her sunglasses.

"Hmm, something is off here. You look—" Ginny paused, her eyes assessing Sofia's face. "Upset."

"What? No." Sofia gazed out the window at students going to class.

"Yes. I know that look. You're upset, and you'd better tell me why." Ginny tapped Sofia's arm to get her attention. "You haven't been in Venice twenty-four hours. What possibly—"

"Fate hates me. Really hates me."

Ginny's hand hid her grin. "The only time you've ever talked about fate—"

"I saw him a few minutes ago at the café," Sofia exclaimed, throwing her arms up. "I mean, come on. What are the odds I'd run into Eduardo Diaz at the same place exactly a year later? Like a gazillion to one. Right?" She sucked in a heavy breath, shaking her head.

"At least a gazillion." Ginny's expression shifted to amusement. "Listen, I don't know the story of you and Eduardo. Milo and I left for vacation right after you two met. I grant you it's pretty crazy to have seen each other today. But hey, it's you and Eduardo. I remember your banter at Milo's party. You two define—"

"And he acted aloof, like I was a mere acquaintance he'd passed a few pleasantries with from the past. I don't get it. Do you get it?" Sofia waited, puzzlement coursing through her.

"Well, I'm not going to meddle here or discuss Milo's friend but—"

"We fell in love and had these amazing experiences together. And we just had another, and he treats me as if—" Sofia's throat tightened with pent-up emotion.

"Need the box of tissues?" Ginny shoved the box across the side table.

"Yeah." Sofia pulled a handful from the container. "I can't decide if I'm going to have a hissy fit or get into a snit, but the cry is definite." Tears trickled down her cheeks.

"Go ahead and let loose. I'm going to slip out to get your fave Italian ginger ale from the vending machine. It's guaranteed to restore your spirits." Ginny hurried out of the office.

Sofia sat stewing. Maybe Eduardo being married accounted for his reserve. Of course, that made perfect sense. Honor defined him. She had a plausible explanation now. One that broke her heart to bits. Eduardo and Isobel joined together as husband and wife. She'd managed to block it out for twelve months. No, she hadn't. "Sofia, pull yourself together. You had a chance encounter. Won't be repeated." She blinked away the tears. "If only we'd gotten another chance to be an us." Her mantra for the past year had been "If only."

Chapter 27

Sofia entered her condo and headed for the shower. She'd crammed a lot into her first day. The symposium meet-and-greet lasted longer than anticipated. Jet lag wrapped around her body as the hot water pulsed from the shower head.

Dressed in her favorite sloppy t-shirt and joggers, Sofia padded out to the kitchen and poured a glass of green tea. Hearing her neighbors' voices chattering outside the hallway, a curious Sofia opened her door. Three residents were standing in their doorframes. Sofia watched as the man with familiar broad shoulders knocked on Rita's door.

"*Ciao*, Rita. Remember me? You baked me a sorry pie?"

Rita bobbed her head, grinning. "Yes, the sorry. Rosa ate your note to Sofia. Sorry. What you need?"

"Do you happen to know which condo is Sofia's? She's back in Venice."

Another door opened. Marie's face appeared. "You want the Sofia? Turn around, signore." Marie pointed.

Eduardo pivoted to see Sofia standing a few feet away. "Found her," he announced to everyone. He smiled in satisfaction. "Sofia, I apologize for showing up, but I brought your hat that you left at the café."

"Thanks for going to the trouble." Sofia took the hat and went to close the door.

Eduardo lifted his hand. "Wait. I'd like to come inside and talk—"

"I don't think that's a good idea. You're married. Go away."

"He's married," Rita repeated to Marie and shook her finger in Eduardo's direction. "You go home to your wife, Signore Sorry."

Sofia closed her door and leaned against it. Emotions flooded her. She heard a light tap and remembered the night Eduardo stood outside her door trying to get a date, with her neighbors' encouragement. Despite her good judgment, Sofia answered. "Would you please just go?"

"Sofia, I am not married. Open the door." Eduardo turned to the women who'd circled him. "I am not married. Okay? You can go home."

"Sofia, he says no married," hollered Rita through the door. "He's still handsome."

"Please. I appreciate your help, but I can handle this," said Eduardo.

The door opened slowly. Sofia kept her grin inside, seeing the women hovering.

Eduardo's voice held amusement. "May I please come inside before the coven of biddies—"

Sofia waved to the women. "Thanks, all of you. Have a good night."

"He no stay the night, Sofia." Rita's finger pointed again.

"Nope. He no stay the night. Just a short visit." Sofia waved and pulled an exasperated Eduardo into the condo. "Okay, you've seen me and managed to create quite the scene out there. What's left to say?"

"Must you take my words so—"

"Literally? Yes."

Eduardo went to the sofa. "May I?"

"No. Just tell me whatever you came to say and then *adios*." Sofia planted her hands on her hips.

Eduardo scrunched his eyebrows thoughtfully. "What's this unkindness? I bring your bonnet home and suffer the biddies, only to hear you say, 'Go away.'"

"Yeah, that sums it up pretty well. Besides, you weren't exactly friendly when we—"

"When destiny brought us together once more? Perhaps I wasn't friendly enough, but the shock of seeing you caused me speechless." Eduardo's hands swiped through his hair.

"Made you speechless." Sofia released a heavy sigh. His nearness was affecting her in ways it shouldn't. It was as if her body had stored the memory of Eduardo's magnetism, and it all came flooding back.

"I know the correct word is made. I tease you a little to change your mood." Eduardo's mouth turned up at the corners.

"Very funny." She fiddled with her hoop earrings.

"Did it work? Maybe you will invite me to sit?" Eduardo pointed to the sofa.

"Why? What's the point? I'm here for a few days. You're here for a few days. It's déjà vu, and I don't do déjà vu. Don't you dare plant yourself on my sofa."

Eduardo sat and folded his arms. "I wish to chat for a few moments. I have no desires to déjà vu with you." He patted the cushion next to him. "I'll take my leave after we catch up."

Sofia joined him, sitting at the farthest end of the sofa. "So? Chat."

"How are you?"

"Dandy," replied Sofia, matching his crossed arms. He wasn't married. Wondering what happened played in her mind. "And you?"

"Good." Eduardo fixated his glance on Sofia's face. "You look uptight and…not happy. Why?"

"It could be because you're sitting in my condo, grilling me like a steak," replied Sofia.

Eduardo frowned but didn't budge. "I see. So, I will try a different way. Sofia, it's nice to see you again. I trust your week in Venice will meet your desires. As for me, I'm happy to assist my uncle and return home to my enterprises." He looked out the glass doors.

"How nice for you." Sofia forced the edginess in her voice. If she didn't look at him, maybe she'd not succumb to his magnetism. Mr. Swoonable, as Ginny labeled Eduardo Diaz, still had his charm.

"Yes, it is nice for me. Let me help you talk to me. 'Tell me, Eduardo, what new enterprises are you involved in at Olivar Siete Colinas?'"

"Would you please stop this charade?" Sofia went to fetch her tea.

Eduardo stood. "Sofia? I apologize. I only wanted to hear you're doing well and happy. I see you have no wish to share this. I shouldn't have pushed myself inside your condo. I'll go now." Eduardo opened the front door and turned. "Enjoy your time in Venice."

"Wait." Sofia hurried to his side. "I'm sorry for being so rude. You were nice enough to bring my hat and suffer the women. Please, stay a few minutes. Let me get you a tea."

Eduardo's eyes held hers. "Really? You want me to remain?"

"I do. Please." Sofia's arm beckoned him to the

sofa. She returned to the kitchen.

Eduardo chose the center of the sofa and sat. "Thank you for the beverage."

Sofia assessed the change in seating and opted for the chair. "You were saying something about new enterprises?"

"Yes, I've begun implementing my plans for the land. We're giving tours now and might construct a small inn next spring based on numbers. My father seems pleased overall, which is good." Eduardo took a sip from the glass.

"Your changes sound exciting and rewarding on all fronts." Sofia refused to ask about Isobel and their marriage. She'd soon need masking tape for her mouth because the words threatened to escape at any moment.

"You grasp the situation perfectly. Thank you." Eduardo scooted to the corner of the sofa, nearer to Sofia. "Now, might I hear news of your work at the museum?"

Sofia tucked her legs, judging his distance to be safe. "The life of museum curator…it's been good overall. I admit the Board of Directors has succeeded in creating obstacles for me to bring in traveling exhibitions. I've not been able to convince them of the benefits yet, but I will. They haven't met my persuasive side yet." A glimmer of a grin came into Sofia's eyes.

"As I recall, you can be most persuasive. I feel sure you'll gain those exhibitions." Eduardo's cell rang. He glanced at the caller and silenced the phone. "Ernesto, my brother. He can wait."

Sofia felt the marriage words rising. Panicked, she jumped from the chair. "Hearing your phone ring reminded me I've got to make an important call." Sofia walked toward the door and waited for Eduardo.

"Yes, of course." He left the tea on the kitchen counter. "Well—"

"Thanks again for rescuing my new straw hat." Sofia made the mistake of looking into those eyes. The eyes that still had the power to melt her within seconds. "I'm glad that you're happy and—" Sofia swallowed as Eduardo slid those eyes up and down her body.

"Maybe I—maybe we could," stammered Eduardo backing out the door.

Isobel's name was a second from slipping from her lips. "Listen, I need to make my call. Thanks again." She gently shoved him out and closed the door as the words escaped. "What about you and Isobel? Did you marry?" Marry? Aaron's face flashed in her mind. Sofia had to return Aaron's call. No doubt she'd spend a sleepless night running the gamut on how it felt seeing Eduardo and the encore of unexplainables.

Chapter 28

The morning sun streamed through Lucia's bakery windows, giving the shop an ethereal golden glow. A steady stream of customers paraded by where Sofia sat, enjoying her favorite brioche and latte. She'd made Lucia her first stop before heading to the symposium. Seeing her friend again brought instant happiness.

"Here I am. I've got two minutes before my bread timers go off. You look wonderful, Sofia Martin. Having you sit here feels like you never left us. How long will you spend in Venice?" Lucia signaled a server to refill a customer's coffee cup.

"I think probably a week. The symposium lasts three days, so I'm going to take advantage of a few vacation days. Promise me you'll make a pizza for us and come upstairs for dinner one evening after work? I love it when we do a girls' night."

"I promise." Lucia's expression grew thoughtful. "Sofia? I must ask you something."

"Sure, okay." A quizzical brow arched above Sofia's left eye. "What's the question?"

"Will you follow your heart this time?"

"Follow my heart? Are you referring to the cookie's message you delivered when I was seeing Eduardo?"

Lucia smiled and nodded. "Well?"

Sofia considered the question and her answer. "I

don't think it applies now. My heart belongs in Boston and—"

Lucia shook her head and reached for Sofia's hand. "Your heart belongs—"

"Lucia? Come quick. The oven's talking loud beeps," called out a voice from the kitchen.

"I must run care for the beeps. Our talkings of the heart must wait, my friend." Lucia squeezed Sofia's shoulder affectionately and took off.

"Follow my heart," repeated Sofia, adding a sigh. Eduardo's face, not Aaron's, was what came to her. Her phone chat with Aaron the night before had felt stilted and lacked something. Did she love him? The answer was it depended on how love was defined. Sofia held zero hope of ever feeling toward any man the way she felt for Eduardo. She'd forgiven herself countless times for comparing every man she'd dated in the last year to him. The guy she'd followed her heart to lead her right down misery lane…a path she'd never take again.

Gathering her laptop bag and tote, Sofia waved to Lucia. Time to focus on the conference, make new connections, and renew others. She soaked up Venice's vibe as she walked the cobblestone walkways. The city had no peers. The canals served as roads and defined the lifestyles of the residents. Observing a boat owner unload merchandise on a store's floating dock, Sofia missed the two men approaching a bank's entrance.

"Sofia?"

She turned to see Eduardo and his uncle. "At the risk of sounding like a cliché, we meet again." Sofia nodded to the older gentleman.

"It appears so." Eduardo's teeth seemed to bite out the words. "Sofia Martin, I would like to introduce you to my uncle, Señor Mateo Diaz."

"Señorita Martin." Mateo bowed and kissed Sofia's hand. "Please excuse me. I must go inside for a meeting. Eduardo, follow me soon. Yes?"

"Yes, Tio Mateo. I'm right behind." Eduardo turned to Sofia. "I do not understand why we must see each other again?"

Sofia bit her lip. "I can't explain it. Let's just say goodbye and not talk more—"

"You made it known to me last night you had no wish for future exchanges." Eduardo inhaled.

"Look, I just see no point in seeing each other—"

Eduardo threw his arms up. "Is this fate? Is it destiny? Perhaps both, I think, have come to bother us. And I, for one, do not seek complications in my life, especially women ones."

Sofia felt the brusqueness of his words. "Clearly. Please know, Señor Diaz, I don't seek complications in my life either, especially men ones. If you'll excuse me, I've got a conference to attend, and your uncle is waiting." Sofia lifted her chin and marched down the walkway, bringing her huff along. What a moody clod Eduardo had turned into. "Good riddance to him," she said aloud to a friendly pigeon following her. Sofia burst into laughter at her labeling Eduardo as a moody clod. His moods since their first meeting may seem mercurial, but a clod would never define Eduardo Diaz. Even moody, he remained dashingly handsome and way too alluring.

****

Ginny's spur-of-the-moment call to come for dinner was too irresistible to turn down. Milo's homemade noodles and fresh marinara had countless times brought Sofia to their dinner table. She'd rushed to the condo after her last meeting to change into a lavender sundress.

The tiny daisies on her shawl reminded her of Eduardo. "Nope. Not wearing it." Sofia tossed it aside and grabbed a turquoise lacey shawl Melody had given her. "Lace." The almost identical shade to the lace dress Eduardo bought to surprise her. "Does everything in my world have to remind me of him?" Throwing the shawl on top of the other discarded one, her eyes peered inside the closet. "A white denim vest? My last option, and it's going to work." Sofia slipped it on, punctuated the action with a groan, and rushed out the door bringing a dessert from Lucia's.

****

Sofia tossed the salad and sprinkled grated parmesan only to halt hearing *his* voice entering the townhouse. She waited for Ginny to pull the fennel bread from the oven. "Ginny? What have you done? You invited Eduardo?" Sofia approached her friend, holding the salad tongs as a weapon.

"Don't attack me. Go after Milo. He's the instigator of this dinner soirée."

"You've no clue what a bad idea this is," said Sofia.

"I'm really sorry. I told Milo he'd regret— Hi, Eduardo. Good to see you." Ginny leaned her cheek in for a kiss. "Say hello to Sofia while I scoot past to the dining room. Dinner's ready."

Before Eduardo could open his mouth, Sofia handed him the large wooden salad bowl. "Bring this." She sashayed out of the kitchen carrying the empty pasta bowls. "Destiny, you've got a screw loose," Sofia muttered under her breath, thinking how strange they were getting an encore of last year's dinner at Milo and Ginny's.

Eduardo's manners were still impeccable as he held Sofia's chair before taking his place.

"So, tell us, how's the symposium so far?" asked Milo, spooning pasta into the first bowl and passing it to Sofia.

"Thanks. This looks divine as always. I enjoyed today and met some fascinating people. I was paired for the afternoon session with a guy who's super accomplished and published. We clicked." Sofia reached for the breadbasket.

"What's this clicked?" asked a frowning Eduardo as he leaned over to grind fresh pepper on Sofia's pasta.

Ginny and Milo exchanged amused looks but said nothing.

Sofia watched in disbelief as Eduardo ground the exact amount of fresh pepper for her taste. The unexplainables were mischief-making again. "Clicked means Rick and I bonded."

"Bonded? What's bonded? Like you want to date this Rick?" Eduardo sprinkled extra parmesan on Sofia's pasta and passed the bowl absently to Ginny's outstretched hand.

Sofia chewed a bite of the oil-drenched bread. She'd put a stop to Eduardo's prying. "Date Rick. There's an idea." Sofia pretended to ponder it. "Yes, I might ask Rick to have a gelato tomorrow evening."

"You don't know this man's character. Asking to share a gelato isn't wise." Eduardo spun his noodles against his spoon like a whirling dervish, cutting his eyes over at Sofia. "You must reconsider."

"Nope. I'm not reconsidering." Sofia bestowed a bright smile Eduardo's way. "Ginny, would you pass the sea salt? Everything tastes amazing."

"Fine. I shall take you for the gelato tomorrow night. It's settled." Eduardo turned to Milo. "Did you hear bank rates rose today again?"

Sofia tapped Eduardo's arm. "Excuse me. I don't want you to take me for gelato or anything else tomorrow evening. In fact, when dinner is over, I don't wish—"

Eduardo placed his water goblet on the table and looked at Sofia. "When dinner is over, I shall escort you home, as I did before. It will be late and unsafe for you to walk unattended."

"He's right, Sofia. Eduardo needs to walk you back to the condo," said Milo.

"Honestly, it's not necessary. I can get a water taxi."

"Sofia." Eduardo's voice was laced with concern. "Please allow me—"

"Okay, okay. Walk me home, but no gelato tomorrow night. I've got plans," replied Sofia.

Eduardo fixed his gaze on Sofia. "You haven't made these plans yet. We must discuss this Rick during the walk. Our hosts need not listen more to us." Eduardo turned back to Milo. "We signed the papers for the venture—"

"I agree. I'm sorry, Ginny and Milo. It seems Eduardo and I are at cross purposes, which will be rectified later this evening." Sofia speared a cucumber and winked at Ginny.

****

"Did you tell Sofia in private our big news?" asked

Milo, placing the plates in the dishwasher.

"No, I'd planned for us to tell them both tonight during our celebratory dinner. I guess we'll invite them back for a do-over when they stop fighting fate. Those two sure can put on a comedy show. Tonight's performance will be hard to top." Ginny glanced off. "Um, Milo?"

"Yes, my lovely wife."

"Did we ever carry on like Sofia and Eduardo?"

"Of course not. We found other ways to communicate, which proved most satisfying. That's their problem. Frustration." Milo put his arms around Ginny. "You married an Italian man. We know how to please our women."

"Is that a fact?" Ginny grinned, spun around, and kissed the dimple on Milo's chin.

"I'd say yes, without a single doubt."

Chapter 29

An evening breeze kissed by dampness found Sofia and Eduardo as they walked the first few minutes wrapped in silence. They'd declared an unspoken standoff, yet sparks still danced around them for those able to see. Charcoal-colored clouds gathered in the inky sky, but neither noticed, so lost were they in thought. The first fat drops of rain splattered the sidewalk, creating a polka dot painting on the concrete and piercing their hush.

Eduardo's eyes spied a bistro a few yards ahead. His arm protectively went around Sofia's waist. "Hurry. Shall we step in here until the rain passes?"

Sofia stole a fast glance. Droplets of water cascaded down his enviable high cheekbones. "Good idea. I'm half soaked already." Her fingers resisted the urge to sweep the wet spikes of black hair from his forehead as he held the door for her.

Stepping inside the cozy but lively restaurant, Sofia felt an instant connection. A band of four stood on a dais playing upbeat music, a favorite of Venetians. Due to the late hour and interrupting rain, the bistro enjoyed few customers. The musicians seemed to take no notice and played as if they were auditioning.

Eduardo motioned to the hostess and held up two fingers. "We'll have to find something to order to earn our place here." A smile claimed his face. He pointed to the table where the hostess waited.

Passing by the band, the drummer waved his sticks at her and winked. Sofia waved back and grinned. Catching Eduardo's brief scowl pleased her for some reason.

Eduardo divided his attention between studying the menu and Sofia. His mouth thinned before he spoke. "Do you prefer sweet or salty?"

"As in appetizer or dessert?" asked Sofia, focused on the menu.

"Yes," came Eduardo's curt reply. "For me, I think sweet since you dropped the dessert bringing it to the table. We were cheated of the pinza cake."

"You know it's rude of you to bring that up again. Accidents happen. I didn't see the dog's toy lying on the floor waiting to trip me." Sofia handed Eduardo her menu. "Sweet. And you pick for me since you're paying. And no gelato. I'll have one tomorrow evening."

Eduardo nodded as the server approached. "We'll have two tiramisus and decaf coffees. *Grazie*." His mouth compressed into a hard line. "Let us finish this gelato discussion once and for all."

Sofia sipped her water and glanced at the band. Why was Eduardo acting so possessively? They wouldn't see each other after tonight. "There's nothing to discuss. My personal life and my plans, while in Venice, belong to me. Put that in your pipe and smoke it."

"Your words yet again make no sense to me. I do not smoke a pipe. It is a habit that bothers others. My mother suffered my father's pipe for many years. I care only for your safety."

"Forget the whole pipe thing." Sofia waved a dismissive hand. "I've got my safety covered. Here's our dessert." Sofia sat back as the server placed the decadent tiramisu in front of her. "This is huge. We should have split one."

"We can split it now." Eduardo glanced at the server. "Would you please box this?"

"Of course." The server disappeared into the kitchen.

"Oh my gosh, this tastes like heaven." Sofia closed her eyes for a second, savoring the first bite.

Eduardo scooped a generous amount onto his spoon. "It's delicious."

"Hang on. Your bites are huge. Hand me the knife." Sofia divided the dessert into half and scooted Eduardo's piece his way. "There. Stay away from mine." Sofia smiled sweetly.

A spontaneous laugh broke through his lips, only to have the scowl return, seeing a band member approaching Sofia.

"*Ciao.*" The drummer's eyes rested on a surprised Sofia. "I notice your liking our playing tonight. So, I was wondering if you have a favorite song the band might play for you?"

Eduardo cocked an eyebrow at Sofia. "Darling? A song we might dance to?"

"What?" Her eyes darted between both men as her mind scrambled for a reply. "Surprise me with any Italian song. Something zesty. Yes, I'm quite smitten with those." Sofia dazzled the drummer with a smile.

"Yes, we enjoy playing the zesty songs you say. I'll make sure to include one in the next set." The drummer paused. "Thanks for letting me intrude."

"And thank you for the kindness. I look forward to hearing your rendition of a song." *Good job, Sofia, handling that awkward moment*. The drummer returned to the dais. Sofia released a pent-up breath.

Eduardo took a bite of his dessert, only to put his spoon down. "I find little to like about this night. Little."

"Well, let me give you something to like. The genre I chose isn't for dancing. You'll not have another complication feeling obligated to—"

"Hold you close? Alas, I find all songs danceable." Eduardo's expression turned wistful.

"I disagree." Sofia held imagined ground. "I find some songs—"

"Listen. Your request plays now for you…for us. Come. I'll show you our dance." Eduardo scooted his chair back.

"Would you please sit down? I'm not dancing. What are you doing?" Sofia felt his hands pulling her from the seat. "This feels like complications to me."

"It's merely a dance, Sofia. Read nothing more into it." Eduardo clasped her hand and found a carefree rhythm to match the music's tempo. He released her, only to bring her back closer into his chest.

"What kind of dance do you call this craziness?" asked Sofia when Eduardo placed both hands on her hips, encouraging her to sway with him.

His laughter rang out. "I call it the Zesty Sofia."

Was his face nestling in her hair? Yes, it was. "Complications," Sofia whispered in his ear. "You're calling complications to us."

"I think not. The music has ended," answered Eduardo, escorting her back to the table.

Sofia waved to the drummer as they passed him.

"Are you ready to go? It's getting late, and the rain has stopped." Eduardo pocketed his cell phone and left money to cover their bill.

"Yep, my jet lag hasn't released me yet. Plus, it's been a long but interesting day." Sofia grabbed the dessert box before heading outside for the three-block walk.

The rain had bathed the City of Canals and awakened the fragrances from the many flowerpots and window boxes along the sidewalk. Sofia inhaled deeply and sighed. "No place smells like Venice."

"This is true, but you'd like Granada even more. We have the Sierra Nevada mountains as a backdrop and many flowers. It's beautiful."

"It sounds very nice. Tell me more about your home."

Eduardo nodded. "Southern Spain possesses a unique charm. We have the climate of the Mediterranean, which olives and flowers like very much. You must visit one day and see for yourself. You will find it to your liking, Sofia. I know this."

"I'm sure you're right, and I'd adore visiting Granada." Sofia tried to adjust her tote and balance the dessert box.

"Here, I shall carry our box." Eduardo's voice softened. "So, what's your conference schedule?"

"For the next two days, I'll attend different workshops and meetings until around five o'clock. I'm looking forward to your friend Tomas's presentation on the history of the cameo. He and I have kept in touch since you introduced me to his gallery."

"I'm pleased to have brought you together. What

about your evenings?" asked Eduardo.

"Our evenings are free to mingle and get to know attendees on a personal level." Sofia's attention went to a pigeon walking beside her. The bird had the same white freckles down her neck as the pigeon from the afternoon. *It can't possibly be the exact bird.* "Anyway, I've got two intense days, but I'm sure I'll enjoy each moment."

"I see. And after these two intense days? What plans have you made for the rest of your vacation?"

"None yet. I'm keeping my options open and see what presents."

"Yes, I see." Eduardo stopped at a flower vendor packing up for the night. "I'll take this one."

A smile tugged at Sofia's lips as Eduardo handed her a single daisy. "Thank you. Of course, you know it reminds me of you and the daisy petals' disagreement."

Eduardo released a chuckle at the memory. "I remember the stay-or-go plucking. A failure for sure, but one I rectified as you recall."

"You cheated destiny by proclaiming each petal meant *stay*, and as they say, the rest is history." A dose of melancholy swept through her.

"You speak of stay. What's with this bird?" Eduardo tried to shoo the pigeon. "She's quite devoted to our walk."

Sofia grinned. "I think we met each other earlier. She's my duenna. I wish I had something to feed her."

"Your duenna?" Eduardo nodded in amusement. "A pigeon duenna. Very unusual, but workable, I think. Our friend walks with us."

"So I hear." A steady stream of coos followed Eduardo and Sofia to the entrance to her condo. The pigeon twisted her head as if understanding when Sofia bid her good night.

"Well, I'll say good night and goodbye, Eduardo. It was nice seeing you, though still a shock." Sofia reached for the door handle.

"Wait. We have a slight problem here." Eduardo held up the box.

"The tiramisu? No problem." Sofia grinned and snagged the box. "I'll enjoy every bite tomorrow." She waved and hurried up the stairs, hearing his footsteps behind her.

"This isn't a proper resolving."

Sofia spun around after entering the door's security code. "What kind of proper resolving did you have in mind?" Her attention focused on the inner war playing across his face.

"I—" Eduardo hesitated.

"Fine. We don't want complications. You can have the dessert." Sofia shoved the box into his hands and disappeared inside her condo. She smiled, anticipating his signature light tap.

"Sofia? Could you open the door so that we might finish this?"

"No need. We've said goodbye. You've got the dessert. Have a great life, Eduardo Diaz."

"Sofia, I cannot have a great life with things…not right between us. We need more talking." Eduardo laid the box on a nearby hall table.

Rita's door opened. "Signore Sorry, you return with more Sofia troubles?"

"Go back inside, Rita. Everything is fine." Eduardo waved his arm.

"No sounds fine to me," replied Rita. "You are not

good at understanding Sofia. You are handsome but bad at the talk. Should I help?"

Sofia could hear the exchange and had to stifle her laughter.

"Rita, please. I do not need help." Eduardo turned back to Sofia's door. "Sofia? Will you please let me inside for a few minutes? I grow weary of this constant door talking."

"Eduardo, just go. There's no point in us talking. There's no point in us doing anything for that matter." Sofia leaned against the wall. The truth of her words cut deep.

"Sofia? It's Rita. Maybe you let Signore Sorry say his words this once? He's unhappy."

Opening the door, Sofia assessed the two people's faces staring at her. "Okay. Rita, for you, I will let him talk. Come in, Eduardo."

"Is good now. I go home." Rita nodded.

Eduardo blew a loud exhale, shoulders relaxing. "Couldn't you have rented a place where we didn't have a history? These biddies—"

Sofia rolled her eyes heavenward. "One of these biddies got you sitting on my sofa. Now, what is it you still have left to say? I've never met any man who has such a difficult time saying goodbye at a door."

"It's a curse that happens only around you. Normally, I am a man who knows his mind. Ask others." Eduardo jumped up. "Hold on. I left the box outside."

Sofia waited while he snagged the troublemaker and put it inside her fridge. "All set now? Is everything to your liking, Señor Diaz?"

"No. If it were so, I would not find myself on your

sofa having experienced another—what's the word?"

"Humiliation? Embarrassment?" offered Sofia.

"Yes. Both of those," Eduardo's voice lashed out. "I get to the point. We've not finished our discussion about Rick and gelato."

"And again, I've already told you there's absolutely nothing to discuss about Rick and the gelato. So, if we're done, you can go." Sofia went to rise, but Eduardo's hand reached out for her.

"Please, stay. As I said before, I worry about your safety. This Rick—"

"Eduardo, if I say I won't invite Rick out, will you leave?" Sofia's patience had evaporated.

"Perhaps," Eduardo answered, staring into Sofia's eyes. "No, I can't leave yet. Sofia?"

"What?" Her voice rose a few octaves.

"Since you're not going for gelato, would you like to see me tomorrow evening? I can show you more of Venice. We'll make sure to avoid any complications. Just two friends."

"Thank you, but no. I don't know the status of you and Isobel, but I'm clear on my no to seeing more of Venice with you. Time to go." Sofia scurried to open the door.

"Isobel and me?" Eduardo's expression showed confusion. "What does Isobel have to do? I can explain—" Eduardo stood in the foyer.

"Not interested." Sofia gave Eduardo's back a little push past the doorframe. "Thanks again for the dessert and, well, fill in the blank. So long now, and don't bother knocking again. I'm going to bed." Sofia shut the door. She'd had her fill of torment being near Eduardo. Her heart could only stand so much, and the flutters were annoying. Fate had thrown them together and she feared awakened her love for him. A love that had no future...never did...never would.

Chapter 30

Sofia and Ginny enjoyed sharing lunch under the covered patio at the college's food court. They took advantage of Sofia's hour break between workshops to spend extra time together.

Ginny deposited her dill pickle into Sofia's sandwich basket. "You can have this." Her nose wrinkled.

"You love pickles and always beg for mine. What's put you off them?" asked Sofia, a concerned frown appearing on her forehead.

Ginny covered her mouth and shook her head. "Excuse me. Be right back."

Sofia watched as her friend took off inside the Student Community Center. Perplexed, Sofia tried to distract herself from worry. Taking in the scene around her, the strong connection to Venice remained. Munching on the pickle, she heard a familiar cooing sound and glanced down. "No way. You again? How's this possible?"

The pigeon hopped into Ginny's empty chair and continued speaking pigeon to Sofia like they were buddies.

"No, no, get out of the chair." Sofia dropped pieces of her sandwich breadcrumbs onto the grass. "Since you've joined me for lunch, here's yours." She watched as the bird gobbled the morsels. "Why are you following me? Better yet, how can you be following me?"

"Sorry about that. I'm back and revived." Ginny took note of the pigeon. "Making friends?"

"If you only knew." Sofia shook her head, tossing more bread to the bird.

"So, introduce me and tell me what sounds like another one of your strange happenings." Ginny sipped her iced tea.

Sofia's expression changed to bemused. "Meet Mrs. Coo. We became friends yesterday on a walk, and again last night when Eduardo and I were heading to my condo. I can't explain how this bird finds me or why, but there you have it. Mrs. Coo, my very own pigeon girlfriend." Sofia pointed downward. "She seems sweet."

"Surely, it can't be the same pigeon. Their everywhere and—"

"Nope, it's her. See the white markings down her neck? Don't they look like tiny hearts? Anyway, that's how I know her."

"But how does Mrs. Coo find you? I know pigeons have this uncanny radar and homing thing, but Sofia, this is—"

"Weird. I know."

Mrs. Coo watched both women for a few seconds before jumping into the empty chair and chattering her coos.

"Guess we've got a third friend for lunch." Ginny dropped a few broken chips on Mrs. Coo's chair.

"So, what happened a few minutes ago? You turn away from pickles and then run off. Something is amiss." Sofia's face lit up like a stadium. "Ginny? Oh my gosh—"

"Yep. Milo and I are expecting around Christmas. We'd planned to tell you and Eduardo over dinner, but—"

"But we were too busy being rude and obnoxious." Sofia went to Ginny. "If you're not too queasy, stand up so I can give you a ginormous hug. This is the best news ever. You and Milo are going to make amazing parents. I'm so happy for you."

"Thanks for sharing in the joy. Don't squeeze so hard. I'm still feeling—oh no. Gotta dash. We'll talk later," Ginny hollered back while rushing off.

"Boy or girl?" shouted Sofia, laughing.

"Boy. Milo decreed it."

Sofia sat back down. The pigeon hadn't budged. "Well, Mrs. Coo, our friend, Ginny, is going to be a mom and get a special gift at Christmas. Isn't that awesome news?"

"I agree it's awesome news, but do you realize you're talking to a pigeon?" The voice came from behind Sofia.

"Honestly, it's crazy enough that I've got a pigeon following me around, but must you shadow my every move too?" Sofia watched as Eduardo took Ginny's seat.

"You flatter yourself too much, Señorita Martin. I've just ended lunch with Milo, where I learned of the expecting. I'm going to my next appointment, and I happen to see you in discussion with a bird." Eduardo paused and looked at Mrs. Coo. "Is that the same bird as last night? No. Impossible."

"It's her. Mrs. Coo." Sofia beamed a smile, enjoying the confusion playing across Eduardo's too-handsome face.

"She told you her name? You've made quite the bond." Eduardo's teasing tone lightened their exchange. Taking the few remaining chips from Ginny's paper basket, he offered them to the pigeon.

"So it seems. And no, she didn't tell me her name. Aren't those little white hearts around her neck cute?" Sofia smiled, watching Mrs. Coo tilt her head, listening. "Are those raindrop splats on the table?" Sofia looked up and saw a cloudless sky. Drops of water hit her legs. "What the—"

Eduardo jumped up, gathering the lunch trash and tossing it in a nearby can. "It's a malfunctioning sprinkler behind you. Sofia Martin, you invite trouble."

"Don't be ridiculous."

"And if there's a mud pit around here, you'll find it, only without me this time. A thousand pardons, but I'm late to meet my uncle. Enjoy your conference." Eduardo strode away, leaving Sofia with her mouth hanging open.

Wiping off her laptop with a napkin, Sofia marched toward the auditorium and the next guest speaker. She didn't know if her snit was directed at the reference to the mud pit fiasco or Eduardo's quick departure. "You don't have a clue what you want, Eduardo Diaz."

"Coo…coo."

"What are you doing? You can't follow me inside the building. Go home. Find nice Mr. Coo. Just make sure he's not from Spain."

****

Waving goodbye to some of the other curators, a tired Sofia decided to take a water taxi to the condo. Adjusting her laptop case and handbag, she trudged toward the canal a block away. Only one more day of workshops and speakers remained. And while Sofia had hit her saturation point, a sense of sadness enveloped her that time in Venice was ebbing too quickly.

There always seemed something awe-inspiring when riding a boat along any Venice canal. The architecture and lifestyle of the residents were unique in many ways. It was a snapshot of the present and the past, finding a way to coexist. Maybe the city's appeal for her rested there. Sofia took a deeper inhale of the salt air as the boat approached her stop.

Thoughts of dinner kept her company as her condo came into view. She'd turned down two dinner invitations from other curators. Maintaining a level of enthusiasm and energy for a social engagement felt exhausting. No, her mind craved a quiet evening and a pizza. Sofia hurried to her destination.

Lucia squirted cleaner across a countertop. "*Ciao*, Sofia. You've turned into…is it called a psychic?"

"*Ciao*, Lucia. Yes, but I don't think I qualify." Sofia handed the roll of paper towels to her friend.

"I wanted you to stop by, and *voila*, you did. Guess what?" Lucia waved to her server who was leaving. "Tonight is pizza night, and our pies bake as we talk. See? You are psychic. I knew you'd arrive about now if a certain someone didn't take you out again. I gambled. No, I knew it was pizza night." Lucia's eyes glimmered in amusement.

"Strange. I bopped in to suggest we do pizzas." Sofia paused. "You're not baking me another talking cookie, are you?"

"Sorry. Not tonight. Listen, go upstairs and relax while I finish closing up. I'll bring our pizzas in twenty minutes. Okay?"

"Very okay. Dare I ask what topping?"

Lucia arched an eyebrow.

"Nope. Not going to ask. I like surprises." Sofia grabbed a remaining cookie under a glass dome. "Put it on my tab."

She'd washed the day's makeup off her face and changed into jeans and a white t-shirt when the cell phone chimed. "Hi, Melody. How are things?"

"Things are super, if you exclude my hooligan children and their constant fighting. Could someone please explain why a single toy can cause so much grief?" Melody released a heavy sigh.

"I'm not versed in child-rearing or toy envy. Ask me about the cameo's fascinating history and why I think the nineteenth century caused them to regain popularity," said Sofia, applying cherry red lip gloss with her free hand.

"I'll pass. I called to see if you'd booked your return flight yet. And to make sure you're finding time for fun and shopping, especially shopping."

"Not yet. Not yet and not yet." Sofia laughed. "Don't worry, I haven't forgotten you want something in Venetian glass. You'll be pleased to hear I picked it out on my way to the conference this morning. They're delivering it tomorrow."

"Give me a hint. Anything," begged Melody.

"It's your favorite color. Gotta go. Aaron's calling. Hugs, sister." Sofia switched over. "Hi, Aaron. What an unexpected surprise."

"Yeah, it's unexpected for me as well. Listen, my boss sprung a meeting in Seattle on me. The problem is, it overlaps when you're coming back home. I can't make our date for that coming weekend."

"Don't worry about it. I've got plenty to catch up on at the museum. How's everything else?" Sofia flicked on a bedside lamp.

"Good. Everything's good," answered Aaron.

Sofia could tell he wasn't alone and probably still at work. Aaron had the professional voice turned on.

"Listen, I need to go. I'm lunching with some associates at the club. Guess I'll see you in a couple of weeks. Maybe I can call you from Seattle, though it's going to be nonstop meetings."

"Sure, go. Bye." Sofia laid the cell phone on the dresser. Wrinkles formed on her forehead. What bothered her about the exchange? Was it Aaron not asking about the symposium and her time in Venice? Was it she'd not seen him for a couple of weeks? No. What bothered her was not minding either. Sofia heard Lucia's healthy knock. Eduardo's face sparked in her mind's eye. Thinking of him standing outside her door and having the bevy of women still minding his business brought her a laugh. Forcing her thoughts to pizza, Sofia greeted Lucia.

"Two pizzas hot off the brick," said Lucia, heading toward the dining room table.

"They smell fantastic. I've got the table set. What would you like to drink?" Sofia opened the refrigerator.

"Choices?" Lucia opened the first box lid and served Sofia two slices.

"Ginger ale, sparkling water, green tea, and Venice's finest out of the tap."

"Never the tap. Sparkling. It'll help with digestion. Did you know this?"

"No, but it makes sense." Sofia placed two glasses

and bottles on the table. Her gaze landed on the plate. "Wow. Make it double wow. You made me anchovy and sausage. How could you know it's become my new favorite combo?"

"I cannot explain why my hands grabbed those toppings tonight. I did as before and made a simple topping on mine, just in case I got yours wrong. Though, I'd like a slice of yours. It does look good." Lucia held up a slice of pepperoni and toasted Sofia's slice.

"I'm happy to trade half. Want to?"

"Yes. I like variety." Lucia grinned and made the switch while Sofia poured the sparkling water into their glasses. "Perfect."

"Yep, perfect in every way. So, tell me about your day?" Sofia ignored her cell phone ringing. The kind and intuitive Lucia deserved her full attention.

Over the next hour, the two women enjoyed lovely Mozart-style music playing in the background while they caught each other up on the past year. Sofia clapped upon hearing that Lucia's younger sister wanted to become partners at the bakery. The reward was Lucia would finally have some free time.

Questions concerning Eduardo were easily dodged by explaining that spending time with him could open Pandora's box again. It was a box that needed to remain padlocked. Besides, Eduardo held the key, as Sofia reminded herself.

"It's getting late. I should go. My days start early at the bakery," said Lucia.

"Wait. Do you want half of my tiramisu? I brought it home last night. It's yummy."

Lucia gave a brief laugh. "No thanks. I get enough

dessert downstairs. Come and walk me to the door."

Sofia playfully slapped her forehead. "Silly me. Of course, you get desserts. Thanks for the pizza and visit." She kissed Lucia's cheek and waved to Marie's husband, Luis, toting a bag of groceries home. Life was life even in the City of Love.

****

While loading the dinner plates and glasses in the dishwasher, Sofia flicked on the cell's speaker to listen to Ginny's message.

"Sofia, I thought I'd better give you a quick warning. Milo spun some matchmaking yarn to Eduardo that Rick was spending the evening at your condo. I know. His sense of humor is warped, and I can envision the panic in your eyes. I'd kill Milo myself, but he's gonna be a dad, so I'm letting him live. Anyway, Eduardo left a few minutes ago. I think he'll eventually show up there, and in what state, I can't imagine. He told Milo he could not care less who you see and then declared Rick sounded like trouble in the next breath. Good luck, and don't worry—I'm about to take care of Milo for you. I hear the matchmaker coming. Bye." Ginny ended the call.

"Just swell. An encore of Eduardo at my door to mess with my qi. Maybe he'll skip a visit and let his ego win this one," Sofia mumbled, grabbed her mystery book, and cozied into the sofa cushions. The classical music continued to play softly in the background, failing at soothing her mind.

She'd managed to turn three pages before hearing the familiar soft rap. Her heart beat faster. "Stop reacting like you're sixteen. Take a breath. Don't succumb to Swoonable. Be polite and send him home."

Sofia reached for the door handle.

"Eduardo, why are you back here? We said goodbye." He stood in front of her wearing jeans and a yellow polo shirt, showing off every defined muscle. There were a few fresh nicks on his chin. He must have done a fast shave. The thought made her feel warm inside.

"Hello. Can you say, 'Hello, Eduardo?'" His eyes tried to see past Sofia into the condo.

"Hello, Eduardo. Goodbye, Eduardo." His foot blocked her from closing the door. "Go home. Let me enjoy my next few days in Venice without you complicating things."

"Please don't talk so loud. The biddies will come off their nests. May I enter to discuss your enjoyment of Venice? I also want my half of the tiramisu. Do you have company?"

"For Pete's sake. No, I don't have company. Come inside, but only for a few minutes." Sofia padded to the refrigerator to retrieve the dessert. "Get the plates. You can eat and talk."

"Your tone isn't cord…what's the word?" Eduardo set the plates next to the box. He watched as Sofia placed half on each dish.

"Cordial?" offered Sofia.

"Yes, cordial. I speak a few languages, but the English words are many and confusing. Why have a word sound the same and mean different? I believe you call this a homonym. For example, bred and bread. It's confusing. Still, I try—"

"Eduardo?" Sofia handed him a cup of tea.

"Yes?"

"Eat your tiramisu. Your distractions aren't

working on me." Sofia went to the table and sat down, hiding her grin with a napkin.

"I can do better. How was your evening? Did you find gelato?" Eduardo spooned the dessert into his mouth, studying Sofia.

"Are you here because of Rick and gelato? I told you I wouldn't—"

"Milo told me this man came here," blurted Eduardo. "I worry for your safety."

"Milo was pulling your leg." Sofia couldn't hold her laughter back any longer.

Eduardo set his spoon down and glanced at his legs. "My leg wasn't pulled by Milo. What nonsense is this talk?" Eduardo paused. "It is another example of English words making no sense. When your laughter stops, please speak plainly, Sofia."

"Fine. Milo set you up. He made it all up to get a rise out of you."

"You call this plain speak? Set me up? Rise out of me?" Eduardo waved his arm in the air. "Forget it. I understand. There's no Rick tonight, only me showing up here."

"Well, Lucia brought pizza earlier, if you want to count her. Are you going to finish your sweet?"

"No, thank you, I find my taste for it gone." A flicker of impatience showed in his eyes as he moved to the door. "I will not trouble you further. I leave you to enjoy Venice."

The door closed gently behind him, and Sofia's heart sank. "Congratulations, Sofia. You ran off the only man you ever truly loved. And you're still not following your heart." For once, her mind had it right.

She felt a cry coming. Grabbing a box of tissues, Sofia went to bed.

Chapter 31

Sofia stared out the window, watching Venice wake up. The sky glowed an orange shade, which reminded her of a ripe peach. A rosy hue tinged the few clouds. She'd dressed for the symposium wrap-up. Dismissal at eleven meant her vacation could officially begin. A frown dressed Sofia's face. "I don't have a clue what I'm going to do for the next few days." An unusual kind of loneliness seemed to color her mood, only to ebb. He was near. Her heart did the funny flutter. Sofia flew to open the door before he could knock, and stood grinning at the sight.

"How did you know I was here?" asked a disheveled Eduardo. "I brought lattes from Lucia's. The bakery wasn't open, but I got her to let me inside." He passed one of the cups to her.

"I just knew. It's one of our unexplainables. Thanks for the coffee, but why are you back here at seven in the morning?" Sofia tried to process his appearance while keeping a straight face.

"Yes, I have an answer. I've been thinking of us since last night. Can we not spend your vacation together without getting in a tangle as before? I assure you I have no plans to romance you, but we have this unexplainable…magnet that wishes us together. It keeps pulling me here." Eduardo pointed to the door.

"On that, we can agree. No one's door here gets

more action than mine, thanks to you." Sofia felt her face flush.

"Don't make the joke." Eduardo tried again. "Would you agree to accompany me to the gardens this afternoon because I want very much—what?"

Sofia covered his mouth. Her eyes danced in merriment and happiness. "Shh, not so loud." Too late. Two doors opened, and faces appeared. "Eduardo, I say yes to the invitation, but you've got something more pressing to attend." Sofia pointed. "Do you realize you're wearing plaid pajama pants and slippers?"

Eduardo glanced down, looking shocked. "See what you do to me? Eduardo Diaz walked the streets of Venice like this. Is too much." He pivoted to leave.

Rita's index finger came to call on Eduardo's arm. "Signore Sorry, you bad to spend the night. You wear the loud pajama pants and shoes in our hallways. Isn't good."

"Rita, I did not spend the night at Sofia's," exclaimed Eduardo, trying to maneuver around her.

"Your hair is a mess," added Marie from across the hall.

Eduardo swiped at his cowlicks and turned to Sofia. "Would you please explain to these two I didn't stay here? No man should suffer such humiliation to see a woman." Eduardo looked at his shoes, groaned, and hurried toward the steps.

Sofia's laughter rang out. "I'll put the ladies straight. Just make sure you don't get stopped for wearing those hideous pajama pants. Come back at noon dressed properly, and we'll go to the gardens," Sofia hollered down the staircase at his retreating back, adoring Eduardo Diaz no matter what state he appeared at her door.

Sofia waved to the women. "He didn't stay over. Don't worry."

"He is too handsome even in the loud pajamas," said Marie.

"We like him for you, Sofia," Rita added before going inside her condo.

Sofia rolled her eyes upward before peeking at her watch. "I've got four hours and forty-nine minutes to figure out how to protect my heart for the next few days."

Chapter 32

Having bid the other attendees farewell, Sofia could officially begin her vacation. The thought of spending the afternoon at the gardens, accompanied by a certain man, had kept her spirits high all morning. Stepping outside the building, Sofia noted the glorious afternoon weather. Not too humid and not too hot, a gift from the Venice gods.

"*Ciao*, Sofia Martin. Surprise. I accompany you to the condo." Eduardo came alongside.

"Surprise for sure." Sofia shook her bewildered head. "I see you're dressed appropriately this time."

"Please do not remind me of this morning ever again. No one must ever hear of such—"

"Our secret. Well, and Lucia, Marie, and Rita's." A smile edged her mouth.

"Enough. Do you want to change before we have our first day together? I have made plans."

"Yeah, I would like to change out of this skirt and jacket. Maybe you could visit with Rita while I—"

"Sofia? I'm warning you." Eduardo's tone couldn't hide his teasing.

As they walked, Eduardo shared his excitement in learning the gardens had a Murano glass exhibit for the weekend. He'd arranged for another picnic lunch delivery for them.

The Eduardo from a year ago had returned, and

that boded badly for Sofia to keep things in check. Everything about her was vulnerable to his charms. The day he'd mapped out screamed complications of the heart and soul.

Sofia felt puzzled about how Eduardo seemed impervious to his past feelings for her. What they'd shared a year ago still held magic and memories which remained unexplainable for her. How had Eduardo managed to harden his passionate nature? Did Isobel play any role? More worrisome, were they still to marry? Maybe today, he'd tell the story of Isobel. Maybe today, she'd feel ready to hear the story. Maybe.

****

Taking her cue from Eduardo's dress in denim jeans and a button-down tan shirt, Sofia grabbed her white jeans and daisy print shirt from the closet. She'd left him occupied on the sofa, conversing in Castellano on his phone. It sounded like Eduardo's uncle needed more financial guidance, judging by the numbers spoken.

Sofia refreshed her makeup and added a splash of gardenia fragrance in honor of the botanical garden visit. Her mind recalled their last visit there and the strange Dina encounter. What did the day have in store for them? She'd happily settle for fun since Eduardo's heart was closed off. He'd assured her of this fact more than once.

Adding the daisy hair barrette, Sofia stole one last glance in the mirror. "Listen, you. Chin up. Keep things light. Have fun over the next few days in Venice. If you play it smart, you can take home memories that won't make you cry for months this time. Right." Sofia entered the living room.

Seeing her, Eduardo stood. His teeth gleamed white against his tan. "I see you wear the daisies for us and the gardens. It's a nice feel."

Sofia met him at the door and snagged the straw tote. "Thank you. I love flowers, all flowers." Skirting his daisy reference to their first encounter at the garden was a smart move. "Score one, Sofia. Keep it fun," she mumbled, heading out.

*****

The thirty-minute drive to the gardens seemed to restore the easy rhythm Sofia and Eduardo enjoyed in the past. While they kept the conversation friendly, their undeniable attraction continued to crackle in the background. Visiting the gardens provided a plethora of beautiful distracting flowers and trees, or so Sofia hoped as they both exited Eduardo's sports car with the picnic blanket.

"There's Roberto with our picnic basket and on time." Eduardo pointed to the left. "I'll come right back."

"Sure." Sofia stood at the entrance gate to the botanical gardens, taking in the afternoon's gift of a gentle breeze. She'd enjoyed hearing more about the olive groves during their drive, as well as Eduardo's plans to increase yield. They'd kept their guards up, and the conversation steered toward their work. Sofia couldn't get a sense of how much land the Diaz family owned, and didn't want to pry. She suspected they were comfortable financially but allowed Spain was a different country than the U.S. in how assets were viewed. Still, Granada sounded beautiful and the lifestyle sublime. Sofia vowed to visit the country one day.

"We have lunch." Eduardo held up the basket. "Shall we eat first?"

Sofia smiled at the idea. "Yep, I'm past hungry. Do we know what's in there?"

Eduardo shook his head. "We do not. Roberto acted like it was some state secret to guard."

"We'll find out soon enough. Can we go to the same private garden as before and hope no one snagged it?" asked Sofia.

"You have to make the arrangement in advance to secure it." Eduardo waited.

"It's okay. We can find someplace else—"

"I made this arrangement earlier. It's ours for an hour. Good?" A grin creased his face.

Sofia stopped her hand from reaching for Eduardo's. "Very good, and thank you for the thoughtfulness." She halted at the directional map. "Which direction? I can't remember?"

"We go toward the rose gardens. We can view them on our way." Eduardo changed hands for the basket. "It is heavy."

Sofia gave a nod. "Must have some good things inside. Anyway, I never get tired of viewing roses. They're one of my favorite flowers, after daisies, of course."

"Observe the apricot ones just there." Eduardo stopped to touch a blossom and read the name of the variety. "Eduardo the Magnificent."

"What? You're nuts." Sofia leaned over to read the name. "Delight."

"Delight is a nice feeling. Let's make it our word this afternoon." Eduardo picked up their walking pace.

Sofia arched a brow. "I'm game. Can you elaborate

on how this works?"

"We find things that delight us, share, and discuss."

"You go first, so I see what the heck this delight game is about." Sofia paused to sniff a white rose with red tips.

"Here is the gate to our private garden." He released the iron lock and waited for Sofia to pass. "This space delights me with memories of our last visit. We had the unexplainables."

Spreading the blanket, she looked up at Eduardo. "I agree. This place is magical and delightful. Will you please bring the basket and sit down? I can't wait to see what's in it."

"Your wish is my command," answered Eduardo. "See? I show off my English humor." Lifting the lid, he inhaled.

"I'm impressed." Sofia unwrapped a sandwich. "Thank you, Roberto. It's a tramezzino with artichoke, roasted eggplant, spinach, and cheese. This must belong to me." Hearing Eduardo's chuckle, she glanced up. "What?"

"For someone who cannot cook, you know food. Hand me the other tramezzino. I want to make sure you don't have mine." Eduardo released the wax paper.

"I claim delight. I've got the best one. This sandwich clearly belongs to me. I know it already." Sofia took a giant bite.

"You are correct this time." Eduardo showed Sofia his lunch. "See? Prosciutto, fresh mozzarella, and marinated red peppers make this an Eduardo delight. Roberto never disappoints." He pulled out a bag of chef-made chips and a container of olives. "Roberto scores another point. Every lunch must have olives from Spain."

Nodding, Sophia took another bite of her sandwich. "Good to know the olive rule."

"You mock the olive?" Eduardo waved a chip at her.

"Never. Such mocking smites of heresy. Give me a green one."

"Open." Eduardo placed a large olive in her mouth. His fingers brushed her lower lip.

Sofia met his eyes, and passion stirred. "Maybe I'd better feed myself the next one."

"Probably best." Eduardo moved the container closer to her. "Still, I felt a delight introducing you to an olive from our grove."

"I can see why. There's a distinctive flavor to this olive. Kind of earthy. I'm having another. You grow nice olives. I wonder if we've got dessert in that cardboard container?"

Eduardo opened the lid. "Zaeti cookies. You love these. But I see an odd number. Roberto's inferior counting might cause us trouble."

Sofia leaned over and counted five. "No problem at all." She broke the odd cookie in half. "Done. Roberto lives to deliver another picnic."

The sun claimed their shade as they finished lunch, encouraging a visit to the Murano glass exhibit and air conditioning. Sofia disposed of their picnic containers while Eduardo returned the blanket to his vehicle. Another couple waited outside to claim the private garden for their enjoyment. Sofia said hello as she exited.

She watched Eduardo walking her way and noted a slight smile flicker across his face when he spied her.

She loved how looking into those intense cognac-colored eyes could clue her to his mood. "Swoonable," Sofia mumbled. Eduardo Diaz was a man who knew his mind, but did he still know his heart the way she remembered from a year ago? He'd done a great job of erecting a wall to keep her out. The reason remained a mystery. Did she want to risk solving it? Somehow, she sensed it tied the answer to Isobel.

Chapter 33

Eduardo dropped his sunglasses in place before reaching Sofia. "Ready to tour the glass? I lifted you a brochure."

How she adored his word choices. She loved everything about him, and that was proving her undoing yet again. Couldn't he get a zit or a patch of gray hair smack on his crown? For a second time, Sofia caught herself wanting to hold his hand. "Thank you. Yes, let's go. I confess to knowing very little about Murano glass. My sister is gaga over it. I'm excited to see this exhibit."

"What is gaga? Another new word for me to learn," Eduardo grumbled.

"You don't need to add this one to your list. Gaga means excited." Sofia studied the brochure as they walked.

"Then why not say excited? Why say the gaga?" Eduardo touched Sofia's waist to have her veer right.

"You know something? That's a good question. I guess we like variety." Sofia scrunched her face. "But I'm going to give your question serious thought." She'd give serious thought to why his hand remained at her back too.

"Perhaps you could show me kindness by speaking plain English until my education is improved."

"Sure. I can do that." Sofia didn't bother reminding

him his English couldn't advance much in the few days they had left together in Venice.

"Here's our glass." Eduardo held the door, allowing two women to exit.

The sunlight streaming into the building created something strikingly beautiful as it played off the colorful glass on display. It was as if someone had sprayed a multitude of rainbows on the floors and walls.

"Eduardo, have you ever seen anything so cool?" Sofia pointed down. "Our shoes are a spectrum of colors. Neat, huh?"

"Very festive," he teased. "I delight in your happiness. The sign leads us here."

"And I delight at your bringing me to see this. So, what's the story of Murano glass?" She felt Eduardo's hand steer her to the first exhibit.

"Murano glass came from the island of Murano, which is made up of a web, no network, of islands in the Venetian Lagoon. You see, glassmaking in Venice goes back to Roman times. By the eighth century, Venice had a reputation as the primo glassmaking center."

Sofia studied the vivid colors and curves of the pieces in front of her. "Wow, you do know your glass history. What else?"

"Well, blowing of the glass is an art. The artisans back then who created these works enjoyed a high standing among the wealthy. Even their children got this elevated status and could marry into the wealthy families of the time. Historically, I think Murano glass has not always been popular. Today it earns our respect. Yes?"

"Most definitely." Sofia moved down the row,

admiring the shapes. "I love the flower and animal designs, but the vases are the most stunning."

"I quite agree. What better to hold nature's blossom beauty than a Murano glass vase?" His eyes never wavered from Sofia.

She broke their spell with a question. "Is all Murano glass marked so that you know it's the real deal?"

"Real deal? Speak plain. Remember?"

"Sorry. How do you know if a piece is authentic?" A smile tugged at her lips.

"Unfortunately, not all glass is marked, so you must rely on an expert to evaluate. Tomas is one such expert on this glass. He wishes to exhibit some pieces at our place in Andalusia."

"Really? Interesting that Tomas is well-versed in jewelry and glass. He spoke at a workshop that I attended on cameos. I like him immensely."

"Yes, he's the real deal, and you should not go gaga over him. He is attached." Eduardo's eyes glinted in amusement.

Sofia straightened up, giving Eduardo her full attention. "Aren't you the fast learner and so clever combining it all into one exchange?"

"Clever me." Eduardo moved them to the next display of colorful bird sculptures.

Sofia tapped his back, and he turned. "I just wanted to say the idea for a glass exhibit at your grove, or whatever you call it, sounds like a fantastic idea. You'll eventually want to consider having a curator of sorts."

"This may be so. Later I will see who."

Sofia nodded, wishing somehow that she'd have the position. Releasing the ridiculous notion, she moved on to study the glass birds. "Which is your favorite?"

"Easy. The pair of swans. They mate for life. You know this, of course."

"Yes, they're most devoted. Humans could learn from them." Sofia adjusted her drooping purse strap.

"Most definitely. Which bird do you choose?" asked Eduardo, focused on the different birds sitting on a large mirror.

"I love them all, but if you force me to choose, it's the owl for wisdom." Sofia moved on to the remaining displays. She kept discovering more things to share as part of their delight game until Eduardo pleaded to cease delighting him.

They ended their garden tour in the butterfly house and watched in awe as countless butterflies flitted from one flower to another. It was an afternoon of color immersion by flowers, birds, glass, and last butterflies. Their spirits were lifted and united in the shared joy of the time spent.

"How about an Italian fruit ice?" asked Eduardo as they left the butterfly house. "I see the cart around the bend."

"I'd love one." Sofia walked in companionable silence, replaying their afternoon. "You know, Eduardo, I feel as if I've been bathed in a rainbow this afternoon. What an extraordinary day you've given me. I'd kiss you my thanks, but we've sworn allegiance to keep us just bosom buddies."

"Perhaps a fast kiss on my cheek would cause no complications," teased Eduardo. He dropped his face low enough for Sofia to deliver.

"If you're sure." She planted a sweet peck on his cheek and took off toward the teenage girl serving the ice. How could such a simple act cause her body to feel like a three-alarm fire? She needed the largest ice on the menu. Sofia read the flavor choices as she reached the cart.

"You must really have the craving or maybe the kiss—"

"Would you stop? It's a craving. I want a large lemon ice," Sofia told the server. "He'll have a large strawberry ice." She turned to a grinning Eduardo. "My treat. And I don't know why I chose strawberry for you."

"Because it's what I always liked since I was three. Unexplainables." Eduardo shrugged. "Thank you for the treat, but I am happy to pay."

"Nope. I'm no moocher. Here you go. One strawberry ice." Sofia grabbed a tiny plastic spoon from the cart and stuck it in the ice.

"What's this new moocher word? I thought you'd promised me—"

"I keep forgetting. Moocher is someone who looks to always take from others for free. That's not me. I don't expect you to pay for everything we do. In fact, I wish you'd let me pay for dinner tonight." The words slipped out. Sofia turned away to take her ice from the server while chastising herself. She'd gone and assumed Eduardo had the evening free and would want to spend it with her. "Bad move, Sofia," she murmured, turning away.

It was his turn to tap her on the shoulder. She turned around, presenting a red face and not from the heat. "Yeah?"

"You wish to dine tonight? You're not tired of my company?" Eduardo stepped aside for three young children to order.

"I'm sorry for blurting out about dinner. Please don't feel any obligation to spend more time with me. Today was wonderful, and I'm sure you've got dinner plans already." Sofia gulped.

"Yes, I do have a plan." Eduardo's attention shifted.

"Kids, you need more money for three," said the server.

"Excuse me, Sofia. A little problem to fix." Eduardo passed the money to the girl. "Here is the extra." He looked down at the three young faces. "Enjoy your treat."

"Señor Diaz, you're a good egg." Sofia caught his frown. "Correction. I meant to say, 'Señor Diaz, you're a nice guy.'" She wanted to add he'd make a good father, but thought better of crossing into new territory. "So, what's your dinner idea? You didn't get to tell me."

"No. Is that a guitar playing?" asked Eduardo turning in the direction of the music.

"Sounds like a guitar to me."

Eduardo grabbed her hand. "Come. Let us go find the music. We love our music. Yes?"

"Yes. Just don't run. I'm not giving up my ice for a guitar or even a fat tuba." Sofia liked that Eduardo didn't let go of her hand as they hurried down a path. She even liked it when his fingers caught her belt loops and tugged her closer to him when a jogger breezed by. *Face it, Sofia Martin, you like Eduardo Diaz touching you anytime…anywhere.*

They discovered the musician playing his guitar under the gazebo. A group of listeners had formed a semi-circle in front of him. Sofia claimed an empty bench a few yards away. The song had a unique melody and beat change that defied description.

The song felt like an unfolding journey with ups and downs. Happy notes on a higher scale, only to transcend to baser notes, much like human emotions. She admired the guitarist's talented playing and interpretation of the piece. "He's letting the guitar speak for him," she whispered to Eduardo.

"Yes, I agree. Ernesto tells me he and his guitar are married, and while I do not understand it, I believe it." Eduardo's cell phone vibrated. He glanced at the screen. "Sofia, my apologies, but this call is from home. I must step away for a few moments."

"Go. I will stay right here and enjoy the music. Take your time."

With a nod, Eduardo hurried down the adjoining path to a wall of hedges that provided privacy.

"I find music often has a way of propelling the spirit to discovering truths like nothing else can. It bypasses the mind's chatter. Do you agree, Sofia?"

A familiar voice came from behind. The woman sat next to Sofia.

Chapter 34

"My gosh, Dina, this is a surprise. What are you doing back on our bench? Do you work at the gardens?" Sofia stared at the woman, trying to process the unexpected. Dina's appearance defined enigma. But then again, so did everything involving Eduardo Diaz.

"Hello again, lovely Sofia. Actually, I guess you could say I work here." Dina's tone sounded nonchalant. "How precious to refer to the bench as ours. Isn't the day spectacular?"

"Yes, I love sunny days most of all." Despite shock and awe running through her, Sofia responded appropriately. She focused on the mundane. Dina was dressed casually in cream linen pants and a silk blouse the color of lemon blossoms. She noticed an unusual rainbow crystal hanging from a long gold chain around Dina's neck. Words returned to Sofia's mouth. "I can't believe what a coincidence—"

"My dear, there's no such thing as coincidence. Destiny sets things in motion, and we react. I hope you're still considering the truth of the words I left with you at our last meeting. I've brought them back today."

"Of course, I remember you telling me about destiny's role and to apply acceptance to what was happening between Eduardo and me last year, but things didn't work out for us." Sofia half-turned to face a smiling Dina.

"Do you recall me sharing that discounting destiny could lead you off the path? And the key was distinguishing the mind's misdirection from destiny's true direction?"

"I confess that part might have slipped by me." Sofia drew a deep breath, then sighed. "Please forgive my boldness. Why are you here? Who are you, Dina? Surely you must know these questions remain unanswered. Especially after the fortune teller brought me a message from you saying my three wishes had been received. From my side of the fence, these encounters seem pretty out there and—"

"Because our time together is short, let me get to the heart, so to speak." Dina folded her hands. "I'm someone who brings you insights and guidance on why you're on earth. Our paths brought us together. Maybe you can see it as we're assisting each other. I'm tapped to illumine the beautiful life that awaits your choosing, and you're giving me the opportunity to realize my purpose. Can you accept my explanation as is?"

The entire exchange felt bizarre, otherworldly. "Do I have a choice?" The retort sprang from Sofia's lips before she could filter it.

"Most certainly. You have free will. Take a moment. Decide if you want to hear what I have to share."

Sofia nodded and sat quietly. One question came to her mind. What did she have to lose by listening to this sage? While the experience of meeting Dina was surreal, Sofia needed to trust and listen. "I'd like to hear what you brought to share. And thank you, Dina, for being willing to do so."

"I'm so pleased you agreed. Now, Eduardo will

soon return, so I must make haste. I'm going to ask you to listen and hold the questions. Okay?" Dina smoothed a wrinkle from her pants.

"Okay." Sofia smiled a little, acknowledging her interrogator nature already had questions bubbling away.

"I'm here to remind you of what you already know. What you came into this life knowing, but so many forget. You're here to love and love well, Sofia. You're here to be loved and loved well. More, you've been blessed to love someone, Eduardo, who cherishes your heart. This is a rare kind of love that exists out of time's constraints."

"Now, you're taking me into a realm—"

Dina raised a hand. "I need you to remember the word I gave you at our last meeting."

"Accept?" answered Sofia, trying to squash her rising skepticism.

Dina smiled knowingly. "Yes, accept. Can you accept and not judge so we might continue? The best is yet to come."

Sofia chuckled. "You know how to sell your program. Okay, I'll accept, even if I don't understand. There's something I need to say."

"Please," said Dina.

"Eduardo and I still seem to share this unusual connection. We sort of know things about each other. Things like food preferences, which there's no rational explanation for us to know. And the weirdest thing has been these mind flashes of us together in another time. We're at a loss to make sense of any of this. We call them unexplainables. I needed to remind you of this part. Sorry. I'm going silent now." Sofia bowed her head slightly.

"Let's delve deeper into this now. Would you agree the flashes, as you refer to them, are an example of slipping out of time's constraints...timeslips?" Dina asked.

"Unless I want to call these hallucinations or some psychotic episode, I think I'd prefer your explanation more. Maybe I tripped the time travel switch." Sofia relied on humor to ground her.

"Maybe you did," agreed Dina. "Back on topic. Despite our first meeting and what we discussed, you chose to return home and abandon a future with Eduardo."

"How did you know? Sorry." Sofia made the sign of zipping her mouth shut.

"You stepped off your true path, Sofia. Take this next statement inside and hold to it. Destiny presents you with a second chance to choose Eduardo and live your life purpose...together. See this as a gift, a rare gift much like the love you both feel."

"Hang on. Eduardo's made it clear that he's not looking for or wanting a relationship with any woman. The last time I checked, I'm still a female. It doesn't matter what I feel if he's closed off."

"My dear Sofia, what you feel matters. You're missing the piece of the puzzle to explain why Eduardo appears closed. Discover it, and you've got the key to unlock the continuing story of Eduardo and Sofia's grand love."

"How do I find this key?" asked Sofia. She sensed Eduardo's return was imminent.

"This answer I can give to you. You've simply forgotten." Dina hesitated, looked into Sofia's eyes, and smiled. "Passion is the fuel for love. If you dare deny passion, then you deny love the necessary power to thrive and continue growing."

"Wow. Those words carry serious weight. I never saw passion in that light. I always equated it with sex." Sofia stared off, letting Dina's meaning find a home in her heart.

"The physical relationship is but one part of passion. Let me explain the genesis of love. A spiritual connection births love's first tendrils. Try seeing love as a seed that needs constant care to prosper. You tend to it by watering, feeding, fertilizing, and communicating. Each of these four aspects unfolds into specific actions and reactions. Having a physical union is an example of a specific action that feeds love. Am I making sense?" asked Dina.

"Yes. Love sounds more complicated to me than understanding subatomic particles."

"Love is…simply complex," replied Dina.

"Simply complex," repeated Sofia. The two words found a place in her mind. "Yep, I agree. So, giving me these pearls of love, what's next? What am I to do with them?"

"As I stated, destiny is giving you and Eduardo a second chance to continue your adventure of loving grandly. Few get to experience such abiding love, Sofia. You both can become a testament to others. It's your true path toward happiness and joy. Let me end our visit by reminding you of your free will to choose. You made those three wishes. If you still want them granted, you must act from a place of your love's devotion to Eduardo. How things turn out for you this time rests in your hands. I've given you the secret to having your heart's desire." Dina stood, bestowing a gentle smile on Sofia.

"I'm awestruck over our second encounter and the wisdom you've gifted me. Whoever you are, I can't begin to express my gratitude. So much gratitude, Dina." Tears trickled down Sofia's cheeks as she moved to embrace the sage. "I want my three wishes granted. I want to see and walk my life's path. I want Eduardo's love for me to bloom. And I want to love Eduardo Diaz right out of this lifetime together and into heaven. My three wishes, as somehow you know."

Dina's smile lit her face. "Yes. And it's the exact recipe for forever love." She squeezed Sofia's hand and walked in Eduardo's direction.

The musician returned to the gazebo. Lifting his guitar, he began strumming a song calling smiles from everyone listening. A frivolity theme carried the notes toward a thoughtful Sofia. She allowed the music to become her vehicle, as Dina suggested. Sofia felt her spirit soar, envisioning Eduardo and her living their future together. "He's my heart's desire. But what is his?"

Chapter 35

"Sofia, I hope you'll forgive my absence. My father and Ernesto drew me into their disagreement over a horse breeding matter. The Diaz men suffer one shared fault." Eduardo's eyes teased a reaction from her.

"I never had time to miss you. I'll bite your hook. What's this one fault?" Sofia arched an eyebrow.

"Hmm, you taunt me back, saying you did not miss me. Okay, we share a fault in how we breed our horses. Three different views and goals make for hot words," said Eduardo.

"I can imagine."

"This matter remains unsettled until my return." Eduardo extended his hand. "The garden closes soon. Shall we? On our walk to my car, you must tell me why my absence wasn't missed. My ego feels an arrow."

Sofia's laugh rang out. "Arrows go for the heart and not the ego. Not to worry, your heart is locked up tight. No arrow will penetrate that wall." Sofia flounced ahead, leaving Eduardo to ponder her words.

He caught up. "I do not pretend to understand the arrow talk, and I've no interest in discussing heart things." Eduardo tapped Sofia's shoulder. "I happen to know a fact that I missed something while away. Please, do tell me."

Sofia halted. "What makes you think you 'know a

fact' you missed?" She felt her curiosity piqued.

"Because a strange lady passed me and said, 'Don't deny destiny.'" Eduardo's eyes narrowed as he searched Sofia's face. "And if it's anything strange, it must involve you...us. Perhaps you might explain this?"

"Was this woman wearing cream-colored linen pants and a pale-yellow blouse?"

"I do not pay attention to her clothes. I noticed a mesmerizing gem sparkling around her neck. It was like a beacon of light?"

"I know the rainbow gem." Sofia swallowed. "That was Dina."

"What? Dina? The Dina from last year who sends messages by a fortune-teller? No." Eduardo pulled Sofia under the canopy of a large oak.

"Yep, the same." Sofia watched as Eduardo leaned heavily against the tree's massive trunk. His hands rubbed his forehead.

"No complications. I don't have time for complications. They didn't end well for us. You know this, Sofia." Eduardo exhaled and continued ministering to his forehead but not the deep furrows between his brows.

Sofia pulled his hands away. "Stop. That's not effective for relieving stress. You have no complications unless you want them. Let's go. I promise not to say another word about Dina."

Eduardo dropped his sunglasses back in place and followed Sofia. "Did she mention my name? Us?"

Sofia shook her head. "Nope. Not answering. Tell me about your dinner plan for us, assuming you're not afraid to hang out with me." She watched Eduardo's hand move toward his face. "No more self-soothing. Hold my hand." She kept them moving forward. "I want to hear your idea."

"Eduardo Diaz is not afraid to hang out with Sofia Martin. I'm fixed."

"You're fixed?"

Eduardo squinted at Sofia's reaction. "Totally. Do not question this fact. No complications will visit us. I declare it."

"Well, okay then. I'm convinced now," Sofia said and wished with all her heart he'd get proved wrong.

Opening the car door, Eduardo waited for Sofia to climb in. He stooped down next to her. "The plan is I cook dinner for us at your place. It will taste good after all the restaurant eating. Yes?" Eduardo's dimples winked at her. He defined complications. Eduardo gave a brief nod.

Sofia waited for him to get into his side of the car. "Yes, I like your plan to cook us dinner. I'll even help."

As he maneuvered the car onto the main road, Sofia turned her attention to the passing scenery. She wondered what thoughts chased the man next to her.

Eduardo drove for a few minutes in silence before replying. "I've decided. You don't cook, but you can chop." He accelerated to change lanes.

"Sure, I'm great at chopping. It's the cooker I avoid." Sofia's happiness took a leap. She had the evening ahead to see where destiny took them.

****

The night held promise as she changed into a black skirt and printed top. Sofia pulled her hair into a ponytail and slipped a black ribbon around the elastic. A fresh application of rose lipstick and a spritz of her signature gardenia fragrance refreshed her natural look.

Sofia wondered what Eduardo's dinner menu entailed. Hopefully, nothing squid-like. She gave a little shiver just thinking about their shape. Glancing at her watch, she hurried to set the table. Eduardo promised to return and bring all the fixings by eight o'clock.

Another wonder came calling as she brewed pomegranate green tea. Where could things lead with only a few days left in Venice? Dina said destiny was presenting her with a second chance with Eduardo. Well, destiny had plenty of orchestrating to do to achieve the goal. Like overcoming Eduardo's proclamation that he didn't want women's complications interfering in his life.

Looking at her reflection in the microwave glass, Sofia pointed and shook her finger. "You're going to stay focused in the moment and see where each one takes you. Whoever this Dina is, she's captured your attention and shared profound teachings. You have enough proof things aren't always what they seem in the world." Sofia reached for two glasses, only to return to the microwave glass. "And don't waste time trying to make sense of what's happening to you. Accept."

A knock at the door broke Sofia's chat with the microwave. "Hi, Lucia. What ya got there?"

"*Ciao*, my friend." Lucia passed a box to Sofia. "Your Eduardo, who I now call Pajama Man from his morning visit to the bakery, called to order this dessert."

"Yeah, he looked quite the mess when he showed up at my door. His plaid house slippers and matching pajama pants were bright enough to light Venice."

Lucia giggled. "My customers waiting outside for

me to open seemed to enjoy the fashion show. Anyway, he asked me to drop this off before I locked up."

"Thanks so much. Hope you have a good evening." Sofia turned.

Lucia started to walk away. "I almost forgot. Don't peek inside."

"Okay. No looking." Sofia went to close the door.

"Stay open," hollered Eduardo, coming up the stairs. "*Ciao*, Lucia," he said, passing her on the stairs.

Sofia stood smiling to herself, watching Eduardo juggle the grocery bags. "Here, let me take one of those off your hands."

"Please. Am I late? The market checker had issues," explained Eduardo, heading to the kitchen.

"Nope. You're perfect."

"See? Finally, you realize this fact about me. Now let me show you more of my perfection by cooking you an authentic dinner from my region of Spain." Eduardo began opening cabinets.

"An authentic meal? Now I'm excited." His passion for worthy endeavors was a character trait she admired. Noticing his damp hair and change of clothes told her he'd put extra effort into their evening. Sofia tapped him on the arm. "What exactly are you searching for?"

"A skillet, a bowl, and flat sheets. Do you have such things in this tiny kitchen?" Eduardo stood and faced the cabinets.

"Let's see. Here's a skillet of sorts and a small bowl. Will they work?" Sofia enjoyed watching Eduardo's kitchen frenzy.

His mouth thinned, taking in the two items. "The skillet couldn't handle an egg, and the bowl is an insult to itself in size. I'll return." Eduardo went out the front door.

A curious and amused Sofia trailed behind.

Eduardo's eyebrow arched as he considered the doors in front of him. Sending a wink Sofia's way, his knuckles rapped on the first door.

"Signore Sorry, what calls you to my condo?" asked Rita, holding a slotted spoon.

"May I borrow a skillet, bowl, and sheet pan? Sofia's place isn't equipped for anything but takeaway."

"You wish to cook for Sofia? Is very nice. Wait here." Rita left her door ajar.

Eduardo nodded.

Sofia heard locks being released, followed by Marie's face appearing. Sofia hid her grin. Eduardo was activating the biddies.

"Signore Handsome, what's your need? I help." Marie waved to Sofia.

"I need kitchen pieces. Rita's peering to see what she can give me."

"Signore Sorry, I have one skillet free to use. Here's a bowl and flat pan." Rita passed the items to Eduardo.

"Thank you. Everything will work but the skillet. I need one this size." Eduard made a circle with his hands.

"Is too big for two people dinner." Rita shook her head. "You need this size." She made a smaller circle with her hands.

Eduardo shook his head. "No, no. It's a special dish. Bigger is better. Marie, do you own such a skillet?"

Marie bobbed her head and then frowned. "It's cooking Luis's dinner now. I must tend to it. You'll figure it out." She shrugged and closed the door.

Eduardo exhaled frustration. "Thanks, Rita. I'll bring back your bowl and sheet later."

Returning to Sofia's side, Eduardo asked, "I don't suppose you know the other neighbors?"

"Nope. There's one place you missed looking. Let's give it a squint." Sofia hurried to pull the small portable island with storage underneath from the corner. She bent down and opened both doors. "*Voila*. Skillets, pans, and nesting bowls."

"Now, I prepare your Patatas a lo Eduardo. The dinner is saved."

"Oh, happy day. I'll return these two items to Rita and then help chop." Sofia left Eduardo humming an unknown tune as his wooden spoon kept a beat on the pans.

****

Having been exiled from the kitchen, Sofia sat at the dining table, admiring how Eduardo had thought of everything. Two yellow candles and a matching single rose served as the table's centerpiece. The fact he chose her favorite color, yellow, wasn't lost in her heart. Sofia stole a peek over her shoulder as Eduardo ladled something into their bowls. A flash hit her.

They were back in the same period as before and stretched out on a blanket surrounded by a field of yellow wildflowers. The sun beamed down on them like a spotlight. Eduardo was feeding her bites of a cookie and bestowing a kiss after each one. Sofia's heart lurched as she saw the same gold locket hanging from her neck and the diamond filigree ring on her left ring finger. Clearly, the jewelry pieces held some significance to the vision, but what? And more importantly, why had the visions returned? Dina told her they were like timeslips. She hadn't begun to process the meaning or implications of such a thing. Hearing Eduardo's singing stop, the image closed.

"Dinner begins. First, I serve the gazpacho, Señorita Martin. You'll find it refreshing." Eduardo set the bowls on each placemat and lit the candles.

Sofia lifted her spoon. "What a lovely presentation you've made for our dinner. I'm crazy for gazpacho, and you even have croutons on top with a dollop of sour cream."

"Somehow, I know you like the gazpacho. It's why I chose it. I confess to ordering it prepared. Still?" Eduardo turned a questioning gaze her way.

"Still, it's amazing and perfect." She spooned another bite. "Just the perfect amount of garlic and onion."

"Yes, perfect," repeated Eduardo. His eyes held a meaningful look for a brief second. "Sofia, after dinner, I wish to discuss a few more things. Okay?"

"Sure, but why don't we talk now? I'm adept at eating and conversing." She poured more tea from the pitcher into her glass. "Since my year in Venice, I discovered that I love anything pomegranate. So, talk to me."

"The talk isn't right for dinner. I will bring our main course." Eduardo went to the kitchen.

Sofia waited for his return. "I'm staring at a plate of Patatas a lo Eduardo. Tell me what's in—"

"Ah, you have the sliced potatoes sautéed with Spanish onions, garlic, red peppers, and the finest of olive oil, of course, from Spain."

"Of course," replied Sofia forking a potato. "And the meat?"

"It's Serrano ham. I think you like my recipe." Eduardo cut the slice of ham and speared a pepper. "I must make this when I return home."

Sofia tried and failed to envision Eduardo cooking in a small kitchen near his father's house. "When are you leaving?" Sofia felt an emptiness seep into her heart, dreading his answer.

"It's part of our discussion. Please, enjoy the food. Have you made your plane reservation?" asked Eduardo.

"Yes, I made it this morning. I fly home Monday, which gives me three full days of vacation." Sofia's appetite evaporated with her last words. A second chance for her and Eduardo seemed as elusive as trying to capture a butterfly.

Chapter 36

"Thank you for making such a wonderful dinner for me. And the surprise of Lucia making a Basque cheesecake was pure deliciousness. Don't tell Milo, but I choose Spanish cuisine over Italian. There's so much variety in flavors and ingredients." Sitting on one end of the sofa, Sofia tucked her legs under her.

"I'm pleased you picked mine as the preferred." Eduardo set his tea glass on the coffee table and twisted to face Sofia. "I can no longer delay this discussion. Someone hangs between us. Maybe more than one someone. Allow me to explain some things and then ask some things. Yes?"

"You've got the stage." Anxiety slipped to the forefront, and she waited with bated breath.

"Stage? Never mind more of the confusing English." A hint of a smile played on his lips.

"It just means you've got my full attention, which is what I should have said. Sorry. Continue." Sofia squeezed his forearm and pulled back, seeing surprise register on his face.

"First, I wish to discuss the story of Isobel and me."

Sofia's throat constricted. Isobel, her nemesis. The reason she turned down Eduardo's proposal and got on the plane. "Okay, Isobel and you."

"A couple of weeks after you left, Isobel came

home. Our families were planning the wedding. I spent my days running the groves and missing you. I was a miserable man who no one cared to get around." Eduardo's eyes narrowed thoughtfully.

"Hard to imagine." Sofia tried to interject humor for them both.

"Yes, is true and more. I didn't want this marriage, but without you, I saw no reason to object. I wouldn't act selfishly and bring pain to Isobel or our parents. I planned to make my life about work, and I still do."

"Yes, you've been consistent in not wanting to have any serious relationship with a woman. So, what happened?" Sofia swallowed the words she wanted to say.

"What happened is I saw Isobel kissing a man at the Granada airport." Eduardo stood and walked to the window. "I waited for him to board the plane before approaching Isobel."

"I bet she about dropped her teeth. No, cancel that. I bet she was shocked to see you."

"Both of those things. I took her for a coffee so we could get honest. The bottom line is we said we love each other only as brother and sister. We agreed to go together and tell our families that we didn't wish to marry." Eduardo faced Sofia. "It was the happiest and saddest day of my life."

Sofia looked up. "Why?" Her voice filled with emotion. "Tell me why."

Eduardo knelt in front of Sofia. "The happiest day because I was free to marry you. The saddest day because you already cared for another man." He returned to the window and pressed a hand to his forehead. "Your love for me wasn't lasting."

"Hold on. What are you talking about, Eduardo Diaz? I understand you and Isobel realized the mistake of letting your families force you into marriage and all. Using your best English, tell me from the beginning your story about another man and me."

Eduardo spun around. Anger and pain shone on his face. "It is very simple. I texted you that Isobel and I were finished and that I was free to marry you. I told you I loved you and asked you to call me so we could make our plans to unite again."

There was an edge to his voice that troubled Sofia. "I want to hear it all before I respond."

Eduardo gazed at Sofia before answering. "You texted me back that you'd found someone else and were madly in love." Eduardo exhaled loudly. "Madly, you said. Remember? You told me to never contact you again and wished me well."

Confusion wrapped around Sofia, while waiting for Eduardo to finish.

"You see, that made for the saddest day because my Sofia's love wasn't constant. It wasn't forever after all."

"Eduardo, I never—"

"Please, I must finish this." His tone turned icy to match his eyes. "I vowed never to allow such weakness to enter me here." Eduardo touched his heart. "Never again will I trust a woman's love. A fool I am only once. Still, I come around you."

"Please, sit next to me." Sofia watched him hesitate as he struggled to gain control of his emotions.

He chose to sit at the opposite end. "Okay, you've got the stage." His lips smiled a little, but the look in his eyes remained distant.

"I didn't send you that text message, but I have a good idea who did." Sofia's anger rose, but not at Eduardo.

"You expect me to believe—"

"I expect you to extend me the same courtesy and listen to the truth." Sofia's emotions were close to bubbling out all over them.

"Apologies. I listen." Eduardo leaned back into the sofa cushions and folded his arms.

"I had an administrator who was bitter she didn't get the curator's job. She'd been at the museum for twenty years and felt entitled. After I returned to Boston and assumed the position, I began noticing small things she'd do to reflect badly on me. She became more emboldened, and well, it doesn't matter what she attempted. What matters is it must have been her that somehow gained access to my cell phone code and answered you." Sofia felt the first tears pooling in her eyes.

"You're telling me this woman is who texted me?" asked Eduardo.

"Yes, because it wasn't me who answered you. How could you ever think I would fall in love with anyone else? And in two or three weeks no less." Sofia jumped up.

"Where are you leaving me for?" asked Eduardo, returning to his window.

"I'm leaving you for a box of tissues. You're about to witness me having the biggest cry, probably of any woman on the planet. If you're as smart as you want me to believe, this would be a good time to hightail it out here."

"I don't know how to hightail it," Eduardo said to

the window. "I don't know how to do anything right now but wait for this discussion to make sense." Lifting his arms in the air, he continued, "Women require too much of men. Too many complications. Always the complications. I want none of it." Eduardo looked over his shoulder. Sofia's bedroom door was closed. Releasing a heavy sigh, he strode to her door.

"Sofia? Sofia? Do I hear crying?" Eduardo cracked the door open. "Sofia?"

She sat on the side of the bed with a pile of tissues surrounding her. "What?"

Eduardo sat next to her and reached for her hand. "Sofia, what happened to us is in the past. People interfered with our happiness."

"Ya think?" Sofia wiped her eyes. "All I can say is Shakespeare's *Romeo and Juliet* don't have anything on us with suffering under others' hands. The only thing we escaped was the draught of poison and a shiny dagger."

Eduardo's laugh rang out. "Let us hope we'll be spared such a fate. I can't leave this earth now. Let's put this all behind us. I have much work to accomplish at the groves. Speaking of them, I still have one question left to ask you."

Sofia faced him. How could he seem so collected, dismissive, and rakishly handsome in this lousy moment for them? She felt the hideous red splotches on her face popping out and quickly covered her face with her hands. "What question? Will I need more tissues?" Sofia mumbled.

Eduardo pulled her hands away. "Look at me. I want to see your deep blue eyes when I ask you something."

"No, I look dreadful." Sofia twisted away.

"Very well. I shall wait on the sofa until you're not dreadful." Eduardo smiled as he said it.

Sofia splashed cold water on her face. She'd hoped after hearing she hadn't betrayed their love, he'd see things differently. Clearly, that wasn't the case. He'd had a year of hurt believing she loved another. Sofia found him in the living room. "Okay, let's get this over with. What's the question?" She plopped down next to him.

"Hey, it's a nice question," answered Eduardo.

"Would you just please ask it before the grim reaper comes for us?"

"Grim? Never mind. You distract me by teasing. Sofia, I would like to invite you to Olivar Siete Colinas for the weekend. It is my pleasure to present my family's home to you. You mentioned how much you wanted to visit Spain. If you agree, we must leave in the morning and return Sunday afternoon."

Surprise colored Sofia's face, and she took a few gulps. "You're inviting me to your home for the weekend? I thought you didn't want any complications from women?" She tried to contain her happiness.

"We'll have no complications. All will work fine. You'll come as my friend. Only my friend. No threads," explained Eduardo.

"You mean no strings, and I accept," replied Sofia before he changed his mind.

Eduardo studied her in the dim light and grinned. "Yes? You'll go as friends? No threads or strings?"

"Yes, I'd love to go. No threads. No strings. Just friends." She'd say yes, no matter what caveats he pinned on them. She could work with friends. It was her chance to break through the walls he'd erected around his heart. Even with him discovering how fate duped them, he showed no interest in rekindling their romance or their love. She had no plans to give up on them, especially after Dina's visit. Spending more time with Eduardo was destiny finally throwing her a possibility for…something. "So, what's the schedule?"

"Yes, I shall give you the details now. I'll come by at seven o'clock. Apologies for the early time, but I've got a meeting I cannot miss."

Sofia nodded.

"I look forward to introducing you to my homeland. You may rely on enjoying your visit." Eduardo rose. "Is this agreeable?"

"Of course. I will be ready at seven, and thank you again for inviting me. I doubt I'll sleep much tonight."

Eduardo's forehead furrowed. "Why is this?"

"Silly, because of my excitement to see Spain and the olive groves." Sofia walked him to the entrance. "Hold on. Don't I need a plane ticket?"

"It's taken care of."

"So, you were pretty confident that I'd say yes if you got the ticket in advance." Sofia tilted her nose in the air and quickly added a bright smile. She'd not blow this by one of her reactive blurts.

"Let me say it like this, Sofia Martin. I rely on my confidence in many matters. Good night. Sleep well." Eduardo glanced back before closing the door behind him.

"Sleep well. Fat chance." Sofia hurried into her bedroom to pack her few things. She assumed her casual wardrobe would suffice to visit a farm or grove in this case. Nothing fancy-sounding there. Her focus was one dashing, swoonable man's company she'd be keeping over the next few days. Sofia gave herself a little hug and looked heavenward. "Stars, how about aligning right this time? Being star-crossed is fine for Romeo and Juliet, but not me and Eduardo."

Chapter 37

The morning sun defined glorious and ushered in a day of promise. Eduardo and Sofia ducked into Lucia's bakery, grabbing a sack of breakfast rolls, two hot lattes, and her wishes for a safe journey.

Stepping onto the sidewalk, the couple stopped short, staring dumbfounded.

"I don't believe this. It's Mrs. Coo." Sofia pinched off a piece of the roll from the bag and offered it to the pigeon. "Mrs. Coo, you're amazing, and you just made my day."

"Please tell me the unexplainables aren't coming for us again. This pigeon must live nearby." Eduardo shook his head. "Come, our water taxi is waiting for us."

"Yep, let's go. Bye, Mrs. Coo. Thanks for the morning greeting."

Eduardo glanced over his shoulder and groaned. "She's following us."

"Uh-oh." Sofia stopped. "Mrs. Coo, go home to Mr. Coo. We're leaving for a few days. You're off duty."

"Coo, coo." The pigeon bobbed her head.

"Come on. She'll figure things out," said Eduardo.

"She hasn't yet. We've got a tail." Sofia laughed. "Sorry."

Eduardo broke into a grin. "Maybe if we walk

faster."

"I can't go faster than this. I've got my tote weighing three tons."

"And who's got the heavy carryon? Me, your pack mule," teased Eduardo.

"Is she still—?"

"Of course. Mrs. Coo is most devoted. Here's our boat." Eduardo handed the luggage to the boatman and helped Sofia board.

Blowing a kiss to the pigeon seemed to clue her the visit was ending. Sofia watched Mrs. Coo take flight. "Such a sweetie. She's flown the coop." Sofia pointed up. "That's another funny, which obviously you don't get judging by your expression."

"When I'm around you, Sofia, there's much I do not get. The pigeon is but one example. There are many more. So, tell me. Are you a good passenger to fly?"

"The best. I love takeoffs most of all. The power of the jet engine. Soaring is thrilling. Why? Are you a nervous flyer? Because if you are, I've got motion sickness pills in my tote that I—"

"Sofia? I, too, am good flying. I just wanted to make sure of you."

They enjoyed the scenic ride along Venice's canals. Boats hauling goods moved with ease around gondolas. There seemed to be a kind of unspoken rhythm and protocol for boats. And while the water had a chop, their ride was easy and relaxed to the dock. Sofia viewed it as good juju for their flight.

"Let me help you off the boat." Eduardo extended his hand to Sofia.

"Thanks. Can you take my tote?" Sofia failed at ignoring the heart flutter from his touch. *No time for this nonsense.*

"My car is still parked in the lot, so we'll take it to the airport," said Eduardo. He waved to the water taxi boatman. "We will walk the few blocks."

****

Sofia waited for Eduardo to get situated inside the car. "Do we have time to drink our lattes and eat our sweet rolls on the way?" She reached for the bag.

"Yes, if you don't mind working the gear shift for me." Eduardo cut a grin Sofia's way as he started the engine.

"Um, that might be a problem. I don't shift so great." Sofia took a sip of her warm coffee.

"In fact, I don't shift at all."

"Good to know this now. I'll manage. Hand me my cup, please." Eduardo maneuvered onto the main road.

"So, I forgot to ask. How long is our flight?" Sofia bit into her roll. "Lucia is one wonderful baker."

"Ah, yes, she is. The flight is about three hours, depending on things. Longer than you thought, yes?"

"I'll say. Now I understand why we had to get up with the birds." Sofia nodded and continued eating. She'd have Eduardo all to herself, trapped in a passenger seat next to her. Things were definitely looking more star-friendly. Maybe the Romeo and Juliet curse was broken.

"We'll arrive at my home in the afternoon. After my meeting, I have something in mind you might enjoy doing." Eduardo turned into the airport's back entrance.

"I'd love a tour of the olive groves. Can we fit that in today?" Sofia frowned at where they were headed.

"Of course, we can do a short tour. I'm pleased you're interested. Why the face?"

Sofia motioned behind her. "You made a wrong turn. The departure lane—"

"No, I'm doing right. Trust me. I've done this many times, Sofia." Eduardo slowed the car as he approached an enormous hangar and pulled into a private parking slot. "Time to fly."

Sofia grabbed Eduardo's arm. "Hold the fort. Exactly time to fly what? I don't see—oh, my stars and garters." Sofia gulped air as she watched the hangar's electric doors open and a private jet moved toward them. "We aren't flying commercial?"

"Correct. No commercial. Hop out, and let us get on board." Eduardo came around to Sofia's side of the car. He handed the luggage to an attendant.

Sofia pulled Eduardo to the side. "Look, this is super expensive. If you want to change our plans, flying commercial is fine by me. Curators aren't paid that well." Sofia stared at the jet. "I gotta be honest. I can't afford to pay my half—"

"Sofia?" Eduardo moved her toward the plane.

"Yes?" She heard the catch in her voice as she tried to process boarding her first private jet. Thoughts ran around her mind like mice on a wheel. Who was Eduardo Diaz?

"You don't need to pay for anything. Prepare yourself for a few unexpected learnings about me."

"But I can't have you picking up the tab for me."

"Please." Eduardo pointed to the plane's steps. His amusement was evident. "After you, Señorita Martin."

Sofia entered the plane's plush interior, taking in the comfortable upholstered tan sofas, chairs, and navy carpet. Technology's accouterments were on display. Behind a partition, she spied a kitchen and sleeping area. Grabbing a few more gulps of air, Sofia turned back to Eduardo. He was in a discussion with the pilot and attendant. Should she stand or sit? Moving toward the swivel chair, she glanced into the cockpit. Spying the plethora of screens and gauges earned her more gulps. At this rate, she was seconds away from looking like a blowfish full of air. Eduardo wasn't kidding when he warned her to prepare for "learnings" about him.

"Apologies. We needed to confirm the flight plan." Eduardo removed his jacket and handed it to the smiling attendant. "Sofia, this is Amos. If you desire anything, just ask him."

"Ask Amos. Got it." She watched Eduardo move toward the cockpit. "Hang on a sec. Where are you going?"

"Somone's got to fly the plane," responded Eduardo.

Sofia flopped down into the chair and pointed to the pilot. "Isn't that his job?" she asked in a shaky voice. Another gulp or two should help soothe her nerves.

All three men enjoyed a chuckle.

"It's his job when I need or want it to be." Eduardo nodded to the pilot, who disappeared upfront.

Sofia pointed at Eduardo. "You're telling me *you* can fly this jet? That *you* intend to fly this jet?" She paused to gather her next question. "Are you also going to tell me this is *your* jet?" Sofia grabbed a magazine and fanned herself.

"Yes. And I'll tell you something else. Since you told me how much you like takeoffs, you're going to sit in the cockpit for the takeoff." Eduardo pulled Sofia from the chair. "Pretty epic, huh? No corrector needed.

I learned this yesterday from Ginny."

"Maybe me in the cockpit isn't such an epic idea. I'm feeling kind of woozy from eating too much air." She was gently propelled through the cockpit door and placed in a jump seat.

"Eating the air? Whatever are you talking about, Sofia?" Eduardo buckled her in, wearing a concerned expression.

"Señor Diaz, we've got clearance. Time to roll." The copilot talked to the tower.

"We're rolling?" Sofia craned her neck to look out the window. She watched as Eduardo took control of the plane and her life. "We're rolling," she murmured. "I may never recover from the shock of this, Eduardo." She indulged herself in swallowing more air and welcomed the light-headedness as he taxied them down the runway.

Eduardo glanced back at her before going full throttle. "Get ready. I bring you the first thrill on your visit to Spain."

Sofia managed a nod. "Just make sure you bring me down in one piece that's breathing." She waited for what came next. "Me and my big mouth telling him I loved takeoffs." Sofia looked longingly at the sofa in the next compartment. "A nice stretch out is what I need. And oxygen. Amos has got oxygen back there. I need the whole canister, pronto."

"Is she talking to us?" Eduardo asked the copilot.

He shook his head. "I'd call it babbling. Wheels up."

Sensing they were airborne, Sofia opened her eyes just as Eduardo banked a turn. "Whoa. What a view of Venice."

"She's back to normal function," said the copilot to Eduardo.

Sofia watched as the men tapped screens. Their Castellano exchange of words left her clueless, but all seemed copasetic. If Eduardo hated complications, she made a mental note to ask him why he was a pilot. Too many complicated instruments sat in front of both men.

Eduardo stole a glance back at Sofia and winked. "Pretty cool, huh?" His dimples came next with a smile.

Sofia nodded, awarding him two thumbs up. "Swoonable, you don't play fair," she said, knowing he couldn't hear her.

Chapter 38

A few hours later, Sofia stepped off the plane. Her breath caught as she paused, taking in the landscape. In the distance, the Sierra Nevada mountains were bathed in peach and coral hues by the sun. Snow dressed the peaks like melting marshmallows. She noted Granada sat at the foot of the mountains, enjoying their protection. Eduardo had shared that four rivers converged there, providing treasured resources to the residents and farmers. The topography was spectacular. She felt instant love for the area and its rich culture.

Sofia waited in the shade outside the hangar for Eduardo to give instructions for his plane. Her mind still reeled from the fact he owned and flew a jet. Ginny never indicated anything about Eduardo's financial means or family, but then she'd never asked. She twisted her hair into a bun and clipped it, knowing she was minutes from discovering more about Eduardo and his world. Excitement bubbled inside her.

Eduardo came alongside. "Pardon the wait, but I had to ensure the plane's readiness for our return on Sunday."

"It's fine. I was taking in the natural beauty all around. From what I can see, Granada is pretty amazing. So, now what happens?" She noticed her bags were stacked beside Eduardo's weekend bag a few feet away.

"Here comes our ride." Eduardo signaled to the driver.

Sofia watched as a large black SUV pulled within a few yards of them. A man dressed in a white shirt, black tie, and cap approached.

"*Hola*, Señor Diaz." He nodded to Sofia before attending to the luggage.

"Thanks, Paco. Let's get inside out of the heat." Eduardo opened the door and helped Sofia step up into the vehicle.

"How far is your home from here?" Sofia adjusted her seatbelt and placed her straw tote between them.

"Fifty or so minutes. It depends if Paco has eaten recently." Eduardo glanced Paco's way. "You see by his looks that food is a passion."

Sofia stole a glance out the window as Paco loaded her suitcase. "He's not obese, but I do spy a bit of a paunch," Sofia whispered and returned the grin.

As they rode through Granada, Eduardo shared facts about the town. "I bet you didn't know Granada was a Muslim kingdom for like eight hundred years? The influence is everywhere."

Sofia shook her head. "But I do know the word Granada means pomegranate."

"Correct. Did you know we enjoy about two hundred and fifty days of the sun each year? It makes for happy olives. The river off in the distance is called Genil. We have a long history and beautiful palaces to prove this true. We won't have time this weekend, but you must see one day the Alhambra Fortress."

"That would be fantastic. Everything here looks so colorful and vibrant. The architecture and flora are unique in so many ways. I've never seen any place like this before." Sofia inhaled, feeling an unusual connection to the area.

"To torment you, I will tell you there are hidden gardens all over Granada. You love the gardens. This I know." Eduardo's eyes sparked with amusement as he said it.

"Hidden gardens. I'm in love. I may marry this place." The words left her before she could stop them.

"I'm not sure our priests would perform such rites. We could ask," teased Eduardo, answering his cell phone.

Sofia gazed out the window as the countryside replaced the urban areas. The rolling hills were carpeted in a vibrant green with olive trees. It reminded her of the countless orange groves in Central Florida. Sofia had always felt abiding respect for what nature's goodness provided for humans. The gifts were often taken for granted.

Paco held up a bottle of mineral water with one hand. "Yes?"

"*Sí, gracias.*" Sofia took a sip of the cold liquid and offered it to Eduardo. The intimate gesture surprised them both. She watched Eduardo end the call and turn to her.

"You like to share this? Okay, we can." Eduardo waved off Paco's second bottle.

"I handed it to you without thinking." Sofia blushed. "Please, Paco has a drink for you."

Eduardo's eyes held a puzzled look. "We can share." His full lips drank from the place hers had just sipped from.

More heat flamed into her cheeks, and she looked away. How could sharing a drink turn into something so suggestive? She'd need to do a better job filtering her words and actions or risk scaring Eduardo away. He'd invited her for the weekend as a friend. She'd better deliver her best performance and let destiny take care of…whatever destiny did.

Eduardo moved the bottle in Sofia's direction.

"No, it's yours to enjoy. I'm not really thirsty. How much longer until we arrive at Olivar Siete Colinas?"

Eduardo capped the drink and placed it in the cupholder. "We're actually here."

Sofia caught Paco's amused expression in the rearview mirror.

"We're here? I don't see your house. All I see are countless acres of lovely olive trees basking in the sun." She pulled her sunglasses off and squinted. "Is that your house up ahead on the knoll?"

Eduardo shook his head. "It is TJ and Lola's place."

Sofia bobbed her head. She wasn't going to act nosey and ask who TJ and Lola were. They passed the two-story stucco home with the red-tiled roof. "It's quite nice, but I'm sure your home nice is too."

Paco's spontaneous laughter echoed in the SUV. Eduardo sent a frown to his driver.

"What's so funny?" asked Sofia, feeling confused.

"Nothing. Ignore Paco. He laughs too much."

"I think you're dodging me." Sofia's mouth pulled to the side.

"What's this dodging?" Eduardo waved his hand. "Doesn't matter. Do you know Spain is the largest producer of olive oil in the world?"

"Not Italy?"

"Please. It's Spain that holds this distinction. And

Spain is second in consuming the oil. Impressive, yes?"

"I'd say Spain takes growing and consuming olive oil seriously." Sofia gazed out the window, seeing a few homes scattered amongst the many acres of trees. "Um, Eduardo, I assume like in the States, you may drive on other people's property to get to yours. Is that what we're doing? Cutting across Lola and TJ's land to get to your house?"

Paco released another guffaw from the front seat.

Sofia peeked around the headrest at the man. She leaned over to whisper in Eduardo's ear. "He does seem to have a slight problem with spontaneous laughter. Is it some psychological ailment?"

A smile played about Eduardo's lips. "I don't think Paco suffers from any head maladies. To answer your question, we're indeed still on Diaz land. TJ and Lola's home belongs to my family. They're employed by us, but we see them as family."

Sofia bit her lip, finally catching on. "Things are falling into place now. Clearly, I had you pegged all wrong." The Diaz family owned a heap of property, a jet, more than one house, and she was a middle-class girl from Boston who happened to land a curator's position.

"I don't understand." Eduardo directed a frown in Sofia's direction.

"I thought you were probably upper-middle class. You know, comfortable. I suspect I've got it wrong." Sofia shrugged.

"No, no, we are comfortable. You are right."

Paco released another laugh, spewing his water.

"Enough, Paco. This is private talking," said Eduardo. "Sofia, my family is most comfortable. Look straight ahead. You'll see our comfortable home."

Sofia turned her attention outside the windshield. She felt her jaw drop. A Spanish-style mansion with rich tan stucco and a terracotta-tiled roof grew closer and larger by the second. Impeccably maintained gardens flanked the long driveway. A round fountain that could pass for a swimming pool greeted her and something else.

As Sofia's eyes fixed upon the estate, a wash of familiarity found her. Dismissing the ludicrous notion, she turned to Eduardo. "See? Didn't I say a moment ago I bet you had a nice home too?" Tapping into humor served her well under these unexpected circumstances.

Eduardo gave a brief laugh. "I'm glad you think so."

Paco stopped the vehicle in front of the most beautiful carved walnut, arched double doors Sofia's eyes had ever seen. Her mind struggled to take in the surrounding luxury and opulence. She'd seen grand estates like this one in international architecture magazines.

"Shall we go inside so you can judge the rest of our home?" asked Eduardo. He nodded as Paco went to unload their cases.

"Very funny. It's all breathtakingly beautiful. Every inch I see is amazing." Sofia spun around. "Eduardo, your family—you're so—you own so much. I had no clue."

Eduardo's eyes captured Sophia's. "I know this. What must you think of me? I let you buy me gelato and pay for—"

Sofia slapped his arm. "Stop it. You're making me

feel more ridiculous." She glanced at Paco. "Well, at least now I know why he was laughing and that he doesn't suffer from emotional outbursts."

"Let's get you settled. I have a business meeting with my father and Ernesto soon. You can unpack and perhaps enjoy a siesta until I'm free. Yes?"

"Now that I'm mentally prepared for you to dazzle me, Diaz, lead the way." Sofia's voice held amusement until a butler opened the double doors. "My gosh, I'm so not prepared. Eduardo, this grandeur—" She swallowed and stared at the imposing winding staircase and gleaming marble floors.

"Like I said, we're comfortable here." Eduardo shot Sofia a smirk before turning his attention to the butler. "You're looking well, Winston. Would you mind showing my friend, Señorita Sofia Martin, to her room?"

"Thank you, Señor Diaz. It's my pleasure to assist Señorita Martin." Winston dipped his head toward Sofia.

Hearing his British accent, Sofia nodded. "Thank you, Winston. I fear I'm going to need a compass and a map to find my way around Olivar Siete Colinas." Sofia caught Eduardo's eye. "I'm glad you find my shock and awe so entertaining. Go to your meeting and leave me in peace with Winston."

"Very well. I shall find in you a couple of hours and give you a tour of my humble home." Eduardo smiled at the butler.

Winston cleared his throat and looked away.

"I'm on to you, Diaz. Now that we're on your turf, I'm getting paid back for the constant corrector." Sofia's nose took a tilt.

Eduardo did the unexpected and hugged Sofia into him. "Winston, she's…I believe the word is sassy. But you will like her, given plenty of time."

"Yes, sir. I'm sure I like her now," answered Winston.

Sofia watched Eduardo disappear through an arched doorway before turning her bright smile on the butler. "Would you mind leading the way to my humble room?"

"My pleasure." Winston's eyes sparkled. "Please follow me. I'll have your luggage brought up."

Head held high, Sofia tried to capture a befitting elegant style as she traveled the grand staircase to the second floor. Wide hallways that resembled art galleries veered off in three directions. Mediterranean-designed chairs and settees bordered the walls as she followed a silent Winston. Sofia smiled at the housekeepers in passing and wondered how many employees cared for Olivar Siete Colinas.

Winston halted in front of the double wood-paneled doors. The unique antique lead crystal knobs caught the natural light from tall glass windows nearby. They reflected two beautiful rainbows on the solid cream wool runner. "Here is your suite, Señorita Sofia, as chosen by Señor Eduardo. I hope you'll find it to your liking."

"Thank you. I'm sure everything is perfect." Sofia entered.

Winston motioned a young man to place Sofia's luggage inside the sitting room.

"I will leave you now. Please ask me or any of the attendants for anything you need. Welcome to Olivar Siete Colinas." Winston closed the doors gently.

Sofia moved around the sitting room, taking in the richly hued color scheme of caramel and yellow. Vibrant floral-patterned plush area rugs covered the terracotta tile floors. A bank of tall arched glass doors led to an expansive balcony overlooking the east gardens.

She stepped out, taking in the ceramic urns of vibrant red flowers and two chaises inviting relaxation. Gardeners were tending to new plantings and cleaning a cement pond. Going back inside, she moved toward another set of double doors. Entering the massive bedroom, Sofia froze in place as her eyes and mind tried to interpret what she saw.

Chapter 39

Sitting on the gold-brocaded chaise, the room had no doubt been redecorated countless times. Still, the interior design features remained identical to the vision she'd had of them in this same bedroom. Even the doors opening to the balcony and intricately carved ivy molding matched the image. Sofia sat transfixed, staring at the one indisputable proof she couldn't dismiss. The same landscape mural of Olivar Siete Colinas spring gardens stared back at her in the now. "Just swell. Another major unexplainable, and I've got to sleep with it for two nights."

Releasing a loud breath, Sofia dared a migraine to intrude on her revelation day. "Do something resembling normal, and you'll feel better." Seeing her luggage, she arranged her things and ventured toward the bath suite, finding a grandiose marble tub with columns on each side. Pillows and candles set a romantic mood, and elegant antique light fixtures complemented the décor. The Spanish and Moorish influences were undeniable.

Standing at the vanity, Sofia opened her cosmetic bag. The ornately carved mirror was kind. The image it reflected was a face flushed the color of love and not one pale, dazed, and confused. She'd let a fresh application of makeup cover it all.

A wardrobe change followed. A cheerful sundress

should convince Eduardo everything was dandy, unless she blabbed the latest unexplainable. "Just friends. He wants you as a friend. Remember it." She pointed to her image and realized hunger and thirst demanded her attention.

Sofia closed her suite's doors and felt the nudge to turn in the opposite direction of the staircase. Walking along the hallway, she made a right turn and discovered a modest set of stairs. "I think this leads to the kitchen."

"It does, but how did you know this, Sofia? Did you find a compass and map?" Eduardo came from behind wearing a smile.

"Trust me. It's better if we call it a hunch and not question this further." Sofia noticed he'd changed into jeans and a white polo shirt. She felt relief seeing casual dress acceptable at the estate.

"I shall trust you. You seek the kitchen? Let me go too." They walked down the steps next to one another.

"Your meeting didn't last as long as you expected."

"No. My cousin Juan appeared and interrupted. We have until dinner to acquaint you with Olivar Siete Colinas. If you like, I shall give you choices of things we can enjoy." Eduardo hesitated as Sofia took the lead.

Without thinking, Sofia turned and meandered along the hallway maze, continuing her chatter. "By all means, give me choices."

"Sofia? Please halt."

She glanced back. "What? I'm starving and thirsty. Please talk and walk."

"How do you know where to go? You realize I've been following *you*?" Eduardo's deep voice echoed in the hallway.

"I don't know. I guessed the way. Yeah, I guessed." Sofia tugged on Eduardo's arm. "Come on. The sooner you feed and hydrate me, the sooner we can go play."

"You're trying to distract me. Because you're my guest, I won't push answers for the moment." Eduardo pointed to the kitchen entrance.

"Smart you. Goodness. I'm going to marry this kitchen too. Any chef would covet creating culinary magic in this space."

Eduardo looped his arm around Sofia's waist. "Hola, Lola. Meet a hungry Sofia Martin."

"Hi, Lola," said Sofia, still marveling at the well-appointed kitchen.

"Hello and welcome."

"Lola keeps our home running like a—"

"Cuckoo clock," giggled Lola.

"No, like a fine clock as Winston tells it," said Eduardo.

"Please excuse. The delivery men arrive. Very nice to meet you, Miss Sofia."

"Nice to meet you, Lola." Sofia spied fresh-baked cookies on a tray, waiting for a buttercream frosting. "Can we visit them?"

"We can try. Chef Inez rules this kitchen, so we must sneak them." Eduardo grabbed two napkins and piled a few cookies on each. He pulled two mineral waters from a beverage cooler. "Here. Take yours. I hear her voice. Let us hurry outside before she takes them from us."

Sofia juggled the cookies and drink as they rushed out a side door onto a veranda. "Who is this Inez?"

"Let's sit at this table," said Eduardo. "I tell you

now. Inez was Ernesto's and my Nanny Inez. She was a very tough nanny."

"Really?" asked an amused Sofia.

"Do not scoff at the Nanny Inez. We had a bad boy chair she made us sit in when we acted badly."

"Fascinating to imagine. Please continue." Sofia devoured the first cookie, enjoying the story.

"I think we acted out too often. I believe Inez still has the chair in the nursery wing and still threatens to bring it out when she disapproves of us. Anyway, once we got older, Inez dreamed of becoming a chef. My father paid for her chef school. She graduated and chose to return here and care for us differently. She's still tough, but only in the kitchen now."

"What a wonderful testimonial to her affection and devotion to you all. You have the most caring relationship with your—extended family." Sofia sensed everyone working for the Diazes was treated respectfully and gratefully.

"You'll meet Inez at dinner. Make sure you brag about each course." Eduardo took another bite and chuckled. "Yes, bragging is very good to do. I change the subject. What do you think of our view?"

"Are you kidding? You've got a magnificent view of the hills and mountains. Do I spy a swimming pool off to the left?"

"Yes. Would you like to swim?" Eduardo took a drink.

"Is swimming one of my choices? What else enjoyable can you recommend?" Sophia noticed a sensual glint flash in Eduardo's eyes. His attraction meter was showing a slight activity, which gave her hope. Rewarding Eduardo with a smile, she rephrased the question. "How about naming some things?"

"Very well. I can offer you a tour of the groves, a visit to Ernesto's prized labyrinth, or a walk in the gardens. We'll have more time tomorrow. I can take you to our lake or even Granada, if you like. Perhaps you like something I say?" asked Eduardo.

"I like it all. Since I don't have a swimsuit, I guess the pool isn't a choice." Sofia's eyes looked longingly at the indigo-blue water.

"Is a choice, my Sofia. We have new bathing suits in the pool house for our guests. You choose one, and we swim." Eduardo ate his last cookie. His eyes studied Sofia. "You want the water. This I know. This we shall do."

"Wait. I do want the pool, but I'd also really like to see the gardens. Can we fit in both?" She didn't miss that Eduardo had slipped and called her his Sofia. Another sign to collect.

"But of course. I'll go change and meet you at the pool in fifteen minutes."

Sofia watched Eduardo walk away and greet two gardeners in passing. He moved with the grace of a panther. Just being with him flipped switches in her body she didn't know existed. The pool beckoned. Time to find a one-piece bathing suit.

Entering the cabana provided another feast for her eyes. The grandeur in design matched the estate. A brass plate over an archway stated Damas. Sofia entered an expansive spa-like area. A massage table sat in a corner with shelves of towels and potions. She chose one of the three well-appointed dressing rooms displaying bathing suits in all colors. Marble-tiled showers adjoined each dressing room. Sofia pulled a green suit from a hanger and held it up to herself, looking in the mirror. "Nope. I'd look like a toad in this one." Spying a yellow one-piece, she smiled and slipped into it. Glancing in the mirror once more, she nodded, grabbed a coral-striped towel, and hurried toward the pool. With any luck, she'd beat Eduardo and have the luxury of easing into the water her way.

Approaching the pool, Sofia saw a man dive into the sparkling turquoise water. At the same time, another man sat in a lounger, fooling with his cell phone. Both had the same dark hair and olive skin as Eduardo. She placed a smile on her face and walked toward them. "Hello there. May I join you both?"

"Of course. You must be Sofia, Eduardo's friend. He told us you were visiting for the weekend. I'm his brother, Ernesto." Laying his phone aside, he stood and extended his hand.

"It's nice to finally meet you." Sofia clasped his hand briefly and noticed who she assumed was the cousin coming her way.

"You'll have to meet my wife, Maude. She and her mother will return tomorrow."

"I'd like to," said Sofia.

"You will like meeting me far more. I'm Juan, the cousin to these subpar Diaz men." A grinning Juan grabbed a towel and mopped his face.

"Hi, Juan. So, I take it to mean you're the primo Diaz man?" teased Sofia. She liked Juan's lighthearted nature.

"Juan isn't primo to anything but himself," replied Eduardo from behind. "Pay no attention to him. He annoys like a fly."

"Do you hear the unkindness? Maybe you'd prefer

my delightful company to Eduardo's sullen self. Besides, American women fascinate me. You're all so confident."

"Enough, Juan. Sofia is my guest and will not suffer you like I do."

"I'm not suffering one bit. I already like your cousin." Sofia seized this unexpected chance to awaken Eduardo's jealousy.

"And I like you right back, Sofia." Juan turned to an amused-faced Ernesto. "I've changed my mind. I will stay for dinner tonight. My father can wait for my return to Venice another day or so."

Sofia noticed Eduardo's scowl and pushed a little more. "I met Señor Mateo briefly. Venice is such an amazing city. How great you get to call it home."

"Yes, Mateo is my father. I quite agree about Venice. Perhaps I can show you around a bit when you return? I'm confident I'm a better tour guide than my cousin."

"Sofia will not have time for you to show her anything. She leaves for Boston on Monday. Shall we swim?" Eduardo's expression held irritation.

Ignoring Eduardo, Sofia responded, "Actually, I don't leave until after lunch."

Eduardo reached for her hand. "Never mind this talk. Let's take a dip and then walk the gardens."

"Just when things were becoming interesting," Ernesto piped up. "I'm getting my guitar and will serenade you all with a few new songs I've written."

"Playing is good. Sofia and I enjoy the music. Yes?" Eduardo motioned for Sofia to lead the way to the pool.

"Yes, a swim and hearing you play sound perfect."

Sofia gave a flirty wave to Juan.

Eduardo's surly expression told her the jealousy arrow scored a hit.

"The water looks so inviting." Sofia waded to her waist, and not hearing Eduardo, she turned. Arms folded, he glared as Juan moved toward the diving board. She hid her grin and swam into deeper water.

The sound of a second splash got Sofia's attention. Seeing Eduardo and Juan beginning a lap race brought back her amusement. *Boys and competition go together like peanut butter and jelly*, she thought. Rolling her eyes at them, Sofia moved to the side as they swam toward her at Olympic speed.

Juan stopped swimming when he reached Sofia. "Let him win. I'd rather talk more to you." His eyes twinkled with mischief and amusement.

"I'm flattered." Sofia flipped on her back and floated. She heard Eduardo splashing their way and grabbed another virtual arrow from her quiver. "What do you want to talk about?"

Juan winked. "I can tell you things about Eduardo, things you should know."

"For example?" Sofia released the arrow, expecting Eduardo to react any second.

"I don't care for this talk of me," voiced Eduardo as he treaded water next to Sofia.

Ignoring him, Juan replied, "For example, he cheats at sports to win."

"I do not cheat. I do not have to. I can easily beat you, cousin. I'm a natural."

"So you say. Here's another fact. Eduardo cares more for being with his olives than he does being around most people." Juan's teeth flashed her way.

Sofia's eyebrow arched toward Eduardo. "Well?"

"This may be true, but only of late." Eduardo grabbed a float big enough for two. "Sofia?"

"You want me to get on that ginormous float with you?" Sofia's fingers squished the red canvas.

"Yes, we can float and ignore my cousin." His eyes narrowed, glaring at Juan.

"Tell you what. Let me swim a few laps in peace, and I will join you in a few minutes. Agreed?" Sofia didn't wait for his answer but took off swimming her first leg. Eduardo's interest in her had made a shift whether he realized it or not. Destiny was helping her cause. She spent the next fifteen minutes alternating strokes and wondering how she and Eduardo could make things work if his love for her were to ever activate again. As she swam past him, he reached for her arm.

"Please join me."

"Okay. I got my laps in." Sofia dunked her hair back into the water.

Eduardo offered a hand and lifted Sofia onto the float like she was a feather.

"We have been spared from more Juan. He has returned to his lounger, where Ernesto is about to play for us. Sit next to me." Eduardo shifted on the float and patted the empty place.

Sofia scooted in and realized their legs touching was unavoidable, as was her reaction to Eduardo's nearness. The brief moment his eyes caught hers showed his inner war raged. She sucked in a breath and willed her focus on Ernesto's playing. "He's an excellent musician and composer. Do you hear a local influence in the song?"

Eduardo nodded. "You and music are so simpatico. Yes, Ernesto tells me he has abandoned the Celtic style since returning to Spain. His music muses have him playing the Spanish guitar. The song reminds me of the Andalusian copla from our region."

"Hey, Ernesto." Sofia waved her arm in the air to get his attention. "I love your song and playing. You need to consider recording."

"Thanks, Sofia." Ernesto continued strumming, but a smile as wide as Granada's Genil River found his face.

Sofia stretched out and trailed her hands in the water as the float glided them around the pool. "Music is his passion. What is your passion? What brings you joy, Eduardo?" She knew her question would cause him to pause.

Eduardo stared off. "Riding my horse over the land and…"

"What? Don't hold back. I want to know more about you." Sofia waited, unsure if he would answer.

Eduardo turned to face her. "I tell this only to you," said Eduardo, as a meaningful look came into his eyes. "My passion stirs when I hold a pen and journal in my hand."

Sofia immediately recalled Eduardo's leather journal by his side on the night he proposed. She'd never gotten to discover what it held or meant. "You get joy from writing?"

"Yes, very much joy. Say no more." Eduardo rolled off the float into the water.

Sofia leaned over the side, her face inches from his. "I want to say more. What do you write?" she whispered.

Eduardo released a breath. "My thoughts. My observations. My philosophy." His fingers tucked a lock of Sofia's hair behind her ear.

His touch set off the flutters. Sofia looked into his eyes. "You're a true romantic, belonging in another time." Sofia recalled the book he was reading at the gardens a year ago.

"I fear this may be so." Eduardo shrugged.

"Know what? You're my version of Don Quixote." Sofia splashed water on his face to cool the moment.

"I can only aspire." Eduardo released the words and Sofia from the float.

She surfaced, surprised by the dunking. "Eduardo Diaz, you don't play fair." And this time, she wanted him to hear the words. Sofia pushed him under, only to see Eduardo rise like a phoenix, lifting her into the air. His laughter rang out.

"Don't you dare toss me. No!" screeched Sofia as she splashed into the water.

"Need rescuing? I'm your man," hollered Juan from his chair.

Sofia waved to Juan and Ernesto. "No, I'm solving this problem my way." She swam to the steps and got out. "Señor Diaz, you will get payback for that stunt. Count on it." Sofia marched off to the pool house to change. She kept her grin hidden.

The gardens were calling her name, and she'd soon find out why.

Chapter 40

Sofia waited for Eduardo at the garden gate closest to the pool. The incredible beauty of Olivar Siete Colinas was steeped in many generations of the Diaz family's devotion and commitment. She realized both were needed to carry the lineage and heritage forward. And yet Eduardo and Isobel defied a joining of lands to honor love first. A sadness flowed through Sofia as she assumed Isobel married the man she loved. However, Eduardo chose to marry Olivar Siete Colinas because fate had cast a cruel blow. Once again, Sofia pondered if Eduardo's carefully erected emotional walls would crumble given a reason. Hearing footsteps, she turned.

"I expected to find Juan by your side, proposing you spend time in his company." Eduardo released the gate's latch.

"No, the guys took off. If you hadn't convinced me you have no interest in love, much less me, I'd ask if you're jealous." The words came before Sofia could stop them.

"Me, jealous of Juan?" Eduardo released a scoff. "I don't want him annoying you."

"He hasn't. I like Juan." Sofia hid her disappointment in Eduardo's tepid response. "So, I'd love to hear about the gardens and anything else you want to share. You've got the most amazing place to call home."

"This is true, Sofia. Olivar Siete Colinas has been home to the Diaz family for hundreds of years. Each generation is brought up to respect and honor our responsibility to the olives."

"Your father chose well in having you take over. By the way, when will I have the pleasure of meeting him?" She paused at a bed of mixed flowers in full bloom.

"Pleasure isn't the word I would choose, but tonight at dinner, you will meet him. Fortunately, Juan will serve as a distraction and help keep my father entertained."

"I assume Maude—"

"Ernesto said Maude and perhaps her mother will join us tomorrow for breakfast. Now, shall I introduce you to the gardens and a possible surprise?" Eduardo leaned down and pulled a weed.

"You pulling a weed is a surprise." Sofia chuckled while pulling one and handing it to Eduardo.

"Why surprise? It was there." Eduardo set a slow pace.

"Why not call the nearby gardeners and ask them to tend?" Sofia was setting him up to understand how he viewed his role.

"Makes no sense what you say. Why should I take more time to do such an act when, in a few seconds, I take care of the problem?" Eduardo looked confused.

"As the Man of de Olivar, I would think—"

"Sofia, you tease me. I am not a man of flaunting. I am a man who loves his land and cares for it and its weeds." Eduardo touched Sofia's waist. "You know me. You know us."

"I do. I wanted to hear you say the man I knew a

year ago still lived inside there." Sofia touched his chest and made the mistake of looking into his eyes. Eduardo's charisma caught her in an instant.

"He does. And I'm probably going to regret this, but—" Eduardo pulled Sofia toward him and kissed her thoroughly. The longing hit them full force and kept the kiss alive.

Sofia pulled away. "I don't regret your kiss." She strolled toward another gate where a rock wall blocked her view. "At least not yet," Sofia tossed over her shoulder.

Eduardo joined her and again lifted the gate's lever. "Not yet? What do you mean, not yet? Is that meant as an insult to how I kiss?" He let go of the gate's latch.

Sofia pulled her mouth sideways, pretending to consider. "Well, you did seem a little rusty in the kissing department."

"Rusty? Kissing department? Will you ever speak plain English to me?" Eduardo lifted his palm.

Sofia planted her hands on her hips. "I meant your kiss wasn't as nice as what I remembered last year. Maybe you're out of practice or something. It's no big—what are you—" Her body was swept back into Eduardo's arms for an encore, only this time he brought the fireworks and sparklers.

He released her. "Is the rusty gone?" Passion still colored his face.

Sofia grabbed hold of the gate and took a breath. "Rusty is gone. Rusty has left the house."

"Left the house? More crazy English. I kissed you like Eduardo." He fiddled with the gate handle. "Come, let me test some possible magic." He furrowed his black brows.

"I think you just did," whispered Sofia, waiting to enter the garden area.

Eduardo held the gate open. "I am called to bring you here this day. I resisted but failed."

"Why should you resist bringing me to a garden? Never mind." Sofia turned her attention to whatever awaited.

"I may have to tell a story," Eduardo said, "should the unexplainables come to us. We must find out, Sofia. It is important." Eduardo closed the creaking gate.

Sofia paused, reading his anxious expression. Confusion followed her inside, only to become amplified by yet another unexplainable. She spun around, bumping into Eduardo's chest. His arms reached to steady her. "What is this place? *The Secret Garden?*" Sofia asked, referring to the childhood story by author Frances Hodgson Burnett. "It looks unkempt, and the flowers droopy sad—"

"Yes, I know. Let's observe first and see if anything happens. Then I shall try to explain." Eduardo's look shifted from serious to amazement.

Sofia followed his gaze and watched as what looked like a kaleidoscope of wildflowers became enlivened as if lit from within. The vibrant yellow, orange, purple, and red blossoms glistened like drops of rain had formed prisms on each petal. They swayed in unison with a gentle breeze as if in greeting. The palm tree fronds joined in a kind of fan dance. A group of colorful butterflies appeared, flitting around, visiting the flowers. "What is happening here, Eduardo? Is this some animated—"

"No, I'm afraid this is very much real." He rubbed

his forehead as they continued walking.

Sofia pointed to more flowers coming to life as she approached. A lovely floral fragrance bloomed into the air. "Come on. Don't mess with a Boston girl. This isn't real. You've got some special effects wired to entertain new visitors." Sofia reached down and touched the velvet petal of a golden rose. "It feels like a real rose, but the color—"

"Trust me, Sofia, no tricks. I didn't think this would happen. It changes everything." Eduardo's tone sounded resolute.

Sofia stopped. "Whatever do you mean? You're acting as crazy as this scene around us."

Eduardo pointed at two wrought-iron chairs. "Do you want to hear the unexplainable now or later? No matter when you choose, I must tell you the story of this garden."

Sofia studied Eduardo's countenance and found him awash in anxiety. "You know, I'm choosing later. I sense you're not ready to tell me this story for whatever reason. Let's wait until you are." Sofia continued strolling toward the exit, taking in the flora's finale. Based on past experiences, especially with Dina, the fortune-teller, the gondolier, and Mrs. Coo, the enchanted garden would be added to the list.

Leaving Eduardo standing in the same spot, Sofia ventured outside the rock wall to what resembled a rectangular-shaped maze of perfectly trimmed tall shrubs. The pebbled walkway contrasted with the wall of green. Sofia sauntered along, knowing Eduardo could call out and she'd hear him. Somehow, she arrived back at the starting point. "Okay, I refuse to get bested by a Spanish shrub maze. This calls for a do-over. I won't let my mind wander this time." Sofia chose a different direction and heard his footsteps.

"Would you like to know the way out? I can show you." Eduardo came alongside.

Sofia noticed his face seemed more relaxed. "Yes, I would appreciate a little help here. I'm curious." Sofia walked next to Eduardo.

"Why curious?"

"Do all the Diaz gardens act and look peculiar? If yes, I think I've toured enough of them." Sofia held out a hand to Eduardo, and he took it.

"An excellent question. Alas, your answer waits for later." Eduardo led them to a veranda on the side of the estate.

"Shall we sit or siesta?"

"Neither. Let's sip something frothy and citrusy. And if time permits, could we visit one of the olive groves? Then you can be rid of me until dinner."

"As my guest, I must grant your wish. Relax for a few minutes. I shall return." Eduardo headed inside the glass doors.

Sofia chose the most comfortable chair and gave over to her thoughts. Did Eduardo regret their kissing? He didn't seem inclined to repeat it. Nor was he still presenting his swoonable persona. Something happened in the enchanted garden, which altered his mood. Sofia could only hope, given time, he'd confide in her. Meanwhile, she'd enjoy reconnecting with Olivar Siete Colinas. Reconnecting? Eduardo wasn't alone in having unexplainable stories to share. She was collecting a passel of them.

Chapter 41

Sofia drew in a long inhale and took in her surroundings. The drowsy afternoon sun painted the mountains in apricots and corals. Fluffy cumulus clouds floated by, their edges tinged in silvery gray. A gardener humming a song activated the sprinkler system and returned to his wheelbarrow of new plants. Sofia closed her eyes, thinking even the veranda had a familiarity for her. In that moment, the flash came. She was stepping off the veranda and running toward the enchanted garden. Eduardo chased after her. A smile graced his face as she entered the gate and awakened the flora.

"Maybe you've changed your mind and want the siesta?" asked Eduardo.

Sofia opened her eyes to him, holding a frosted glass of a rosy-colored drink. "No siesta. I was day tripping. What's this luscious drink?"

"Pomegranate lemonade. You will love it, says Chef Inez, who asked about the missing cookies." Eduardo sat next to Sofia.

"Did you confess?" Sofia took a sip. "So good."

"I did not confess. You remember Inez has the chair, which I refuse to sit in."

"Surely it's too small for—"

"No. Inez upgraded the chair as we grew. The size fits Ernesto and me, and he was last to get exiled there."

Eduardo's eyes glinted.

Sofia lowered her voice. "And how long ago was this?"

Eduardo leaned his head closer. "Last month. Shh." His fingers covered his mouth.

"What? No way. You're teasing me."

"Perhaps. Perhaps not. Why not ask him over dinner?" suggested Eduardo.

"Maybe I will, but I'm warning you. I'll tell him you put me up to it." Sofia stared into her glass. Should she tell Eduardo about the visions at Olivar Siete Colinas or wait for him to tell the garden story? His mood seemed light again. Better to wait for his cue.

Eduardo finished his drink and set the goblet on the table. "So, you wish to see an olive grove?"

"Yes, but only if you will give a proper tour. It will provide me with dinner conversation. You've avoided informing me on what to expect tonight."

"I shall deliver you a proper tour as you requested. As for dinner, you dress nice, prepare for a long meal of courses and boring conversation." Eduardo lifted his hand. "I forgot Juan is dining at our table. Not boring. Annoying."

"The Diaz dinner doesn't sound so daunting. I think I can manage a table full of men quite nicely. It is a table full of men tonight?" asked Sofia, taunting him a bit.

"Yes. As I said earlier, breakfast has Maude at our table." Eduardo stood. "Shall we go?"

"Sure. Am I dressed okay to meet olives?" Sofia glanced at her sandals.

"All except for your shoes, but I had the problem cared for." Eduardo crooked his arm, inviting Sofia to hold on.

"What does that mean?" Sofia's heart sang, being close to him.

"Soon enough, my curious one." Eduardo pointed to a parked white SUV. "I'm driving you to our oldest grove."

"Lovely." Sofia climbed inside and spied her sneakers and socks in the backseat. "Eduardo, you anticipate my every need. Thank you for the thoughtfulness and for inviting me to your home."

Eduardo nodded, started the engine, and drove a short distance from the estate. He parked the vehicle off the narrow road, where hundreds of olive trees covered a hillside. "Step outside, and we can walk a bit. I shall speak of the olives."

Sofia slipped on her sneakers and met him at the first row of trees beside a large machine. "I'm ready for Olive Trees 101." The sun had found a cloud and shaded her face. She regretted leaving her sunglasses in the pool house. Using her hand, she made a sun visor and followed Eduardo into the grove.

"Our region of Spain may go a month or so without a drip of rain," explained Eduardo, touching a leaf.

"A drop of rain." Sofia shrugged. "Sorry old habits die hard. So, the trees don't mind being thirsty. How cooperative of them."

Eduardo laughed. "Yes, a drop of rain, so we can drip irrigate. Drip is correct. Do not object."

Sofia pretended to zip her mouth.

"To continue, the olives, meant to become oil, or golden liquid, as many call them, are treated carefully. You see, we hand harvest this grove. The piece of equipment behind us is called a—"

"A shaker. Right? It shakes the olives to the ground." Sofia covered her mouth. "I swear I don't know where those words—"

"I know. More unexplainables in our day. Yes, the equipment shakes the olives from the tree. It doesn't belong in this grove, which means I must investigate later. Anyway, we harvest around October or November and use netting to treat the fruit gently. We also prune a couple of times each year to keep the trees healthy."

"What are these?" Sofia pointed to gadgets on the ground.

"Those are what you call probes. They report humidity and temperature, both important to keep the trees happy. We are conservationists at heart and watch carefully for soil erosion. As for history, it is believed they cultivated olive trees back in Roman times. The Diaz family honors history."

"Goodness." Sofia waved her hands along the branch. "These trees have good juju."

"The trees have this juju because they know my family protects and cares for them. No developer or golf course will take our trees. We make the commitment as a family to this land for many, many years."

"And now the baton has passed to you." Sofia studied Eduardo's features. "This is where you belong." She thought about his willingness to move to Boston a year ago. Seeing him amongst the olives proved it would have been a terrible mistake. "You have a bond here. I sense it."

"Yes, Sofia." Eduardo faced her. "Do you not bond with Boston?"

Sofia considered his question and turned, taking in the hills and mountains, feeling like they were embracing her. "No, I don't think I have such a bond." She didn't venture further into how she felt standing next to him, looking at acres of olive trees as the sun dipped behind the mountain range.

"Come. I think you have heard enough for this day about olive groves. I must return you home so you can enjoy quiet time before dinner at nine. Besides, I've some business matters needing attention." Eduardo offered his hand to her as they walked a few yards back to the SUV.

"Eduardo?"

"Yes, my Sofia. What do you wish to say?"

"Could we go someplace quiet and sit for a few minutes? I'm ready to share more of my unexplainable visions. And after I tell you my part, maybe you'll explain what happened in the enchanted garden?" Sofia didn't wait for his reply but climbed inside the vehicle. She noticed her hands trembling and quickly clasped them in her lap, wondering if he'd call her "my Sofia" after she blew his mind yet again.

Eduardo stopped the vehicle in front of a white gazebo near the main estate's entrance. "Is this acceptable?"

"It's lovely." Sofia took a breath and moved to claim a seat.

Eduardo's dark eyes settled directly on hers. "I will listen now."

She could feel a swirl of nervousness move through her. "This sharing isn't easy because we're only together a couple more—never mind. I'm just going to say it."

"I'm ready."

"I have three unexplainables to add to our list. First, my bedroom is the same room I saw in my visions. Seeing the mural confirmed it." Sofia saw Eduardo's expression unchanged. "Second, I sort of knew the way to the kitchen. Also, I can probably take you to the study and dining room. I don't know how I know, but I do." She paused to see if Eduardo would respond. "Why aren't you freaking out hearing this?"

Eduardo's gaze wandered down Sofia's body. "Because it is us. The us that gives me no peace. I fight this war here." His fingers thumped his chest. "What is the last vision?"

"It's the garden. I had a vision of the garden and how it welcomed me." Sofia couldn't take her eyes off Eduardo. She watched as he stood observing the two swans in a nearby pond. Sofia felt panic wash over her. Maybe she shouldn't have told him of the flashbacks or whatever they were. What if he asked her to return to Venice? What if he'd had his fill of their unexplainables? Hot tears welled up. She was hopelessly in love with Eduardo Diaz, and it seemed her love had no future except in the past.

Eduardo sat next to her. "I regret for us these complications and more of the unexplainables. I believe your sights are true. I still cannot explain why they visit you. I cannot explain where they come from, but I grasp what the garden tells us."

Sofia's face wrinkled in confusion. "Whatever do you mean? Gardens don't talk. Maybe Inez slipped something in your lemonade." Sofia scooted closer and sent him a teasing smile. "Did you hear flowers chatting?"

"You must listen to what I'm about to tell you. Then you will see my problem." Eduardo's eyebrows came together thoughtfully. "Sofia, the garden awakening happens only when the lady of Olivar Siete Colinas enters the space. My grandmother and dear mother would visit, and the garden greeted them in the same way as you. The enchanted gardens have behaved quietly since my mother passed. Little life there as you saw at first." Eduardo lifted his hand. "You see now my complications."

"Just give me a sec to process what I think you're saying." Sofia inhaled a deep breath. "Are you telling me the big show of flora was for me? No."

"Yes, for you."

"But I'm not the lady of the manor. I'm a girl from Boston visiting—"

"Who has the visions of being in my home at another time. Who the flowers greeted, showing happiness. You understand?" asked Eduardo.

"So, you think because I have these flashes, it means I was the mistress during that other time? And the garden remembers and is welcoming me back? Now, I know you're tripping on lemonade." Sofia rose and walked to the SUV to get a bottle of water. She'd grant anyone that the universe held unlimited mysteries, and anything was possible, but not when it involved her…like this.

Eduardo came alongside. He stroked her arm. "Sofia? Can you sit a few more moments so I can say more?"

"Say more? What next? The fountains dance at midnight when I approach them?" asked Sofia, feeling her wits abandoning her.

Eduardo drew in a sharp breath. "Believe me, I do not welcome these complications into my life. I had everything running smoothly until your return."

"Hey, Señor Diaz, I don't appreciate being labeled the cause of our complications. You might want to look at your part here, Señor. It's not my bizarre garden trying to greet you like a long-lost patron." Sofia stomped back to the gazebo, noting the swans now sleeping together a few feet away, mated and devoted for life. She thought of Aaron and felt nothing but kindness toward him. Eduardo approached, and her heart skipped a beat. "Ridiculous garden. Ridiculous flashes. Ridiculous, all of it," she mumbled under her breath.

"Sofia?"

She sat once more.

"What now? More complications you want to lay at my feet?" Exasperation claimed her mood. She took a long drink.

"I do not understand how to lay complications at your feet, though there is plenty of room for them." Eduardo glanced down and cocked a grin.

Sofia glared, suspecting the source of his amusement. "Don't you dare bring up last year and you measuring my feet as too big. I'm still mad at you for letting that salesperson think I had enormous dogs." Sofia glanced over at Eduardo. "You're asking for it, buddy." Sofia smacked his upper arm.

"Hey, I ask for nothing." Eduardo rubbed his arm. "You provide me free the laughs." He hesitated. The serious tone returned. "Now, I must state the last complication, which you do not see."

"Fine. What's the last one?" Sofia bent down and

retied her sneaker.

"We are still talking about the flowers recognizing the lady of the garden. Yes?"

"Sure, if you're fixated on this," answered Sofia absently.

"I do not think so much the garden recognized you from what we call another time. No, Sofia, I believe the garden sees you as the next Señora of Olivar Siete Colinas." Eduardo sat looking at her, his face unreadable.

Sofia's mouth dropped open. "The garden sees me as the next lady of the manor? You can't be serious." Her fingers turned Eduardo's face her way. "My gosh, you are serious."

"Yes, Sofia, I'm most serious and most troubled. The garden has tapped you to become my wife. My wife," Eduardo repeated, shaking his head. "No complication before comes close to this one. You agree?" He folded his arms across his chest and exhaled loudly, waking the swans.

Sofia read Eduardo's body language. He wasn't interested in having her in his life, or he'd not object to the garden's insane message. "I agree this complication is a doozy, but you don't have to do anything. I'm clear that too much time has passed for us, and your desires are different now. You only see me as a friend who's visiting over the weekend. I accept it." Sofia paused. "Besides, I have my personal life in Boston waiting for me to return." She lowered her voice to get his attention. "I've got Aaron expecting an answer to his marriage proposal."

Eduardo jumped up. "Aaron? Who is this, Aaron? Why have I not heard of him before now?"

"Relax. Aaron is my complication. Let's focus on what's in front of us." Whiplash still defined Eduardo's behavior. One minute she thought he still had feelings for her, and the next, he was an ice cube. Sofia thought his outburst had a jealousy stamp, just like earlier, when Juan's friendliness struck a nerve.

Eduardo paced in a small circle but said nothing more.

"Hey, I've got a question. If the garden validates the next lady of Olivar Siete Colinas, what happened when Isobel visited?" Sofia tapped her chin, pondering the question. "I mean, what about Isobel and your father proclaiming her the chosen one for you?"

Eduardo stopped a few feet from Sofia. "You ask an excellent question. The garden made silent for Isobel, but my father overrode it because of wanting our lands to join." His mouth thinned. "No one outside our family knows of the garden's behavior except the ones affected."

"So, you're saying your father knows this flora phenomenon because it involves the male descendants. Your mom lit the place up, and now you—"

"And now I have been shown who the garden wishes to follow my mother."

"Why can't you tell the garden gods to choose someone local that you could love?" suggested Sofia, hating herself.

"No, Sofia, I cannot control this. You're the one." Eduardo ran his hands through his black hair and looked at his watch. "I find no more time to discuss our complications. We must go now. Do not trouble yourself further on this subject."

Once inside the vehicle, Sofia posed one final

question. "Do you plan to tell your father what's happened? I can't imagine he's going to welcome this news any more than you."

"Yes, I must tell him. My father and I usually see things differently. It's always been so. I cannot predict his reply."

Sofia sensed he'd closed the topic when he pointed out Juan and Ernesto playing tennis as they drove past. "They seem to find their fun," she observed.

"Sometimes too much fun." Eduardo left the SUV at the estate's front entrance and accompanied Sofia inside. "Do what pleases you until dinner. I will see you then."

"Do what pleases me," Sofia repeated softly, watching the man she loved so desperately disappear through an archway. "If I did what pleases me, Eduardo Diaz, your world would tilt on its axis."

Chapter 42

Sofia wandered upstairs to her suite, taking the load of woes. No one seemed around, save a housekeeper pushing a cleaning cart down the hall. Hearing her phone ding an email, Sofia answered Melody, confirming her plans to fly home on Monday. Tossing the phone on the sitting room's chair, she felt a tug toward the balcony. She stepped outside in time to overhear an exchange below between Ernesto and Eduardo.

"Brother, you're in a mess. You've proclaimed to everyone marriage is not what you seek. And now you tell me the garden liked Sofia, which means you need to marry her." Ernesto laughed.

"I do not like being directed by Father, much less flowers on marriage. You know this after Isobel." Eduardo's voice sounded sharp.

Sofia stayed far enough back so they couldn't see her if they glanced up.

"I like Sofia. She's pretty, classy, smart, and fun. I think the flowers are a lot wiser than you." Ernesto laughed again.

"You insult my intelligence?" asked Eduardo.

"I was trying to. Listen, I need to grab a shower. You'll figure everything out. You always do. Good luck when you speak with our father on this subject. My advice is to wait until he's met Sofia. Let destiny—"

"Do not speak of destiny to me. You have no idea how destiny can torment." Eduardo waved his arm in the air. "Go to your shower. I'm late for my meeting, worrying over these Sofia matters."

"See you at dinner, brother. It should prove quite the show, especially having Juan at the table. He's taken by…your friend."

Sofia stood digesting Eduardo's words. He resisted anyone or anything telling him what to do. She had no doubt now the garden's welcome had the opposite effect on her and Eduardo having a future. If anything, it had pushed him further away. "You're such a rebellious man. Finally, I discover a trait in you I don't like."

Releasing a huff, Sofia grabbed her sunhat and made the kitchen her first stop. She still had a couple of hours before making her dining debut. The craving for another cookie and more of the lemonade spurred her on. She'd chase it with fresh air, ample space to vent, and whatever divine guidance could offer her.

Sofia poked her head around the kitchen doorframe and saw three women buzzing like bees around the room. Two she recognized from the earlier cookie raid. The third person could be Inez. *Battle stations. Full steam ahead. Remember to compliment her,* Sofia thought and marched into the kitchen wearing a friendly smile.

Hearing someone enter her domain, Inez pivoted to see Sofia. "Señorita Martin. I've been expecting you."

"You have?" Sofia noted how the nanny-turned-chef had flawless English.

Inez lifted the dome from the cookies. "You had a nice sample earlier but without the buttercream frosting.

I knew you'd return asking for the fully dressed cookie. Eduardo just left, getting his hand smacked for trying to pilfer more." Inez chuckled.

"I'd say you've still got his number and know how to manage him. I could use some pointers." Sofia clapped her hand over her mouth. "Forget I said that." She heard the two younger cooks' giggles.

"First, let's get you a few of my special buttercream delights. Then would you like to visit a few minutes on the patio?" Inez reached for a small plate and placed three cookies on it.

"I'd love both." Sofia accepted the plate and napkin and followed Inez out the side door to the chairs and table.

"You mustn't tell Eduardo I gave you cookies. We women must stick together when it comes to the Diaz men. Forget I said that." Inez smiled. "We're now even on the keep-quiet score."

"I need all the allies I can muster. I like you, Chef Inez, and appreciate this chance to chat." Sofia bit into the cookie. "This tastes like ambrosia. The frosting flavor is—"

"Cherries, coconut, and pineapple pureed into cream cheese. Ambrosia is exactly what I call this cookie. I like you back, Sofia Martin." Inez stole a cookie off Sofia's plate. "Tell me, what brings you in search of Eduardo's nanny? And don't say you didn't come to me. You did."

A grin flickered on Sofia's lips. "Maybe I did seek you out subconsciously. I could use some guidance from someone who knows Eduardo. I guess I'm at a complete loss over him and me."

"It shows on your pretty face. Please trust me."

Inez sat back in her chair.

Sofia gave a brief nod. "We met a year ago, and to say it was magical is an understatement. I fell instantly in love, and if I'm honest, I still am. We were star-crossed then, and it appears we still are." Sofia paused. "And I can't believe I just confessed this to you."

Inez's eyes softened. "I'm so glad you did. I know a little of your star-crossed love because Eduardo sought my counsel when he returned home last year. He was quite bereft at losing you. Of course, I knew he and Isobel weren't a match. She's lovely but could never hold her own with Eduardo, even as children. Anyway, if you're interested in my input, I'm happy to share it."

"I'm more than interested. I'm desperate. Time is closing in on us finding our way back to each other. Eduardo has been giving me mixed signals since we found each other again. One minute he's calling me his Sofia and the next, he's waving his arms wildly in the air like a referee and declaring he wants no women complications."

Amusement glinted in Inez's eyes. "I recognize his behavior. Let me tell you what it means. Eduardo loves you, Sofia. He loves you so much that he closed himself off to feeling much of anything once you parted. Instead, Eduardo operates from his head and no longer engages his heart. You've entered his world again, and his heart awakened for you. He's trying, and failing miserably by all accounts, to deny this fact."

"How do you know he's failing at denying us?" asked Sofia, holding her hope close.

"That's easy. Earlier, I witnessed Juan's flirting when you all were at the pool. I overheard him tell Ernesto he's plotting a coup to win you at dinner. Now mind this, Juan is all fun and means no harm. In fact, Juan is working on your behalf, if you understand me."

"Are we talking about the strategy to make Eduardo jealous?" Sofia reached for another cookie. Her spirits felt buoyed.

"We are, but more it's about helping Eduardo realize his heart's desire. That's Sofia Martin and only Sofia Martin." Inez squeezed Sofia's hand. "Dear girl, if I didn't think you two belonged together and here at Olivar Siete Colinas, you wouldn't find me sitting here. What you share is a rare kind of grand love. In full bloom, it will be something to behold."

"I pray you're right," said Sofia. Her voice was laced with emotion.

"I am right. I'm always right. Ask the boys." Inez chuckled. "Understand this. I love Eduardo like my own son. I want what's best for him, and you're what's best for him."

"How can you tell? We've only just met, Inez. I could be some gold digger or—"

"The enchanted garden knows you. Eduardo loves you. I need no other proof."

Sofia choked hearing Inez speak of the garden. "How do you know the garden's ways or what happened there earlier? Eduardo said no one but family—"

"Darling girl, I've lived, loved, and cried amongst this family for decades. They're my only family. Of course I know of this unusual, otherworldly kind of connection spanning generations. It's been a guiding principle for the Diaz to have happy love and marriages, and when ignored, the opposite. I'm sensitive to how strange this all must seem to you."

"It's only another unexplainable to add to my growing list." Sofia waved her hand in a mock dismissive gesture. "I'm close to giving up on ever finding answers to what happens between Eduardo and me. What do they say? Ignorance is bliss? I'm so blissful it's a wonder I can form a sentence." Sofia grew quiet. "Inez, I love Eduardo so much. I will never love anyone but him. I can only hope he finds his way to loving me." Tears threatened to spill.

Inez extended her hand across the table. "Listen. By all means, show Eduardo and tell him your true feelings. Then give him time to trust. Expect his behavior to challenge your love. I leave you with those words. Remember them, Sofia. Rise to this challenge, and destiny will see you joined." Inez stood. "Now, I have a dinner to oversee and a troublemaking Juan to nanny."

"The Diaz family is blessed to have you here. So very blessed." Sofia's gaze softened toward Inez. "I don't know how I can ever thank you for such wise counsel."

"You can thank me by loving Eduardo well and long. He's a fine man and deserves nothing less from you." Inez walked a few steps and turned back. "May I recommend the labyrinth for some extra guidance? Take the stone path by the white fence. It's about a ten-minute walk, but well worth the effort."

"Great idea. I'll head there now. See you a bit later. And I plan to brag a lot on the dinner." Sofia bit her lip, grinning.

"I shall count on it." Inez disappeared into the kitchen.

Sofia took into the labyrinth Inez's words on

expecting Eduardo to challenge her love. She came out full of uncertainty in herself. How much more of his whiplash behavior could she handle emotionally? Eduardo Diaz wasn't the only one dealing with trust issues. She had a heart full of them.

****

Staring inside the antique walnut wardrobe, Sofia envisioned gowns hanging. Today it held a simple black A-line dress and her favorite yellow daisy belted dress. "Black is probably best for a formal dining room and meeting the head honcho of the Diaz family."

Sofia had just fastened her gold button earrings when she heard the familiar-sounding knock on the door. Putting on her smile, Sofia answered, "Come in."

"I came to escort you to—" His eyes ran up and down her body. "You look beautiful. Sofia. What you do to me." Eduardo came closer, allowing his hand to caress her cheek.

Sofia sucked in a breath, willing her body to not react...yet. "Why don't you tell me, Señor Diaz?" she asked, her lips tremulous.

Eduardo inclined his head. "You stir things which need not be stirred. Right this moment, I wish to kiss you, my Sofia. Help us resist—"

Sofia put her fingers to Eduardo's lips to stop his next words. "I think resisting is highly overrated. In fact, when it comes to us, I think resisting isn't advised." Sofia stood on tiptoes and bestowed a kiss as light as a butterfly's wing to a surprised Eduardo.

"Sorry to interrupt," said Ernesto outside the door.

Sofia and Eduardo pulled away.

"The dinner gong sounded five minutes ago. Father sent me to find you." Ernesto's smile was wide enough to reach Boston. "Don't waste time trying to explain away what I just saw. See you downstairs."

"More complications," exclaimed Eduardo, looking up at the ceiling. "Let us go to dinner, Sofia."

"Yes, I'm ready." The tone of his voice clued Sofia the wall was up once more. As they walked downstairs, she congratulated herself on taking Inez's advice. She'd given Eduardo a sampling of how she felt. The telling part needed to wait. He wasn't ready to hear declarations of the heart, but the body's primal urges she'd pursue. Eduardo was a passionate man.

Entering the dining room, Sofia took in the large carved decorated table with an elegance she'd only seen in movies. An assortment of white flowers from the gardens were thoughtfully arranged in gold-colored ceramic vases. Tiered brass candelabras welcomed lit tapers and cast a kind light upon the room. Sage green damask placemats held gold-rimmed empty porcelain plates and crystal goblets waiting for the tardy diners. Sofia glimpsed three pairs of male eyes turned her way.

"Forgive our late arrival." Eduardo dipped his head toward Hector Diaz, seated at the head of the table. "Father, I'd like to introduce you to Señorita Sofia Martin. Sofia, this is my father, Señor Hector Diaz." Eduardo seated Sofia in the empty chair next to Juan.

"Good evening, Señor Diaz. Forgive me for speaking only English, but my Castellano is sadly lacking. It's shameful." Sofia grabbed a short breath. "Personally, I believe my country's schools should put far more emphasis on learning other languages. Also, I feel strongly we shouldn't expect the world to speak English and—"

"Sofia?" Eduardo touched her arm. "No apologies.

You may feel free to converse tonight in English."

Hector cleared his throat.

Sofia chastised herself for the embarrassing rambling. She offered Hector a tepid smile. "Let me try this again. Señor Diaz, it's indeed a pleasure to meet you. Thank you for the opportunity to visit your estate this weekend. It's lovely here." Sofia placed the linen napkin in her lap. She observed Hector sitting for an eternity, judging her.

A slow smile found Señor Diaz's mouth. A laugh erupted, causing Juan to join in. Sofia observed an exchange of puzzled looks between Eduardo and Ernesto. Still, no one spoke. Unable to cope with the silence, Sofia's voice returned. "I'm looking forward to Inez's dinner very much. Her cookies are so—"

A deep voice sounding like Eduardo's interrupted Sofia's chatter. "Sofia, it's my pleasure to meet you and have you as a guest in our humble home." Hector rose and approached her. He reached for a crystal pitcher resting on the buffet and poured water into her goblet. "Allow me to serve you. Please, call me Hector."

Juan choked on the water but stayed silent.

"Thank you, Hector." Sofia smiled up at the man, taking in his features. He was an older version of Eduardo in every way. There was something in his eyes that made her feel they'd forged a connection. Sofia stole a glance at Eduardo sitting at the other end of the table. His face showed no emotion, which contrasted Ernesto and Juan's amusement.

Hector sat again in his chair. "Sofia, I think you'll enjoy your first dinner with us. Inez created the menu, especially for you. We'll have our first course now."

"How thoughtful of her." Sofia reached for a slice

of lime and dropped it into her goblet.

A server dressed in black appeared carrying a soup tureen. He ladled chicken noodle soup first into Sofia's bowl.

"Thank you. I adore any noodle soup. Don't you, Juan?" asked Sofia, trying to strike a friendly atmosphere.

Juan grinned. "I'm a cold-soup kind of man. And I like plenty of spice in all things. Do you?"

Hector cleared his throat again. "Juan."

"It was a simple question, Tio Hector." Juan winked at Sofia.

"I'm a light-on-spice kind of gal," answered Sofia. She smiled reassuringly at Hector, signaling to him that handling Juan wasn't a problem.

Hector ate a spoonful of soup and laid his utensil to the side. "Sofia, are you enjoying your stay so far? Has my son devoted time to showing our groves to you?"

"Yes, Eduardo has been most devoted—"

Ernesto burst into laughter, drawing attention his way.

"Ernesto, whatever caused such an eruption is unacceptable. I will thank you to allow Sofia the courtesy of your silence." Hector smiled at Sofia. "Forgive him. Please continue. You were saying?"

"It's okay." Judging by the scowl on Eduardo's face, it wasn't okay. "I was saying your son—the older one sitting at the other end of the table and looking irritated at who-knows-what—has given me a wonderful day."

Hector directed a frown toward Eduardo.

"Tio, should I ask Inez to bring the bad boy chair around?" asked Juan, not bothering to contain his amusement.

"*Manda narices!*" voiced Eduardo. He pushed his bowl to the side as Inez entered the room.

Hector's hand motioned to Inez to wait. "Ignore his response. It merely shows indignation. Please finish your telling of the day, Sofia."

Inez looked at Sofia, signaling her the opportunity to act.

"Of course, Hector." Sofia paused, letting her eyes assess the scene. "I'll ignore these gentlemen's antics and focus on you. We swam, and I suffered only a minor mishap under Eduardo's care. I especially enjoyed seeing the older grove. Your son is quite versed in the olive's history and future. Truly, I've enjoyed every moment so far."

"Excellent. I expect the men at this table to extend you every hospitality."

Sofia snuck a peek at each surprised face and finished the last of her soup.

Juan piped up first. "I'd like to volunteer to take Sofia around tomorrow."

Two servers entered carrying trays.

Eduardo jumped in. "Sofia's my guest, cousin. I shall see to her day's enjoyment."

"If you say so, cousin, but perhaps Sofia might prefer my company. Shall we ask her?" suggested Juan.

Hector's throat-clearing didn't halt the exchange.

Eduardo pushed his chair back. "You don't need to—"

"Juan, thank you for the kind offer. I promise to seek you out posthaste if Eduardo fails to—"

"Enough. What does this posthaste mean?" Eduardo's voice echoed.

"Posthaste means fast, without delay." Sofia turned to Inez. "Something smells heavenly on those trays. Chef Inez, whatever masterpiece of perfection have you created?"

"I've taken the liberty of helping you to feel at home by preparing fried chicken in a buttermilk crust, mashed potatoes with gravy, your famous recipe for Boston baked beans cooked in our Serrano ham, and homemade biscuits with pomegranate jam. Dessert is what you call Boston Cream Pie. We're serving family style this evening, approved by Señor Diaz." Inez motioned to the servers to place the platters and bowls on the table.

Sofia scooted her chair back to see Inez. "What a wonderful menu by a wonderful chef and two of my Boston favorites too. Thank you for bringing me a taste of home."

The unexpected acknowledgement lit Inez's face in happiness. "You're quite welcome. Everyone, enjoy." Inez departed, leaving the servers to attend.

"Sofia, if you want more American food out of Inez's kitchen, I will extend my stay." Juan accepted the bowl of potatoes from the staff and scooped a mound onto his plate.

The server spoke to Sofia in Castellano.

"He's asking if you prefer a large spoon to eat your meal?" explained Juan. He leaned in and whispered to Sofia.

Smiling up at the woman server, Sofia replied, "*Prefiero como can losdedos.*"

The server's expression looked shocked and confused.

Ernesto's laughter rang out.

Hector coughed. "Eduardo, please see to this."

"Sofia, corrector needed." A smile tugged at Eduardo's lips. "My Sofia, you replied you prefer to eat with your fingers."

Sofia turned to Juan. "You're so bad. You need the naughty boy chair. No biscuits for you either." Sofia accepted the large breadbasket from the server. She took two biscuits and sent them down to Hector.

Juan reached for the air. "Hey, bring the basket back—"

"Let's give Inez's dinner the respect it deserves." Hector's eyes focused in Juan's direction before turning to the platter heaped with fried chicken.

The rest of the dinner discussion turned to Sofia's work as a curator and current world affairs. Sofia relished their impassioned exchange over conservation and climate change. While agreement on the global problem was unanimous, everyone diverged on answers to address the issues. Sofia was not surprised to discover how much she aligned with Eduardo's input and ideas. What pleased her the most was the way Eduardo kept looking at her. Maybe he'd have time for a stroll after dinner. Maybe she'd kiss him again. Maybe he'd kiss her back. And maybe destiny would send them into slumber, having awakened passion.

Chapter 43

Bidding everyone good night, Sofia walked toward the kitchen to find Inez sitting in front of her laptop typing. "I'm back in your domain to thank you again for the home-cooked dinner and the wise guidance."

Inez glanced up and removed her glasses. "You're welcome for both."

Sofia pivoted to leave.

"Before you go, I want to compliment you on winning Hector's approval. He's not an easy man to know or spend time around. Who you met tonight is someone we seldom see. Well done, Sofia. And all by being yourself, your lovely self."

"Thank you for the unexpected compliment. I had no idea what to expect from Hector Diaz. I was pleasantly surprised to find him so likable." Sofia punctuated her assessment with a faint smile.

Inez closed her laptop and rose. "I'll say good night. Tomorrow should bring some female support. Maude returns for the required attendance at Saturday's breakfast. She's a cute young woman possessing a fiery brand over Ernesto when needed. You'll like her." Inez waved to the kitchen staff.

"I'm sure I will. Good night, Inez." Sofia stepped through the veranda's open doors and onto a gravel walkway. Sleep seemed as elusive as Eduardo. She'd follow the pathway lights and see where they led her.

"Finally, I discover you." Eduardo appeared from the shadows. "You left the table before I could ask you to take a walk."

"Yep, here I am. Want to go somewhere with me?" Sofia came alongside him.

"I must since I stand before you. However, my Sofia, I do not think you want to continue in this direction to somewhere." A smile flickered on Eduardo's lips.

"No?" asked Sofia.

"Not unless you want to meet Inez's hens and a mean rooster. They were supposed to provide food but turned into pets."

Sofia couldn't resist a laugh. "I think I'll skip those introductions. Can you suggest somewhere a little less farm-like?"

"I can, but first we should change into more flexible clothes. Yes?" Eduardo tilted an eyebrow.

"Yes, flexible clothes." Sofia wasn't sure what he meant, but she'd go along because it meant more time in his company. She'd fly a kite from a bell tower if it meant standing next to Eduardo. "As usual, you've got me intrigued." Sofia reached for his hand. "Do you know a shortcut back to your humble home?"

Eduardo nodded and kissed her hand. "I know such a cut. It's a secret door you can't tell on."

Sofia zipped her lips. "I promise not to tell on it."

****

Fifteen minutes later, they converged in the hallway, each wearing jogging clothes the same shade of navy.

"Well, this is just weird." Sofia looked at her outfit and then at Eduardo's.

"Shh, no talking. We don't want to attract Ernesto or Juan." Eduardo crouched and walked, pretending to sneak.

"Would you stop? We're stealthy enough in dark colors," Sofia whispered and pulled him upright.

Downstairs, as they passed Hector's study, his door opened. Peering at them both, a quizzical expression replaced the frown. "My son, are you burglarizing your own home?"

"No, it's Ernesto's pride and joy we plan to take possession of. Come, Sofia. He'll only ask more questions if we remain here."

They heard Hector's laughter as they slipped out a side door.

"My father never laughs," said Eduardo as they walked. "Tonight, you awakened this in him. You cast spells over all the Diaz men, Sofia Martin. Don't deny. It is so." Eduardo pointed. "We go to the right."

"I disagree," Sofia answered, a bit breathless at the pace. "My spells don't work on you."

"They work, but I'm strong. I resist." He paused. "We're here." Eduardo shined a flashlight ahead.

"What in all we call glorious is that structure?" Sofia's mouth dropped open as her eyes stared upward. A double-decker, brown-stained wood structure resembling a treehouse, without a tree, stared back.

"You're meeting Ernesto's Stargazing Station from when he was a teenager. You love the stars. You talk of them often."

Sofia tapped Eduardo's shoulder. "Hang on a sec. I talk about us being star-crossed, which has nothing to do with stargazing."

"Stars mean the same. Gazing or crossing, they're

still stars." His eyes glimmered in the moonlight.

"Whatever." Sofia watched as Eduardo put his first foot on what resembled a ladder nailed to posts. "Hold the fort. Is it safe to climb those boards? I don't know if this is such a great idea."

"It is a great idea because I wish to please my Sofia and her love for stars. You'll remember once you look at the telescope. Give me your hand."

"I don't think I'm going to remember something I've never done. What are you doing?"

Eduardo's hand pulled on Sofia's sleeve. "Your hand? I need your hand to guide you up the first few steps. Then it's easy."

Sofia tentatively put her hand in his and pulled it away. "No. Can't we look at the stars down here? Get the telescope." She pointed. "There's a nice flat place. It's perfect. I love it."

"No, I cannot bring the scope down myself without risking damage. I beg you. Don't make me throw you over my shoulder." Eduardo wriggled his hand. "Trust me. I would never let harm come to you."

Sofia released a sigh. Those words sounded like caring words to her ears. "You don't play fair, Eduardo Diaz," she mumbled. It was becoming another one of her mantras. "Okay, I'm coming. Get out of my way because once I start up, I ain't stopping." She chuckled, seeing Eduardo fly up the last few rungs to the landing. Flipping on his belly, he dangled his arms down for her to grab.

"You did a good job. Now, we look to the stars." Eduardo studied the night sky and uncovered the telescope, positioning it. "You like to see our moon first? It's big, and I can find it."

"I'm not feeling too confident in your astronomy skills if the moon is your best offer." A wry grin touched her lips as she watched Eduardo swing the instrument toward the full moon and adjust the scope. Sofia couldn't tell him she'd prefer observing him all night than some dead, gray rock dogging earth.

"Got it. Yes. Come see the craters."

Sofia bent down and peered through the eyepiece lens. "How cool. I see the craters in real-time, unlike a video or a photo."

"Look left. You can see the mountains," instructed Eduardo.

"Simply spectacular," breathed Sofia. "You're right. I do feel an affinity to stargazing."

"I know this. Here, let me show you the stars." Eduardo flipped levers and made more adjustments.

"You already have," whispered Sofia to herself.

For the next thirty minutes, they traveled the galaxy shoulder to shoulder, sharing the excitement in what they observed. Clouds began to roll in like a curtain closing on a show. Neither wanted to let the night end.

Eduardo stored the telescope. "If you're not tired, let's go down for a hammock swing."

"A hammock swing sounds good." Sofia waited while Eduardo went first. He struggled to help place her feet on the rungs.

"Can you turn your foot sideways? It is not sitting properly on the step." Eduardo pushed on Sofia's heel.

"Don't you dare say my feet are too big for this ladder. These same feet took me up in nanoseconds." Sofia found her position and made it to the third step.

Eduardo stared up from the ground. "I see this as

Sofia's coordination of the feet—"

"Hush. I need to focus." Once both feet were safely planted, she faced him. "I'm a natural climber, just like you told Juan you're a natural winner. So, no more wisecracks. Listen. Do you hear music?" asked Sofia.

"Alas, I hear the gondolier Angelo's music whenever I'm with you. It haunts me day and night. Do you remember him?"

"I do. How could I not? He played a song…an us song. Still, don't you hear music off in the distance?" Sofia tilted her head listening. "Yes, it sounds like music you'd hear in a planetarium."

"If you don't talk, I may hear too." Eduardo stood still, listening. "Ah, yes. It is Ernesto's guitar and Juan's violin. They're playing outside. Is nice. Is romantic. Maybe too romantic."

Sofia felt pulled into Eduardo's chest, followed by his lips finding hers. He tenderly kissed her flushed cheeks before releasing her.

"My resistance slid. Apologies."

"Your resistance slipped, and I didn't mind." Sofia touched his face.

"Aaron would mind." Eduardo's voice turned cool.

"Aaron?" repeated Sofia, trying to shift gears.

Eduardo climbed into the hammock. Without waiting for an invitation, she joined him. Lying side by side, they said nothing. The swinging motion helped soothe their emotions.

"Will you not speak of him?" asked Eduardo.

"Answer me something first. Do you care enough to have me speak of him?"

"Though I have this war inside me, I must answer truthfully. I do care."

Sofia clasped Eduardo's hand and stole an extra breath. "Aaron is a guy in Boston who I've been seeing regularly. He keeps proposing, and I keep saying no."

"You have a history with this, no?" Eduardo said, his face unreadable.

"True, but a proposal to me must have certain things, which I don't care to elaborate on right now. Anyway, Aaron proposed again before I flew to Venice, and I promised him an answer when I returned."

"You needed time because you're considering saying yes to this Aaron?" asked Eduardo, trying to sit up in the hammock.

"No, I needed time because I wanted to make my trip and not deal with his reaction. He'd call me constantly, trying to get me to change my mind. I know the drill. It's exhausting."

"Perhaps I am not so worried." Eduardo stretched back out. He slipped his arm under Sofia's shoulders and pulled her closer.

She snuggled up against him, taking in his signature citrus scent. "Anyway, when I get back to Boston, I'm going to end things once and for all. He needs to understand I like him and nothing more." She stole a sniff of Eduardo's cheek.

"You sniff me?"

"Just a wee sniff. What is the scent? It reminds me of fresh-squeezed lemons and limes."

"You say I smell of fruits?" Eduardo sat up again. "What—"

Sofia laughed, and her fingers touched his lips. "I didn't mean you smelled like fruit. I love your scent. What is it?"

"My aftershave. It lingers too long, and I smell to

you like a fruit." Eduardo tried to stand, but instead, he sent the hammock swinging. "Even now, I'm not allowed to resist you."

Sofia savored fate, giving her more minutes back in his embrace. "Eduardo, you smell great, just the way I remembered you for the last year. You're all masculine and—"

Eduardo's mouth found hers, bringing a pent-up passion that took them both back to the stars for the next minutes.

While Sofia grasped the concept of timelessness, a fresh memory came calling. She and Eduardo were riding horses across Olivar Siete Colinas's land with wild abandon. She opened her eyes to wonder. Was it the past or the future?

Chapter 44

The night sky, which Sofia had fixated on, finally gave way to morning light. She'd devoted the last hours to asking and waiting for any guidance on whether they had a future together. Her mind didn't have answers. What she'd expected to happen, sitting in the chaise, letting the breeze's voice keep her company, she couldn't say.

Declaring her bedroom exile ended, Sofia did morning ablutions before stepping into her flowered sundress and white sandals. She'd devised her plan. The first stop was the kitchen for an espresso, followed by a stroll in any garden but the trouble-causing one.

When Eduardo had kissed her good night, he said family breakfast was at eight o'clock. It was barely seven. That gave her an hour to luxuriate amongst the normal-behaving flora. One hour to let nature's colors paint her day. Sofia hurried down the stairs, mindful to keep her footsteps light and not call attention to her movements.

A woman's head was bent over a glass bowl, creating a cloud of white flour puffs as her hand stirred. Sofia smiled and moved toward what looked like an espresso machine.

"Good morning, Miss Sofia. You're visiting my domain early." Inez entered and reached for a bright orange cup.

"Yes, I longed to hear the hiss of an espresso machine and think I've discovered one here." Sofia watched as Inez put the cup under the dispenser and punched numbers on a screen.

"The hiss is coming. Cream is already on the tray to your right. Can I offer you anything else? A biscotti?" Inez nodded to one of the cooks.

"No, thank you. The espresso will get me out of your way and to the gardens."

"Don't forget, breakfast is served at eight sharp. And you might like to stroll past the pool toward the edible flower garden. Eduardo added this recently to entice me to expand my culinary creativity."

"An edible flower garden? This I must see." Sofia smiled and slipped out the door, taking her cup along for company. It took her a full ten minutes to find the garden and the perfect little wood chair to wile away the next hour. Sofia adored Olivar Siete Colinas and how the welcome feeling seemed to wrap around her. Even Hector Diaz had been charming and delightful.

For a moment, Sofia tried on the idea of living at the estate, and feelings of joy washed over her. "Stop dreaming of the impossible. Eduardo may kiss you like a man in love, but his head is calling the tune. And it's a tune that excludes women complications." She sighed and reached for a pale-yellow rose petal. The bloom reminded her of the night Eduardo proposed. Boy, she'd blown that proposal. Sofia studied the petal and guessed it was safe to eat since it lived in the edible garden. A tiny bite couldn't hurt.

"An early breakfast?" asked Eduardo.

Sofia could see his hair was damp from a shower and curling around his ears. "A small sampling is all. I wouldn't want to spoil my appetite for the homemade sweet rolls I just saw coming to life in a bowl."

Eduardo stooped at her feet. "My Sofia, we didn't sleep last night. This is not good. I see the shadows under your eyes. It's the complications. Yes?" His fingers stroked her cheek.

"I suppose." What could she say? *Eduardo, I love you beyond reason and want you to stop fighting being an us.* He'd see such a declaration as forcing her will upon him. "Have you told Hector about the enchanted garden encounter?"

Eduardo shook his head and watched a bumblebee choose a flower. "I will speak of this after breakfast. It cannot wait."

"I'm sorry to bring complications to your life, Eduardo. Truly I am. If you'd like for me to fly out today, I can." Sofia's throat tightened with emotion as the words left her.

"Leave? No. I do not wish such a thing. Come, my Sofia. Let us enjoy breakfast, and you can meet Maude."

"I'm looking forward to it." Sofia accepted Eduardo's arm as they walked toward the home.

"After I speak with my father, would you like to take a horseback ride to the lake? I promised to show it to you today." Eduardo paused. "Perhaps you do not ride?"

"I would love to see the lake. As for riding, it's been a long time, but I'm game." What had come over her? She'd never ridden, except for maybe a pony at a carnival when six years old. A merry-go-round with plastic horses at the yearly Revolutionary War Festival didn't count…until today. "Yes, siree, a nice, easygoing mare will do nicely. Emphasis on easygoing."

"I know the perfect horse for you. We will enjoy a simple day without worries or—"

"Complications," supplied Sofia, and gave a slight groan. Progress with Eduardo was proving slower than a tortoise climbing a hill on a hot day.

Breakfast was delightful, and the mood of everyone at the table was as light as Inez's croissants. Discussion centered around new grove plantings and Ernesto's breeding plans for the estate's Andalucian horses.

Maude, a vivacious redhead, offered input on the barn renovations and included Sofia in ideas for the barn manager's quarters and a bunk room for the groom and others. Her Irish brogue was endearing, as were the freckles dancing across her face when Maude explained the difference between cool colors versus warm to the disinterested men.

An amused Sofia felt drawn into the doings as if she were a part of the Diaz family. As the minutes ticked by, a sad reminder came calling as Sofia sat sipping her tea. Tomorrow morning, every person surrounding her would become a memory when the time came to say goodbye. Before the tears came, bringing embarrassment, Sofia excused herself to change for the horseback ride.

She stopped at the conservatory. The vibrant green of the plants caught her eye as the sun's rays doused them in stripes of shimmering gold. Sofia paused a moment to sit on the velvet cushioned circular sofa. The negative ions coming from the plants helped restore her composure before it was time to jump her next emotional hurdle. Mounting a horse and then attempting to drive it in the right direction called for a hefty dose of luck. "Drive a horse sounds wrong. Steer it maybe?" Sofia mumbled aloud.

A smiling Maude joined Sofia. "Sounds like Eduardo has you agreeing to a horseback ride. That'll be fun." Maude studied Sofia's expression. "No, it's not going to be fun. You can't ride."

"Not a lick." Sofia rolled her eyes upward. "I can't even talk horse." Hysterical laughter claimed her.

Maude joined in. "Are you sure this is a good idea? Olivar Siete Colinas's horses are demanding."

"Like Olivar Siete Colinas's men?" asked Sofia, her expression quickly changing to somber.

Maude twisted her mouth to the side. "Like one particular man, I'll say yes. He would be yours and not mine." Maude squeezed Sofia's hand. "Listen, I only have a second. I know about the garden and you. It probably sounds like malarkey but does the garden proclamation matter?"

"I—"

"Sofia, it doesn't matter. What matters is how you and Eduardo feel about each other. He's hardheaded, but you know this. Eduardo is also a most sincere and honest man. You love him. I see it. I recognize it. It's the same look I had when Ernesto and I struggled to find our way to each other living in different countries. Me in Ireland and him in Spain doesn't make for easy dating. So, I understand."

"But at least Ernesto didn't deny his feelings."

"No, but he fretted over displeasing his father. It caused a temporary wedge, but I solved that soon enough. I took him to Cork, near my home, and made him kiss the Blarney Stone." A brief laugh broke from

Maude.

"No, you didn't." Sofia shook her head, laughing.

"I surely did. Irish girls know their way around their men. He kissed it and went home to negotiate a happy ending for us with Señor Hector."

"I bow to the women of Ireland," said Sofia. "Eduardo's problem isn't so much Hector—at least not yet. It's him wanting to avoid any and all complications from a woman. In this case, said woman is me. His words. Not mine."

"I bring help. Here. Take this shamrock. I've been waiting to know who it belongs to. It's for you." Maude passed the four-leaf clover to Sofia's open hand.

"A clover?"

"Not just any clover, an Irish good luck clover. It awakens the fairies. Promise me you'll keep it with you."

"I will. I'd cart around a toad if I thought it would help Eduardo see us in a true light."

Maude gave a brief sympathetic nod. "I love a good stout Irish proverb on such an occasion as this. Ready? 'Don't fear an ill wind if your haystacks are tied down.'"

Sofia released a chuckle. "I guess I need to tend to my haystacks because I sense the wind is about to blow." She tucked the clover into her dress pocket.

Maude rose. "Since you took kindly to that saying, I'll be a leaving you with another one. 'You'll never plow a field by turnin' it over in your mind.'"

"I keep being told the mind isn't our friend. It's about time that I believe it. Thank you, Maude. I hope our paths cross again soon. We'll see if the clover and Irish fairies agree."

"The shamrock will give you the luck of the Irish, and the rest is up to you and destiny. Bye for now, Sofia Martin of Boston." Maude jogged toward Ernesto's waiting vehicle.

Sofia sat quietly, ignoring the bubbling thoughts meant to torment her. Instead, she closed her eyes and hoped the horse-riding vision would return. This time, she'd pay close attention to other things besides Eduardo Diaz. Seeing how she'd dressed to ride the gray Andalusian might ease her fretting, especially if seeing herself riding.

When no insight came, Sofia headed upstairs to change into jeans and a cotton shirt. That was as close to riding attire as would come from her suitcase. An idea came calling. Maybe grabbing a fast check on the internet about how to ride a horse would be wise. After all, how hard could it be once sitting atop the steed? "I just need to hold the reins and tell it to giddyup in Castellano. You can do this. Piece of cake." Sofia pulled on her jeans and tucked the clover into her back pocket.

Chapter 45

Eduardo found Sofia standing coin in hand at the fountain outside the front entrance. "You plan to make more wishes? You must see this is not a wishing fountain. No coins are in the water, my Sofia."

"I can see the fountain has nothing except a few leaves. A coin would add a bit of flair. Don't you think?" Sophia set a lighthearted mood to counteract her fear of mounting a horse. Her research on horseback riding had painted a failing picture.

"No coins in this Diaz fountain." Eduardo grinned and pointed. "The barn is but a five-minute walk."

Judging by his mood, the talk with Hector must have gone pretty well, thought Sofia. She'd wait to inquire until sitting on the beast and needing a distraction from her rising fear. Seeing the barn up ahead, Sofia took a few extra gulps of air.

"Why are you eating the air again, Sofia? You did this on the plane from your nerves. Is there something you want to tell me?" Eduardo frowned, looking sideways at Sofia.

"Nope. I'm just loving Olivar Siete Colinas's clean air. Couldn't help myself wanting to eat some."

"I think you're a little bit loco." Eduardo approached a wiry middle-aged man holding two reins attached to horses. "TJ, would you help my friend, Sofia, to mount Chile?"

"Did you say her name is Chile? As in a hot pepper?" Sofia's throat sounded raspy, like she'd swallowed one.

"Yes, Chile's her name because she is fiery. Right, TJ?" Eduardo checked his saddle before climbing up.

"Si, Señor Diaz, Chile is one hot mamacita." TJ helped Sofia into the saddle.

"Uh, Eduardo, maybe me and Chile need a few minutes to walk around the ring over there. You know, girl-to-girl chatter." Sofia settled into the saddle seat like she'd been in the riding stratosphere forever.

"No time for girl chatter," said Eduardo. "TJ, can you strap the lunch bag on back of Rio?"

Where had her self-preservation desire gone? Without waiting for another thought, Sofia's mouth emitted a horse command. She trotted off, alternating gulping and whooping. "I can flat ride you, Mamacita Chile. I don't know how, but it seems we're simpatico." Sofia glanced over her shoulder, seeing Eduardo riding at full gallop to catch up. Her hands pulled on the reins and slowed Chile.

Eduardo came alongside and adjusted his hat. "How did you know to ride this direction to the lake?"

"I—don't know. Lucky guess?" suggested Sofia, rewarding him with a sunlit smile.

"No guess. It's an unexplainable back to torment us. First, you know the way around the home, then the garden welcomes you, and now you show me to my own lake. Is too much, Sofia." Eduardo waved one arm.

"Since you're feeling loaded with unexplainables, let me add one more. I can ride Chile, like really ride her." Sofia beamed with another smile.

"You already told me you could ride—why is your

head shaking no?"

"I can only ride a pony, preferably a plastic one on a carousel."

"What nonsense. I saw you gallop away and ride like—still you say no?"

"Nope. I've never been on a horse, Eduardo, except in one of my flashes I rode with you here at the estate. I agree it's crazy, so let's do what we always do: Ignore it and enjoy the day."

"Do I have a choice?" Eduardo's voice held a bitter note.

Sofia refused to let their time together crash. "You always have a choice. But if you're a good host, you'll choose to show me a lovely lake…again," Sofia added, to desensitize them a tad from the unexplainables.

Eduardo slowly released his breath. "You see." He lifted one arm. "You cast more spells on me. Okay, we will do as planned."

"Super. Follow me," said Sofia, tossing her hair back. "Let's go visit the lake, Chile, and you can have a cool drink."

"Who are you, Sofia Martin?" hollered Eduardo to Sofia's back.

"I know the answer, and so do you, Señor Diaz." Sofia nudged Chile's flanks, and they set off. The riding soreness would hit her tomorrow, but for now, the outdoors in Eduardo's company lay ahead.

They rode in companionable silence for the next minutes, tossing sideways smiles at each other. It was a new day, offering new experiences and new memories to make. Still, on a different level, the day felt like an encore to Sofia. And she suspected Eduardo thought it too. Instead of feeling relaxed around the awareness, it added unspoken angst until the lake came into view.

"Eduardo, what a lovely setting! It's a slice of heaven." Sofia slowed Chile and rested her hands on the saddle's horn. A deep exhale of pure bliss escaped her lips.

"Yes, heaven. Only good lives at the lake. I have visited often since being a young boy." Eduardo paused and turned his head toward Sofia.

"Like you just said, only good lives here. And I want to bask in such goodness…now." Sofia's laughter rang out before taking off in a gallop.

The water looked almost opalescent as she led Chile to drink. "Is it the light making the lake appear like liquid black opals?" She reached down and swirled her fingers in the water.

Eduardo stood next to her. "Is beautiful, to be sure. It's the minerals that color it so, and the sunlight draws you to see. Let us tie the horses, and we can explore."

Sofia wrapped Chile's reins around a sturdy branch. On impulse, she opened the saddlebag and grabbed a drink and an apple. "Here you go, Miss Chile. A nice apple to cool your jets." Sofia heard Eduardo chuckle as he tied Rio to the next tree.

"Ready to explore?" Eduardo unscrewed the lid on his water bottle and took a long drink.

"I'm ready to walk some of these saddle kinks away." Sofia stretched one leg out to the side. "What's to explore?" Her eyes took in the trees around the lake along with a couple of canoes nearby turned upside down on the bank. Nothing remarkable.

"It's what you don't see that invites you to explore." Eduardo pulled Sofia close and pressed his lips to her forehead.

Taken aback by the surprise kiss, her face warmed. Grabbing a calming breath, Sofia replied, "Sounds mysterious. Show me." Her mind refused to let Eduardo think the kiss even warranted a response. It was time for a new tactic. Sofia recognized her advantage of being a woman with a toolbox full of ideas.

"Let's head toward the stand of ash and alder trees," said Eduardo, taking Sofia's hand.

"Okay." Sofia liked the feel of having his strong hand in hers.

"Did you know these trees prefer a home near water? A few months ago, I saw to the planting of more here." Eduardo pointed across the lake.

"I confess to knowing very little about trees, except that I like keeping company with them. They make me feel happy and energized." Sofia inhaled.

"My family has always believed in caring for the tall friends. I take this cherishing most seriously. We need trees to survive as well as the honeybee. You know this, yes?" asked Eduardo. His brow furrowed, waiting for Sofia's answer.

"Yes, those facts I do know. I like the name tall friends." Sofia felt the shade's coolness embrace her as they entered the woods.

"Do you know this little tree?" Eduardo touched the leaves.

"Nope. Introduce me." Her finger brushed a leaf.

"This is a group of figs that my grandfather planted. He loved to fish the lake and eat figs and almonds for his lunch. I asked Inez to pack some for us today to go with the cheese and bread. Good?"

"Very good. Now, I'm hungry." Sofia made a smacking sound.

"We'll eat soon. First, I must show you an unexplainable."

"Another one? You don't like them. They make you crabby," said Sofia, slowing their pace.

"This is true, but I must rise to this occasion for us. Let me show you. It's only a few more yards." Eduardo tugged Sofia along.

Eduardo led her into a section showcasing a different variety of tree. "These trees are cork oak. I will not discuss their value, for I only wish to show you one value. See this special tree?"

"Yep. I see it." Sofia tapped her chin. "You want me to ask you why it's special."

Eduardo grinned and crooked his finger. "Step around to this side and see for yourself."

Sofia stared at a carved heart bearing the initials E.D. and S.D. with a date: March 16, 1847. She shook a bewildered head at Eduardo. "What—?"

"My fifth great-grandfather carved this heart of love for his wife."

Sofia collapsed onto a tree stump and scanned Eduardo's face. "You didn't carve this to mess with my head?"

"This kind of messing I do not do. This kind of messing is being done to us. How do we explain this, my Sofia?" Eduardo's fingers traced the heart. "Who you see in the visions is us. The us of then and the us of now. Yes?"

Sofia felt her eyes sting. Now wasn't the time for some big cry. She pinched her arm to break the emotion ready to spill over. "It's an us, in a manner of speaking."

"What do you mean?" Eduardo pulled Sofia up and

placed both hands on her shoulders. His eyes bored into hers. "Do you see us?"

"I believe so. It's us dressed for the time. Your hair is longer, and you have whiskers. I'm…fancy." Sofia felt the pulse in her throat and stepped out of his embrace to gain a clear mind. "Eduardo? Are we somehow thinking we're the same—no, it's some bizarre coincidence. Did you just assume E.D. meant Eduardo? Maybe his name was—"

"I'm no fool except around you. Let me explain." Eduardo thrust both hands into his jean pockets.

"Don't explain. I'm not ready. I'd much rather hear how the meeting went with your father. Did he reject the whole garden extravaganza? Did you convince him you control your destiny and not a few posies?" Sofia tried to interject a lightness.

"Hardly. If his arthritic knee would let him dance, I think he would have. Instead, he produced our old family Bible showing me the Diaz family names. He pointed to Eduardo and Sofia's signatures and said, 'A sign to marry, my son.'"

"You're kidding. Eduardo and Sofia were married and in your old family Bible?" Sofia shook her head. "Well, that's pretty incredible. Literally and figuratively." Sofia's hand hid her smile.

"You hide the face, but I know what is there. I see no funny in this complication. Eduardo Diaz does not get told who—"

"Who to marry, except I recall someone named Isobel you were promised to. That fact caused me to choose a flight to Boston over my own happiness. You were going to marry her." Sofia's hands found her hips.

"You remember wrong. I proposed, and you

rejected me." Eduardo's tone changed.

Sofia balled her fist. "I rejected the proposal. I didn't reject you."

"You are splitting the mane."

"I am not splitting the mane. Oh, you make me so crazy. I'm not splitting hairs, you man from Andalusia. You had agreed to marry Isobel. Your family expected you to marry Isobel and not some museum curator from Boston. I loved you so much that I chose your honor over my happiness. Then what did you do? You sent me some email or text saying the marriage is off and let's get back together. You got a reply from that administrator saying I was in love with someone else, and you never even questioned it. And you stopped there. You made no further attempts to reach me."

"Why would I question your telling me to get lost? I do not push a woman to care for me."

"It wasn't me who told you to get lost. You thought so little of my love that you believed a text. And for some reason that defies all logic, you ignore the fact I didn't rush home and find someone else. My admin lied to you. I'm standing here having never married."

Eduardo's eyes flared. "Perhaps in that moment. But you found Aaron, and he's proposed."

Sofia held up her hand in protest of his interrupting. "Forget Aaron. Let me finish. You believed I'd moved on, and it hurt you. So, you decided to close off your heart and declare no woman will have your love."

"And with a good reason. After you, my life needs no female complications. Women cannot be trusted. I have no wish to experience such sadness again. I have no wish to discuss our past any longer. We keep things as they are now. No strings. No threads either." Eduardo gave a dismissive shrug of his shoulders.

"Well, that's just dandy by me, but let me tell you something. I wouldn't want your piecrust promise of love, even if you served it on one of your fancy silver platters and threw a dozen of Inez's ambrosia cookies on top. What are you doing?"

"I'm going to silence you my way," said Eduardo, sweeping Sofia up into his arms. He covered her protests with his full lips and turned her unspoken words into tiny moans.

Sofia came up for air. "You don't play fair, Eduardo Diaz, and this changes nothing."

"This may be true."

Sofia declared a truce out of a different kind of hunger…food. She vowed to revisit his declarations when alone and able to evaluate what he truly meant. After all, she reasoned, her heart needed protecting as well.

They wiled away the afternoon, holding neutral ground and savoring a simple picnic lunch and a leisurely canoe ride. Getting to know each other on a social level proved meaningful. The physical, emotional, spiritual levels transcended time, but they discovered the world each inhabited looked different from their individual perspectives. Shared values seem to meld with their contrasting lifestyles. And through the intellectual bonding, Sofia and Eduardo tried to pierce the veil of complications and unexplainables until egos and others clouded their world once more.

As they prepared for the ride home, Sofia remembered her clandestine actions right after arriving at the lake. She'd set in motion the payback scheme for

Eduardo's tossing her at the pool the day before. Despite the impasse Sofia feared they'd reached in their relationship, she would let her trick unfold. It would give them some comic relief to remember.

Eduardo glanced at his watch. "It's almost three. I must get to a video conference meeting with Tomas. Shall we go?"

"Sure. Be sure and say hello to Tomas. Since you need to rush back, how about a race?" Sofia's eyes danced in merriment.

"A race? And you not experienced on a horse? An easy win for me. I accept. Come stand next to me, so we start at the same time. You may count us. Yes?" Eduardo bent down, ready to run toward Rio fifty yards away.

"Don't be so sure, Diaz. I'm a woman, a cunningly clever woman." Sofia planted her right foot. "Ready. Set. Go." She took off running toward Chile. She grinned as she pulled herself onto the saddle, hearing Eduardo shouting.

"What have you done to my reins?"

Sofia patted her shoulder. "Good job, Sofia." She watched him struggling to untangle the reins' knots from around the branch. "That's what you call a payback, Eduardo Diaz, for tossing me in the pool. Seems I'm the natural winner here. See ya at home!"

Sofia trotted off, leaving her happy spirit behind. Reality caught up and jumped on the saddle with her. A crushing reality that could no longer be denied. It demanded a quick decision from her.

Chapter 46

Sofia slipped in the west door, not wanting to enter Olivar Siete Colinas's main entrance looking disheveled from her ride. As she approached the study door, Hector appeared.

"Sofia, might I have a word?" Hector stood aside, his face unreadable.

"Of course." Sofia held her head high and entered the room. Her mind wondered what the elder Diaz could possibly have to say.

"Please, take a seat. May I offer you some refreshment?" asked Hector.

"No, but thank you." Sofia folded her hands in her lap and waited.

"Let me get straight to it. I owe you an apology."

"An apology? I'm afraid I don't understand." Sofia pressed a hand to her temples, feeling the first twinge of a migraine.

"I recognize now the mistake I made interfering in my son's desire to marry you as opposed to Isobel. I make no mistake by telling you Eduardo's mother and I had an arranged marriage. In time, I came to love her deeply. I assumed Eduardo would do the same with Isobel, but I was wrong in every way. I'm sorry, Sofia."

"Thank you for being so gracious in saying this." Sofia sat stunned by Hector's words.

"Yes, well, I wish to give you and Eduardo my

blessing to marry. I found myself liking you from the moment we met. You're a delightful and intelligent woman who fits and belongs here, if it's your desire." Hector studied Sofia for a moment. "Eduardo has impeccable taste, and I hear so does the Garden of Enchantment."

"I'm honored by your blessing and welcome, but I fear it comes too late, Señor Hector. For you see, Eduardo has no wish for any serious relationship. Since we reconnected, he's made it very clear that he only wishes for friendship. I love him too much to remain here. I'm going to see about arranging a flight back to Venice. Over the last days, I kept hoping Eduardo might trust his heart and our love."

"The stubborn mule has not? It's all my fault. Apologies."

Sofia felt a smile break through. Hector and Eduardo were so much alike. "The stubborn mule has not." Sofia rose. "Thank you for the lovely hospitality you've extended me." She walked around to where he sat, bent down, and kissed his cheek. "I'm going to say goodbye, Hector. Maybe one day our paths will cross again."

"My son is a bigger fool than I thought." Hector released a heavy sigh. "I prefer not to say goodbye. See you later, Señorita Sofia Martin."

As she stepped into the wide hallway, Sofia sucked in a breath full of pent-up emotion. Her eyes stung from unshed tears. What should she do next? Go to her room and pack? Say goodbye to Inez? She had this short window to leave while Eduardo was in a conference. Facing him wasn't an option. She'd reached her emotional limit. Everyone who'd conspired to help her and Eduardo lean into their destiny needed to admit defeat. "I'm going back to Boston," Sofia said aloud.

"When are you planning this escape?" asked a grinning Juan coming from behind.

Sofia pivoted. "You're one stealthy man. As soon as I can pack and get a ride to the airport. Care to be my knight in shining armor?"

"Depends. Will it fire up Eduardo?" Juan craned his neck around the corner. "He's not around, I hope?"

"No. He's having a meeting. And it might fire him up. Hard to tell. I don't want to cause you—"

Juan laughed. "You misunderstood. If it fires him up, I'm in. He needs a lesson. I get the sense he's blown things with you. What a fool."

"So I keep hearing." Sofia headed toward the back stairs with Juan. "Can you give me a lift?"

"I can do better. I'm planning on flying out today. You can hitch a ride. Meet me at the garage in an hour. Will that work for you?"

"Works for me. Thank you, Juan." She hurried to her suite.

****

Sofia managed to get her bags to the kitchen without being seen. Saying goodbye to Inez would complete her final checklist. She'd left a heartfelt note for Eduardo, thanking him for the weekend and explaining why she was returning to Venice. Freeing them of more complications and unexplainables seemed wise. She loved him beyond reason, but it wasn't enough. Absent his love, they had no future, only a past.

Wiping at her tears, Sofia stuffed the tissue into her pocket. "Is Inez around?" she asked the young woman chopping carrots. Not knowing enough Castellano, Sofia hoped hearing Inez's name would get her directed.

"I'm here." Inez came out of the pantry holding a legal pad and pen. "More ambrosia cookies?" Her eyes narrowed, seeing the travel bags. "You're leaving, Sofia? This is unexpected."

"Yes, and I wanted to say goodbye and to thank you." Sofia pulled the tissue out.

"Let's step outside for a moment," said Inez.

Sofia followed and collapsed in the cushioned chair.

"Tell me."

"I tried, but Eduardo refuses to give way to his heart, Inez. If anything, the garden's big display and his father's nudge to pay attention to it caused him to close off even more. I mean, when he kisses me, I feel his passion. His desire. Then he shuts it all down and declares he wants no women complications. If I stay, it'll only hurt more. Do you understand?"

Inez patted Sofia's hand. "I'm a woman. I understand. I also know my Eduardo. You two belong together. Let me give you some words to take with you. I read somewhere the fated life is one we've chosen to be born into. The destiny life is the one our spirit picks. When you get back to Venice and can get quiet without distractions here, make sure you're listening to your spirit, your higher self, and not your head. Okay?"

"Yes, okay. You've given me insights to mull. How did you become so wise?" Sofia sniffed and stood.

"By living fearlessly and fully, dear. I hope you find your way back to us." Inez kissed Sofia's cheek and went inside.

Sofia spied the dark SUV approaching as she drew closer to the garage. Paco was behind the wheel.

Juan lowered the window. "Your chariot, Señorita Sofia."

"Thanks again for letting me tag along." Sofia waved to Paco when he got out to load her cases.

"I'm happy for the company, though I must warn you my plane is much smaller than Eduardo's." Juan answered his cell phone.

Panic washed over Sofia, envisioning herself strapped into a two-seater for hours. She must really want to run away badly. She looked for a peppermint to settle her stomach, already anticipating the bumpy flight.

Juan disconnected. "Sorry, my father was confirming my return plans. You don't look so good. Are you okay, Sofia?" Concern was evident in his expression.

"Juan, just how big is your plane? It's not a two-seater?" Sofia accidentally swallowed her peppermint whole and tried not to choke.

Juan's laughter attracted Paco's attention. Once again, the rearview mirror provided the driver's entertainment.

"No, my plane is a small but well-equipped jet. You shouldn't worry."

"Well equipped with a pilot?" asked Sofia in a quivering voice.

Juan twisted in his seat. His white teeth gleamed. "Well equipped with a pilot and an attendant. Do not fret. I plan to keep you entertained with my sparkling wit and charm. By the time we land, Eduardo will pale in your eyes." Juan's teasing helped Sofia move past her worries.

"You're wonderful, Juan Diaz, and some lucky woman will surely snag you soon." Sofia inhaled and looked out the window, saying goodbye to Olivar Siete Colinas and the man who didn't want her love.

Chapter 47

Dropping Sofia's note on the floor, Eduardo ran out of his bedroom and down the stairs. Was he too late to stop her from leaving? Standing in the driveway, he felt an aching loneliness fill the empty spaces left behind by Sofia. She'd had enough of his wishy-washy behavior.

"She's gone, son." Hector came to stand beside Eduardo. "And we are all the worse for it."

Eduardo said nothing. He kept staring down the long driveway as if he could will Sofia back.

"Let me give you some fatherly advice. Decide what matters in your life and chart a course. This applies to all aspects of your life, Eduardo. Until you do this, I suggest you leave Sofia alone. She doesn't deserve the man who stands next to me. She deserves the man you've yet to become." Hector walked back inside.

"*Manda narices*! My own father chooses Sofia over me. Complications find me even when she's gone." Eduardo waved his arms skyward. "I don't need these distractions." He stomped off toward the garage. He had time to go check on the new irrigation system before sunset.

Seeing Paco preparing to wash the SUV, Eduardo approached him.

Paco released the sprayer. "Too bad Señorita Sofia

left us so soon."

Eduardo groaned. "Not you too. Did you take her to the airport?" He grabbed the keys off the hook and headed toward the truck.

Paco took the car sponge and began washing. "*Si*, I drove Señor Juan and Señorita Sofia. They fly together to Venice."

Eduardo spun around. "What? Juan flew Sofia? I cannot believe this. Where is family loyalty?" He felt anger rising along with his blood pressure.

Paco gave a shrug. "We all like Sofia *mucho*."

"I've heard enough." Eduardo got in the pickup truck, taking his feelings of family betrayal to the grove. "I'm glad she's gone. Now I can focus on the estate and projects I want to do," he told the windshield.

Sofia's face haunted him as he drove. Her beautiful face, her eyes the color of the Adriatic Sea, and a smile that rivaled the sun in brightness found a small opening into his heart.

"Leave me in peace," he spoke the words in a low, pained voice.

****

A somber cloud hovered over Eduardo and Hector as they dined in silence. Neither tasted nor enjoyed Inez's culinary efforts. Instead, the two men feasted on glaring at each other from opposite ends of the table.

"I find my appetite missing. Excuse me." Eduardo tossed the linen napkin next to his half-eaten entrée.

"For me the same," said Hector rising. "I have some correspondence to do. Good night, Eduardo."

Inez poked her head into the dining room, seeing Eduardo alone. "Meet me on the veranda. I have your bowl of crow to eat for dessert."

"I do not eat the crow…ever." Eduardo sighed. He'd do as asked by the woman who held his respect and affection. He had always sought Inez's counsel when he lacked direction. Clearly, his compass was lost.

"Here's your hot chocolate. I made it the way you always like it: extra whipped cream and chocolate drizzle." Inez set the steaming mug in front of Eduardo and took a seat.

Eduardo's eyebrow lifted. He waited for Inez's scolding as he sipped.

"Don't worry. Your bowl of crow is nearby waiting. I'm listening." Inez lifted a cup of tea to her lips.

"You know Sofia left. She sees no future for us because I want no complications—"

Inez stood. "Eduardo, when you're ready to stop hiding behind your so-called complications and open your heart, let me know. In the meantime, I've got a kitchen to tidy before my favorite television series comes on."

"Wait. You cannot leave me without advice. I am unhappy and angry. Now Juan has whisked Sofia away."

"Your behavior sent Sofia away. This isn't about Juan." Inez paused at the door. "Eduardo, I love you as if you were my son. You know this. And because I love you, I'm going to ask you the one question which will reveal your next step. You get to choose whether to answer it or remain as you are, a man alone."

Eduardo released an exasperated breath. "What is this all-important question for me?"

Inez returned and bent down, looking directly into

Eduardo's eyes. "When did you stop loving Sofia?" Back ramrod straight, she disappeared inside. Eduardo missed seeing her Cheshire grin.

He swirled the liquid in the cup and let his thoughts take him prisoner once again. The tightness in his chest came from the arrow's bull's-eye. Inez scored a direct hit on his heart by asking one simply complex question.

The stars pierced the dark sky with pinpoints of light. The moonbeams acted in concert, drawing Eduardo's attention to the Garden of Enchantment. He felt a nudge to stroll there and ponder Inez's question.

Solar lights were scattered around the garden giving off a subtle glow. He noticed many of the blossoms appeared as if they were sleeping. The liveliness they exhibited for Sofia was as absent as she. It was as if her leaving brought them great sadness, as it did the other people in Eduardo's life. Given time, Ernesto and Maude would surely make their feelings known regarding Sofia. Everyone faulted him. "Why am I not allowed to seek a peaceful life, free of the complications and unexplainables that Sofia brings me? What man wants such things?"

Eduardo sat on the bench and rubbed his neck muscles. Inez's question troubled him. "When did I stop loving Sofia?" His throat felt like it was in a vise. Truth had its own way of coming out and bringing answers. "Stop loving Sofia? I cannot ever stop loving my Sofia. I only pretend to myself to do this. I allowed fear of being hurt again to cause me to behave—I am the biggest fool. Even the flowers dislike me this night. I dislike me."

Heading toward the kitchen at a fast clip, Eduardo found Inez. "What nonsense you spoke. I never stopped loving my Sofia. I hid my love. That is all. I shall make my plan to bring her back. Bake more ambrosia cookies." He lifted Inez into the air. "Make lots of cookies."

Inez's laughter rang out. "Put me down at once, Eduardo. Now that you've come to your senses, we both have our work cut out for us. Scat! And don't you dare return without our Sofia by your side."

Eduardo disappeared into his study. He knew the first thing he must do. Picking up his leather-bound journal, he let his heart dictate.

Chapter 48

The flight back to Venice with Juan had proven uneventful. Possessing the impeccable Diaz manners, Juan had insisted on seeing her safely home. The biddies, as Eduardo referred to her neighbors, greeted a confused Juan with a scolding. They misinterpreted him as a suitor, which activated their loyalty to Eduardo. While amusing, the scene left Sofia feeling more bereft and questioning her decision to leave Olivar Siete Colinas.

She'd called Ginny earlier in the morning to arrange a goodbye dinner, only to hear she and Milo had to leave unexpectantly to visit his new nephew. Ginny was engrossed in holding the baby, and Sofia knew the timing was off to cry on her friend's shoulder. And Lucia's bakery was closed on Sundays, leaving Sofia alone on her last day in Venice.

She stirred honey into her cup of raspberry tea. Moving to the balcony, she absently watched alfresco diners ordering lunch. Their smiling Sunday faces contrasted with her profoundly sad one. Tomorrow she would fly home and resume living a life that no longer held any appeal. Melody's earlier phone call saying she was preparing her sister's favorite meal as a homecoming didn't bring Sofia even a tiny bit of joy.

A familiar knock brought Sofia out of her doldrums, causing her heart to patter. "Impossible. It can't—" The knock returned. Flying to the door, Sofia halted. If Eduardo truly was on the other side, nothing but more heartache waited by letting him inside. Pushing her shoulders back, she answered, "Who's there?"

"It's me, Eduardo. Please, Sofia, we must talk."

Sofia heard her neighbors' front doors opening and let the grin escape.

Rita spoke first. "Señor Sorry, you have much trouble. Sofia has a new suitor."

"What? No, you are mistaken. Rita, leave me to this." Eduardo tried to shoo her away.

Marie tapped him on the shoulder. "Is true. You may have lost your Sofia to this other very tall and handsome—"

"Enough of such ridiculous talk, Marie. Would you two meddlers please let me talk to Sofia in peace?"

Both women stood on each side of Eduardo, fingers pointed and moving.

"You ask Sofia about her new man. Go on," said Rita.

"Fine. Sofia, did you have a man here last night?" Eduardo's exasperation was evident by his tone.

Sofia rolled her eyes heavenward. "Yes. Why should you care? You want no complications or me in your life. Now please go."

"See? We tell you the truth. A very handsome man," said Rita.

"Sofia, who was this man these two biddies are carrying on about? I must know immediately. I warn you. Do not play with my feelings." Eduardo tried the doorknob and found it locked.

She couldn't let him suffer more. "It was Juan. He

was seeing me home. Okay? Now go."

"Juan." Eduardo turned to Rita and Marie. "It was my cousin. He's no *problemo*. Now scoot home and let me try to get Sofia to open her door. Why am I always outside this door? It is too much for one man such as me." Eduardo waved his hand in exasperation. "You women have caused me enough trouble. Go with yourselves."

"Señor Sorry, you make your own troubles. We think you are not so smart. We maybe think our Sofia should not allow you inside." Rita's finger punctuated her words.

"You may be right, but I am smart now and standing here trying to convince Sofia this is so. You are not helping. Please leave me to this." Eduardo rapped on the door once more. "Sofia, you must show me some pity. I wish to beg—"

"It's good you beg the forgiveness for whatever you have done this time, Señor Sorry," said Rita with approval.

Sofia heard Eduardo's Italian fly and couldn't understand a word. She listened to the doors close and silence return.

"Eduardo? What did you say to my friends?" asked Sofia. Her happiness over his arrival soared until she reminded herself that he didn't want a real relationship. Somehow, she'd hold her ground.

"I told them if they would go home and leave us alone to work things out, I would have Lucia bring them pizzas. Now, my Sofia, take this door from us."

"Lucia is closed today, and they know this." Sofia didn't bother to correct his "take the door from us." What did it matter? "You charmed Rita and Marie, but it won't work on me. You're not coming inside, Eduardo, so you might as well leave."

Eduardo swiped his fingers through his hair, which had become his trademark act of frustration around Sofia. "I understand you are upset with me. I am upset with me too. More than you are. It is true. We must talk."

Sofia heard only silence. Had he left? Her heart sank to the bottom floor.

"My Sofia? Are you there?"

"Yes." Just hearing his deep voice say "My Sofia" melted her.

"Good. I shall return at eight o'clock to take you for dinner. Perhaps you will feel nicer toward me. Eight o'clock, Sofia."

She knew Eduardo had departed, but he would return. Sofia danced around the living room. She'd held ground but knew that come eight o'clock, her door would open to him.

Chapter 49

For some reason that Sofia still couldn't fathom, she'd packed the lovely lace dress Eduardo had surprised her with last year. Moments ago, a strong nudge to wear it came calling. She succumbed at the last minute and hurried to change from the sundress. Glancing in the mirror, the image of that last night together rushed in. The night Eduardo offered to walk away from his life and commitments in Spain, all for her. Given a do-over, would she accept his proposal? No. Her reasons were high-minded then and still held true.

At promptly eight o'clock, Eduardo's knock returned. Sofia opened the door to him wearing a tux and his signature charming, dimpled expression.

"Good evening, Señorita Martin." Eduardo's cognac-colored eyes stayed fixed upon the lace dress as he spoke. "You wear what I—" He stopped talking.

"You dressed in a tux as before." Sofia said nothing more.

"I think this means you decided to say yes to dinner." Eduardo's voice held a hopeful tone.

"Yes, I found myself dressing and realized another part of me had taken control of my actions." Sofia smiled at him with doubt in her eyes.

"Perhaps, my Sofia, the other part was your heart? Shall we go before the biddies appear?"

Sofia signaled Eduardo as she locked the door.

He turned to see two faces peeking out. "I take my Sofia for dinner. Do not trouble yourselves." Eduardo offered Sofia his arm. "Shall we?"

"Yes. Good night, Rita and Marie." Sofia ignored Eduardo's arm. Instead, both hands held her clutch.

"Señor Sorry, you try harder," shouted Rita, watching them go down the stairs.

Eduardo released a loud exhale. "Those two give me no peace. We go this way."

Sofia's lips quirked. "Those two women are your biggest supporters. Ask Juan."

"If you say it is so, then I must accept." Eduardo touched Sofia's elbow, slowing her pace. "You look lovely tonight. Seeing you in the dress removed my breath."

"You mean took your breath. Thank you, Eduardo. And you look most handsome in the tux, though I'm confused why you're dressed so formally for a simple dinner and quick talk. What you have to say can't take but a few minutes."

Eduardo shook his head, steering them around a group of tourists snapping photos. "No, that is wrong. What I have to say to you will take eternity."

Sofia heard a sound and looked down. "Look! It's Mrs. Coo. I can't believe my eyes."

"She brings us, Mr. Coo, to say hello. They form a couple," said an amused Eduardo.

"Indeed, they are a couple." Sofia pulled out her phone and took their picture. "I want to have this to remember them by. Mrs. Coo, you're one remarkable pigeon. Thank you for finding me and saying hello again."

"We must go. I'm sure we will see her more." Eduardo's eyes looked kindly at the two birds.

"I hope so." Sofia began walking, knowing the Coos were following. After a few minutes had passed, she asked, "Where are we dining?"

"Here." Eduardo released the wrought iron gates and stood aside.

"Here? As in the same here where Luigi served us the incredible meal and the yellow roses—" Sofia stopped all movement as her eyes tried to take in the scene.

Eduardo accepted the yellow rose corsage from the server and pinned it to Sofia's dress.

She sniffed the blooms. "You've recreated our last night in Venice, as it was a year ago. Even my favorite yellow color for the corsage. I don't understand, Eduardo."

"You will soon understand, my Sofia. I wish tonight to be perfect for us. I must do my part, for it's a very big part I play. Please, Luigi has our table waiting." Eduardo escorted Sofia to her chair.

The decorations were exactly as she remembered them. The twinkling gold lights woven around a canopy of greenery became their ceiling, and potted yellow flowers defined the area. Even Luigi's three musicians had returned and began playing a romantic piece.

Sofia's eyes found Eduardo's. "It's all so beautiful but—"

"Please wait until you hear what I have to say. First, let us enjoy our dinner and music. Can we do this?" asked Eduardo.

Dinner and music she could handle. It's what Eduardo had flown to Venice to say that filled her with uncertainty. Was he going to make some insane invitation she become—what exactly? He wasn't married, so mistress wasn't the word. Why had she agreed to dinner? "Eduardo, maybe this isn't such a good idea. I mean, it's lovely and all but—"

"Sofia, please. Can you not trust me a little to care for us tonight?" Eduardo's hand rested gently on hers. "Stay for us."

She could feel his eyes searching her face. He'd said the word *us* twice. "I'll stay for us."

Eduardo masterfully steered the conversation to facts about Venice as they enjoyed the encore of each delicious course served. He made no mention of her hasty departure or anyone back at Olivar Siete Colinas.

Sofia turned down Eduardo's invitation to dance. Being in his arms was a mistake she chose to avoid. She remembered all too well how it activated the flutters. And in the present moment, her anger and disappointment at his inability to love overrode the annoying reminder of her love.

Eduardo watched Sofia eat the last bite of carrot cake. "Did you enjoy the food?"

"Very much. Thank you." Sofia glimpsed the trio leaving quietly through an archway.

"Would you agree to listen to my words? I have many to give to you, my Sofia." Eduardo rose and held out his right hand.

Sofia stood. "I'll listen to whatever you have to say, but I can't imagine it changing anything for us."

"Come, Sofia. We return to the special place as before. The fountain is there waiting, and I have a coin should you wish for it."

The metal bench sat in the exact spot where he'd

professed and confessed. The fountain bubbled, and so did the memories for both. Their fate rested in how the next moments unfolded. Destiny, in its glorious way, had delivered them a second chance.

Sitting on the bench, Eduardo touched Sofia's cheek. "You are looking at a man who has come to apologize for his actions and words. Some might even say you are looking at a man who was a fool but is no longer. I apologize for so many mistakes."

"Some might be right. What precisely are you apologizing for?" Sofia removed his hand from her cheek.

"I made a mess of us. I hid my feelings from myself and you. Of course, being the fool, I did not know I was doing this. I focused on the complications and unexplainables that followed us everywhere. I could find no peace, no understanding for such strangeness." Eduardo's eyes narrowed thoughtfully.

Sofia waited, not wanting to interrupt his catharsis. Their future rested in the next moments.

Eduardo tilted her chin up to look at him. "From the moment my eyes saw the miracle of your return to Venice to last night, I fought an inner war like you cannot know, my Sofia. I didn't want to risk feeling such pain again as when you left me. I pretended not to care." Eduardo caressed Sofia's cheek. "But I do care. I never stopped caring or loving. You must believe me."

"Oh, Eduardo, I'd like to believe you, but I know the pressure you're under from your father and what happened in the garden. How do I know you're not acting from a place of honor again like with Isobel?"

"You are right to question my feelings. It does not matter what my father says or how the flowers speak of you. Yes, I tried to build the walls, as you say, but they crumbled. My heart would have none of it." Eduardo reached for Sofia's hand and kissed it. "My heart wanted you, has always wanted you."

"Are you truly sure?" Sofia watched as Eduardo produced a velvet jewelry box. He held up a vintage gold heart locket on a chain. Sofia gave a slight gasp, recognizing it as the one she saw in her vision.

"This locket is very old and special." Eduardo's voice softened. "I offer you my heart to keep forever." His eyes roamed over her hair and face. "Will you accept it?"

Sofia glanced at the fountain, still not allowing Eduardo's declaration to claim her love. "It's a beautiful piece." This wasn't the time to tell him of the vision. "I need a moment to reflect on what you've shared. I'll take the coin now."

A solemn Eduardo nodded and placed the coin in her palm. "For us."

Sofia went to the fountain and closed her eyes. "Please give me a tangible sign to believe Eduardo's able to love me. That his love is the rare forever kind." She released the coin and her hope.

Sofia sat on the bench. "Do you have anything more to say?"

Eduardo nodded and handed Sofia the leather-bound journal. It was the same one she'd seen before. "You desire more proof of my true feelings and thoughts. Here you will find what you seek. I shall return in a few minutes to ask you my last question."

An emotional Sophia opened the diary's first page and saw Eduardo's handwriting detailing the first day they met. She flipped through the pages reading snippets of how he was falling in love and agonizing about making it work. Scattered along with the pages, she saw he'd written poems to her. Tears ran down her cheeks as the depth of Eduardo's love unfolded. Knowing he would return soon, Sofia skipped to the final pages. There it all was. Her sign was provided in a journal. She'd read enough for now. She closed it and waited for the man she loved.

Eduardo returned, his expression hopeful. "Did your wish come true?"

"Yes, my wish came true." Sofia dabbed her eyes.

"Surely you cannot doubt I am in love with you. You read my heart's journaling."

"Yes. Thank you for sharing your most private and beautiful words. Now it's my turn." Sofia hesitated, gathering her thoughts. "I believe in your love. More, I believe our love is the rarest kind of love. A grand kind of love which defies time. And while we don't understand the unexplainables, they're a gift. Gifts to us that will continue for eternity, I pray."

"Does this mean I may hang the locket around your neck? You accept my love and my heart?" asked Eduardo.

Sofia smiled and lifted her hair. "Yes, and yes."

Eduardo pulled Sofia into his arms and let his kiss imprint his happiness. "My Sofia?"

"What's your one last question?" Sofia answered, grabbing a breath and touching the charm. Were her three wishes made last year about to come true? So far, two had. She watched as Eduardo got on bended knee. Wish three smiled up at her.

"My Sofia, please say you will marry me? Spend all your days and more by my side? I promise to love and cherish you for always like no other man could ever do."

Sofia's happiness escaped as she threw her arms around Eduardo. "Yes, I will marry you, Eduardo Diaz."

Eduardo reached in his pocket. He placed the canary diamond filigree ring on Sofia's finger. "This ring has been worn by the wives of Olivar Siete Colinas for many generations."

"I know." Sofia turned her hand, admiring the diamond flashing up to her. "Welcome home."

Eduardo sighed. "Another unexplainable?"

Sofia nodded. "Most definitely."

Chapter 50

Leaving the courtyard, Eduardo and Sofia stepped onto the cobblestone walk. The night's darkness changed Venice's mood. People bustled toward restaurants and other activities. Laughter rang out from a group seated outside a bistro. A mist of happiness seemed to drift down, touching everyone as if the City of Love celebrated the joining of Sofia and Eduardo.

"It is too beautiful of a night for us to say good night to it. There's something left we must do." Eduardo pulled Sofia closer to his side and kissed the top of her head.

She looked up at him, wearing a curious expression. "I don't suppose you'll tell me."

"No. It will take up the surprise."

"Take away the surprise," replied Sofia staring at Eduardo's handsome face. She hoped to spend a lifetime correcting her charming man.

Eduardo's lips curled into a smile.

"Coo coo," came the sound at their feet.

"It's the Coos. Join us. You two love birds. We've taken our *coo* from you and decided to become a couple." Sofia's laugh was framed in joy.

Eduardo looked behind and saw the two pigeons following along. "It would not surprise me to wake up at Olivar Siete Colinas and see them perched on our bedroom windowsill. Speaking of the estate, would you agree to move there? I ask because if you want me in Boston—"

Sofia stopped and touched his lips. "I can't think of any place I'd rather live. Though, my work—"

Eduardo touched her lips. "This was to be a surprise, but Tomas and I have been working on a plan this day. I know how much passion you feel for antique jewelry. Would you like to curate a small museum and traveling exhibits at Olivar Siete Colinas? If yes, Tomas awaits a meeting soon."

Sofia jumped, throwing her arms around Eduardo's neck and causing the Coos to flap their wings. "I love your idea. I love you. Yes, I want to contribute and play a role in running things. Kiss me, you handsome charmer."

"My most sincere pleasure." Eduardo delivered extra on the passion.

Onlookers paused to smile and cheer the couple before continuing.

Eduardo took up Sofia's hand and glanced at the canal. "Beautiful Venice. We must go and make no more spectacles."

Sofia laughed. "No more spectacles…for at least five minutes." She breathed in more joy. "Yes, the water glistens under the moon as if fairy dust has been sprinkled. You see our devoted Coos are still accompanying us?"

"Not for much longer. We arrive now for a boat ride." Eduardo pointed at the line of gondolas.

"How perfect. A gondola ride just as before—oh my stars and garters. Is that?"

They stared in amazement as the same gondolier, Angelo, beckoned them to board.

Standing in the shadows, a smiling Dina and the fortune-teller nodded to each other in approval.

"Hello again, Sofia and Eduardo. I've been waiting a long time for your return. Shall we take another ride this night?"

"Hi, Angelo. What fate to find you here. Yes, we'd love more time in your gondola." Sofia clasped his arm as he helped her board.

Eduardo shook the gondolier's hand and stepped into the boat. "Thank you, Angelo. You make our special night complete."

Angelo hummed as he steered them into the same secluded lagoon as before. He rested the rowing oar. "Tonight's words have been waiting for you both." He paused making eye contact with Eduardo and then Sofia.

"I say again, a grand love such as yours cannot be denied. Destiny proclaims this forever joining of two. You understand me now?"

Sofia and Eduardo nodded and drew closer.

"Now I play you the last version of your song…your song for always, 'Venetian Rhapsody.'" Angelo reached for his mandolin and touched a button on his cell phone, awakening the musical accompaniment.

Eduardo's arms wrapped Sofia in love's embrace. The song swept them away once more with its haunting passion.

The melody lingered into the night as Angelo steered them home.

Walking away from the boat arm in arm, Sofia and Eduardo turned back to wave farewell to Angelo. Surprise colored both of their faces. Angelo and the gondola had disappeared, along with Mr. and Mrs. Coo.

Eduardo pulled Sofia closer. "More unexplainables."

"Something tells me we'd better get used to them." Sofia sealed the words with a tender kiss, lighting love's eternal flame.

A word about the author…

As an author, Tonya's moved by the effect humor and narratives have on readers. That observation illuminates why her stories often convey messages inviting personal exploration. She is enthusiastic about crafting stories with beguiling characters, adding dashes of snappy humor, and engaging dialogue that leaves her fingerprint on each page.

When Tonya relocated to the mountains, she found fresh writing ideas waiting. From her favorite porch chair gazing at a tranquil lake, the nudge to scribe her first novel came calling. From her beach chair, she got the idea for a cozy series, Shell Isle Mysteries. Tonya confesses new respect for a chair's ability to motivate writers. She chases her writing joy from the mountains to the seashore.

The Shell Isle Mystery Series introduces three novels: *Baubles to Die For, Red, White, and Boom* and *Murder by Numbers*. The characters of Page and Betsy keep chattering to Tonya, so expect future stories in this collection.

Tonya's other books include *Old Mountain Cassie: The Three Lessons*, *A Secret Gift*, and *Welcome to Charm*.

Her fiction and nonfiction stories are published in numerous anthologies, e-magazines, local press, and literary magazines. She's a member of Poets and Writers. Tonya Penrose is her fiction pen name.

Visit:
Website: http://www.tonyawrites.com
Twitter: @TonyaWrites